Dread Naughts

A GameLit/LitRPG Novel
of Time Travel and Alternate Realities

Head Hoppers, Book 5

MK Eidson
Emila H Thicke

EPOSIC

This volume of Head Hoppers is dedicated to the real Ken St. Andre, in whatever timeline he may reside. How his work has inspired us is beyond description.

I'd rather be lucky than good.

LEFTY GOMEZ

TABLE OF CONTENTS

The Head Hoppers Series

CHAPTER ONE

Kevin: The Level Thirty List

Dr. Splat holds the syringe containing a dose of a sedative meant to knock me out. I need to be in Khertaan asap. He rolls up my sleeve and touches the needle to my arm. I know to expect a slight pinch.

An alarm blares, and the pinch doesn't come.

"We're too late." Dr. Splat grits his teeth. "Megan Wright is awake in her room."

I jump to my feet. "The Shadow Gaunt killed her?" Damn. I should have been there for her. I could have helped her get away, at the very least. If the Shadow Gaunt has killed her, she's going through some seriously debilitating mental and emotional shit right now. "Nigel, what's the status on Megan Wright?"

The AI installed in Dr. Splat's van replies in its suave masculine robotic voice. "Megan Wright's avatar, Mithabel, was killed, thereby waking Megan."

"How did Mithabel die?"

"She was killed by a fireball spell cast by the Wizard Bradford of party XStorm, who has been awarded over a billion XP for the encounter."

"A billion XP?" That's more than a single PC would be worth, even a high-level one. "Why so many?"

"Mithabel's death was worth over a quarter of a billion XP. Because of the dual-nature of Mithabel and Megan, both die when one dies, thus doubling the XP award. The other half-billion XP were awarded due to the death of Dylan at the hand of Priestess Yuni of party XStorm, which triggered the death of Debra Jones, who was in a dual-avatar situation with Dylan. Together, the four deaths earned those involved over a billion XP.

"Interestingly, every PC in the game and many NPCs received the billion-plus XP for the kill, many who were clearly uninvolved in the encounter. Why this award was made is unclear."

"Did Megan and Debra receive the billion XP?"

"They are slated to receive it upon respawning."

I rub the back of my neck. "Most curious."

"Should I investigate?"

Dr. Splat lays aside the syringe. "Please do, Nigel." The doctor is as curious about what has happened as I am.

Emma the Elf Wizard peers over the edge of the top bunk bed. "Does this mean we're not going to visit the other world? And where's Fauna? Shouldn't she be here by now?"

With a giggle, the shadow baby, Spooky, peeks over the edge, too.

"Fauna is on her way here and should show up any moment. We do still need to go into Khertaan. But I need to make sure Megan goes back in, too."

"Emma." Spooky touches the Elf Wizard's nose and laughs. Then she waves her arm around. "Fauna."

"Very good, you know our names." The Elf Wizard strokes the shadow baby's hair. "Fauna will be here soon."

What must shadow baby hair feel like?

It's against policy to talk to the contestants in their bedrooms except under special circumstances, and I'm making the executive decision that this is one of those circumstances. "Nigel, turn on the crystal ball in Megan Wright's room and patch me in."

An image of Megan Wright's bedroom pops up in the lower right corner of my view. Light shines through an overhead window, a clear indication the resident is awake and moving about.

She's bent over at the waist and rummaging in her closet, her back to me.

I whistle... to get her attention. "Megan, it's me, Kev. We need to talk."

"Kev." Straightening, she swings around, battle axe in hand, and gazes at me, though in actuality she's looking into the crystal ball located in her room. She should be seeing my image in it, peering out at her. She grins, a bit flush. "It's good to see you. I'm just... I'm looking... Mithabel's magic sword isn't here. She must have had it equipped when we died, and now it's lost in equipment limbo. She won't be happy with me."

Though overly wrought about her missing weapon, the blond contestant isn't demonstrating the symptoms expected of someone killed by a Shadow Gaunt. She's not mumbling incoherently or staring into space—showing no signs of severe emotional trauma. I trust Nigel, but it's a relief to have visual proof of her escape from the Shadow Gaunt. She owes more than she realizes to the Wizard Bradford of XStorm.

Nigel interjects. "Six PCs and five NPCs have reached level thirty in Khertaan—all the members of XStorm, all the NPC members of MAD, and one PC member of MAD, the Viking Archer, Amarynth. As soon as Mithabel, Megan, Dylan, and Debra respawn, they will also advance to level thirty."

"That's good news." And all the more reason for Megan Wright to get back to sleep.

"Moreover, the Shadow Gaunt has reached level thirty."

3

I sit up—disrupting my crystal ball connection to Megan Wright. "The Gaunt received the billion XP?"

"Affirmative. It was instrumental in the deaths of the four avatars, and thus received the same XP as those who delivered the fatal blows."

"Shit. Has the Shadow Gaunt released the Dread Naughts yet?" Please say, *no.*

"Negative."

I sigh with relief. "I need to get into Khertaan, along with Megan Wright. We need to stop the Gaunt before it releases those things."

"The Dread Naughts have already been released by the NPC named Charli."

"*What?*" Fear demolishes my relief. How is this even possible? "Collect what information you can on Charli, please. In the meantime, patch me back in to Megan's crystal ball."

The blond is rummaging in the closet again.

I give her another whistle. "Sorry about the interruption, Megan. Do you know the NPC named Charli?"

"The Cowgirl. Yeah. Sweet, upbeat girl, brimming with optimism. Why do you ask?"

"Did she express any hostility towards any PCs?"

"No. Mithabel was none too pleased with Charli after the girl killed Dylan—for the Longest Survivor bounty, with Dylan's permission—but other than that, everyone seems to like her and she seems to like everyone."

Nigel interrupts again. "The System is executing an emergency update. All players are awakening in their rooms this instant. No estimate has been entered for the expected downtime, and no restart has been scheduled. Everyone is locked out of Khertaan indefinitely, including you."

Shit, shit, shit, shit, shit. I'm afraid to ask my next question. "Where are the Dread Naughts now?"

"They are no longer registered in the System."

"And the Shadow Gaunt?"

"The same."

"Make sure Mr. Freeman is aware of the situation, Nigel."

"Acknowledged."

I suck in a deep breath and focus on Megan Wright's concerned face. I blow out the breath.

"What's wrong, Kev?"

"The war for the multiverse just took a sharp one-eighty. A level thirty Shadow Gaunt and an army of Dread Naughts have escaped Khertaan. They could be anywhere in the multiverse now, their only goal to destroy everything. You're gonna need to fight them with what you have right now. You can't respawn and pick up level thirty until we can restart the System, and we're not even sure why it went into update mode to begin with. But hang tight, and I'll come to your room—be there in a few minutes."

I jump to my feet, careful not to hit my head on the upper bunk. "Emma and Spooky, wait here for Fauna, and don't go anywhere until I get back. Nigel, what do you have on Charli?"

I slip out of the van and walk while the AI talks.

"She's a Cowgirl, level 30 Guide, level 21 Shadow Wizard. Her high average and better attributes are Sensing, Constitution, Agility, Willpower, Understanding, Logic, Sanity, Intuition, Memory, Charisma, Temperance, and Optimism. Her low average and worse attributes are Brawn, Toughness, Faith, Conscience, and Morals. All other attributes fall in the average range. Her traits are Stubbornness, Mental Armor level 4, Complex Personality level 3, and Ambidexterity. In addition to her class and subclass skills, she has one spell, Shadow Warrior. Equipment-wise, her weapons are a Wizard's Staff and a pair of cursed Shadow Gauntlets. She wears a Long Skirt, Culottes, a Blouse, Sandals, and a Wide-brimmed Hat, none of which serves as armor. Her only other possessions are Ezmerelda's Ring and a Map of Khertaan.

"Her history shows her as traveling with party MAD, initially as a story asset but quickly integrated into the party as a full member. She helped parties MAD and Quantized to find Ezmerelda's hut, where each party secured quests. At one point she had a cursed Shadow Stone in her possession, which she could morph into other small items. Using it as a dagger, she killed Dylan and collected the Longest Survivor bounty. She no longer carries the Shadow Stone, which was consumed in the creation of the Shadow Gauntlets she wears. Also consumed during that process were some ashes she collected from a Scarecrow and a Shadow Marble given to her by the PC Yuni from party XStorm. The Shadow Gauntlets granted a spell to Charli that she used to release the Dread Naughts.

"Charli traveled apart from other parties for a while, but her logs don't show anything peculiar during that time. She met party TimeTrippers, which at the time was comprised entirely of unregistered avatars. She traveled with TimeTrippers for several hours, though much of that time she is shown as being unconscious.

"She became a member of TimeTrippers, but a glitch in the System allowed her to remain in party MAD, which enabled both parties to gain XP when either party did. It gets worse. Charli was added to all parties by an unauthorized script executed by a developer with user name Raphael. Moreover, Raphael added Charli to the party creation template, so that all parties created afterward would automatically include Charli. This caused all XP earned by *any* party to funnel through Charli and be earned by *every* party. This is clearly why every party in Khertaan earned the billion XP when Mithabel and Dylan were killed."

Goodness gracious. "Good work, Nigel." I reach the elevator doors. "Where is Charli now?"

"She's no longer in the game. When the System went into update mode, it booted her out along with the Dread Naughts and anyone else who reached level thirty. Any of them could be anywhere in the multiverse now."

"Get me a list of everyone, PCs and NPCs, who reached level thirty, Nigel. Avatar names, player names for the PCs, kindreds, classes, and levels. And get me anything you can find on developer Raphael, too, please."

"Affirmative."

"And see what you can find on this PC, Yuni, where she got the item she gave to Charli, and what reasons she had for delivering it to her."

"On it. I have something on developer Raphael. He reported in as arriving late for work, but doesn't show up in the building access logs. In other words, he never made it in for work today. Records show he was involved in a car accident en route to work this morning, was admitted to the hospital, and has not been released. Yet actions were taken by someone logged into his account today, and not remotely. I'm also noticing atypical actions taken by someone logged into the account of a user named Ivanhoe, who created special quests and tasks for avatars Yuni, Charli, and Slithy."

"What are the natures of these quests?"

Nigel pauses. "Ivanhoe created the quest for Yuni to deliver the Shadow Marble to Charli. He then took advantage of rule loopholes to arrange for Charli to release the Dread Naughts before the Shadow Gaunt could, choosing Charli because of her subclass, Shadow Wizard. As for the special Slithy quest...."

"What?"

"I don't know. The details are locked by user Ivanhoe."

"Unlock them. And get me more info on Ivanhoe."

"Affirmative. It may take some time."

"Report as soon as you know more."

None of the elevators are on their way down. I missed Fauna somehow. I punch the button for the eleventh floor, where Megan Wright's room is located. "Fauna, where are you?"

"Can't talk. Busy."

"Kevin." Nigel already has something. "Mr. Freeman requires your presence in his office now. Your elevator has been overridden to deliver you to the thirtieth floor."

Arrggh. Megan is waiting for me. "Patch me through to Megan's crystal ball, Nigel."

7

Megan sits on the end of her bed, staring down at equipment scattered at her feet. "Hey, Kev." She jumps to her feet and sprints to the crystal ball. "You almost here? I've been trying to raise Debra on the mirror, and it's not working like it did before."

"Lots of things aren't working like they did before, Meg. Listen, my boss has called me to his office, and I have to go. So it will be a bit before I get to your room. Just hang tight, okay?"

"It's not like I can leave. Believe me, I've tried."

"I'll be there as soon as I can."

"I have the list of level thirty PCs and NPCs you asked for, Kevin." It's Nigel again.

"Read it to me."

"Party XStorm first: *ChrisCross*, PC, player Christopher Warden. He's an Elitist, level 30 Martial Artist, level 21 Psyon. Has a Magical Companion, *Lance*, an Electric Serpent, level 30 Electric Warrior, level 21 Rogue. *Ruby*, PC, player Gloria Rubio. She's a Centaur, level 30 Fighter, level 21 Barbarian. Has a Faithful Companion, *Penelope*, a Goth, level 30 Fighter, level 21 Guide. *Bradford*, PC, player Saiko Haru. He's Asian, level 30 Fire Wizard, level 21 Life-Stealer. *Yuni*, PC, player Saiko Aimi, twin sister of Saiko Haru. She's Asian, level 30 Priestess of War, level 21 Anjai.

"Party MAD next: *Amarynth*, PC, player Anna Milligan. Viking, level 30 Archer, level 21 Crossbow Specialist. Has a Magical Companion, *Rolag*, a Pseudo Code Dragon—"

"A what?" I've heard of pseudo code and pseudo dragons....

"A Pseudo Code Dragon. A foot high at the shoulder, wingspan of four feet and eight inches, weighs thirty pounds. Some developer had fun with the kindred name."

"Sorry for interrupting. Please, continue, Nigel."

"Yes. *Rolag*, a Pseudo Code Dragon, level 30 Winged Fighter, level 21 Were-Giant."

"Whoa." This is getting more amusing by the second. "A Were-Giant Pseudo Code Dragon?"

"Affirmative. Using his Were-Giant skills, Rolag can grow as large as nine feet at the shoulder, weighing five tons, with a wingspan of forty-two feet. Moreover, Amarynth maxed out her Magical Companion trait and assigned all four levels to Rolag, lowering his combat heartbeat cool down period to two seconds."

"Geez. I would hate to be on his bad side. Continue with the list, please."

"Also in party MAD is *Zyekt*, NPC Angel. He's a level 30 Psyon, level 21 Life-Stealer. Has a Faithful Companion, *Niav*, a Mouse. She's a level 30 Guide, level 21 Mentalist. Then there's *Charli* the Cowgirl NPC, level 30 Guide, level 21 Shadow Wizard.

"That's it for XStorm and MAD. I already mentioned the *Shadow Gaunt*. It's a level 30 Anjai, level 21 Psyon. It's registered in the System as an NPC rather than a PC, which allowed it to ignore the player requirement to go to sleep in order to respawn.

"Finally, there's one other PC who reached level 30. Avatar name is *Kylie*; player name is Kendra McKenzie. She's in party TimeTrippers. She was initially unregistered, considered an illegal avatar, but developer Raphael... or someone logged in as him... made her legal, along with all the other unregistered avatars in TimeTrippers. He then locked the change with a special password. Mr. Freeman can unlock it, but I can't.

"Kylie is an Angel, level 30 Spirit Warrior, level 21 Barbarian. You may find this interesting. Her HP is in the negative by nearly thirty thousand points. But she has the Pain Tolerant trait at level four, which prevented her from dying. Her activity log shows that her body was smashed to a pulp in a rock fall trap, but with Charli's help she was extricated. Afterward, Kylie regenerated, restoring her body to working order, despite being so far in the negative on her HP that she may never heal. You may find it interesting that Kylie doesn't have the Regeneration trait or any item that would grant it to her. It's as though she suddenly gained the ability, used it long enough to restore herself, and then lost it."

My elevator nears the thirtieth floor. "See what you can find on how Kylie managed to regenerate. And get me info on all the members of party TimeTrippers."

"Affirmative."

"Keep looking for more info on Yuni, too."

"Yes. Still working on that."

The elevator car stops. It's time to see the big guy, Mr. Franklin Freeman. I don't like being called to his office, because it's never for anything good—like a promotion.

CHAPTER TWO

Ronnie: Personal Hell

They murdered Nick and Greelia before my eyes. It doesn't matter whether the murdered couple were *the* Nick and Greelia I knew—they were still people and didn't deserve to die merely to prove a point to me, the point being that Queen Jean is Evil Incarnate and has no compulsions against abusing her power.

What grander quest can there be than to depose an Evil Ruler? It's up to me to bring down the Queen. Can I kill Mel's mother if it comes to that? And it may, because unlike the empty vessel of Nick she destroyed, this Jean is the real deal, fully aware of the multiverse and timelines, manipulating them to her benefit.

I must be willing to do whatever is necessary to stop her.

I'm not in possession of dice. When I last called for a saving roll, no dice magically showed up to roll my Luck, because Queen Jean has scripted a nice, long life in hell for me, ordering me to be stripped and tossed into some lonely cell, and the key thrown away. If it's up to her, I'll be occupying a windowless cell with metal bars set six inches apart and no one else around—a scripted epilogue to a failed adventure, the final paragraph at the end of a solo game describing one's degree of success or failure. Her script has me failing miserably—a tragedy with no possibility of a Happy Ever After ending.

I'm from a T&T campaign world where food and drink for PCs aren't considerations. I don't need nourishment and won't dehydrate. The Queen understands something about role-playing, having been married to Nick in a timeline where he loved gaming. She understands enough to know I'll stay alive if left unattended. No guard will ever bring me anything to eat or drink or otherwise enjoy. I'll be alone, bored out of my skull, for eternity. Or so says her scripted ending for me. I'm only guessing, but I can't think of a worse finale for me. If she has something worse in mind for me, then may the T&T gods help me, please.

With five rifles and four motorcycles in my invisible inventory, I'm not totally devoid of resources. But I don't want to tip my hand too early. I'd like to have a decent chance to succeed at whatever plan I attempt first.

Attired in green nurse uniforms, four female guards armed with rifles escort me along a hallway extravagantly wide and tall, spacious enough it could easily accommodate two Arachnid Behemoths marching side by side. Armed, uniformed guards line the walls, spaced one every thirty feet. If I were to make a run for it, even on one of the motorcycles, I'd be gunned down before I reached an exit, especially since I see no exits other than at the extreme ends of the hallway.

Given that I have effectively no experience using a rifle, trying to blast my way to freedom has about the same chance of success as digging my way out of a prison cell with my bare fingers. Trying to blast my way to freedom, however, has the greater chance of ending in character death, with no possibility for a sequel. So I'll bide my time.

Life-sized photos line the marble walls to my right, the bases of their thin-edged, twelve-foot tall and eight-foot wide gilded frames touching the floor. There's a photo of Queen Jean seated on her throne and holding a scepter. I could almost swear her eyes follow me as I walk by. There's another photo of her standing in a pose with a finger resting against her raised chin. Another shows her and Princess Karen standing side by side before a sign reading *Golden Minnow State Park*. When was *that* picture taken?

In another photo, the royal duo ride horses sidesaddle under a canopy of cherry blossoms, looking like they're about to ride out of the picture and into the hall. Another shows the pair from behind, seated in a stadium watching two armored gladiators in a life-and-death struggle, one of them about to run the other through with his sword. Glancing back at the camera, Princess Karen is caught mid-clap, her eyes bright with excitement, eager to see blood spilled. That's not the Princess Karen I know, who doesn't claim to be a Princess at all and doesn't go by the name Karen, but identifies as a man named Mel.

Did Mel, Erica, and Gondra find the real Greelia? I can't for a second believe the real Greelia was the one Queen Jean had murdered next to me. I and my Luck failed to assist, but perhaps the three persisted without me and succeeded in their search for the real Greelia despite my ill fortune.

I've always been good at keeping my cool, not letting rage consume me. I inherited that from my player, Ulric. Whatever happened to him?

The further I walk down this forsaken hallway and view the photos, the more difficult it becomes to repress my anger. Mel—aka Princess Karen—is portrayed as delighting in death, destruction, and torture. Pulling wings off butterflies, holding the back legs of a piglet in one hand while chopping off its ear with a hatchet in the other, or standing with a foot resting on the neck of a disemboweled man. In each photo, a malicious grin is pasted across the face of the Princess in pink. This is so wrong. Mel is not this kind of person.

In every photo depicting Queen Jean, the woman keeps her chin up and expression noncommittal, even when shown in the same picture as Princess Karen at her most cruel. In one photo, the Queen sits on her throne, her eyes fixed on the camera, while in profile at her feet a fully clothed Princess Karen straddles a naked man in a sexual position, gripping the hilt of a bloody dagger dripping on the man's chest.

Naked men feature more and more often in the photos we pass, with Princess Karen engaging with them in some lewd manner — always without the sex act itself being on display. The naked man is always debased and tortured by the Princess, and his face turned away from the camera.

Though the hallway continues on into infinite distance, the photos come to an end. The last one depicts a jail cell, the door hanging open. Princess Karen sits on a polished wooden bench at the rear of the cell, a freshly painted puke-green concrete wall rising above her bowed back. Long blond curls flow down from a silver crown over the shoulders of a lacy pink gown. The Princess wears a bored expression, her arms resting on her spread thighs, her gown dipping down to cover her privates. From one hand, a dagger dangles between her legs.

The guards come to a halt before the photo. "Strip, prisoner."

"No, thanks."

Heavy footfalls sound directly behind me. Strong hands lay hold of my tunic and tear it off me from the back, stripping the buttons in the front and ripping the cloth where there aren't any buttons. My pants are taken next, torn along the seams. I have no underwear or footwear. Rough hands plant themselves on my shoulders and shove. I stumble towards the life-sized photo of Princess Karen.

The heavy footfalls follow me. My instincts cry that if I'm to do anything, I need to do it now. I materialize a bike, turn it sharp to the left, and hop on. The back wheel smokes as it burns rubber on the marble floor for half a second before catching and propelling me forward.

Shots ring out as I race back the way I came down the hallway — a nude adventurer riding his motorcycle. There are too many guards, I have too far to go, and without dice there's no way for me to use my Luck.

I call for a saving roll anyway.

No dice materialize. I didn't expect them to. Is my attempted escape part of my scripted ending?

Holding a scepter, Queen Jean stands in the middle of the hallway ahead of me. I veer right to go around her. She raises the scepter, and a wall of flame rises before me. I'm racing too fast to avoid it.

The flames don't burn as I ride through them.

Exiting on the other side of the flames, I see the life-sized photo of the bored Princess two inches ahead of the front bike wheel. I can't avoid a collision.

There's no collision. The bike races through the open door of a jail cell, headed for Princess Karen, who doesn't flinch. Acting on impulse, I put on the brakes. The back wheel skids to the right and the bike goes down, metal and rubber screeching on marble. I tumble free and roll across the floor, coming to a stop at the feet of the Princess, the bike stopping just out of my reach. I'm on my back, as vulnerable as I can be, looking up at the Princess and the dangling dagger.

The Princess drags her lower lip under her upper incisors, her eyes hungering for mischief. "Welcome to your personal hell, Ronnie. Your adventure has come to an end, and this is your epilogue, frozen forever in time."

There's a saying in my world: *The best ending for an adventurer is to die adventuring. The worst ending is to never die.* I understand now.

CHAPTER THREE

Erica: Yesterday's Garbage

I've never seen someone wolf down as many chocolate kisses and sweet buns as Nick is doing, washing it all down with gulps of soda, and not the diet kind. He's famished, but he's not having a breakfast for champions.

Closing his eyes briefly, Nick draws a deep breath. "Okay, I'm good. So… any words of wisdom, Gondra? Pitting my will alone against the combined wills of Jean, Seth, and Greelia seems destined to failure."

The cloaked Lizardman reclines in a cushioned rocking chair. "I'd forgotten how comfortable this kind of furniture could be."

Susie climbs into his lap. "You look funny."

Gondra chuckles. "I was born this way. What's your excuse?"

She laughs. "I don't look funny."

"You do to me. Where are your scales? You should have scales on your face. See, I have scales on my face. Why don't you have them on yours?"

"I'm normal."

Gondra looks up. "On my world, so was I." He lowers his gaze onto Nick. "You *can't* do it, because you aren't fully you. I still need to find Greelia. Seeded in her is your determination, and without it, there's no way you can match her, much less overpower the three of them." The Lizardman turns to me. "Think you can find her and take me to her? Can we try again? Nick can help in the role Ronnie failed in."

"About Ronnie...." I grimace. "Did I lose him? Is his absence my fault?"

Gondra flicks his forked tongue. "What happened to Ronnie was no one's fault. He tried something for which he knew there was a chance of failure, but he tried anyway... and failed. Where he ended up, I don't know. I doubt it was anywhere good."

What the reptile man has to say doesn't diminish the guilt in my gut. "I want to find him. I need to know he's safe. I can't go after Greelia until we have Ronnie back. His absence will be too much of a distraction, and if I'm distracted, it's not going to work."

Nick pops another chocolate kiss in his mouth. "But you know where Greelia is, don't you?"

"Yeah." I reach for one of the chocolates, and he begrudgingly gives me one. I relish its dark sweetness before finally swallowing. "She's in the nexus you created, where you left Morrow. In case you've forgotten, you created the nexus to bind the broken timelines together. Someone needs to occupy the nexus at all times or it will collapse and the timelines will break again. Morrow left the nexus so you could come here. But Greelia is still in there, and she'll stay there as long as she's not distracted. If we go there and disturb her, she might leave, and if that happens, someone else will have to stay, at least until the broken timelines are fixed more permanently."

"It's all coming back to me." Nick unwraps one end of a sweet bun. He's *still* hungry.... "Okay, so, Gondra, how much time do we have to save Ronnie before we have to go to the nexus?"

Gondra holds up a clawed, scaly forefinger. "We may be out of time already." He jumps to his feet, holding Susie. "Follow me." He rushes down the hall towards Kendra's bedroom.

We reach the bedroom door just as it bursts open. Framed in the doorway stands an Angel holding a length of glowing blue rope with a noose tied at one end. Peering under her arm at us is the painted white face of a clown, with bulbous red nose and star-shaped blue glasses.

"Kylie?" Nick gasps. He does a double take. "Where's Kendra? And who's this clown?"

Golden blond hair in tight curls frames the Angel's pale face. White angelic wings lie folded against her back. She's dressed in the sexiest, blackest, skin-tightest leather outfit I've ever seen. I'm jealous of how she fills it. And her eyes... they're so hypnotic, I can't decipher them, can't even know their color. She oozes sexiness, confidence, and power. There's no way I can compete with her for Nick's affections—if she wants him, he's as good as hers.

"I'm both Kylie and Kendra, my dear, so call me whichever name you like." She beckons to him, to my Nicky Nick, and he rushes to her. They kiss and hug and feel each other like two people who've spent a lifetime becoming comfortable touching each other. In this timeline, they have.

I fight to suppress the jealousy. I'm the intruder in this timeline, not Kylie or Kendra or whomever this sexy woman is.

Whatever happens to the multiverse, I'll never be able to stay in this timeline. If this one ends up being the only one, there will be no place in it for me. I'll take off my Cosmic Cloak and then force Nick to look at me and say my name, banishing me forever. I couldn't bear a lifetime of watching him live with another woman in his arms and her lips on his mouth.

The clown slips past Kylie and offers me his hand. I don't take it, because I don't trust clowns. He chuckles. "Aren't you the wise one. My name is Georgie. Where, pray, are we? And where did Slithy, Rancor, and our Ghoul Dragon go?"

The door to Susie's bedroom opens, and out stumbles Glynda—that is, future-Susie, but not as far-future as the one who called herself Super Glynda. Glynda moans, holding her head. "What year is this?"

Gondra flicks his tongue. "It's 1997."

If that's true, I haven't been born yet. I'm definitely an intruder in this timeline.

"Thanks." Glynda gropes like she's blind until Susie grabs her hand. The future-girl picks up her past self. "Listen, Suze. Some day, all of this will make sense. I'm not there yet. But I'll get there. Super Glynda told me. Then again, maybe she's full of shit."

"Om, you said a bad word."

"I know. I'm sorry. I'll see you around, little me." She sets down Susie and looks around at the rest of us as though only just noticing we were there. She waves. "Bye, Dad. Bye, Mom. Give 'em hell. Everyone is counting on you." She turns to Gondra. "I time-shifted, didn't I?"

His reptilian grin looks menacing. "More than once. But now you're back. Be careful. You're bound to time-shift again."

"I'll do my best. Tell Dad he needs to send Morrow back into Khertaan and join up with Slithy asap." She turns to me, wiping sleep from her eyes. Hesitating, her eyes betray her sadness. Or is that sympathy? For me? "Be brave, Erica. There is no victory without you." She waves farewell, the gesture directed solely at me. Even her grin is sad.

Then she's gone, as though she were never there.

She'd avoided making eye contact with Mel or speaking to him.

Nick and Kylie break their embrace, though not in time to say goodbye to their time-traveling daughter.

Sadness wells inside me. I want to cry, but I won't. *Be brave,* Glynda said to me. *Be brave.*

If there's no victory without me, I'm pretty damned important, huh? So why do I feel like yesterday's garbage?

CHAPTER FOUR

Slithy: Dragon

I'm crouching on the back of a Black Ghoul Dragon, gripping its bony spine to keep myself from flying off as it speeds through the air over a territory called the Sands of Time. I'm not afraid of falling. One of my Mentalist skills is Levitation. If the Dragon were to spill me, I could hover in the air until Mom circled the Dragon around to fetch me. Or I could float to the ground and walk on foot if it came to that. Not that I could see where I'm going, but I have some other Mentalist skills to help me know where to go, should I ever find myself going it alone.

Dad's Woodpecker Familiar, Rancor, grips my right shoulder with sharp talons. They smart, but don't cause any actual damage. Party members can't hurt each other in Khertaan.

Mom is in Spirit Form, or so she says. Spirit Form allows her to see in the dark, so she's the eyes for the group as we begin our journey through the darkness to the city of Caravel, where I'll finish my last quest, the one that will catapult the three of us to level thirty. That is, it will raise me to level thirty, along with any who accompany me to the end.

Both Mom and Rancor can fly, but I can't. Mom could carry me, but the Dragon flies faster than she can, so we're riding it. A sense of urgency compels me to reach Caravel as quickly as possible.

Marta rides beside me on her crooked broom. She's a Dark Elf witch, mid-twenties, with a long, pointy nose bearing a prominent wart. She wears a brown robe and a black, pointy-but-crooked hat. Very witch-trope-fulfilling. She's my personal support AI, which no one else in Khertaan can see or hear. I don't always see her, either, since she stays out of the way if I'm in an encounter. Even though she's nearly as dark of complexion and dress as our surroundings, I see her clearly now, because that's how the support AIs work.

The sight of her keeps me sane. I'd be going out of my mind otherwise, enveloped by darkness.

"Ha ha." Rancor the Woodpecker laughs all the time, regardless of the seriousness of the situation. "How long to the city?"

Mom doesn't answer. She's got something on her mind. It's probably Dad. The two of them came into Khertaan together, Morrow the Punk Lightning Wizard and Kylie the Angel Spirit Warrior. I came into the game with them, Slithy the Frogkin Mentalist. Then Dad and I died, and our Cowgirl Guide, Charli, lost consciousness. Mom was left in custody of Charli's sleeping body and had to push on without us, aided by a co-opted Arachnid Behemoth she named Spyder. I only recently rejoined her, but Dad still isn't back.

Charli regained consciousness before I respawned. Upon waking, she aged four years and had a Cave Goblin baby girl named Britta. The weirdest things can happen in Khertaan.

Our flight to Caravel is barely under way when Marta flies over and hangs on her broom upside down and backwards, facing me as we continue forward. "Congratulations, girlie. You've just received over a billion XP. You're now level twenty-nine. You're 46% of the way to level thirty." She returns to flying beside me, upright but still facing backward, grinning like she's hoping I find her amusing. I don't feel like smiling, but her attempt at humor has lightened my mood, and I give her a weak smile.

"Ha ha." Rancor loosens his grip on my shoulder briefly, clamping tight again when the wind threatens to pull him free of his perch. "I just got a bunch of XP. Put me to level twenty-nine. What was that for?"

"I don't know, but I got a giant XP boost, too," Mom says. "We're still far from Caravel, so it can't be due to our quest, but I'm at level thirty now."

"Wow, Mom. I'm level twenty-nine, like Rancor. Do you feel any different?"

"Not really."

Marta the witch flies close again. "Hey, girlie. An emergency System update is in process. No estimate of when the update will be finished. All avatars are to be booted out while the update proceeds."

My Intuition sparks. "ODYSSEY, if you can keep some part of Khertaan running while the System is updated, do it." I need to reach Caravel as soon as possible, and if there's not even an estimate for a completion time, who knows how long I'll be shut out?

"Attempting...." The nanobot collective remains silent for two seconds. The sky brightens, returning to normal daylight. "Action complete. All level twenty-nine and lower PCs and NPCs will remain active in Khertaan during the update."

But.... "Mom?" I can't see her while she's in Spirit Form, so I don't know if she's still with us. The Dragon beneath me goes into a spin as it flies forward. It's trying to dislodge me. "*Mom.*"

"Kylie is no longer in Khertaan," Marta informs me.

"The intent of the System update was to boot out all those who had reached level thirty," ODYSSEY says. "I couldn't override the System objective. She was one of the eleven targeted for expulsion."

The sinews along the Black Ghoul Dragon's spine stretch as it bends its neck. No longer under Mom's control, it intends to make a breath attack against its riders. "Fly, Rancor!" I use my Teleport Self skill to vacate the premises, reentering the physical domain a hundred yards higher in the air, and then activate Levitate to keep from falling.

Below, the Dragon flies in a circle around Rancor. A noxious cloud spews from the Dragon's mouth to swallow the Woodpecker.

"Ha ha, it worked. I'm fine. What happened to Kylie?"

I sigh with relief that Rancor is okay.

The cloud dissipates, revealing the Woodpecker, frozen in space, not even flapping his wings.

"Mom was booted out of the game. The Dragon isn't under her control now and has turned on us. What ability are you using?" It's not one I've seen him use before.

The Dragon continues to circle Rancor, occasionally snapping at him or breathing poison. The mook's fangs and breath attacks have no effect on the Woodpecker.

"Ha ha, I activated my Discarnate Psi power. I'm insubstantial and can't be hurt, but I can't do anything, either, not even move. I can stay this way indefinitely without expending more Psi points, but once I stop the effect, I'll have to spend more Psi if I want to start it again."

"Keep it active for now." I turn on my Displace skill, so if the Dragon comes after me, it won't know exactly where I am. This might be a good time to use my Predict skill. Now that I'm level twenty-nine, I can use it seven times a day. I invoke it, concentrating on the Dragon.

In my mind's eye, the Dragon continues to circle Rancor and attack as it's now doing. This being a prediction, I don't know how much to trust it, but I'm thinking the undead beast is operating solely on automatic. After all, the System is in update mode, unable to provide live combat updates to mooks.

"Rancor, seriously, keep doing what you're doing. ODYSSEY, can you reprogram the Dragon to be on our side, like you did with Spyder?"

"I will try…."

I don't move from my position, not wanting to do anything that might draw the Dragon's attention. If it notices me, it's internal AI might be smart enough to prompt it to come up here instead of wasting its time on Rancor.

"It's not working," ODYSSEY reports. "Spyder was different, in that it didn't originate in Khertaan and wasn't properly classified as a mook. The Black Ghoul Dragon is properly classified, and I can't change it. I might be able to if the System weren't in update mode, but… I'm sorry."

"Then how do we defeat it? And by *we*, I mean *me*."

Marta flies before me. "Pertinent information has just unlocked. The Black Ghoul Dragon can be damaged only in the physical or spiritual domains. It is immune to poison and mind-influencing skills, and is completely devoid of emotion. Kylie's control of it was spiritual in nature, not mental, and so it worked. But the Displace skill you're using won't fool it. Neither will your Mislead skill. None of your Psi powers, such as Mind Spear, will affect it. Your Anticipate and Predict skills will work normally, because they feed you with information rather than attempting to influence the mook's mind.

"Also consider your Martial Artist class. You have the skills Bare Hands Ignore Armor, Bare Hands Fast Attack, and Bare Hands Stun. These might be your best skills to use against the Dragon."

"Right, I'll take on the Dragon with my bare hands." I suppress a laugh.

"You could ask for help," ODYSSEY says.

"Who's around to ask?"

"They don't need to be around. You can ask someone to head hop in and lend you their skills. Maybe someone with a spiritual attack form."

I'd forgotten about head hopping. "Rancor, stay put. I'll get some assistance. Maybe."

Marta wags a finger. "Don't ask for it over local chat, girlie. The mook will hear you, too, and you could draw its attention."

"Right. Thanks." I check the party roster. Mom, Dad, and Charli are all on it, but marked as unavailable for chat. The only ones on the roster available for me to chat with other than Rancor are Spyder and Britta, Charli's daughter. "Spyder or Britta, if you are in a position to head hop to me, I need your help."

"Where's Mommy?" Britta's voice is tinged with apprehension.

"Good to hear your voice, Slithy," says Spyder. "Charli simply vanished, along with everyone in parties MAD and XStorm. Quantized is trying to calm Britta, but she's frantic without her mother. I can't do the head hopping thing, sadly, but Britta did it for Kylie, so she knows how. If we can calm her, maybe she can help you."

I need to give it a try. "Britta, my name is Slithy. We met before. I'm your Mommy's friend and your friend, too. Would you like me to take you to your Mommy?"

"Yes. Go to Mommy."

"I can take you, Britta, but I need your help first. Will you help me?"

"Yes."

"She's actually saying, *yes*, now, instead of *aagh*," says Spyder. "And speaking sentences of more than two words."

"Thank you, Britta. Do you like Spyder?"

"Yes. Spyder is nice."

"I want you to be safe while you help me, Britta. Will you sit by Spyder, please?"

"Yes. Sit by Spyder."

The Arachnid Behemoth tells me when Britta is sitting next to her.

"Britta, I need you to come into my head. You did it for Kylie before. Now do it for me. This is how you help me so I can take you to your Mommy. Will you do it?"

"Yes. Head hop."

I accept her request and get a mental picture of her that's more realistic than her chat icon. Though her mentality is that of a toddler, she has the appearance of a young, green-skinned Cave

25

Goblin woman. She's wearing a suit of Leather Armor, rather than cavorting about in the nude like she had been when I briefly met her. "Hi, Britta. Thank you for helping me. Do you see that Dragon?" Now that she's in my head, she can see through my eyes.

Britta's mouth forms the word, *oh*. "Yes. *Dragon*."

"We need to kill it, or it's going to kill me, and then I can't take you to your Mommy. Can you lend me all your abilities, please?"

She nods vigorously.

A long list appears in my view. Marta gestures, and all the skills that duplicate my own fade from the list. Both Britta and I are level twenty-nine Mentalists, so all her Mentalist skills are a wash for me. Her subclass is Assassin, at level twenty. "What can you tell me about her Assassin skills, Marta?"

The witch grimaces. "Nothing much there of value against undead mooks. Vitals Strike, Disguise, Hide, Ranged Vitals Strike, Poison Touch—none of them will help against a Black Ghoul Dragon. Flight Speed will give you mobility in the air. Inspect Character and Locate Character will do nothing against the Dragon."

"Britta has the Locate Character skill?"

"That's what it says, girlie."

I can understand why the young woman is so frantic, especially given her childish mentality. Her skill isn't working to locate her Mom. Or maybe it is working, but Britta can't go where her skill tells her Charli is.

The girl's traits are Claws Attack, Dark Sight, Special Movement - Burrow, Regeneration level 3, Shadow Self level 2, and Iron Will level 2. I doubt the Claws Attack is as good as my Martial Artist Bare Hands skills. The Shadow Self trait is grayed out, unavailable. "What does Shadow Self do?"

"At level two," says Marta, "it can create two Shadow Self copies of the character. Britta only has one Shadow Self activated, but since the trait is in use, you can't use it."

Other than Flight Speed, the only ability Britta has that sounds useful isn't available to me. "Just curious, what abilities does a Shadow Self have?"

"All the character's abilities are duplicated for the Shadow Self. It and the character share a single XP pool and share hit point pools in all domains. But each has her own combat heartbeat and cool down period, and each tracks her own skill and trait usage counts and expended Auni and Psi points. If the trait were available to you, you could have two copies of yourself helping you. Triple the damage in a third of the time."

I huff. This head hop was all for nothing. "We're back to square one. ODYSSEY, can anyone else head hop to me?"

"Only members of your party can head hop to you. Rancor could do it. He can't transfer his Psi Powers skill, as it enables his Discarnate power, which he needs to remain incorporeal and thus impervious to the Dragon's attacks. On the good side, the Discarnate power freezes him in place. If he head hops and loses consciousness, he'll still remain suspended in place and thus continue drawing the Dragon's attacks."

I relay what ODYSSEY told me to Rancor.

"Ha ha, let's do it."

I accept Rancor's request. His list of abilities replaces Britta's. The girl is busy watching the Dragon through my eyes, and it's just as well she stays occupied, keeping her out of trouble here and elsewhere. "Which of these are useful in our situation, Marta?"

The witch scans Rancor's abilities list. "The Psi-Warrior defensive skills could help against the physical damage dealt by the Dragon's fangs, but not against poison breath or the spiritual damage also dealt by its fangs. The Psi-Melee Weapon skill and Psi-Fast Melee Weapon would serve to deal both physical and mental damage to the mook, except that it's immune to mental damage, and its armor would apply against the physical damage dealt. You'll be reduced to zero spiritual hit points long before you succumb to physical attacks, so all the skills that help you against physical or mental attacks are of next to no value. That goes for all

27

the Tank skills Rancor has. The only Tank skill he has that could be of much real help is the Stun skill, which would stack with your Bare Hands Stun skill. If you can keep the Dragon stunned, you could keep beating up on it.

"Moving to Rancor's traits.... His Flight trait won't help as much as the Flight Speed skill from Britta. She gives you a faster speed. His Beak Attack is less effective than your Bare Hands attack. His Peck Wood trait won't help, since the Dragon isn't made of wood. Wakeful and Death Tolerant are interesting, but of no use in defeating the Dragon. That leaves Power Strike level four. There's some real meat with this trait. Each level doubles the damage dealt. At level four, the total multiplier is sixteen."

"Ha ha, go for it, Slithy. It's either that, or you go on without me, which would make me really sad."

"I'm not leaving you behind, Rancor." So that's it. "Okay, Marta, tally up all my damage dealing bonuses."

"You got it, girlie. Using your bare hands, each attack is at +30 and ignores up to 24 points of the Dragon's scaly armor, so you'll get at least 24 points of damage through with each attack. On the face of it, that's not much, compared to what some other fighter types can do. But your level 20 Bare Hands Fast Attack gives you two extra attacks per combat heartbeat. One combat heartbeat is normally equal to ten seconds, but you have the Time Sense trait at level four, allowing you to shorten your combat heartbeats by four seconds each. So, every six seconds, you can deliver three attacks. In nine seconds, less time than the normal combat heartbeat, you could deliver six attacks, all of them ignoring up to 24 points of armor, for a minimum delivery of 144 damage.

"That's not taking into account Rancor's skills and traits. His level 30 Melee Damage skill will increase your Bare Hands Attack by 30, and then his Power Strike will multiply it all by 16. You'll still only ignore 24 points of armor per strike, but each strike will be delivering 60 times 16, or 960 points of damage total. We can hope the Dragon's armor is less than 960. That's a good bet. If you total everything, within nine seconds you could deliver a total of 5760 points of damage, minus some if its armor value is greater than 24. Sadly, it's armor will reduce the amount of damage dealt per hit, so whatever it's armor rating is, it's effectively six times that against your six attacks.

"Now, before you ask, no, I don't know how much armor or hit points the Dragon has. After your first strike, I'll be able to tell you more. But at that point, you're rather committed."

Despite all the damage I'll be able to do in a short amount of time, I'm not feeling confident. "If it breathes on me once, I'm a goner. I have no defense against spiritual damage."

"The Dragon's poison needs to enter your system to affect you, girlie. As a Khertaan avatar, you don't need to breathe, but the poison can still get inside you. If only you had some trait that could block unwanted foreign substances from entering your system."

"Ah." Being a Frogkin, I have the Hold Breath trait at level two, plenty high enough to ensure I can block the Dragon's poisonous breath for far longer than this encounter will last. "So, I only need to worry about its fangs." My confidence is returning.

"Keep in mind," ODYSSEY interjects, "if you die, you can't respawn until the System finishes its update. If you want my opinion, it's unlikely the System has any intention of ending update mode. Once you're out, you're not likely coming back in."

"Great." I've lost confidence again. But I said I'm not leaving Rancor, and I'm keeping my word to him. "Okay, tell me how the Psi-Melee Weapon works."

Marta cackles. "Indeed, girlie. Don't discount it. Even though the mental damage it delivers will have no effect and the Dragon's armor will absorb some of the physical damage, the weapon deals 81 physical damage total when adding in Rancor's level 30 Melee Damage skill. Coupled with the level 34 Psi-Fast Melee Weapon skill, you'll get two additional attacks with it per combat heartbeat. That's 243 damage per combat heartbeat before applying the Power Strike trait, which brings the total up to 1296 per strike, or 3888 for the three strikes you can deliver in one combat heartbeat. In fact, with all your skills and traits working together, you can deal an attack every second, three with Bare Hands, three with the Psi-Melee Weapon, after which you terminate your combat heartbeat with Time Sense and start over. All total, every six seconds you can deliver 6768 damage, 72 of which ignores armor."

I'm feeling better again about my chances. "But how do I come into possession of the Psi-Melee Weapon? I don't have one in inventory."

Rancor answers that question. "Ha ha, you summon it when you want it and dismiss it when you don't. Very handy."

"Okay, okay." I resist the urge to close my eyes for even a second, since I don't want to disturb Britta, as she is still enthralled by the Dragon's movements.

I watch the Dragon closely for a couple of combat heartbeats, using my Time Sense trait to count the seconds between its attacks. It breathes once every ten seconds and tries to bite once every twenty seconds, losing a fang attack every other round due to the need to reorient itself after each one. Oh, I've so got this.

Using Anticipate to fix a target location, I start my Hold Breath trait and activate Teleport Self. I'm above the Dragon's back. It's in the middle of reorienting itself to come at Rancor again, and it just finished breathing two seconds ago, so I have time. I'm already three seconds into my current combat heartbeat. Flying along with the mook and staying tight on its spine, I smack it with my open palm. Once. Before I can smack it again, the Dragon erupts into a spray of pixels.

I laugh so hard. That was too damn easy. The careful planning was way overkill, but gave me the confidence I needed. I couldn't have done it like I did without Britta's Flight Speed skill or Rancor's Power Strike trait and Melee Damage skill, though I happily didn't need his Psi-Melee Weapon skills.

Add smacking a Dragon to death to my list of accomplishments. I can't stop laughing.

And damn, that little Woodpecker is way more impressive than I've given him credit for.

I want the Power Strike trait for my own. And the Flight Speed skill. And level 30 Melee Damage. *That was such a rush.*

"Congratulations, girlie, you earned one million XP for that kill. You're still only 46% of the way to level thirty. Rancor is at 49%, and Britta is at 50%."

The Cave Goblin girl is closer to level thirty than either Rancor or me. Amazing.

Rancor leaves my head.

Britta doesn't. "We find Mommy?"

"Ha ha, thanks, Slithy." Rancor breaks from his frozen state and joins me, wings aflutter. "We're not that far from Minook. Maybe we should go back and invite everyone else to join us. Make every PC and NPC level thirty. It's not like we have a Dragon to ride now, anyway."

I scan the horizon and spot the tower Kylie was headed for. "Now that I can see it, I could Teleport to the tower if I wanted. But I'm not going without you, Rancor, I promise. And we need to take Britta along. Spyder should go, too—maybe her being there will give her levels.

"So, yeah, we're going back, and we might as well, like you say, invite everyone." I bring up global chat. "Hello, all PCs and NPCs in Khertaan, this is Slithy from party TimeTrippers. Anyone who would like to accompany me on a quest guaranteed to take everyone who finishes it to class level thirty, meet me near the mouth of the cave in Minook. I'll be there in a few minutes. We'll head out on the quest ten minutes from now, sharp." I use my Time Sense trait to start a ten minute timer. To Britta, I say, "It's a long trip to where your Mommy is, but we're going. Just stay with me, and we'll get there. Okay?"

"Yes. Go to Mommy."

I wish my Mom and Dad were with me, too.

CHAPTER FIVE

Fauna: Desert Battle

I don't want to run into Kevin or Dr. Splat, so I take the elevator to the basement. I'd like to see Emma and Spooky, but I know they're safe, and what I need to do can't wait. I take the exit ramp out of the basement.

Random flashes of sunlight pierce the dark dome above as metal spiders larger than houses vie to dominate in the battle to break through. The Behemoths swarm across the invisible shell protecting the tower and its inhabitants. The van where I was to meet Kevin isn't in sight—it's parked on the opposite side of the tower.

I race forward, covering the distance to the edge of the protected area as fast as my hoofed legs will carry me, my shiny brown gunne cradled across my blue armored chest. Nearing the lower reach of the dome, I don't break my stride. There is no good place to do what I must do, no place where the Behemoth presence is less dense.

Blue, yellow, silver. I've repeated the sequence in my head since leaving Mr. Freeman on the thirtieth floor. I'm ten strides from the dome, my path clear to it. I want to get this right the first time. "Khenn Arrth, may I have a saving roll on Intelligence, please?"

Thunder rumbles, as the Trollgodfather rolls the dice for me off in his distant abode. I hope the roll was a success, and will soon find out. I turn my gaze on the blue button. It lights up, and I hold for a moment to lock it in. Then I move to the yellow, and then the silver, until all three are blazing.

Whoosh. The blue coating covering my armor retreats into the control panel, leaving my armor white. An inverted bowl of silver energy forms directly over my head, the rim expanding until it extends to the ground, creating an enclosing shell, through the interior of which streak miniature lightning bolts, some of them a mere inch from my face.

According to what Mr. Freeman told me during my fifteen minute training session, I'm now surrounded by a force field destabilization shell that will last for three seconds. The shell blurs my vision, but the tower's protective dome lies before me, so I leap forward, kicking my goat legs as hard as I can.

The dome evaporates where my silvery shell touches it. I tumble through the opening, even as a sharpened leg of immense proportions stabs the desert sands beside me. I'm not optimally protected at the moment, since my armor is white. I come up on my hooves as the three lit buttons on my sleeve panel dim. The silver shell becomes a brief shower of silver rain and is gone.

Metal spider legs slash and stab all around me. I focus on the blue button.... Before it can activate, a spider leg smacks me across the chest like a club, and I go flying across the sand, away from the dome. My gunne flies from my hand as pain shoots through my breast and arms. I've probably lost Constitution points, but I don't think many. I don't have my character sheet, so I can't check.

Spider legs stab the sand all around me, giant abdomens and thoraxes bobbing overhead. Springing up, I focus on the blue button, holding the focus, and the protective coating flows from the control panel, changing my armor from white to blue. An Arachnid limb stabs at my right leg, and the pointed tip slides across my armor, not even scratching it, shunted aside by the boost from blue. I even manage to stay on my hooves.

Dodging flailing spider legs, I dart across the sand. I can't avoid them all, and am knocked off track twice, but I get back up and keep going. I need my gunne back in hand, or I'm doomed.

A spider leg plunges into the sand next to the weapon as I reach it. Grabbing up the gunne, I aim straight up at the point where thorax meets abdomen. Depressing the trigger, I hold it down.

The weapon doesn't fire. Instead, a red light springs from the gunne's control panel. As Mr. Freeman had instructed, I stare into the retina scanner from where the red light is emitting. Is this necessary because I lost possession of the weapon and then regained it? It takes but a second to reset the weapon, but it feels like forever.

Again, I aim straight up and depress the trigger. Copper projectiles six inches long and half that in diameter stream from the end of the barrel, pounding into the Behemoth's chitinous armor. I expected some kick against my shoulder, but there isn't any.

Goat pies. When our group back in my original T&T world killed one of these things, it exploded. If I kill one at close range, can my armor protect me from the blast? As I recall, the heat of the Behemoth's death explosion was intense.

My ammo runs out. While I aim at the ground to reload, I select the red button on my armor for heat protection. Running to stay directly beneath my moving target, I train my stream of bullets on the same area as before. Even at maximum power, my bullets aren't doing much to the Behemoth. Their chitin is too tough.

How did we kill the Behemoth back in my original world? Greelia had put a blade in the creature's eye. The jostling of the blade kept delivering damage to the Behemoth inside its head, until it died.

Dodging flailing spider legs, I search for a spider head. Spotting one, I aim for its eye and open fire. The first few bullets miss but help me adjust my aim. Five huge bullets plunge one after the other into the Behemoth's skull before the creature explodes. I clap my gunne against my chest and close my eyes to the ensuing blast of flames.

The sand trembles and melts beneath me. I'm bowled over and go rolling, but this time keep hold of my gunne. I don't feel the heat at all—or any pain, really, for that matter. Either I'm fully protected by the armor, or adrenaline has me pumped and I don't feel a goat-blessed thing.

Opening my eyes, I jump to my hooves. Thankfully, no flames linger in the area. I locate another spider head, and loose another stream of bullets larger than my fist. *Thwack*, goes each missile that tears through the Behemoth's vulnerable spot. After five *thwacks*, spider number two goes bye bye. Once more I'm knocked off my hooves, and once more I protect my gunne to keep from losing it.

Spider leg attacks aren't so random now but deliberately aiming for me, as though I'd not been seen as a threat before. I'm noticed now. I switch the armor to blue—sharp-and-pointy deflection mode.

A leg stabs at my chest. I'm thrown off balance, but still feel immensely *powerful* when the spider spear fails to pierce my heart. Blessed Goat Mother, *what a rush*.

A web of chain metal hits me while I'm down, covering me. It closes up as it drags me across the sand. Still in possession of my gunne, I can't aim it effectively, though plenty of Behemoth heads loom around me.

Lifted into the air, caught in the giant spider's web, I don't panic. I've never been more calm and clear-headed.

I get a good look through the chain mesh.

The protective dome over the tower is gone. The Arachnid Behemoths swarm over the building, stabbing and smashing windows and bricks and slaying armed guards like flies. The Behemoths want inside, and before long they'll be there.

My force field destabilizer created a weak spot in the dome, and the Behemoths exploited it. The entire dome is down and all those in and on the tower—plus my friends in the van—are about to die. I still don't panic. Mr. Freeman knew the risks, and he'd taken them. What has happened isn't my fault. It's his. I'm following orders to the best of my ability, and I will keep on doing so.

Chopping sounds echo in the distance. Angling my head isn't easy, but I catch sight of a fleet of metal birds approaching. Rather than flapping wings, blades twirl in circles over their backs. Are they coming to fight the Behemoths or join them? Whichever the case, I need to get free of this web now.

I can't see my gunne's control panel, but my finger is on the trigger, and the gunne isn't pointing at me. I squeeze the trigger, and bullets scream as they striate the metal chains holding me. The webbing might give way eventually, but I need something to deliver an area attack and can deal more damage to metal.

Maybe acid…? But attacking at close range like this, there's a chance of it hitting me. I needed to switch my armor. What color had Mr. Freeman said was resistant to acid? Black. I'm sure of it. But I can't see the black buttons on my armor or weapon. I ask the Trollgodfather for some appropriate saving rolls.

Somewhere, cosmic dice roll on a cosmic table top, and thunder rolls down from the sky, though not loud enough to mask the constant whir of the metal birds. Thunder rumbles three times in total—for three saving rolls attempted.

The layout for the buttons springs to mind. The outlines of the buttons under my fingertips allow me to locate the button I know to be black, and I push it.

The color drains from my armor, turning my suit white. Then the white sweeps through a continuum of shades of gray, turning black in a fraction of a second. I pushed the correct button.

Now for the ammo selection. I find the gunne's control panel with my fingers and make my weapon black. It's nice I can verify my selections by the color of my equipment, rather than needing to see the buttons.

Perhaps too trusting in my armor, I keep my eyes open as I pull the trigger. Black liquid splashes in my face, but doesn't burn or blind me. I keep the trigger down until I run out of ammo and the liquid blast stops.

The chopping sounds grow ever louder while I wait.

With a groan, the metal webbing opens up, dumping me out. Before I hit the sand, I glance at my armor control panel and switch to blue stab-prevention mode.

Landing on my back slams the breath from my lungs.

My vision blurs as the tip of a Behemoth leg descends on me, aimed at my head. Stunned from the fall, I can't react in time, and the spear-like limb strikes my forehead. My upper body is pushed into the sand, but my blue-boosted armor prevents me from being skewered through the brain, and the tip of the leg slips across my scalp and off me. Sand rushes in to cover my face.

Thankfully, as I told Mr. Freeman, I don't need to breathe. I'm blind and half-buried but keep my calm. Clenching my gunne between my knees and using both hands, I dig at the sand covering my head.

My vision clears. I strain to rise, but can't. I clear away more sand until I can lift my noggin.

Another Behemoth leg steps on my gut, and I sink further, bearing the full weight of the sharpened limb on my belly button. The spider spear doesn't pierce me, but I scream at the pain of immense pressure. Then the leg lifts, leaving me still alive but buried in the sand. *Goat pies.*

Wriggling my fingers, I work to move whatever sand I can. Something big and heavy strikes my right arm but glances off, while stirring the sand sufficiently for me to free my limb. Another something strikes my right leg, but slips aside without pushing me deeper. With my right hand, I clear away enough sand to free my left arm, while Behemoth legs pound the sand about me. If they're trying to hit me, they're not doing a good job. They must be occupied with something more important than me. I'm collateral at this point.

Grabbing my gunne from between my knees, I aim it down to reload it, effectively pointing the weapon at myself. At the same time, I blindly finger the armor control pad with my left hand, find what I believe is the black button, and press it. I'm leaving myself vulnerable to spear attack, but it won't be for long. Still aiming the gunne at myself, I pull the trigger.

Sand melts away above and around me. The chopping of the metal birds slams into me, deafening. I activate slash-and-stab-resistance as a Behemoth leg swipes by overhead.

Flames billow in a brilliant red mass across the opening of my sandy pit, pouring down upon me, bathing me in its heat.

For how long does my fear of fire paralyze me? I don't know, but it has finally let go.

My armor is blue….

Not the red kind needed to protect me against fire….

Yet I don't feel any burning pain.

Thunder rumbles. I must be in need of a saving roll.

The memory hits me. My character sheet, now in Khenn Arrth's custody, states that even though I'm afraid of fire, I'm unaffected by fire-based effects. I don't need the armor to fireproof me. I'm already fireproof.

Holy Mother Goat.

Legs, abdomens, and thoraxes flash across my vision. Keeping my armor blue and my gunne black, I stay in my pit and shoot acid at anything that comes in sight. I don't shoot straight up, as the acid would fall back on me.

Smoke rises from scorched Behemoth legs. Fire continues to explode above me, which I take to mean the giant spiders are dying, but I can't verify.

The sun's rays dim. The chopping of the metal birds overwhelms all other sound.

One metal bird passes over me. A beam of light shines from the bird, sweeping across the sand. A large gunne mounted on the belly of the bird fires bullets at the Behemoths.

A solitary sphere about six inches in diameter arcs down from the bird. Sitting up, I watch its descent. It hits the sand not far away. Fire bursts outward, creating an expanding fiery dome. It swells across the sand, swallowing Behemoths in its rage. Closing my eyes, I drop into my hole.

I peek two seconds later. The fire has passed, though smoke fills the air. I sit up to see what kind of dent the bomb made on the Behemoth army. *Goat pies*, I can't tell a difference. If any Behemoths were killed, others have already filled the gap.

A second metal bird follows in the wake of the first, firing bullets and tossing a spherical bomb. I steel my nerves and force myself to watch as the bomb explodes. Flames gust around me without harming me. Sadly, they have no effect on the Behemoths, either. The bullets from the birds pass right through the spiders. I was hoping for help, but my hopes lie burning on the sand.

Behind the two metal birds comes a third one, also firing bullets. As a bomb arcs out, a web lashes up at the bird. It tangles with the spinning blades atop the bird, slowing the spin. Ropes dangle from the bird and people drop along the lines to the sand as the bird careens away. It crashes below my line of sight, but the resulting explosion tosses debris into the sky.

Jumping to my hooves, I run towards the people on the ground, firing acid at the Behemoths I pass, causing what damage I can with a quick blast before moving on. The soldiers I'm running to have their own gunnes and use them to pepper the Arachnids with all manner of ammunition types, including fire, acid, copper bullets, silver bullets, and grenades.

But their attacks pass through the spiders like they're ghosts. The Behemoths pay no attention to their attackers, who rush closer, not giving up hope their attacks will be effective to some degree.

Other metal birds flood the darkening sky, dropping more and more soldiers. They'll only get themselves killed.

Glass shatters at the top of the tower. The Behemoths have broken the plate glass window of Mr. Freeman's office. They're too big to crawl through, but they've found a weak spot, and they've proven they're good at exploiting them.

Chunks of stone fall from the tower as Arachnid Behemoth legs slam into the exterior wall, most of them focused on the floors housing the contestants.

"Halt!" A soldier shouts at me as I approach on the outskirts of the Behemoth gathering. He does a double take as it registers in his brain that I'm not human, and he aims his gunne at me. "You…. Drop your weapon…. Come with me…."

I don't comply. There's no need for me to go any closer, and I shout from where I am. "You aren't hurting them. They aren't even paying you any attention. If they do notice you, you're dead without the right gear. Your normal equipment won't cut it with these things. And if one does happen to die, watch out—they explode."

The Behemoths aren't paying me much attention now, either. I've given what warning I can, and hope it passes to all the soldiers and their metal birds. I head back into the fray. The soldier behind me shouts for me to stop, but I don't listen, spraying acid on another Behemoth.

A spider eyeball burns out from my acid attack. Thunder rumbles and inspiration strikes. Switching to grenade launcher and loading the new ammo, I then aim for the empty eye socket and fire.

My aim is true, and the grenade flies through the eye socket into the Behemoth's head. It detonates on impact, taking the monster's head off from the inside. The Behemoth explodes, the force of which slams me onto my butt on the sand. I close my eyes to the fire enveloping me as I manually switch my weapon to acid. I'm onto something here.

The soldier I'd conversed with lies burning on the sand. Other soldiers run to his aid. I hope he lives. I didn't mean for him to get hurt, but he chose not to listen to me.

Another soldier runs my way. I wave him away and shout for him not to come any closer, but he doesn't listen. He'll get himself hurt, too, if not killed.

Three Behemoths turn to face me and lumber my way. *Goat pies.* "Get away," I shout at the approaching soldier. "You're going to die." I shoot acid at the head of the closest spider as it stabs at me. Its attack throws me backwards across the sand, but I'm not hurt. I switch again to grenade launcher, reload, and wait for the shot. "Get the goat cheese away, soldier!"

"How are you killing them?"

"I'm special. You're not. Now go, all of you! *Please*."

Hearing the desperation in my voice, he turns and runs.

The wounded spider closes on me. I roll to my left to get a clear shot, and pull the trigger. "Fire in the hole!"

The soldier running away dives onto the sand, lying flat.

Kaboom. Closing my eyes to the fire, I switch my gunne to acid once more. It may take a while, but I know how to efficiently kill these damned Behemoths now, and I'll take out as many as I can before I'm dead.

The shadows of dusk creep further across the sand. I can see just fine. My character sheet says I can see in the dark. That helps. Means I can keep right on fighting.

The other two Behemoths facing me go down one after the other, victims of my grenade-in-the-burned-out-eye-socket trick. I don't miss my targets.

Larger and larger chunks of stone fall from the tower walls. I don't know how much longer the structure will stand.

A dozen Behemoths break off the group attacking the base of the tower and head my way. Bring it on!

I hope Emma, Spooky, Kevin, Dr. Splat, Mr. Freeman, the contestants, and all the other people in or around the tower are all right. Please, Khenn Arrth, don't let my friends die.

Thunder rumbles as the cosmic dice roll.

CHAPTER SIX

Yuni: Tuni

The last thing I remember is Inuki informing me of an emergency update. The game was to resume after the update. So I guess the game has resumed.

But I'm lying in a bed in a dimly lit room that looks exactly like the bedroom in which my player, Saiko Aimi, goes to sleep when she wants me to respawn in Khertaan. Why am I here? I should be in Minook. Perhaps I'm in an inn in Minook… in a room looking exactly like Aimi's bedroom? I don't think so. Something isn't right.

Right before the emergency update, we were facing the threat of thousands of level thirty mooks called Dread Naughts, released by Charli, though she claims she didn't do it on purpose. She gained the ability to perform the summons because of the artifact I brought her as part of a special quest I received back in Maron. I'd earned two-hundred-million XP for delivering the artifact to her, though it was two-hundred-million XP I didn't need—not that I knew it at the time. According to Inuki, everyone in my party gained enough XP to reach level thirty when Bradford and I killed Mithabel and Dylan.

I roll over to stare at the creature sharing my bed. He's a roly-poly feline—a ball of long, white fur with four paws, a whiskered head, two protruding triangular ears, and a three-inch stub of a tail. He's poised on his tail, the tip of which rests on the bed. His underside faces me, and I can see the soles of his paws. "Where are we, Inuki?"

"You've graduated from Khertaan. It's time to take the fight to another world! You're in the Fanciful Pegasus tower."

"What are you saying?" I know what he's saying, but I'm not ready to believe it.

He makes a smug face—something common for him. "You're not in Khertaan anymore. This room exists in two worlds at once. The question is, which world will you choose to defend?"

I sit up. I'm wearing my slick red Leather Armor with cutouts exposing the flesh on either side of my tummy. My outfit includes platform boots.

Under the Leather is a thin suit of red Quilted Armor, with cutouts in the same places as the Leather. As I understand it, people on Earth often wear Quilted Armor under Leather Armor to prevent chafing. Being from Khertaan, I don't chafe. I wear the Quilted for the small boost it gives to my armor value. I stand and stretch my legs.

On a small table rests a pocket watch stopped at three o'clock, a mirror, a wand, and a candle holder with a burned out candle—all items that Aimi has seen before, but I haven't.

How am I not Aimi? Or am I?

Against the wall opposite the bed rests a crystal ball on a wooden stand. The ball measures two feet in diameter. To the right of it is the door to the closet in which Aimi typically finds my equipment. To the left is a door that's always locked to my player.

I glance in the closet first. There's nothing in it.

Inuki bounces beside me, his stub tail the only part of him touching the floor. "Your Cudgel is in your inventory."

My inventory grid pops into view, with one item stashed — my Cudgel. I call it to hand and turn to the other door. It slides open at my touch. That was unexpected.

Beyond the door, a hallway lined with dark veneer leads to the right. Framed photos hang on the walls. Saiko Aimi features in each photo, whether portrait or snapshot. In one picture, she stands next to her brother, Saiko Haru. They look comfortable beside one another, like they're glad to be family. That's how I feel about Bradford. Where is he now? Where's the rest of my party?

I visit each photo, running my fingers over them. They call to Aimi in an attempt to draw her out of me, but I can't allow it — I can't let her consciousness dominate me. I am Yuni, level thirty Priestess of War, level twenty-one Anjai, and it was me, not Aimi, who did the work to become who and what I am now. I am her subconsciousness awakened. It is my responsibility and privilege to save the world that Aimi could not.

Leaving the photos behind, I approach another closed door. I touch it. A prompt overlays my view: *Choose your target world: Destin or Earth.*

Now I understand the photos. I return to them, and select one with a view of the outdoors. Which world did Saiko Aimi come from, Destin or Earth? I want to choose hers, for that's the one I most want to save.

To know the truth, I must allow her to speak. "Which world do you call home, Aimi?"

She replies in my mind, her voice calm. "You should not need to ask."

"Khertaan is my home, so I do need to ask. Will you tell me, or will you force me to guess?"

"There is a version of me on each world. It is for you to choose which one to save."

I stare at the photo longer. Dressed in a two-piece bikini, Aimi builds a sandcastle on an ocean beach. I touch the bikini. My average Intuition tells me it isn't from Destin. "I should choose Earth."

Returning to the door, I pause to pull up my character sheet. I haven't looked it over since turning level thirty.

My level twenty-one Anjai subclass has picked up a new skill, level 1 Split Body. I ask Inuki about it.

"Here's what I have on it, musume: *Allows character to create an autonomous copy of the character's self, to which character is telepathically connected. If any two or more of your selves agree, they may share each other's senses to see, hear, feel, etc., what any of them do. All selves share an XP pool, hit point pools in all domains, and a single inventory space. If any self gains a skill or trait, all selves gain it. Buffs and debuffs only affect the selves they are placed on.*

"*A newly created self is not automatically a member of any party, and is free to join any party according to normal party rules. Once a self is split off using this skill, it cannot be recalled. While this skill is inherited by all selves it creates, the total number of selves created through use of this skill may not exceed the level of the skill.*"

Interesting. I can create a copy of myself. Ha! I might not have to choose between Earth and Destin after all. I could split off a copy of my body and go to both. Why not?

I've earned more trait and attribute points. I boost my Metal Resistance trait to the max level of four, which makes me immune to all attacks made against me with metal objects. My Passion attribute is low average, so I put my last two earned attribute points on it, raising it to nine, the minimum value needed to put me in the average range. Just doing that makes me feel better about myself.

I have another skill I've yet to use. "Inuki, how many followers can I recruit with my level eight Followers skill?"

"Six-hundred-forty."

"Wow." I should recruit some followers. They might be a ton of help. "What can you tell me about the Followers skill?"

"Here's the info I have: *PCs and mooks can't be made your followers. Anyone you wish to designate as your follower must be willing, and must allow you to touch their face.*

"*Once someone becomes your follower, they inherit your traits, including your kindred traits. They automatically and continually benefit from your Morale skill, gaining its bonus on all actions they undertake.*

"*You gain two new actions pertaining to followers: Grant Skill and Transfer Auni. I don't have more info on those actions, sorry, but you can guess their effects from their names.*

"*Your followers are* **your** *followers, not followers of your Goddess. If they don't believe in your Goddess and her precepts, that's neither here nor there, unless it matters to you. Any follower who no longer wants to be your follower is automatically removed from your followers list. You can strike anyone from your followers list any time you like, opening up more slots for new ones.*

"*Lastly, a special chat channel is created for you and your followers.*"

"Chat channels… now there's an idea." I try to bring up the list of chat channels, but nothing pops into view.

"*Chat channels only work in Khertaan, musume. There are no chat channels available in this room or on Earth or Destin. If you want to talk with someone, you'll need to find another way.*"

"But I still get the special followers chat channel, right?"

Inuki grimaces. "*Not on Earth or Destin. Sorry.*"

I'm so alone. I wish I knew whether Dylan and Mithabel are all right, and I miss my twin brother. But I won't find any of them if I stay in this hallway. It's time to go… after one final item of business.

I invoke Split Body… and turn into a blob of goop.

The blob divides into two blobs, one remaining inside my Armor, and the other flowing across the floor. Then the half of me inside the Armor reshapes, filling the Armor, including the platform boots, everything back in place. The Cudgel lies beside me, and I pick it up. I have the sense of being the original me.

The other half of the goop-blob reshapes into a naked duplicate of me. Oh, gosh.

She looks herself over and then looks at me with raised eyebrows. "So I'm Yuni v2, it seems. Would have been nice if the skill made duplicates of our equipment, too. So, you've got Quilted Armor inside the Leather. Mind letting me wear the Quilted?"

"That would be for the best." I stash the Quilted Armor. The Leather Armor magically adjusts to lay against my skin.

Yuni v2 jumps to her feet and equips the red Quilted. Her feet remain bare, but I'm not giving up my platform boots. Being of the Anjai class, we don't need footwear, but I have my style.

She looks herself over and nods. "It will have to do. So… which of us is off to Earth and which to Destin?"

"You're the duplicate. I'll let you choose."

"Great. I'll go to Destin."

She knows I wanted to go to Earth. "Thanks. Hey, maybe we can meet up some time somewhere."

She grins. "That would be nice. Um… I have one request before you go."

I gesture for her to spit it out.

"I don't want to be referred to as Yuni v2. I need my own name."

With a fake frown, I shrug. "How about Tuni?"

"Like Yuni, but with a *two* sound instead of a *you* sound. I like it. Tuni it is."

"Great." I give her a brief hug. I'm accustomed to having a twin brother, but not a twin sister. Here I was feeling so lonely, and now that I have company, we're parting ways. I'm just going to go. "Well, I'm off to Earth, then." I reach to touch the door.

"Um… one more thing, Yuni. Do you mind if I stay right here and watch through your eyes for a while before I depart for Destin?"

"I don't mind."

"Great."

I don't feel her presence in my head, just an internal acknowledgment that my duplicate is aware of what I'm aware of. Keeping my back to Tuni, I hold up three fingers in front of my chest and look down at them. I attempt to telepathically project to her, "How many fingers am I holding up?" I want to see the telepathy and senses sharing at work.

"Three." Her words enter my head without her speaking them. "We good, Yuni?"

"We're good, Tuni." I wave at my own face... she's looking through my eyes, so she'll see the wave. Then I touch the door.

CHAPTER SEVEN

Yuni: Beach Battle

The door opens on the scene from the photo—a brightly lit ocean beach, a sandcastle spread before me. Stepping through, I find myself standing on wet sand in my red Leather Armor.

A man wearing only swimming trunks approaches me, running along the beach. He smiles as he draws within earshot. "Cool outfit."

I give him the sweetest smile I can muster. "I'm Yuni." I focus on my Followers skill. "Who are you?"

He comes to a stop three feet away. Water beads on his tattooed skin. He's six inches taller than me, lean, and not overly muscular. "Hi, Yuni. I'm Guy. I gotta tell you, you look outta this world."

"I'm looking for people to be my followers."

"Oh, yeah? Is Yuni your social media name? I'll be glad to add you."

I smile at his interpretation of my request. "Do you know how to fight?"

"I'm a lover, not a fighter." He raises and lowers his eyebrows at me.

Being a Priestess of War, I've got a certain type of follower in mind, but I'm eager to have my first one. "I'm mainly looking for fighters, but other roles are welcome, too. Are you a healer, perchance?"

He strums an air guitar. "I'm a musician."

Hmm, that's interesting. "May I touch your face?"

"May I touch yours?"

"Sure."

He leans close, puckering his lips. That's *not* what I meant, but at this point I don't care. I put my lips to his and give him a soft kiss as I stroke his cheek with my right hand. I don't allow him to hold the kiss, and as I pull away, I whisper, "Athlea, Goddess of War, may I introduce my first follower, Guy."

He stares at me. "I'm not religious...." Then his eyes mellow and his expression softens. "But that doesn't matter, does it? I'm happy to be considered one of your followers, Yuni. If there's ever anything I can do for you, just let me know."

"Congratulations, musume. You have your first follower." Inuki bounces on his tail.

Guy smirks at Inuki. "Is that a talking cat?"

"You can see him?" I didn't expect that anyone on Earth could see my support AI. While in Khertaan, no one ever saw him but me.

"Why shouldn't I?" Guy kneels to pet Inuki on the head. "What's your name, little fellow?"

Am I in some alternate version of Earth where a talking cat wouldn't shock the shit out of someone? Guy is more impressed than surprised.

"My name is Inuki. Thanks for asking, Guy."

"Hey, Inuki. I don't know what technology created you, but you are one cool cat. Your fur feels like... real, dude." Guy stands and gestures at me. "So... I'm your first follower, hey? Cool. Like I said, if you ever need anything, let me know. You got a phone? I'll give you my number."

"Sorry, I… lost mine." Saiko Aimi had a smart phone, but I have no idea what became of it. "Tell me your number anyway. Inuki will remember it if I don't."

"Wow, versatile little critter." Guy rattles off a string of numbers. "See you around, Yuni. Text me and I'll put you in one of my videos, if you don't mind wearing your outfit for it. I'm getting ideas already just looking at you."

"I just might take you up on that." I'm being serious. Of course, it all depends on whether there is a tomorrow, but it's good to act as though there will be.

I spend the next hour talking to people from all walks of life. Some of them aren't at all what I'm looking for as followers, but I find a dozen worthy souls, counting Guy, who agree to follow me, all of them thinking I'm a social media influencer who had the bad luck of losing her smart phone before coming to the beach in red Leather Armor. Inuki is a hit with everyone we meet.

"Inuki, give me a summary of my followers, please."

"Happy to, musume. Here are their names and the little we know about what they do."

Destiny - dancer and vocalist
Lana - martial artist
Guy - musician (possible guitarist)
Michelle - novelist (probably fantasy)
Bethany - nurse
Sharice - nurse
Daisuke - surfer
Evan - surfer
Joseph - surfer
Mya - surfer
Tara - surfer
Jamie - wrestler

"I got my phone here, Yuni." Wearing a two-piece bikini and a smile, the novelist, Michelle, runs towards me from where she has an umbrella set up. "Want me to video you? I can send it to your phone when you find it."

"Um… sure." Why not? Something good might even come of it. I pose, flex a muscle, and summon my Cudgel from inventory into my hand. To an observer, my weapon suddenly appeared in my grasp.

Michelle's eyes widen. "How did you do that?"

"Watch this." I raise the Cudgel over my head. "Athlea, Goddess of War, enchant my weapon for my followers to see."

The Cudgel turns black, bleeding wisps of dark mists.

"Whoa." Michelle steps closer, her eyes wider yet, recording the weapon close up. "That is so slick."

"Record me, too." My fat cat AI jumps up and down, waving a paw.

"But of course." Michelle backs up to get a wider shot. "Can I post this now, pretty please? My friends will just die."

"Sure." Of course, she doesn't mean her friends will literally die from seeing the video. I don't have that kind of power over people, and wouldn't want it. But I sense that I can do things no one else on Earth can. I'm a powered person. It's enough to make one heady.

Michelle punches buttons on her phone.

Cries of despair fall from the heavens as a large shadow darkens the day to dusk. The eyes of all beach-goers turn to the sky. Loosing their own screams, everyone in sight flees, except Michelle, Inuki, me, and a half-dozen fearless surfers.

Michelle punches more buttons on her phone and aims it at the sky. "Is this your doing, Yuni?"

"No. It may be dangerous, Michelle."

"But you're not afraid." She continues recording.

"Not yet."

The dark mook descends upon us. An aliform oblong creature, ten feet in length and as slender as my waist, it spreads wings like shredded fans twenty feet to either side. Beady black eyes glare at us from a shadowy beaked head as the mook floats earthward. "Worthless humans." It's voice has an echoing quality and might be in my head. "You may as well slit your own throats now."

I instinctively know what this mook is. Its name was mentioned right before I left Khertaan. Like me, it was released from there and chose to come here. My guess is no matter where I had chosen to go, whether on Destin or on Earth, I'd have run into one or more of these damned creatures eventually. "Inuki, what is that?"

"It's as you guessed, musume. A Dread Naught. This one is of the Flitter variety."

"There are multiple varieties?"

"From the information I have, yes. There are also Burners, Creepers, Divers, and Lungers. Each variety has its own set of kindred traits, which someone with the Monster Lore skill might be able to describe. All varieties have two traits in common: Dread and Emotional Armor. All Dread Naughts are level thirty mooks."

Dang. Though I'm level thirty, I don't like the idea of facing an enemy that's also level thirty. But here we are, and I can't run away like nearly everyone else has.

"You really aren't causing this, Yuni?" Michelle's hand trembles.

"This is a real menace, Michelle, and it's the reason why I'm here—to eradicate it from the face of the Earth so it can't hurt anyone."

Michelle gasps. "You're a powered hero?" A deeper admiration grows in her gaze.

Everyone else has vacated the beach. Some people are still on the water, surfing. I bet they're my followers, emboldened by the Morale boost they automatically get from me. *Please don't let them be harmed by this creature.*

"Be courageous, Michelle, but be careful. Leave if you feel you must, and if I tell you to run, then run."

"You got it, boss."

The Flitter repulses me to my core. Left to its own devices, it will kill everyone it can and lead the rest to the brink of suicide. The

Dread Naughts don't exist only to destroy. They play a sick game, their objective to coax as many people as possible into destroying themselves. And this beach is only one stop among many intended stops on the mook's journey across the planet.

Like black ink swirling across the sky, smudging the clouds and staining the sun, darkness exudes from the Dread Naught's fringed wings.

High in the distance, more tendrils of blackness spread out, marking the presence of other Dread Naught Flitters. Is anyone else from Khertaan confronting them? Or am I the only one on the planet with the power to face them? Surely I'm not the only one who chose Earth as my destination. But I might be the only one who arrived on this beach.

I raise my hands, one brandishing the Cudgel, still darkly enchanted. "Athlea, Goddess of War, hear me and lay your blessing upon me in this darkest hour, that I may demonstrate your full glory." I'm invoking my Morale skill, which Michelle, being my follower, enjoys without my instigation. But I need to invoke it if I'm to benefit from the effect.

As I finish my request to Athlea, an inky vine descends from the Flitter and swipes at me. I call upon my Courage and Presence skills to resist any debuffs it attempts to lay upon me, and bash at the tendril with my weapon. I connect with nothing, my Cudgel passing through the dark vine, which lashes across my chest.

I don't believe I affected it, and I feel nothing from its attack on me, but I need to know for sure. "Inuki, status."

"The Flitter attempted to Demoralize you, musume, to cancel your Morale bonus. The attempt failed, due to your combined Courage and Presence skills."

"And what about my attack against it?" My cool down timer is going, and my Cudgel Attack action is unavailable until my next combat heartbeat.

"Sadly, musume, the appendage you attacked wasn't an appendage, but a visual conveyance method for the Demoralize. It wasn't an actual part of the mook's body. You attacked the equivalent of an illusion that can't be disbelieved. Your Detect Anomaly skill could conceivably have determined the tendril's true nature, but only if you focused on it."

Well, I can do that now.

A dark vine descends in Michelle's direction. Focusing, I see it's of a similar nature to the one that attacked me—not an actual part of the mook's body, and so not something that deals damage or can be damaged, but visually conveys a spell or skill. Michelle trains her phone camera on it, uncertainty clouding her face. I don't tell her to run, though I wouldn't blame her if she did.

"Inuki, what effect is the Flitter attempting now?"

"I can often ascertain a tendril's intended effect after the action resolves. Before then, your guesses are as good as mine, musume."

Michelle steels her jaw as the Flitter's tendril floats in front of her face. Taking a step back, her hands trembling, she continues recording.

I don't know how exactly it works, but I attempt to use my new Grant Skill action, granting Michelle my Courage skill. The Grant Skill action is added to my cool down list for the current combat heartbeat.

Her hands stop shaking, and she stands her ground, exhaling loudly.

The tip of the tendril touches the phone. It strokes Michelle's fingers, moving from there to the back of her right hand and then over her wrist and along her forearm. Tickling her elbow, it follows the curve of her upper arm to her right shoulder.

Then the dark vine twines around Michelle's throat.

My nerves cry for me to attack the tendril, but I know it won't do any good. As much as I want to intervene, I can't. It's like trying to stop a spell—once the magic locks onto its target, the only thing that can stop it is the resistance of the target itself and any buffs on the target. Michelle must defend herself and prove to herself that she can. I've given her Courage. When she became my follower, she gained not only my Morale bonus, but my traits—Spiritual Armor and Pain Tolerant at level one, Wakeful at level three, and Metal Resistance at level four. Not shabby for an Earthling novelist.

"I'm seriously getting ideas for a novel from this." Michelle pokes some buttons on her upheld phone, and takes a selfie of her wearing the Flitter tendril like a scarf.

"Novels are naught but lies," says the echoing voice of the Flitter. "Those who write them contribute nothing to society—or worse, dilute the world's knowledge, planting crazy, useless ideas in their readers' minds."

"You're wrong." Michelle slips the fingers of her left hand between the tendril and her neck. She tugs, and the tendril slips free. "Novels hold a mirror before us, showing us where we've been, where we are, and where we're headed. They free the mind of the burdens of everyday responsibilities, granting a necessary respite from the daily grind, without indulging in alcohol or drugs. You attempt to rob me of my passion, Dark One, but I see you for what you are, because I've written about such as you."

The dark vine dissolves to dust as my cool down timer expires, and my next combat heartbeat begins.

The Flitter screeches. Dark mists rise from the sand to swirl around Michelle. She gasps, not from pain, but surprise.

"Michelle is at 45% HP, musume. The Flitter cast a Harm spell, using its Ranged Spells skill to extend the range beyond touch."

Bam, one more attack like that, and my follower is dead. I lay a hand on her and cast Healing, pumping 20 Auni into it, hoping it's overkill. She's got the Courage to face death and the ability to withstand much of the pain, but I *don't* want her to die.

"She's back to full HP, musume."

Fantastic. "Run, Michelle. If you stay here, you'll die, and I can't allow that."

She takes a step back, but doesn't flee. I don't have time to argue with her. I Shapeshift to Crow and launch into the sky. I don't have ranged attacks like this mook does, so I have to take the attack to it. I can fly without turning into a Crow, but by combining my Flight

Speed and Wind Control skills with my bird form, I'm faster and more maneuverable.

"Come, puny human. You can do nothing to me." An echoing laugh accompanies the Flitter's words.

This monster thinks I'm human. Ha. I'm a Khertaan Asian. Slight difference.

I focus on my Wind Control skill to push me upward even faster, reaching the Flitter before my combat heartbeat resets. My Cudgel is already enchanted. Clutching it in my talons, I swing.

My weapon drags, like the Flitter is only partly tangible. I've connected with its body, and my enchanted weapon should do some amount of damage.

"Though magical, your attack failed to harm the enemy, musume. It has no hit points in the physical, mental, or spiritual domains, and is thus immune to those types of damage. In the emotional domain, it is heavily armored."

Damn. I have one second left in my combat heartbeat, and so can still take one action not on cool down. There's no time to think about it. I lunge, intending to cast Enervate from inside the intangible mook, since my range is touch. I choose the emotional domain for the damage type and put twenty points of Auni into the spell, which should deliver about fifty percent more damage than I did with the Cudgel.

The mook flaps its wings, raising a gust of wind meant to repel me. It stresses my already active Wind Control, but doesn't overpower it.

I'm inside the mook.

With twenty Auni powering the Enervate spell, it should deal over a hundred and fifty points of damage. What percentage that represents of the mook's total EP depends on how many EP it has, of course. I just hope I get past its armor and do *something*.

"The mook's EP stands at 100%, musume. It can be damaged in the emotional domain, but your attack failed to overcome its Emotional Armor."

Holy Mother of War.

My cool down timer resets, as does the mook's.

I sense it's attack on me as I cast my Enervate spell on it. It's not trying to repel or avoid me, but is intent on damaging me. I put all my remaining 144 Auni into the Enervate. This might be my one and only chance to defeat this monster. If my spell doesn't bring it down this time, I'm screwed.

Invisible forces tug at my soul, trying to rip off a piece, like they could strip from me something of what makes me who I am. It's a strong pull, and one I can't take a defensive action against.

You are Yuni, Priestess of War and an Anjai, says Saiko Aimi from deep inside me. *Let no one and nothing make you doubt it.*

Thank you, player.

My Enervate spell activates. I propel myself away from the mook. If what I've done doesn't defeat it, I've little hope to do so — escape will be the only action left to me in this encounter.

The Dread Naught shrieks its pain. Similar screams sound in the distance.

All the shrieks cut short, not only here, but those far away, as the Flitter above me implodes. Dark tendrils on the distant horizon fold in on themselves.

An explosion rocks the beach. Surging winds blast outward from the Flitter's point of implosion. My Wind Control pushes some of the gusting forces aside, so I don't take the full brunt of the attack, but I still feel it in my little Crow body.

"The Flitter is defeated, musume, as are the three Shadow Selves it created to wreak havoc elsewhere. Your HP is at 70%. Your follower Michelle, is at 13% HP and lies unconscious on the beach. She would likely be dead if not for your Wind Control absorbing a portion of the blast damage."

I dive toward her prone figure. She's on her back, her eyes closed. Her hands lie on her chest, her fingers curled as though holding the phone that's no longer in her grasp, but lying ten feet away. Landing, I switch back to human form, kneel beside her, and check for a pulse, to assure myself she lives. "Keep me updated on her status, Inuki."

"You're not listening to me, musume."

My attention *was* all on Michelle. "What is it?"

"Joseph is at 3% HP and Mya is at 2%. They need your help. Your other three surfer followers, I regret to inform you, are dead. Joseph and Mya are lucky to be alive. They did not have the benefit of your Wind Control buffer."

It can't be… three Earthling humans dead.

Saiko Aimi stirs inside me. *Face it, Yuni. There will be many more deaths before it's over. You can't save them all.*

Tuni is still watching and listening, but says nothing. She's trying to be no more intrusive than necessary, which I appreciate.

Aimi is right, of course. But it feels like the deaths of these three followers should have been preventable. If they hadn't been my followers, they'd have fled the beach like everyone else. Their automatically boosted Morale made them overconfident.

Five surfers float not far from shore, face down. None of them are moving, but with my Detect Anomaly skill, I determine which two still have life remaining.

In Khertaan, when someone dies, their bodies turn to pixels, free to respawn later, if they have lives remaining. Earthlings don't pixelize or respawn. I don't even know if *I* can respawn if I die on this world. The life forces of three Earthling surfers are gone forever, and their corpses remain as proof.

I grab an arm in each hand and drag the two still-living bodies to shore. Rolling them onto their backs, I tend to Mya first, since her HP is lowest.

I know some basic lifesaving techniques, says Aimi. *Let me try to save them.*

I give control of my motor functions over to her, and she gets to work.

Mya sputters and opens her eyes. "What…?"

"Thank the Goddess you're alive. Rest while I help Joseph." Aimi bends over the male surfer.

Mya sits up. "Where's Tara? Evan? Daisuke?"

"I'm sorry, Mya. They're gone."

Looking out to the waves, she gasps. Struggling to rise, she chokes.

Aimi must do what she can to help Joseph.

After a moment, he stirs, coughing up water.

Mya stumbles towards the shoreline, words gurgling in her throat. "Tara. No. *Tara.*"

I am a Priestess of War, and deaths are to be expected when War is waged. But I wasn't prepared for the harsh realities of War on Earth. I must keep fighting, but I have no right to ask these Earthlings to follow me into danger.

Tuni decides to speak. "There were thousands of Dread Naughts released in Khertaan. We should assume half of them came to Earth, and the other half went to Destin. You've dealt with *one* of them, and spent all your Auni to do it. You need help, with no idea whether any other Khertaan PCs will come to your aid, or when they will come if they do. Perhaps I should come to Earth rather than go to Destin."

"She's right, musume," Inuki sits beside Joseph, patting his shoulder. "Can you alone save this world? Not if this encounter was any indication. And who is to say whether anyone from Khertaan will help Destin if not Tuni? Can you deny the people of both worlds a chance to join this fight if they will? You both need many followers and to teach them. Grant them many skills, more than just Courage.

"But in the meantime, you need to get some healing, for yourself and the three followers whose lives you saved. You have two nurse followers who will help at your request. They can't be too far away. I have their phone numbers, and Michelle's phone lies on the ground just over there."

CHAPTER EIGHT

Amarynth: Companions

Barney, my personal support AI, tosses his hair out of his face. He's dressed in jeans, t-shirt, and leather boots, and has a British accent. "It's your choice, love. Earth or Destin. They both need help."

"Why are all these photos of Anna Milligan on the walls?"

"That's for you to figure out, love."

"You're not of much help, are you? Well, I know nothing of Destin, so I choose Earth. I just go out this door to be on Earth? Where on Earth will I be?"

"That's for you to figure out, love."

I see. I examine the photos closer. Some are of Anna at work, some are at home, and a few are in outdoor settings. "Are Mithabel and Dylan making similar choices now, too?"

"They haven't graduated from Khertaan yet, love, so… no. When the System update is finished and they're allowed to respawn, they will receive the necessary XP to reach level thirty, at which time they will graduate from Khertaan, too. Until then, you can either wait for them, or venture out alone."

"What about Charli...? And Rolag? Where are they?" I don't relish traveling without company. Where's the fun in that?

Barney grimaces. "Charli reached level thirty, but she isn't a PC, love, and so has no bedroom at this facility in which to awaken. I don't know her fate. As for Rolag, he was the instantiation of your Magical Companion trait. Perhaps if you concentrate on the trait, you can summon him."

"Well, then...." I close my eyes and turn my focus inward, picturing my Pseudo Code Dragon friend.

"Hey, Amarynth." It's his little reptilian voice.

I open my eyes.

Rolag crouches on the hallway floor.

I kneel beside him and give his long neck a hug. "I'm so happy to see you, my friend."

"Thanks for calling." He winds his neck around mine. "Where are we?"

"In the Fanciful Pegasus facility, where Anna Milligan went to sleep to pass her awareness to me in Khertaan."

I'm right here, Anna says in my head. *But don't ask me how I got to this place. Those memories are fuzzy.*

"I remember this hallway. It led into Khertaan. But my support AI says now it will lead to one of two places, Earth or Destin. I've chosen to go to Earth, but I don't feel quite ready."

"Cheers, Rolag." My AI waves at the Pseudo Code Dragon. "I'm Barney, Amarynth's personal support AI."

"Glad to meet you, Barney."

"Um, what...?" I look from Rolag to Barney and then back to Rolag. "You can see him?"

The Dragon squints and points his tail. "Yeah. He's right there."

"Well, that's new." I turn to Barney again. "So.... Oh. I get it. Things are different now. Which means... I'm going to try something." I close my eyes and turn my focus inward once more, this time concentrating on my High Social Status trait. It was the trait that brought Charli to me in the beginning, way back in the starting city of Voorton. I picture her, not as I saw her last—an eighteen-year-old mother—but as I remember her the most—the fourteen-year-old star-struck girl who wheedled her way into party MAD as our Cowgirl Guide. Instead of long blond strands flowing over her shoulders, I see her brown pigtails swinging beneath the brim of her Cowgirl hat. I imagine her voice, the reverence it held for me as she called me....

"Milady."

Her voice is so real... so close. I want to believe she's here, in the hallway with Rolag and me, but I'm afraid to open my eyes... afraid she's only in my head and that opening my eyes will prove it.

Fingers touch the back of my hand, then slip to my waist. Small arms pull me into a hug. She's crying, seeking comfort from me.

I slide my arms behind her shoulders and hold her snugly against my armored chest. "Is it really you, Charli?"

She nods, her head still pressed against my Leather. "Yes, Milady. I've missed you so much."

I open my eyes to verify the truth. Her Cowgirl hat lies tilted back but remains on her head, hiding her from my gaze. I step back and hold her at arm's length. Her fourteen-year-old eyes gaze up at me with longing. Anna Milligan never married. She had no children. She doesn't think Earth is a good place for kids. Maybe she's right. But Charli is like a daughter to me, the closest to one that either Anna or I will ever have. There's no one on Earth or any other world I love more.

Mithabel had claimed more than once the NPCs in Khertaan weren't real. But Charli is here, with me, outside of Khertaan—feeling, sounding, and looking as real as anything else I consider real. Mithabel can have her opinions, but we all choose our own beliefs. And I choose to believe Charli is as real as I am. After all, I'm not Anna Milligan. I'm Amarynth, Viking Archer and Crossbow Specialist, trained to level thirty in Khertaan, but now headed to Earth to combat an alien invasion.

But not yet. Charli and I hug again. We don't speak. Words would ruin the moment.

CHAPTER NINE

Charli: To the Office

No longer suspended in the darkness of limbo, I'm trembling with emotion, my arms around my hero and role model, Lady Amarynth. She drew me back into the light. I'm alive, with mobility and awareness of my surroundings.

She brought me to her in my first persona, that of a fourteen-year-old Cowgirl. It's the way she remembers me, so I get it. And maybe it's best I stay in this persona—not only for Lady Amarynth, but for my own sanity. In my second persona, that of an eighteen-year-old Cowgirl, I'm a mother, but my child is not with me. If I were to switch to Eighteen, I'd be out of my mind with worry until I could reunite with my daughter, Britta—who manifested as a green-skinned Cave Goblin woman and doesn't look like she could possibly be my daughter.

Even in my fourteen-year-old persona, I want the best for Britta. I don't want her floundering in the darkness of limbo like I was. Perhaps I can bring her to me the same way Lady Amarynth summoned me. Keeping my arms around the Lady, I close my eyes and picture my little girl. The last time I saw her, she had the appearance of an eighteen-year-old and the mentality of a toddler. But that was her disguise, beneath which she was still a baby, in which case having the mentality of a toddler was quite impressive.

Try as I might, I can't bring Britta into focus. My mental image of her flits from adult to baby and back, never stabilizing. If I gave Eighteen control of my faculties, perhaps she could do better, but if she failed, I'd never get control back from her, and she'd be so distraught, she'd be no good to anyone. Besides which, I know nothing about where I am. Maybe it isn't even safe for Britta to be here.

As I step back to take in my new environment, I consign Britta to the recesses of my mind. She's not forgotten, but my memory of her won't be a distraction, either.

Rolag sidles up to me. "How about a hug from the runt of the party?"

"Oh, it's so good to see you again, Rolag." I relish the squeeze of his neck around mine for a minute.

"Hello, Charli." A man with a strange accent extends a hand for a shake. "I'm Barney, Amarynth's personal support AI. I feel like we've met before, because we traveled together in Khertaan a good deal, but you never saw me. We support AIs are typically invisible in Khertaan to all but the one we're assigned to. I'm glad to make your acquaintance officially. You mean a lot to Amarynth, and thus to me, too."

I shake his hand. It's true, I've never seen this fellow in my life, but the knowing look in his eyes says he's known me for years. It's like I'm meeting a stalker.

Lady Amarynth clears her throat. "Well... we're all here, as much as can be of party MAD at this time...." She turns to Barney. "Maybe that's not true. You said Mithabel and Dylan couldn't join us, but Zyekt and Niav were in our party. Did they reach level thirty?"

Barney nods. "Indeed."

"Give me another second." Lady Amarynth closes her eyes and holds her arms out to either side, palms up. She says nothing. We all know what she's thinking and attempting.

We wait….

A short Angel man stands next to the Lady, holding her right hand. A pink Mouse with pink eyes sits on her left palm. I clap at her achievement. The Lady opens her eyes.

The Angel is Zyekt, a Psyon and Life-Stealer. Sounds ominous. The Mouse is Niav, a female Guide and Mentalist. Our merry little band has two level-thirty Guides—me and Niav. Gosh, between the two of us, we should always know where we're going.

Amarynth isn't finished. "I'm on a roll, so let me keep trying." She stands apart from the rest of us and takes the position, eyes closed and arms upraised. Who is she focusing on now?

After a few minutes, she shakes her head. "It's no use. I was hoping I could bring Britta here for you, Charli, but I can't. Tried Mithabel and Dylan, too, on the off chance it might work. It didn't, as you can see. I think it only works on NPCs who reached level thirty. I'm guessing we're it. It's on us to save Earth."

This prompts a discussion about Earth, which I already know about, having traveled there with Nick, the father of my child and—in one Earth timeline—my husband. But Rolag, Zyekt, and Niav are curious. Barney meanders behind Lady Amarynth, adding occasional commentary.

Everyone is on board with the idea of saving Earth, though no one is sure exactly what we're saving it from. Every time someone tries to delve into the nature of the danger we could be facing, Barney leads the conversation in another direction.

I confront him. "What do you not want us to know, Mister?"

He grimaces and turns sad eyes on me. "Something you don't want to know, love."

I poke him in the chest with a finger. "Tell us what you're hiding."

He turns an imploring gaze on Lady Amarynth.

She shrugs. "I'm curious, too."

His gaze comes back to me. "I warn you, it won't be pleasant for you to hear, Charli."

Poke, poke, poke. "Tell me."

"Tell us all, Barney." Lady Amarynth has given her support AI a direct command, so now he's got to say.

He keeps his eyes trained on mine. "It's something your Eighteen persona knows, and seems to have successfully kept from you. She released the Dread Naughts that we must now fight."

I don't believe him. "Why would you say that?" NPCs from Khertaan can't lie, but can support AIs? I wouldn't think so, but how can what he's saying be true? "You're lying. Or joking. Or something...."

"It's the truth." He turns away from me. "I didn't want to tell you. I knew the truth would not be compatible with your Fourteen persona code and memory."

Accessing Eighteen's memory banks, I stagger under the weight of the truth. She *did* summon the Dread Naughts. She didn't mean to. "Yuni brought her a Shadow Marble. Once she possessed it, a force possessed her, taking her through the steps to perform the summoning."

Barney still faces away from me. "If I may add something to ease your pain...?"

I want to respond in the affirmative, but can't find my voice.

Lady Amarynth speaks on my behalf. "Please do, Barney."

"The Dread Naughts would have been released anyway. The Shadow Gaunt reached level thirty, giving him the power to summon them. But you did it first, Charli, mere moments before he gained the ability. You stopped him. It's said the Dread Naughts will not physically harm the one who released them. And so, in that light, you did a good thing. The Shadow Gaunt isn't protected against the Dread Naughts, but you are."

The Angel Zyekt asks the question I'm wondering. "And what if Charli attacks the Dread Naughts? Is she still protected from them then?"

Barney faces the group again and nods. "Yes, according to legend."

Lady Amarynth scoffs. "Legends have a way of stretching the truth."

"As you say, love."

I have one more question, and no one else thinks to ask it, so I must. "Is only my Eighteen persona protected from the Dread Naughts, or are all my personae protected?"

Rolag tilts his head. "How many personae do you have? You talk as if you have more than two."

I hold up four fingers. "I only had one—the one you see here—for the longest time. I had the Complex Personality trait since day one, and never understood it. Then I found myself wishing I was older, and suddenly Eighteen manifested. Later, my Complex Personality trait hit level two, giving me the right to create another persona, but I've kept the slot in reserve. I thought that would be it, but when I hit level thirty, the trait rose to level three, giving me yet another empty slot. So, I have two personae set, and can choose two more. I'm waiting to decide what they are until I feel a need for them."

Niav the Mouse squeaks. "That's amazing. What are the limitations on who you can become? Could you have a male persona? An old lady persona? What about a Cave Goblin persona?"

"I don't know." I tug on Lady Amarynth's hand. "Can we go save the Earth now?"

Zyekt holds up a hand like he's stopping traffic. "We've all just hit level thirty. Can we go over what skills we picked up?"

Lady Amarynth nods. "Sounds good to me. Will you start, Zyekt?"

The Angel looks pleased. "I now have a Create Undead skill I picked up for my Life-Stealer class. As for traits, my Meditative Focus is maxed out. My Auni Connection trait is at level three, which means each Auni I expend is worth eight." He looks to the Mouse. "Go ahead and tell them yours."

Niav wiggles her nose. "My newest skill is Clairvoyance. I also have some other skills I should mention. I've had them a while but no call to use them. In addition to Teleport Self, I also have a skill called Stone Teleport, which isn't for teleporting stone objects, but for teleporting to areas of stone, and I can take others with me. We just have to be connected, holding hands like when Zyekt takes us flying. I maxed out my Burrowing Special Movement trait, so if we're in need of a quick hole or even a tunnel, I'm your Mouse. Also, I want to say that since Charli and I are both Guides, we each have the Hide Party skill at level 10. I don't know if they will stack, but here's hoping. I'm assuming the skill will work for our group, since we're all in party MAD, or at least we were back in Khertaan."

Barney shakes his head. "Parties can't be formed or maintained on Earth like they are in Khertaan. But the skill will apply to whatever group you're traveling with on Earth, so it actually works better there. Same goes for Destin, should you find yourself on that world."

We continue around the circle. Lady Amarynth gained a Multi-Deflect Crossbow skill, which means she can deflect two crossbow missiles per combat heartbeat instead of one, which she doesn't think is that useful. Her Increased Movement trait is at level three, which gives her the ability to move four times faster than I can. She must wear her Boots of Silence if she moves at a speed of 3x or 4x, or she sounds like a locomotive. Luckily, the Boots are still in her possession. They grant her an additional level in Increased Movement, so she can actually move at five times my speed. Wow.

Another trait Lady Amarynth has is Magical Companion, which she maxed out, and assigned all four levels of it to Rolag. This means Rolag's combat heartbeat has a cool down period of two seconds. Any action he takes, he has to wait at most two seconds to use it again if he wants. This is blowing my mind.

As for Rolag, we're all blown away by what the little critter can do, and can't wait to see some of it demonstrated. He's a Winged Fighter and a Were-Giant. At his normal size, he's a foot high at the shoulder. With his Enlarge skill, he can grow to nine feet high at the shoulder—what I think of as an actual Dragon.

As a support AI, Barney doesn't have classes or levels. He can't attack or be attacked, but could carry any one of us if necessary. He's also able to fly, and is never far from Lady Amarynth.

I take my turn last. My newest skill is Shadow Dome, which allows me to create a protective, magical, ten-foot-radius dome-shaped force field that can only readily be penetrated by shadow-related creatures or magic. Since I'm only level twenty-one in my Shadow Wizard subclass, it's possible something or someone of level twenty-two or higher could get through, but it wouldn't be automatic. The skill is at level one, so I can only create one protective dome per encounter.

As for my traits, I've already mentioned my Complex Personality trait at level three. I've also got Mental Armor maxed out at level four, providing me two-hundred points of armor against damage from mental and psionic attacks.

"Okay, good." Zyekt seems to have taken the role of strategic leader. "Before we go anywhere, let's assess our strengths and weaknesses in dealing and absorbing damage types. Let's all go around again and state what kind of damage we can do and what kind we're protected against."

I quickly get lost about who can do what. But Zyekt seems to have it all in his head, so that's good.

We gather at the end of the hallway before the exit door and take hands, with Lady Amarynth in front. "To my office, on Earth." She touches the door, and it slides open. We walk forward into a blinding light.

The brilliance fades, and we're in a hallway with fluorescent lights overhead. Cubicles with desks sit to either side of me. The people occupying the desks turn curious stares at us. One of them laughs. "Anna Milligan? You look like you just came from a LARP session."

"Call me Amarynth." The Viking Archer woman waves her crossbow.

I make the correction on her behalf. "It's *Lady* Amarynth. She's being modest."

A woman walks over to Zyekt, standing half again his height. "Your Angel costume is quite convincing." She strokes one of his wings. "I'm Shirley... and I'm single."

"Everyone," says another woman seated at a desk, "take a look at the news. It's on all the sites."

Our group crowds around the closest desk. The person occupying it turns her computer screen towards us.

The view on the screen is from a helicopter flying over a downtown area with tall buildings. Traffic is at a standstill and people scramble to flee.

Dozens of metal serpents twenty feet long and three feet thick slither through the streets, attacking unlucky pedestrians. I recognize the Ferro Serpents—Boss Monsters from the Grassy Brassy Field, the first territory we explored in Khertaan.

Above them, a shadowy creature a good ten feet long and not even a foot thick flies between buildings. My Monster Lore tells me it's a Dread Naught, of the Flitter variety. The Dread Naught's fringed wings ride the breeze, spanning four times the length of its body. Dark tendrils stretch down from its belly, catching fleeing people around the throats. Many of those caught in this manner fall on their knees and bow to the Flitter. The tendrils then release them and search out others. Some who are caught don't kneel, but collapse to the ground where they lie in a broken heap.

Though the Flitter moves with ease in seeming slow motion, the screaming people can't move fast enough to escape its reach, especially since some of the Ferro Serpents serve to corral people towards it. The Dread Naught reaches through windows into buildings and pulls out occupants, dropping them to the sidewalks below. The monster doesn't discriminate—its victims come from all manner of ethnic backgrounds, genders, heights, weights, and ages. The slower a person moves—such as the elderly, mothers carrying children, and people in wheelchairs—the sooner the Flitter catches them.

"Where is that?" Lady Amarynth leans close to the computer screen. She straightens. "Anna Milligan knows the place. Let's go. Shirley, let me borrow your car."

The addressed woman pales. "Are you crazy, Anna? They're saying this is really happening. It's not a LARP thing."

"All the more reason we need to get down there—*now*. I'm serious."

"She is." With a flap of his wings, Zyekt lifts off the floor and stares into Shirley's eyes. "Give her your keys."

With a gulp, Shirley hands them over without further argument.

CHAPTER TEN

Charli: City Battle

We pile into the vehicle, Lady Amarynth in the driver's seat, with Rolag in the middle up front and Zyekt in the front passenger seat, Niav on his shoulder as usual. I sit in the back with Barney.

As Lady Amarynth backs the car out of the parking spot, someone runs up and slaps the trunk. The Lady brakes and leans out the window. "Please step back…. Oh, it's you. Good, maybe you can make yourself useful for a change. Get in."

My door opens, and I scoot to the middle of the back seat. A familiar man climbs in to sit next to me—ChrisCross, the PC avatar that Mithabel dislikes so much. Strapping a seatbelt across his shoulder, he nods at me. "ChrisCross at your service. Elitist Martial Artist and Psyon. You might want to strap in."

I glare at him for a moment before grabbing my seatbelt and hooking it.

A red-headed, freckled girl a couple years older than me knocks at the Elitist's window.

He rolls it down. "You okay, Bucky?"

She wears overalls with suspenders. "Let me hold on to the door frame, pretty boy."

"Knock yourself out." He looks back to me. "She's my support AI. She'll be fine out there. It's not like I could get rid of her if I wanted, you know." He points his chin at my hands, on which I'm wearing the Shadow Gauntlets I used back in Khertaan to summon the Dread Naughts we're now having to fight. He raises an eyebrow. "Nice gloves. What's your name?"

"I'm Charli."

"Oh? Sorry, but I thought you were older. I nearly removed you from the XStorm party list. Yuni talked me out of it. How'd you get added to all the parties, anyway?"

"I don't know."

"Well, you helped us out, XP-wise. Thanks for that, though I think it helped everyone else more than it did us. I mean, it was XStorm who earned the billion-plus XP there at the end. We'd have reached level thirty even without you. Not to take away from anything you did."

Zyekt cranes his neck to look over the back of his seat. His wings are folded tight against his back, but stick up in his face. "Hello, ChrisCross. Do you remember all of us? I'm Zyekt, Angel Psyon and Life-Stealer. Nice to know another Psyon. This is my Mouse Companion, Niav, Guide and Mentalist. Of course you remember Amarynth and her Companion, Rolag. Back there on the other side of Charli from you is Barney, Amarynth's support AI. I'm taking stock of all our strengths and weaknesses. Mind telling us your traits and Martial Artist skills?"

ChrisCross shrugs. "Nah, I don't mind. My Elitist kindred trait is Emotional Trigger. I tended to be the target of every mook our party fought, because of that trait. People and monsters… neither of them like me, and it throws them all off their game, so it works out for me. My other traits are Natural Weapon - Bare Hands at level four, Magical Companion at level one, and Combat Reflexes at level three."

The Angel cranes his neck more. "Where's your Companion?"

The Elitist shrugs. "I'll summon Lance when I need him. Haven't needed him on Earth yet, and I wasn't in the mood to explain an Electric Serpent to the humans of this world. How are people not freaking out over the little Dragon?"

"Tell me your Martial Artist skills," says Zyekt, "and then you can tell me Lance's abilities."

ChrisCross rolls the list off his tongue. In addition to Tough Skin at level 58, he can deal a ton of damage with his bare hands, and his bare hand attacks ignore armor to a degree. He can also leap a hundred feet, vertically or horizontally, and has a skill at level 8 called Bare Hands Fatality. "I've yet to use the Fatality skill. Not had the need or even an opportunity."

He then relates Lance's traits and skills. His companion can attack with fangs, an electric blade, or a bolt of electricity. If he dies, he explodes in a ball of electricity, and he can kill himself if desired, exploding for even more electrical damage to nearby enemies. This is the first time I've heard about anyone from Khertaan being able to commit suicide. If he were to kill himself on Earth, though, could he respawn? None of us know the answer to that, not even the support AIs.

Lance has Increased Movement at level four, same as Lady Amarynth. Yeah, that's impressive. He's got electric resistance and can transport people through electric fields without them getting hurt. His Rogue skills aren't geared for combat—Improvise, Mislead, Charm, Spot, Anticipate, Identify Item, and Inspect Character. I suppose the Mislead and Anticipate skills could help in combat. He has proved most useful as a Spy, another of his traits.

Turns out, both Lance and Rolag have the Accelerated Healing trait.

And that's it.

We ride along in silence. Bucky flashes me a grin every so often from her position outside the car. These support AIs are weird, both Barney and Bucky. I kinda wish I couldn't see them now, just like I couldn't see them in Khertaan. Even here, they're indestructible, but unable to fight. They have knowledge they sometimes are allowed to share, can carry a body on occasion, and do little else.

The car stops. Lady Amarynth opens her door. "Everyone out."

ဆၢႱၶ႖ၜႱ႖ၶ

Barney gets out on his side, while ChrisCross gets out on his side. They both offer me a hand. I take Barney's.

If something is in the sky, it's blocked from our view by all the tall buildings. I don't hear any aircraft. They either left of their own accord or the Flitter got them.

Lady Amarynth fires her crossbow. A single bolt in flight divides along its length into three bolts, each somehow still the same thickness as the original. The three bolts strike three nearby Ferro Serpents. Back when we first encountered them, they were so powerful compared to us, they killed both Lady Amarynth and Mithabel. They aren't so tough now. One shot from the Lady's crossbow, and all three Serpents erupt into fading pixels.

"Come on." My Viking Archer hero runs down the street. The rest of us follow, but she moves way too fast for us to keep up. Three crossbow bolts later, and she's cleared the immediate area of Ferro Serpents. She takes a pause, staring at the mess ahead of us.

To the extent of my First Person POV, flames devour the buildings lining either side of the street.

We catch up to the Lady and then we all move forward as a group.

Inside the burning structures, giant scaly bodies flash past the windows. We all know what happens when a Ferro Serpent comes in contact with flame. It grows to twice its size. Those inside the burning buildings are twenty feet long.

A man throws himself out a window to escape being swallowed by the Ferro Serpent at his back. At a lower window, the head of a second Ferro Serpent lashes out and snares the man in mid-flight, dragging him back into the building, drawing him into its hinged metal mouth.

A bolt from Lady Amarynth's crossbow splits in two and strikes both Ferro Serpents. They evaporate into nothingness. The swallowed man remains, and he slumps to the floor. Is he still alive? I don't see him rise.

Rolag flies over to peer through the window. He returns, shaking his head. His grim expression says everything.

We continue down the street, Lady Amarynth popping every Ferro Serpent she sees. If all we face are Ferro Serpents, she doesn't need us. But there's a Flitter Dread Naught here somewhere. I wrack my brain for more Monster Lore on the horrid mooks.

Niav, the other Guide in our group, peers at me from Zyekt's shoulder. "The Ferro Serpents...."

I nod. "Yeah. I doubt they're level thirty. They're here because of the Dread Naught. They're either illusions or summoned, and I don't think they're illusions."

The Mouse claws the air. "Right. So this Flitter either has a trait or a skill for commanding them. Kill the Flitter, and the Ferro Serpents should go back to where they came from...."

"Or," I finish for her, "vanish if they're illusions."

"Thanks for the insight, both of you." Lady Amarynth waves for her Pseudo Code Dragon Companion to take to the sky. "Stay low, but find the Dread Naught."

"Wait." I look to Barney. "Can you carry me?"

He glances at Lady Amarynth, and she grants her permission with a nod. Her support AI cradles my fourteen-year-old girl body in his arms like I'm a sack of straw.

I close my eyes and try to forget where I am. "I'll head hop to you, Rolag, and lend you my Hide skill."

"Head hop?" The voice of ChrisCross intrudes on my attempt to focus. "Lending a skill? How does that work?"

Oops. We weren't going to tell anyone else. But that was when we were competing with other parties in Khertaan. Now, the fate of the planet lies in our hands, and we need to pull out all the stops.

The Lady fills him in. "It's a trick we learned in Khertaan. Putting your awareness into the head of another party member, if they're willing, and then lending them your traits and skills. But it leaves your body unconscious, which is why she needs Barney to carry her."

"Bastards...." He doesn't sound as angry as the word slipping from his mouth might indicate. "So that's how MAD got ahead of all the other parties so quickly. I'll be damned.... That's brilliant."

"Go ahead, Charli." The Lady nods at me. "You have my permission." She explains to ChrisCross that head hopping to her Magical Companion can only be done if she allows it.

Nestled against Barney's chest, I focus on transferring my awareness to Rolag.

Even with the Lady's permission and Rolag's willingness, it isn't happening. I'm letting in too many distractions.

I focus harder. It still doesn't work.

Continually trying, I continually fail. To their credit, everyone keeps silent, waiting patiently for the little Cowgirl to do her thing or admit she can't. Maybe it can't be done on Earth...?

Thing is, I *am* a Cowgirl, and the kindred trait for Cowgirls is Stubbornness. So I ain't giving up. I've also got a high average Willpower attribute, and what good is it if I don't push it to its limit?

If head hopping can be done by anyone on Earth, it's going to be me. I give it everything I have.

"Hey there, Charli." Rolag speaks to me telepathically. "Glad to see you found a way in."

I'm looking at the city through his eyes. It worked. I *made* it work. "Hey, Rolag." I transfer my Hide skill to him, and he takes to the air.

The view from his First Person perspective is dizzying, what with him turning his head on his long neck this way and that while flying at high speed. I switch to Third Person POV, and my view quits swaying side to side. With Third Person POV, Rolag should be centered in my view, but I don't see him, which means the Hide skill is working as I'd hoped. I raise the point of origin for my view as high in the air as I can, capturing our surroundings at a wide angle.

I spot our target, a dark mass the length of a normal Ferro Serpent, with stringy wings fanning out, each one twice as long as its body. "The Flitter is to your left."

Rolag stays low but confirms my sighting using Third Person POV himself, and then flies back to the group. "Three streets up and turn left."

Seen from above, our group is such a mixed sort. Dressed in skin tight brown Leather Armor and wielding her Crossbow, Lady Amarynth leads, with the weaponless Angel Zyekt a step back to her right, flying just above the pavement, his white wings scarcely flapping. His pink Companion, the Mouse Niav, rides his shoulder as always. Behind the dwarfish Angel comes ChrisCross, barefoot, dressed only in white Quilted Armor. He appears to be unarmed, but his weapon of choice is Bare Hands, and his fingers flex as though itching to be put to use. To his left, behind the Lady, comes Barney, with me in his arms. The AI doesn't walk, but glides forward, his feet not touching the street. The weight of my body isn't putting the least stress on the AI.

Bringing up the rear is Bucky, the personal support AI for ChrisCross. Manifested as a red-headed girl with freckles, about sixteen-years-old, she's as barefoot as the avatar she serves. Wearing overalls with suspenders, she crouches on a skateboard without wheels—zipping along and occasionally cutting circles. Like Barney and Zyekt, she isn't touching the road's surface.

Do any of the PCs wonder how the System decided on the appearances and personae of their support AIs? Is a support AI in any way a reflection of the PC she or he serves? What does Barney, an older British male tourist, say about Lady Amarynth or her player, Anna Milligan? Likewise, what does Bucky, a freckled teenage girl in overalls and riding a skateboard, say about ChrisCross and Christopher Warden?

It's not something I want to dwell on. Maybe no one else wants to think—or speak—about it, either.

I remain unconscious in Barney's arms, keeping my awareness and Hide skill transferred to Rolag. The little Dragon flies out again, to keep track of the Flitter's movements. When Lady Amarynth and the others reach the third intersection, Rolag tells them to continue to the fourth street, since the Flitter has drifted further over.

The stream of Crossbow Bolts continues from Lady Amarynth, taking out every Ferro Serpent we happen upon. Some of the Serpents occupy buildings that aren't on fire, and those mooks are only ten feet long. Occasionally, someone runs into the street, and Lady Amarynth shouts for them to run away in the direction we came from. No one argues with her or stops to ask for her autograph. Will the people of Earth—when not in the middle of a Dread Naught invasion—treat Lady Amarynth as someone with a High Social Status, a celebrity?

If she saves the world, I'm sure they will.

The Flitter looms ahead. Threads of dark mist stream from the tips of its wings, flowing downward. Some of the threads grab people as they flee from buildings, while other threads snake into buildings through the windows to find victims. Those who the vines grab aren't always killed. Many are released almost immediately and drop to their knees where they stand, their heads and backs bowed, as though worshiping the monster in the sky as a deity.

Rolag hangs back until the group catches up to him. "What's our plan of attack here?"

"Head's up." Zyekt spins to face the building to his right. "They're bringing the fight to us. Attacks are coming from the buildings on both sides of us within ten seconds. More Ferro Serpents to be sure, but something else, too. What, exactly, I can't say. Something invisible and powerful enough to kill us all if we don't kill it first. I recommend an immediate withdrawal."

No one asks how he knows what he just told us. We all have powers and abilities. Some of us can remember what powers others have, and some of us can't. Most of us fall in the latter category.

"We can take it, whatever it is." ChrisCross takes a Martial Artist stance. He faces right and Lady Amarynth trains her Crossbow to the left.

Fire belches from the buildings to either side of us, blowing out the walls. Dust, smoke, and stone debris flood the street. Over-sized Ferro Serpents stream from the breaches.

The dust obscures the road. Rolag hovers above it, his form expanding in my Third Person view as he invokes his Were-Giant ability to Enlarge. His wingspan is over forty feet now, rivaling that of the Flitter. With a few flaps of his massive wings, he clears the dust and smoke from the street.

Lady Amarynth destroys a slew of Ferro Serpents on her side—a single Bolt fired that splits into numerous missiles, each one dousing the life of a Serpent.

ChrisCross runs to meet the Serpents to the right of the group. His motions are a blur as he fells one, two, three, four Serpents in as many seconds. He keeps going, hitting Serpents with the flat of his Hand, each strike demolishing its target. Then a glowing white Psi-Sword appears in his hand, and he strikes down even more Ferro Serpents, after which he dismisses the weapon and returns to slamming Serpents with his Bare Hands. His skills with both Bare Hands attacks and Psi-Weapon attacks and his supporting skills and traits allow him to make an attack every second. Impressive, but still not as great as Lady Amarynth, who slays dozens of enemies in only a few seconds. She keeps her side of the street clear. ChrisCross can't halt the flow on his side.

Zyekt holds up his hands, palms facing to the right. The Ferro Serpents streaming from that side go into slow motion, reducing their emerging numbers to something ChrisCross can handle.

The Angel had mentioned some powerful invisible enemy would be involved in the encounter. Focusing on my Search skill, I scan the area, starting on the Lady's side. If something is hidden there, I don't see it. I scan the other side of the street.

Ah, there it is. A foot-long Serpent hanging back, inside the breach through which the Ferro Serpents are exiting. I lend my Search skill to Rolag.

He surveys the area. "Yeah, I see it. There's one on the left side, too."

I switch to First Person POV to look through his eyes, and see what he sees—a foot-long snake hiding in the breach to the left.

Rolag flies closer to the latter one. He can't go too low because of his enlarged size, but gets close enough for a better view. "It's like a Ferro Serpent, only a lot smaller." He circles over the Lady. "Do you see the small Serpent, Amarynth? It's in the breach."

"I don't see it."

"There's one on your side, too, Zyekt. They're hidden, like you said they might be."

Checking Monster Lore, I find info on three types of small Serpents—Aqua Moccasins, Elemental Serpents, and Stone Snakes—none of which are the type to hang back and observe.

Lady Amarynth strides forward, dropping Ferro Serpents like proverbial flies. The Ferro Serpents don't leave corpses—they pixelize, leaving no proof they were even here.

Sirens sound in the distance. Planes and helicopters dot the horizon. The authorities are on their way. With all the burning buildings around us, they might be too ready to hold a Dragon with a forty-foot wingspan responsible, but only if they see him. I need to stay with Rolag and make sure he remains invisible.

But if law enforcement and the military go after the Flitter in the sky, all they'll achieve are their own deaths.

"I've got super-human ranked Sensing, and I don't see it." Lady Amarynth slays another dozen Ferro Serpents. "Whatever ability it's using to hide must be really high level."

Zyekt flies up for a better view and looks to both sides as he keeps his hands up to slow the procession of Ferro Serpents. "I can't see anything, either."

Perched on the Angel's shoulder, Niav looks both ways. "I see one of them. A small Serpent, but not of a type I can identify, unless it's a baby Ferro Serpent. Oh... it's coming our way."

"ChrisCross, get over here, *now*." Zyekt flies down. "Rolag, be prepared to protect us."

The Elitist Martial Artist runs back to the street, chased by Ferro Serpents. "Someone lend me their Search skill, so I can fight the thing."

Both small Serpents dart out of their respective breaches towards the street. Both of them stop and open their mouths, becoming completely visible. I know what that means. They're preparing an attack.

Rolag shouts a warning. *"They're going to breathe."*

"Stop, Serpents." Zyekt's voice is commanding, hypnotic.

But his Hypnotic Voice trait fails him against these mooks as they draw back their heads, stretching their mouths open even wider. *Ack.* My unconscious body is caught between the two of them. If they're about to attack with fire or acid breath, I'll be pixelized—or whatever happens to level thirty Khertaan NPCs who die on Earth.

Rolag drops from the sky as gouts of flame spew from the gaping mouths of the Serpents. The enlarged Pseudo Code Dragon spreads his wings, draping them over our group. Flames roll over him, blocked from reaching the rest of us. He's highly resistant to flames, and I sense no pain in him from the fire breath attack.

I switch back to Third Person POV. The small Serpents rise a foot off the ground and fly toward us, without wings. Rolag relays what I see to the others.

Lady Amarynth peeks out from beneath Rolag's sheltering wing and takes a quick shot. Several Ferro Serpents pixelize. One of her missiles strikes the small, flying Serpent on her side of the street.

Barney and Bucky give the same status report in unison. "The Dread Naught is still at 100% HP. Its armor absorbed the entire attack."

So, the Flitter isn't the only Dread Naught in the vicinity. These tiny snakes are Dread Naughts, too.

ChrisCross darts out from beneath Rolag's wing, racing at the little Dread Naught closest to him, evading the Ferro Serpents swarming around it. He slams a palm against the fire breather.

The two support AIs chime in with the status. "Dread Naught is at 31% HP."

Dang, ChrisCross *is* bad ass with his Bare Hands.

This Dread Naught must be an Anjai, with the abilities to Hide, Compress its body, Shapeshift to a specific type of beast, and Summon that type of beast—the beast in this case being Ferro Serpents. If the Dread Naught is a Burner, it could breathe fire.

It will also explode if it's killed.

Rolag hears my thoughts and shouts yet another warning. *"Don't kill it, ChrisCross.* It will explode."

A flaming blade appears in the coils of the wounded Serpent's tail, and it thrusts the fiery weapon at ChrisCross. The Elitist doesn't even try to Dodge, and the blade glances off his white Quilted Armor.

Four Ferro Serpents gnash their fangs at him.

He slams his hand against the wounded Serpent once more.

His target explodes, as my Monster Lore said it would.

The other small Serpent on the left side of the road explodes, too. Several small explosions sound down the street. The Burner had duplicates wreaking havoc elsewhere. By killing one, ChrisCross has killed them all.

Every Ferro Serpent in the area vanishes.

Flames from the explosions wash over Rolag's body once more, his wings still spread over us for protection. Because he's invisible to me, it appears as though an invisible dome of force protects us from the explosions.

Unfortunately, ChrisCross is caught in the dying blasts of both Dread Naughts.

The flames die down. ChrisCross still stands, singed. Smoke rises around him.

"Congratulations, the enemy has been defeated and the encounter is over." Barney and Bucky speak in unison from beneath Rolag's wings.

Bucky adds in a loud voice, "You're at 68% HP, pretty boy." She means ChrisCross, of course.

The Martial Artist bows. "I'm happy to have been of service to humanity."

Rolag raises his wings, something I *feel* instead of *see*. With a flapping of his invisible wings, he lifts into the sky. "Charli believes we might have been fighting a Burner Dread Naught with the Anjai class." The Dragon adds *why* I think that.

Everyone he'd been sheltering straightens, except for me, naturally, since I'm still unconscious in Barney's arms. Everyone else thinks my theory is a good one, and the point is made that no matter what we're seeing in an encounter, if we're fighting things from Khertaan, there's a good chance a Dread Naught is nearby.

ChrisCross points to the Flitter, which moved further away from us during our encounter with the Burner. "Can we discuss how we're dealing with that thing? I, for one, can't fly."

CHAPTER ELEVEN

Emma: Tunnel

"Please stay in the van." Dr. Splat sits in the driver's seat, watching the Arachnid Behemoths swarming over the invisible force field between them and us. Their shadows block nearly all the sunlight on this side of the tower.

"We just want to sit up there with you so we can watch, too." I hold Spooky's hand. She's floating in the air beside me as we make our way up front. "Can I climb over this equipment?"

"You won't hurt anything." He motions for me to come forward.

I do my best not to step directly on something that looks like it could fall over. I settle into the front passenger seat, and Spooky settles on my lap. "That's a large force field you have around the tower."

Dr. Splat scoffs. "It's not my work. I don't know where Franklin found the tech, but it's not from Earth or Destin."

"How do we know it will keep holding?"

He harrumphs. "We don't."

"But you feel safe enough in the van, right? We don't need to go into the tower?"

"If they get through the force field, it will only be a matter of time before they bring down the tower."

Forks of electricity play on the inner surface of the dome.

"That's not good." Dr. Splat straps himself in and starts the van. "You're right. We could be better served with a different position. Nigel, alert Franklin that the force field is weakening. I give it two minutes, tops, before it falters and those things start attacking the tower itself."

"Affirmative."

"Strap yourself in, Emma, and hold on tight to Spooky." The doctor drives, staying near the base of the tower. "We'll go around back and take the ramp into the basement. That's the safest place now."

I keep my voice low as I strap in like the doctor ordered. "Khenn Arrth, give me some saving rolls, please, for us to make it into the basement safely."

Thunder rumbles.

A sharpened Arachnid Behemoth leg slams into the ground ahead of us. Dr. Splat swerves to avoid it, as a forest of giant metal spider legs drops into place all around us.

The doctor continues driving and swerving, jostling the equipment in the van, until a large metal spike drives through the roof of the vehicle between him and me, reaching the floor. Dr. Splat revs the engine, but the van goes nowhere... until the Behemoth lifts us from the ground.

"Nigel, target the Behemoth leg spearing the van and sever it with a laser."

"Affirmative."

The van drops four feet to the ground and bounces. "Hang on." Dr. Splat revs the engine again, and this time we move... until another Behemoth leg comes through the roof between the bunk beds. "Another laser strike, Nigel."

"Affirmative."

The van lurches forward again. Dr. Splat struggles to find the best route beneath the spider abdomens to avoid their legs, but evasion grows increasingly difficult. "Nigel, take the wheel. Get us down the basement ramp. You're at liberty to use any weapons at your disposal—just get us down that ramp."

We race between and beneath Behemoth legs, all of them in constant motion, rising and falling, more focused on the tower than on us, fortunately.

Another spider leg comes through the roof over Dr. Splat, but it stops before drilling into his head. He hurriedly unstraps and scoots towards me, only half-occupying the driver's seat. The spider leg wobbles back and forth before falling out. The severed limb slides down the front window and onto the ground. The doctor sighs with relief as he straps back in.

The ramp comes in sight. Nigel gives us the bad news. "The doors are jammed and can't be opened remotely, doctor. Please submit alternative orders."

"Get us as close as possible to any usable door." Dr. Splat peers out the window on his side. He has a better view of the ramp than I do. "The van will have to stay outside."

A chunk of stone plummets to the ground right outside Dr. Splat's window. The van veers away from it. "Recommended course of action is to drive away from the tower, doctor. Put as much distance between you and the Behemoths as possible."

"Right. Do it, Nigel."

"Affirmative." The van makes a sharp turn. "More news, doctor. Military assistance is approaching the tower."

"Hail them and make them aware their weapons won't be effective against the Behemoths."

"Affirmative. I'm also detecting ground opposition to the Behemoths on the far side of the tower. Acid has been found to be an effective weapon against the Behemoths."

Dr. Splat cranes his neck to look in the back. "What does Kevin have in here in the way of acid blasters?"

"There are no such weapons on board, doctor."

If only I had more Auni, I could teleport us all to safety. Thing is, it has only been half an hour since I exhausted my Auni supply, and in that time I've only recharged a total of three points, enough to cast three of my most basic spells, none of which I expect will be of any use under current circumstances.

The van moves away from the tower, weaving among the giant spider legs. The swarm thins. We should soon be clear of it. I dare to hope.

Should I ask for a saving roll, or should I rely entirely on Nigel's capabilities? I'm afraid I'll jinx things if I ask for a saving roll. I hold my breath as the van plunges forward through the animate metal forest.

"Our transmitter has been damaged, doctor, and I am unable to hail the military. They are firing on the Behemoths. It's quite possible they aren't aware of our presence."

Talk about jinxing us....

An explosion rocks the van, throwing it onto its side. Van windows shatter. Dr. Splat is still securely strapped into the driver's seat—above us—moaning softly. The van isn't clear of the swarm, and a Behemoth leg slams against the vehicle's underside.

I should have asked for a saving roll.

Spooky pulls my hair. "Come, Emma." She shoves her hands through the broken glass of the passenger side window and makes a sweeping motion. Where there was desert sand, there's now empty space. She shoves her hands deeper and with an outward sweeping motion displaces more sand. Where the sand goes, I don't know. But she's creating a pit beneath us—one we can drop into and escape this deathtrap we're in.

I remove my seatbelt. "Dr. Splat, can you unstrap? Spooky is digging a pit for us. It's got to be better than staying in here."

"You've got to be kidding me." He waves for me to go. "I'll be right behind you."

The pit is snug and dark—smooth and circular. I go in head first. I drop six feet before hitting bottom.

"Emma. This way."

Where I'm from, Elves like me can't see in the dark. I have a Dark Sight spell, but I don't want to use up my Auni for it. I grope in the direction of Spooky's voice and find an opening into which I crawl. The shadow baby is digging a tunnel, headed deeper into the desert, away from the tower.

It's *amazing* the shadow baby can burrow like this. But it's *maddening*, too, crawling blindly forward on my elbows with sand brushing the top of my head every time I lift it. "Are you with us, Dr. Splat?"

"Right behind you. I had to pull Nigel's module first." His voice is muffled.

I keep my eyes closed, since there's no use in having them open, and I want to avoid getting sand in them. Explosions rock the desert above us, shaking sand loose from the packed walls of the tunnel, but not enough to prevent me from crawling ever onward. Spooky coos as she digs, for which I'm grateful. It's the only way I have to know she's okay and not leaving me behind. Occasionally I call back to Dr. Splat. He's keeping up.

My crawling isn't overly strenuous, and I'm able to recover expended Auni as I go. I recover another three points, for a total of six, before Spooky angles the tunnel up.

As the shadow baby breaches the surface, smoke and other unfamiliar, putrid odors fill my nostrils—I gag on the smell of freedom. The shouts of men echo in the mouth of the tunnel as Spooky vacates it. Human hands reach in to pull me up. I've never seen such a welcome sight or felt so *cared about*.

CHAPTER TWELVE

Megan: Tower Shakes

How long must you wait in this damned bedroom before the System finishes updating? Not only that, but you're *so* not tired. That's not quite true. You're tired of sleeping.

The decision Debra and I made to travel as a pair was not our most shining moment. We'd gotten overconfident and found ourselves outmatched by an enemy the likes of which we'd never faced before.

You faced a Shadow Gaunt.

I don't know what that is.

It attacked your emotional aspect. You became severely depressed—suicidal—and tried to kill yourself with Ghost Maker. Fortunately, PCs can't harm themselves or other party members in Khertaan. If it had taken your EP to zero, you'd have become an undead under its control. Party XStorm took it upon themselves to kill Mithabel and Dylan, thereby also killing you and Debra, to spare all four of you from an undead fate.

That was gracious of them. Which of them killed Mithabel?

The Wizard Bradford killed her. Yuni killed Dylan.

It must have been difficult for Yuni to kill the woman with whom she'd bonded so closely.

To pass the time, I take stock yet again of my equipment. I'm dressed in a two-piece black Bikini, which doesn't serve as armor but allows me as an Anjai—the public name for Khertaan's secretive Ninja class—to take greater advantage of my Natural Armor trait, which more than makes up for the Bikini's lack of armor rating. A suit of brown Leather Armor lies on the floor, but wearing the Leather would remove my special Natural Armor Anjai bonus, while the armor rating of the Leather wouldn't compensate for the loss.

Also on the floor lies the two-piece Bikini Mithabel wore. I've got duplicates of so many items due to a glitch in the System during my previous visits to the bedroom. Mithabel being my primary avatar and me being in the game as a secondary avatar might have confused the System. The glitch didn't make any duplicates this time. Someone must have fixed it.

As an Anjai, I'm great at balance, which allows me to wear High-Heeled Slippers and fight just fine. I'm wearing one pair, and two more pairs sit on the floor, one for Mithabel, if she wants. She went barefoot for a while.

I'm wearing a Ring that Mithabel received from Ezmerelda, the Speaker of Omens. Two more of Ezmerelda's Rings lie on the floor—more duplicated items. They're magical, but I don't know what effects they have other than to make it possible to deal damage to mooks impervious to non-magical attacks. I suppose that effect alone makes them worth wearing. Actually, Mithabel wore the original. The one I'm wearing is a duplicate. I should have offered the other duplicate to Debra.

Then there's the Ogaltha Ring. I don't wear it, because Ezmerelda said not to. I only have one of them, a duplicate, because Mithabel traded the original for a magic sword, Ullullu's Hair, with its wavy blade. The sword isn't here, and I don't relish the conversation I'm sure to have with Mithabel about its loss.

No sense in beating yourself up about it. Except that Mithabel might decide she deserves to wield Ghost Maker, if you ever get back to Khertaan.

Ghost Maker... *my* weapon of choice, a Battle Axe I got at Ye Olde Magic Shoppe in Maron, trading a severed Orc's Ear for it and a few other things: a Map of Safe Routes, given to Charli; a Bracelet of Action, which I'm still wearing and used once to little effect; and a harness to strap a severed Faerie Wing to my back. The Faerie Wing is a duplicate of the one Mithabel slashed off the back of PC Toxxi before the first System update. Mithabel gave the original Wing back to Toxxi, who was able to reattach it, but I've still got the duplicate. I enjoy wearing it. Why not wear it now? I fit it in the harness, slip the harness on, and take a look in the mirror.

You're too big to be a Faerie, and the Wing is only a foot and a half long, if that. No one would believe you can fly using only that one small wing, especially since you can't even flap it.

Hee hee, I know. That's why I love it.

What else do I have? Three coils of Rope. Three Heavy Self Bows—the original one stolen from ChrisCross, the other two duplicated from it. I don't really want to use any of the Bows. They're *tainted*. I don't want anything to do with Christopher Warden or his Elitist avatar. Christopher called Debra a whore. I just sat there and let him say it without coming to her defense. I don't know if I'm more upset with him or myself.

Are you ever going to let that incident go?

I want to. I really do.

Sure you do.

I've got a few more items. While I gave my Khertaan Safe Routes Map to Charli, Mithabel had picked up another one, and I have it now.

There's an Endless Writing Quill and some Parchment. I had used them to write messages for Mithabel when our communications channels were severed, hoping she'd find the parchment in her inventory and read my message, but she'd been too busy to check her inventory. It had been a brilliant idea that fell by the wayside.

How many of your brilliant ideas do fall by the wayside?

Lastly, I have another Battle Axe. This one, Mithabel took from Ger-Alt around the same time she lopped off Toxxi's Faerie Wing. This one is a duplicate, actually. Did Mithabel give the original back to Ger-Alt? It's too much to keep track of. I only have an average Memory.

As I recall, this Axe was enchanted by the Goddess Scintilla in an alcove within the dungeon under the Red Pegasus Inn. I don't know that Mithabel used it much, though, preferring to use the Flamberge she called Ullullu's Hair. Well, if we ever get back into Khertaan, she might have to use this Axe. Whether or not she holds me responsible for the loss of the Flamberge, I'm not giving up Ghost Maker. Too bad it wasn't duplicated.

I weigh Ghost Maker in my hands. Outside Khertaan, I can't stash the weapon to inventory. Maybe I could if I were level 30, but I only reached level 27. Dylan and Debra had reached level 28. Mithabel and I trail behind everyone else on XP.

Don't let it get to you.

I'm not.

You're shaking.

That's not me. It's the floor. It's the whole damned room. What the bloody hell is happening?

You know it can't be good. One might think it an earthquake, but you know better. This has to do with inter-dimensional invaders. You best get your gear on, and hide what you don't use, since you can't stash it.

Holy crap, I can't carry all this junk. I've got to hide nearly all of it.

The tip of a giant metal spider leg scratches across the overhead window. This isn't good. The Arachnid Behemoths have found the Fanciful Pegasus facility and are coming after us contestants before we can attain level 30. They're sure to break into the place before the System finishes its update.

As the spider leg stabs at the glass in an attempt to break it, I grab up the Battle Axe enchanted by Scintilla and try *really hard* to stash it to my inventory. My Willpower is high average, and they say, where there's a will, there's a way. Calling on my extraordinary Temperance, I stay calm while the Behemoth bangs on my window. I focus my mind.

The Battle Axe vanishes.

Slick. I grab up the Ogaltha Ring and try stashing it. It disappears, too. Great. The two Ezmerelda's Rings that I'm not wearing get stashed next.

The Endless Writing Quill and the Parchment won't stash. Dammit, why not? I try again, but they won't go.

Moving on…. The Heavy Self Bows don't stash. Damn. The three coils of Rope do. What the hell? The extra Bikini and two pairs of High-Heeled Slippers don't stash, but the Leather Armor and the Map of Safe Routes in Khertaan do. I try the Quill again. Nope. Nor the Parchment, Heavy Self Bows, Bikini, or High-Heeled Slippers. Those things just don't want to go in.

Fine. I slip off the Faerie Wing harness, pull the Wing out of its holster, and stuff the Bikini, Quill, and Parchment into the bottom of the holster. Then I jam the Wing back in on top of it. Locking it in place takes some teasing and elbow grease, but I do it. Forget the Slippers. Mithabel won't need the Slippers nearly as bad as the Bikini. I toss the Slippers under the covers on the bed.

Should I take a Heavy Self Bow or two? Mithabel and I aren't good with the Bow, but we have no other ranged weapons.

"Megan?"

I turn to the crystal ball from which Kevin speaks to me again. "I'm here, Kev. An Arachnid Behemoth is trying to break into my room."

"That's exactly why I need you to listen very carefully. I'm going to open your door. Follow the hallway to the end, where you'll find another door, which I'm also going to open for you. You'll find yourself in another hallway. Turn left and then take the first right. You'll come to an elevator. I'll have the door open. Get in,

95

and take it all the way to the thirtieth floor. It should make a stop on the way to pick up Debra Jones. Once the two of you reach the top floor, walk straight ahead and enter the room at the end of the hall. I'll be waiting for you both there. Are the Bows you're holding from Khertaan?"

"Yeah." My heart is racing, hearing that Debra is all right. I'll see her soon. How I miss seeing her and interacting with her in more Earthly surroundings.

"Bring them, and any other weapons you have from Khertaan. Now get going. I'll see you in a few."

His image vanishes from the crystal ball. A clicking sounds, and the exit door to my bedroom opens—the door I've never been able to open myself.

The Arachnid Behemoth shatters the window pane, and its long metal leg shoots into the room over the bed. The stone around the window crumbles, and the leg thrusts in farther, spearing the bed.

Good thing you weren't sleeping there.

Please don't let them hurt Debra.

I run out of the bedroom, carrying Ghost Maker and the two Bows in my arms, and speed up the hallway to the second door.

Kaleisha flickers like a dying flame in the doorway. "I'm having trouble manifesting, chief. Sorry. But I need to tell you, if you want to see Debra, choose Destin, not Earth." Then Kaleisha is gone, a fire snuffed out.

Choose Destin? Not Earth? Earth is my home and Debra's, too. Why would either of us want to choose anything over it?

Do you trust Kaleisha?

Of course.

Do you want to see Debra?

Yes.

Then you should follow Kaleisha's advice.

I know. Right, I choose Destin.

A plane of light flashes golden in the doorway. My spine tingles as I pass through to the hallway beyond.

Stone crashes behind me. The Arachnid Behemoth is gaining more and more access into what was once my bedroom. Holy crap. Is the same thing happening in Debra's room? I hope she's already out.

Turn left. There's the door to the room next to mine, labeled Gloria Littlecat. She's got to be another contestant. I try to open the door, but it won't budge. I don't have time to mess with it. Kevin knows how to open the doors for all the contestants, and he'll open them if they need to be opened.

There are the elevators. One of them is open. I get in. The door closes and the car ascends.

I'm starting on the eleventh floor... only nineteen floors to the top. The number over the door counts up. Twelve. Thirteen. Fourteen....

I close my eyes and calm my mind.

The elevator car stops and the door opens. Debra stands before me. She rushes into the car, and we wrap each other in hugs. The elevator door closes on us and the car resumes rising while we keep hugging.

The elevator car trembles. Dammit. We let go of each other and check the floor number. Twenty-one. The Arachnid Behemoths will tear down the building before we make it to the top floor. Twenty-two. Twenty-three. Twenty-four....

The image of Kaleisha wavers in the car for a second. "Take the stairs, chief."

The car rocks in the elevator shaft. Metal shrieks, under stress. I punch the Stop button. The car stops on floor twenty-five. The doors start to open when the car rocks again.

The doors are stuck.

I compress my body and slip into the six-inch gap.

You're compressing your body like an Anjai in Khertaan. Interesting.

I try to push the doors apart enough for Debra to come through. They won't budge. Crap. "Deb, don't panic. I'm gonna try something." I sit on the floor, my back to the wall, close my eyes, and reach out with my mind to her.

You're trying to head hop?

Yes, but it's not working. Dammit.

"Kaleisha, can you hear me?"

My support AI appears briefly, and I can see the disappointment on her face as she vanishes almost immediately.

"Stand back, Deb." I lay down the two Bows I'm carrying and heft Ghost Maker over my shoulder. I chop at the elevator door. I make a dent, but the Battle Axe isn't doing enough damage quickly enough for my liking. "Dammit." I strike again and again, but without any great success. So much for my fancy Battle Axe.

I stash it… or try. It won't stash. Why do some things stash and others don't? I want to try the other Battle Axe, the one enchanted by Scintilla, the Goddess of Light served by both Dylan and Mithabel. I draw it out of inventory. Attacking the door with it does no better than Ghost Maker. Damn. I stash the Scintilla Axe, which works fine.

Kaleisha appears again. "Go to the top floor, chief." Her mouth moves like she's saying more, but she vanishes too quickly.

Debra holds her head high. "Go on, Meg. Let Kevin know the elevator door is stuck. He'll know how to get it open."

"I can't leave you here."

The floor trembles.

"Hurry, Meg, please." Debra's eyes plead with me even more than her voice does.

I hold back the tears. It won't do for Deb to see me cry about this. It would only make her feel worse. "Dammit, Deb, don't you dare die on me."

"Not if you hurry."

The door to the stairway is nearby. I fly up the stairwell.

And now you're flying like an Anjai in Khertaan. Aren't you supposed to be level thirty to operate outside of Khertaan like this?

Hey, I was killing Orc Wizards before I ever entered Khertaan. I'm special. I've always been special.

Then why can't you head hop?

I don't freaking know. Arrggh.

Reaching the top, I pull up short at the top of the stairs as Kaleisha materializes with no problem. "Congratulations, chief. You've reached level thirty."

"I…. What does that mean, exactly?" My AI makes it sound like reaching the thirtieth floor of the Fanciful Pegasus building is equivalent to reaching level thirty in Khertaan. But if that were true, all the contestants could have simply taken an elevator ride to the top floor and never bothered with adventuring in Khertaan.

"No, it's not quite the same, chief, but metaphorically, it is, and the similarities coupled with your expertise and heritage now allow you to operate in Destin as a level thirty Khertaan Anjai. Try head hopping now."

I sit down on the landing and close my eyes, reaching out to Debra.

"Meg?" She lets me in, and I lend her my Compress Body skill. She slips out of the elevator car through the six-inch gap. "Thanks! Where are you now?"

"At the top of the stairs. Here, borrow my Flight Speed skill, too, and come on up."

I watch through her eyes as she flies up the stairwell. She sets down on the landing next to my sleeping body. I take my awareness back and jump to my feet.

Kaleisha is with us, and so is Dylan's support AI, Magnum, a white British butler type from a bygone era, dressed in black and white, wearing a black bow tie. Sporting short, black hair, his appearance is in stark contrast to that of Kaleisha, who manifests as a Jamaican dancer in an electric miniskirt, with a narrow band of electric energy extending around her otherwise bare torso, barely hiding her nipples and leaving next to nothing to the imagination.

Magnum opens the door for us, and motions us through. "If you will, madam." He's addressing Debra, but all of us rush through.

We hurry to another door waiting open for us. Beyond the open door, an Arachnid Behemoth has broken through a plate glass window and has the front quarter of its body inside the building. The urge rises inside me to kill the thing, but it's stuck, unable to come in further, and unable to extract itself. Its head is the wrong end for shooting webs. "Let's leave it. As long as we stay out of the reach of those two front legs, we'll be fine. Let it continue to plug the hole it has made."

"Agreed." Debra waits for me to enter first. I'm the Tank, after all.

CHAPTER THIRTEEN

Megan: Tower Battle

I fly into the office, and the Behemoth flails its front legs, trying to get at me. A desk sits in ruin at the far end of the room, shredded by the Behemoth's fangs. A name plate on the floor reads *Franklin Freeman*. There's no sign of Mr. Freeman or Kevin, but voices come through an open door to my right, one sounding like Kevin.

Kaleisha flies along with me into the next room.

All manner of rifles and big guns line the walls. Holy crap, how many are there? "Kaleisha, please tell Deb to come on in."

Kevin is here, as is a white man in a business suit, looking to be twice my age or older. I assume he's Franklin Freeman. I fly over. "Hey, Kev."

Deb and Magnum join us, and quick introductions are made. The older white man is indeed Franklin Freeman. He nods in understanding when we introduce Kaleisha and Magnum as our support AIs.

A few suits of Armor lie in a pile on a nearby table, not so neatly arranged as the guns on the walls. Kevin hands one to me and one to Deb. He's wearing a similar suit, but his is light green while the one for Deb is pale yellow and the one for me is a light orange. The suits aren't heavy, but there's still too much to them. If I wear one, it will interfere with my Natural Armor skill, assuming my skill operates here the same way it would in Khertaan. "I'm good." I hand the suit back.

Mr. Freeman cocks an eyebrow. "Are you sure? This suit protects from fire, acid, poison gas, bullets, magic, and more. You look smashing in that Bikini, but can it stop an Arachnid Behemoth leg from piercing your tummy?"

"Trust me, I'm good." But on second thought…. "I'll take it just in case, and stash it in inventory."

He's happy to oblige, but insists I wear it long enough to receive some training. I oblige him, slipping it over my Bikini. He turns to Kaleisha and Magnum. "How about you two?"

The support AIs shake their heads. Magnum answers for them both. "Our programming doesn't allow it. But thanks for the offer."

Debra stashes her new suit and then equips it, swapping out her layered Leather and Quilted Armor.

Mr. Freeman gives Deb and me a crash course on how to operate the new armor using a panel of buttons and a retina scanner located on each suit's arm. It's a little complicated, requiring one to activate different settings depending on the kind of attack one needs protection against. With my Natural Armor, I don't need to think about any of that. Once the training session is done, I stash the suit. I really don't think I'll need it.

"Okay, then, who wants a big gun?" Mr. Freeman hefts one and hands it to Deb.

I try again to stash Ghost Maker… and this time it works without effort. I stash the Heavy Self Bows, the extra Bikini, the Quill, and the Parchment without issue. I keep the Severed Faerie Wing strapped on. It symbolizes my unconventionality, just as my Bikini does.

On a hunch, I call for my character sheet. It appears, overlaying my view like it would in Khertaan. The top lines read:

Name: Mithabel V2 aka Megan Wright.
Player: Megan Wright.
Class: Tank, level 30 / Anjai, level 21.
Kindred: Elf. Gender: Female.

Well, isn't this a hoot? I scan down my skills list. Holy crap, I've got a new level one skill. "Kaleisha, what does my Split Body skill do?"

My support AI shakes her head. "The info is locked from access until you exercise the skill at least once."

"Fine." I invoke it.

I become a pile of slimy goo, which divides into two equal halves, both of which reform into a person. I identify with the right half, which still has blond hair. My ears still feel rounded, not pointed like Mithabel's.

The other half of the goo reforms into Mithabel, with her black hair and pointed ears.

We're both naked. The Bikini, Faerie Wing, and Slippers I was wearing lie on the floor. I grab up the Bikini, stash it, and equip it. The new Mithabel gives me a forced smile, which broadens into a wise-ass grin as she equips the duplicate Bikini from our shared inventory.

I pick up the Severed Faerie Wing, stash it, and then easily equip it. She eyes it with a narrowed gaze, but says nothing. I step into the Slippers.

Deb looks from me to my other half. "Mithabel?"

The split-off person holds the Scintilla Battle Axe, having drawn it from our shared inventory. She twirls it. "Mithabel V3 at your service."

Debra scowls. "V3?"

Mithabel V3 nods. "That's what my character sheet says. I'm level 30 Tank and level 21 Anjai." She points her weapon at me.

103

"Thanks for using the Split Body skill to bring me out, Megan. How do you want to address me?"

Kaleisha pirouettes and stops to face me and V3. "The primary Mithabel avatar—V1, if you will—can still become active, though you'll need to reenter Khertaan to make it happen, which isn't possible at the moment. Still, I suggest you keep the name Mithabel for V1, and devise a new name for V3 here. Moreover, the info on the Split Body skill is now unlocked, if you'd like to hear it."

"Please." V3 and I speak at the same time.

Kaleisha reads off info about my ability to create an autonomous copy of myself. We can share each other's senses, and also share other things, very much like how Mithabel and I have always done.

"This is fucking amazing." Mr. Freeman steps closer to V3, for whom I'm still trying to think of a better name. He raises a hand as though to touch her arm, but holds back. "Would you mind if I…?"

"I'm real, mister." She bumps her arm against his hand. "Now, what name shall we use for me?"

I shrug. "You pick."

"Great." She smiles. "Call me Belle. It's *not* short for Mithabel, but spelled out with a double *l*, and an *e* at the end."

A tremor shakes the room. Mr. Freeman hands Belle a big gun. "Glad to meet you, Belle. Take this." He fetches another weapon for me. Deb already has one. Mr. Freeman gives us a crash course on using our new weapons… how to switch between the different weapon types and reload.

The guns have retina scanners, which Mr. Freeman locks into recognizing our individual retinas… except that Belle and I have the same retinas. We can trade off if we want. Belle takes a weapon with a flamethrower ammo type, like Kevin took. Their weapons don't have grenade ammo types, so Deb and I take weapons that do, though we're missing the flamethrower. I try stashing my gun, and it works. Belle stashes hers, and we draw each other's weapon from inventory. Then we hand our original choices back to each other with knowing grins. Belle is already more fun than Mithabel ever was, the sourpuss.

Mr. Freeman holds up a suit. "How about you, Belle? Would you like some adjustable armor, even if only to carry as backup?"

She winks at him. "Yes, please, thank you, Franklin." She gets a light-blue suit, which she stashes in our inventory.

I try not to cringe. Belle isn't behaving the way either Mithabel or I would, and Mr. Freeman is eating it up.

Another tremor hits.

"Lock and load, ladies." Kevin raises his gun. "Time to take the trash to the curb."

We experiment with the different weapon types on the Behemoth stuck in the wrecked plate glass window. According to Kaleisha and Magnum, the acid ammo type works best.

We stop short of killing the mook. I recount how Arachnid Behemoths explode when they die. Our armor would take it, Mr. Freeman assures us, but he'd like to keep what he can of his office intact for as long as he can. He's got work to do after we leave, assuming his laptop still has a network connection.

Kevin waves us to the office exit. "Let's take the fight outside, shall we?" The four of us who are armed and armored head out, leaving Mr. Freeman to comb through the wreckage of his office while avoiding the fangs of a stuck and heavily wounded Behemoth.

Nearing the elevators, Deb and I explain how the one is broken and the other one probably isn't safe to take. Deb opens the door to the stairway. "We need to go down this way."

Kevin balks. "It will take forever to go down thirty flights of stairs." He taps the elevator button. The numbers above the door don't change—neither car is moving. "Okay, let's get moving."

"Hold on." I gesture at Kaleisha. "Can you carry Kevin and fly down the stairwell with him?"

"Affirmative, chief."

Deb's eyes light up. "And Magnum, can you do the same for me?"

"Indeed, madam."

"Then let's go." Belle and I lead the way, flying down the stairwell. Kaleisha and Magnum float down after us, with Kevin and Deb riding piggyback on them.

We reach the first floor and head for the exit.

"Megan, you're with me. We'll go left." Kevin beckons. "Deb and Belle, the two of you stick together and go right. Either team runs into issues, let the other team know right away. Megan and Belle, you're our line of communications." He's referring to the telepathic connection between Belle and me. He was paying attention. Good man. "Remember, acid is our ammo type of choice. Let's go." He looks into a retina scanner by the door, and the door slides open.

A Behemoth leg stabs at him through the open doorway, striking him in the chest. He falls back as the other three of us crowd up to the doorway and open fire on the mook, streaming acid. Kev falls on his back, and the leg pins him down, or tries, slipping off to one side. Kevin rolls away and jumps to his feet like nothing happened. Damn. Could my Natural Armor protect me from a direct pin like that? I don't really know, but neither Belle nor I decide to put on the new suits.

With a screech, the Behemoth backs away. We press the attack, with Kevin joining us after taking a moment to close the door behind us. Two other Behemoths join the first one in stabbing at us.

Bring it on.

Behemoth legs flail, and each of the four of us are hit at least once. Deb loses her footing, but isn't hurt, and hops right back up. None of us have a scratch on us. Twenty seconds into the skirmish, the first of the three Behemoths explodes.

This is the moment of truth. Roiling fire engulfs us.

The flames are gone almost as quickly as they came. All four of us still stand—Belle and I in our Bikinis, and Deb and Kev in their high-tech suits. We all look scorched, but everyone reports being unhurt.

With a four-fold war cry, we open up on the enemy, Kev and me headed left and our friends headed right. Belle and I keep each other updated as we circle around the tower in opposite directions. After a couple minutes, Belle shares a new tactic with me. "Shoot their eyes with acid, and then pop a grenade through the eye socket. Takes them right out."

The tactic allows each team to take out the Behemoths at the rate of one every ten seconds. Even though we're outside Khertaan, all four of us are operating under its rules, with cool down periods and combat heartbeats just like we had there. Apparently so are the Behemoths.

"We've got help," Belle says in my head. "Choppers and soldiers. Strike that. They're having no effect. Wait, there's someone else out here, wearing a suit of high-tech armor like those Franklin gave us."

I pass on the info to Kevin.

"That's Fauna. She's on our side. Franklin gave her armor and a gun, too."

I convey the info to Belle as I Dodge an incoming web. The webs are just as vulnerable to acid as the legs and bodies of the Behemoths, but getting tangled slows us down, so after getting caught once, I do my best to avoid them. Kevin gets tangled a few times, because he's not as good at evading as I am, especially since he can't fly.

Kaleisha offers to let him ride her shoulders piggyback, and he takes her up on it. Sadly, even though Kaleisha can fly, the two of them aren't maneuverable enough, and they keep getting webbed. The reach of the Behemoth's webs is greater than the range of our acid sprays and grenade launchers, so we can't just fly above them and attack from afar.

After Kev jumps off her back, Kaleisha flits about, distracting the Behemoths. She can't do anything to effect them, and their attacks don't effect her, but they keep trying. It's funny to see their webs land on her and then pass right through her like she's nothing but an illusion. She's solid to me and to Kevin, but not to the spiders. I don't understand how it works.

Kevin and I hit a good rhythm, and soon we're making a noticeable impact. The stack of Behemoths on the tower loses altitude, slipping closer and closer to the ground as we whittle down its base. The Arachnid legs are designed to stab and kill, not to adhere to the sides of buildings, so as we clear out the lower tiers, the higher tiers lose the support they need and slide down a tier, then another tier, and another tier, until none of the damned things remain on the ground.

About twenty Behemoths don't fall, but stay on the building, including the one stuck in the plate glass window on the top floor. A few others have legs caught in windows or are wedged into crevices they've created in the stone walls. Without anything to support them from below, they can't get the leverage they need to continue their efforts to widen the breaches they've started. Some may have broken through to contestants' bedrooms, but at the moment it's impossible to tell. We can't kill any of these last twenty until we determine which ones have breached the wall. We don't want to cause damage to any exposed contestants.

Belle and Deb meet up with us half way around the building, along with their new friend, Fauna the hoofed goat lady, and a regiment of soldiers eager to help. The soldiers lost two choppers to the Behemoths before they learned about the webs, but they have other choppers. They'd learned quickly that their weapons weren't having any effect, but they had served as distractions to occupy some Behemoths while Deb and Belle picked off others.

The soldiers lower long cables from the choppers, intending for Belle and I to fly up and wrap them around the spiders, but the cables pass through the Behemoths the same as the soldiers' weapons. Between Deb and me, however, we have five pieces of Rope, which tied together is a little less than 200 feet. We tie the Rope to the cable, and it stays.

One Behemoth at a time, we systematically remove them from the sides of the tower. Belle and I wrap the Rope around a

Behemoth's waist. The chopper cranks on the cable and drags the spider free of the building. I pull the quick release tail to undo the knot. The spider crashes to the ground, but the fall doesn't kill it. Deb and Kev spray its eyes with acid, and Fauna pops a grenade into a hollowed eye socket. The soldiers on the ground stay well back, since they don't have armor to withstand the explosions brought on by each Behemoth death.

The sun sets and two half moons come out by the time we finish, but we clear every one of those twenty Arachnid Behemoths off the building without any casualties among ourselves. Belle and I look in on any contestant rooms that were breached, and either the room has been vacated already, or the contestant is still asleep and breathing. How anyone could sleep through all that commotion is beyond me.

If some contestants are sleeping, does that mean the System has finished its update? Why else would contestants be sleeping? Can contestants sleep during an update, and if they do, what's happening with them and their avatars? I'm just wondering if I could go to sleep now and respawn Mithabel.

The half moons shed enough light for Deb and the others to see by. Belle and I have inherited Mithabel's Dark Sight, which allows us to see just fine in low light conditions. Slick.

"Kevin?" A man calls from the distance. "Is that you?"

"Dr. Splat? I saw the van but not you. Glad you made it out alive." Kev runs towards a group of newcomers. "Are Emma and Spooky with you?"

A female voice replies. "We're here. Is Fauna with you?"

Stashing her own high-tech rifle, the goat lady waves and runs after Kevin. "I'm here, Emma. You missed out on all the fun."

ঌউঙঝ৶ঌউঙ

Introductions are made. Fauna and Emma are manifested table-top role-playing game characters. Spooky is a shadow twin of

Charli's baby, Britta. I hadn't met Britta, but Mithabel did, and I can call on her memories of the girl. Mithabel hadn't known Britta had a shadow twin.

Spooky dug a tunnel to allow Emma and Dr. Splat to escape the conflict when their van was overturned while trying to get away. The baby has skills.

Dr. Splat and the soldiers are natives of Destin. So is Kevin, but he's different because he volunteered for early experiments at Fanciful Pegasus that helped advance the Khertaan program. According to Dr. Splat, my dad was originally from Destin and had volunteered for even earlier experiments before I was born. I don't know if I buy that. I ask how my dad got to Earth to meet my mother, and the explanation goes over my head before the first sentence is fully out of Dr. Splat's mouth.

The leader of the soldiers asks about getting outfitted with equipment like what Kevin is using, and Kevin tells him to come with him to see Mr. Freeman. They'll need to train in Khertaan first, and Kevin doesn't know if the program is finished updating, but Mr. Freeman is the man to talk to.

The soldiers clear out while Kevin takes their leader inside the tower to visit Mr. Freeman. Dr. Splat goes with them, and tells Emma and Spooky to come along so they can get outfitted. Evidently, there will be plenty more inter-dimensional enemies to fight. Fauna, a short woman with goat hooves for feet, excuses herself to accompany Emma. Kaleisha and Magnum make themselves scarce, like they so often do.

So it's me, Deb, and Belle left standing on the charred sands of the battlefield. None of us say anything. We're all a bit overwhelmed by past events. We watch the stars and Destin's two moons in silence.

A dark winged shape flits across the dark sky. I might have missed it if not for my Alertness trait.

"I see them." Belle points.

Instinctively, I know it's an enemy. "We should warn Kevin and the others."

As we watch, ten more winged shapes follow in the wake of the first one.

"I'll tell Franklin." Belle flies up and enters the tower through the broken office window.

A *whoosh* from behind me alerts me to the presence of another threat. An individual mook approaches, not a Boss, but something worse, something called a Dread Naught. I don't know what types of damage it can deal, but my Danger Sense tells me it has access to attack types other than physical. How much more could I learn about approaching enemies if I had the Danger Sense trait at level three or four? I give Deb a head's up.

"Belle, we might need your help here." I telepathically let my duplicate know we're in trouble. "Something big is coming."

A dark shape bursts from the sand near Deb. It's like a giant centipede, five feet thick, towering over her like a double-powered Ferro Serpent. The two of us shoot acid at the monster, but it isn't fazed. It opens its mouth and drives its head down at Deb as though to swallow her.

Not on my watch. I spring up, taking to the air with Ghost Maker in hand, and perform a Block. The head bounces off my magic Battle Axe, thrown off track, and it plunges into the sand.

Deb touches Ghost Maker as I drop beside her. "Scintilla, Goddess of Light, bless this weapon, I beseech you." The weapon already glows, but now it's got an additional orange tint.

The Dread Naught lifts its head from the sand and once more drives at Deb.

I impose myself between them and invoke my Reflect Any Attack action.

If the Dread Naught was harmed as a result, it's not obvious, but I stopped it from harming the woman I love.

Deb steps back. "Goddess, lay your blessing upon us to boost our morale and make you proud."

The monster aims its gaping mouth at Deb. Dammit. I go for a Stun.

My attempted action has no effect whatsoever on the monster. It's still moving.

It screeches.

Debra goes limp and falls where she stands.

The whole world must hear my shout of despair and rage as I swing to kill. Ghost Maker bites deep. The Dread Naught falls beside Deb, lying as still as she. I hack at it with Ghost Maker and keep hacking at it.

CHAPTER FOURTEEN

Ronnie: Out of the Picture

Though I'm naked as a newborn, I have rifles in inventory. I can't bring myself to shoot Princess Karen, no matter how cruel she is and no matter that here inside the inter-dimensional space of this photo, she's only a simulacrum. She has Mel's face, and shooting her would be akin to shooting him. I can't do it, and I don't know that shooting the Princess would buy me a way out of this magical prison, anyway. Besides, I've already made peace with the knowledge I'll likely need to kill Queen Jean to bring peace to the timeline.

I've got one shot at this—literally. Already paralysis is settling into my limbs, but not enough to prevent me from rolling onto my side so I'm facing away from the Princess. I can see the hallway outside the photo. Queen Jean is approaching to survey her handiwork. Such an arrogant woman. Summoning a rifle into my outstretched hands, I take quick aim and pull the trigger.

Taking into consideration the size and distance of my target, I need a level four saving roll or better on Dexterity to hit. With my

Dexterity of 23, I need a 12 or better on the dice… doable, if only I had dice.

With a frown and a slight twitch of her scepter, Queen Jean freezes the action in my prison even as Princess Karen's blade slides between my ribs. The pain is immediate and intense.

The bullet I fired freezes in midair.

I can't move, but I feel the metal blade in my side, stuck in place, never to be removed. I can see what's before me and hear the clomp of Queen Jean's high-heeled slippers on the marble floor as she comes closer. She stops before the magical photo that I've become a part of, assessing it as one might assess a painting by an old master. The trajectory of the bullet is such that, if unfrozen, the projectile would intercept her right between the eyes, and she knows it. She's taunting me, demonstrating how much more powerful she is than I.

Would that I had the ability to unfreeze that bullet. But that's her point. I took my best shot, and with a twitch of her scepter she put a stop to it. Jeaniverse belongs to her, and she can do whatever she wants in this timeline—in control of its very Laws of nature. If she wants a bullet to freeze in midair, then it freezes in midair.

I'm not from her timeline. I bring an aura of Chaos from my world, allowing me to act against her Laws. But for my aura to work, it requires randomization of the correct nature. If only I had two dice to roll and could generate a total of 12 or more for a saving roll, the bullet might spring into action. I'd like to test the theory.

But I don't see anything that could even simulate the roll of two dice. The Queen has no random tics I can take advantage of. The guards in view stand perfectly still. No part of the motorcycle is moving. Both the Princess Karen simulacrum and I are frozen. Queen Jean continues to stare at me—it's like she's reading my mind. It's her timeline, so maybe she has that ability.

She turns to leave, pivoting on one high heel. But before she takes a step further, a man in a hooded gray cloak appears before her, his face hidden in shadow. His fists, however, extend from the cloak. They aren't scaly like Gondra's would be, but covered with what appear to be wriggling, thin gray worms. His voice isn't coarse like Gondra's, but smooth as silk, exuding confidence. "Hello, Jean."

Guards rush in from two sides, their rifles aimed at the man's hooded head. If the stranger wasn't present, the two groups of guards would be pointing rifles at each other. How do they feel about that, or do they even have feelings? Are they basically nothing more than automatons?

Queen Jean raises a hand and holds up three fingers. "Seth." She speaks the name with ice in her voice. "Are you here to surrender?"

"I can understand why you'd make that assumption. No, I'm here to negotiate the terms of your surrender. Basically, you give up, or you die. Do you accept these terms?"

One finger goes down, leaving two up. "You have no power here, Seth. I can easily have you tossed into one of my photos, to amuse myself forever. But you know that, so tell me why you're really here."

His laughter is the definition of haughty. "You can't really believe your guards and their weapons will have any effect on me."

A second finger goes down. "And I can't believe you think an aura of make believe will protect you from me. You can see behind me how that worked out for the latest acquisition to my pictorial menagerie."

She's talking about me.

Seth nods his hooded head. "You're right, of course. You've bested me. But perhaps a truce would be to our mutual benefit?"

Queen Jean keeps the last finger raised. "I'm already winning the battle for domination of the timelines. I don't need a truce with you. I'm trying to think if I'd rather have you in a painting or give my guards some entertainment more to their liking. In Jeaniverse, boredom is so prevalent for those in their line of work."

Seth inclines his head. "Perhaps I would be better as a servant than as decoration or plaything."

"So, *you* have come to surrender." Queen Jean lowers her last finger halfway.

"Your Majesty, please. If I must, I will bend the knee." With his head still bowed and his arms at his side, he slowly lowers onto his knees, making no sudden movements, while the guards keep their rifles trained on his head. Once he's on his knees, he bends forward.

"Your Majesty, please, I beg you." His voice is raised in desperation.

Two dice fall from one of his hands, rolling on the floor. I can't see the total….

The whine of a fired bullet sends a shiver through me an instant before pain flowers through my ribcage, as Princess Karen's blade sinks even deeper before it's yanked free of my flesh.

Queen Jean crumples to the floor as tiny spiders fall by the hundreds onto the guards.

Mindful of the rifle still in my hands, I push the Princess simulacrum away as adrenaline energizes me. She drags her weapon with her, pulling it from my wound. I'm not dead… she didn't lower my Constitution to zero. Generally, no matter the type of attack in Tunnels and Troglodytes—the Laws by which I play—one doesn't continue bleeding out after the initial damage is dealt. It's possible for special weapons to deal a wound that continues to bleed, but no such special rule was written for the simulacrum's weapon. I'm not seeping blood—internally or externally—from the wound she dealt me.

Rolling up on my feet, I catch a better view of the situation inside and outside my photographic cell. Queen Jean lies on the floor, her blood spilled from the back of her head. The bullet I fired no longer hangs in the air—it was freed from its frozen state to continue its trajectory, striking the Queen.

There's no sign of Seth or the Queen's scepter. The guards struggle against webs covering them from head to foot, restricting their movement. Spiders cover everything—floor and guards.

A pair of dice lie on the floor where Seth had knelt. One shows a five and the other shows a two. If that was for my saving roll, it was enough for a third level SR but not fourth level.

But, then, Queen Jean had moved into point blank range, lowering the needed saving roll to level two. The saving roll succeeded, changing the script.

I'm getting a sequel adventure after all.

Princess Karen sits slumped on the bench at the back of the cell, in the same pose she'd had before I entered the picture, her bloody blade dangling in her limp grip.

"You want to get out of here, Princess?"

Her gaze is hollow as she lifts her head. "I've failed my purpose for existing."

"Come on. See what the rest of your world is like." Stashing the rifle, I set the motorcycle upright and climb on, butt naked. I pat the seat behind me. "Climb on."

Her weapon vanishes from her grip, presumably stashed to her inventory. The Princess takes the offered seat, and I rev the bike. The machine has no problem passing from the cell to the hallway, and spiders clear out of my way as I inch forward. Pausing next to the dice, I lean over, touch them, and stash them both.

Spotting my torn clothing, I wheel over to them, touch them, stash them, and equip them on my body. As I'd hoped, stashing and equipping them caused them to mend. Some things are going right for me today.

A hole opens in the floor, and the spiders flow into it like liquid down a drain. Queen Jean's corpse slides into the hole, too. The floor tilts. Guards mummified in spider webs plunge into the unknown depths.

Time for me to go. Revving the bike again, I ride it away from the hole toward the throne room. None of the guards standing at attention against the walls make a move to stop me as the simulacrum Princess and I drive past them.

I reach the end of the hallway and ride the bike into what used to be Queen Jean's throne room, from whence double doors lead outside.

"Welcome, Ronnie." The voice isn't Queen Jean's, but Seth's. Attired in his gray cloak, he sits on the throne, holding the Queen's scepter and wearing her golden crown over his hood, tilted to one side. Gray-skinned, bony alien guards dressed in drab attire and armed with shiny rifles stand at attention around him. Other guards block the double doors. A few spiders crawl atop the stranger's knees and shoulders. "I'm glad to see you're out of the picture. Queen Jean has been taken out of the picture, as well, thanks largely to you. I'm glad I could provide the means for you to make the necessary saving roll."

I stop the bike but stay seated. "*King* Seth, I presume?"

"Not exactly." He examines his fingernails. "I'm known as a Shadow Gaunt. I'm to Seth what you are to Ulric. I'm a PC, if you will. Well… almost. It's complicated."

"So, then, King Shadow Gaunt?"

"Actually, it's more like King Shadow *Gaunts*. Plural. Say hello to some of my other selves."

The spiders on his knees and shoulders jump to the floor. Where each lands, up springs a twin to the Shadow Gaunt. They bow with grand, sweeping gestures.

"These aren't all of me. You met some of my selves earlier. One of them brought you a gift—a pair of dice. He rolled them on your behalf—another gift. And now, thanks to our working together, Queen Jean is gone and Jeaniverse is no more. Welcome to the Shadowverse!"

I'm not one to give away much with facial expressions. "I thank you for your aid in releasing me from my prison. Aside from that, I'm not sure I see much improvement in this world's future."

He exaggerates a pout. "Be nice. I assume you have the dice on your person. Would you mind bringing one out? I'd like you to roll it."

It's because of him that I'm not a permanent fixture in Queen Jean's photo gallery, and he *did* bring me the dice, so I feel some tiny obligation to him. I equip one die onto my open right palm. "Very well, King Shadow Gaunts, here's a die. What am I rolling for?"

"It's to determine your fate, young adventurer, to randomly choose what you'll face when you leave this throne room. Think of it as a roll against a Wandering Monster table."

"And if I don't roll?"

"Then I'll decide your fate for you. Random is more fun, but if you don't roll, I'll do what I must. I'm partial to the Creepers. Very nasty things, some nastier than others, depending on their class and subclass. But, seriously, I doubt you'll be a match for any of the Dread Naughts. Which is why, if you roll a six, you'll face nothing at all. At least, not immediately. I can't make any promises about ten minutes from now."

I climb off the bike, kneel beside it, equip the second die, and roll both of them. They come up two and five. I've just made a level twenty-seven saving roll on Luck.

The seated King chuckles. "Rolling on your Luck to influence the roll for the WM. How clever of you. Well, let's see if it helped. Go on. Roll."

Stashing a die, I roll the other one. It comes up a one.

The King claps slowly. "Ah, a Flitter—the winged type of Dread Naught. You do amuse me, Ronnie, and I will be sad to see you go. But go, you must. Now, off with you. Good luck fighting the Flitter."

The guards blocking the double doors lift the bar and swing the doors open to a hallway that will take me outside. Stashing the die, I ride the motorcycle down the red carpet and exit the throne room. I don't know what a Flitter is, but maybe a rifle will kill it. If not, maybe I can escape it on the bike.

In any event, I hope to take advantage of the level 27 Luck saving roll I made. I hadn't rolled in an attempt to sway the outcome of the WM die roll, but to have a leg up for whatever comes next.

The Princess simulacrum and I ride the motorcycle out of the palace into the darkness of night. The city lights are dead. No stars shine. That's not quite right. The moon and stars blink in and out as foul winged creatures crowd the sky, crying like fledglings kicked out of the nest.

CHAPTER FIFTEEN

Greelia: So Much to Think About

I don't know how I came to own a Cosmic Cloak, as it wants to be called. It sensed my need and responded by manifesting on my body. It's not sentient... or maybe it is. Thoughts pop into my head that I can only attribute to it. We don't carry out conversations, but it casts thoughts at me, and I catch them or not. *You're wearing a Cosmic Cloak* was a thought I caught. The Cloak always addresses me in the second person. That's the easy way to distinguish the thoughts it throws at me from my own thoughts.

With the Cosmic Cloak, I'm able to enter any timeline in the compacted timeline group, whether or not I have an alternate-me living in it. That's a great ability, but the Cloak grants another equally powerful ability—I can *split my awareness* out to multiple incarnations of myself in different timelines. Each real-me is capable of telepathic communication with any other real-me across timelines, and any real-me can see through the eyes or hear through the ears of another real-me, as long as the other real-me permits it.

Beyond that, if I don't have an alternate-me in some timeline, I can make one by splitting part of my awareness off for it. Not that I'd do it much at any given time, because it would spread my awareness too thin. But each split-off part of my awareness grows within its timeline. Over time, I could have a *real, aware* me in every timeline.

You could become a Goddess.

I swear, I can't mull over my situation or reflect on recent events without the Cosmic Cloak making some remark.

You talking to me?

Ugh. I currently have my awareness split out to five versions of me—the one of me in the nexus, or nexus-me; the one of me on the metadisc-turned-metadonut, or meta-me; the one of me living with a version of Nick and Britta in an underground complex of tunnels, or Underverse-me; the one of me in the timeline championed by Jean, or Jeaniverse-me; and the one of me in the timeline championed by Seth, or Sethiverse-me.

You like your Underverse timeline the best, obviously. Which timeline do you find the most despicable?

Both Jeaniverse and Sethiverse are deplorable places. Jeaniverse isn't a nice place for anyone but Queen Jean to live. She's a murderous, sadistic bitch. She found Jeaniverse-me and had me killed—right in front of my friend Ronnie—but not before I drew my awareness back and created another Jeaniverse-me.

Jean clearly doesn't understand the full capabilities of the Cosmic Cloaks. She thinks she has killed me permanently in her timeline and I can't return to spy on Jeaniverse any more. If she were as clever as she is cruel, she'd be a real menace. Everything with her is brute force without reasoning. Despite her timeline growth at the moment, the more clever Seth will eventually subvert her timeline—unless I do it first.

How do you feel about the Sethiverse?

It can't be allowed to become the dominant timeline. Unlike Queen Jean, Seth takes no delight in destruction, killing with ambivalence and efficiency. He's basically a robot designed to destroy—set on autopilot. He has already destroyed nearly all sentient life in Sethiverse, with no shred of remorse.

Sethiverse-me goes by the name Timmy Landers. I'm a Ring Ghoul in that universe, an immortal undead—provided I continue to wear the Ring that empowers me. Susie McKenzie—Nick's daughter in Sethiverse—is my ex-girlfriend. I still exist in that timeline. Susie does, too, but her primary awareness time-shifted out and all that's left of her there is an automaton Susie. Ronnie was there for a while, but he time-shifted out, too, with a friend named Mel. They didn't so much time-shift out as they meta-shifted out, taking their entire physical and metaphysical beings with them. I don't understand how they did it—they don't have Cosmic Cloaks that I can see—and I'm curious whether anyone else can do it. Ronnie and Mel ended up in Jeaniverse, which wasn't much better than being in Sethiverse.

Seth has Sethiverse-me on board his spaceship, Planet Buster. Sadly, the vessel has lived up to its name. Sethiverse is a worse place to be than Jeaniverse, because in Jeaniverse there are other people around, even if they're all in misery. In Sethiverse, there's practically no one left. It's like having to choose between spending my life stranded on a deserted island with a few constantly-complaining friends or being stuck until death in a jail cell with a quiet, convicted serial killer. Jeaniverse is the island, while Sethiverse is the cell. I'll take Jeaniverse over Sethiverse any day.

Sethiverse-me is strapped in a chair on the bridge of Planet Buster. As long as I'm on his bridge, I'm privy to everything he's doing.

Fortunately, not all of my split-awareness selves must wear a Cosmic Cloak. Seth understands the significance of the Cosmic Cloaks better than I do, and definitely better than Jean does. He doesn't realize Timmy Landers is Sethiverse-me, and that's only because Timmy isn't wearing a Cosmic Cloak. If Seth gets any hint that Timmy is an alternate-me, then Timmy is dead, plain and simple.

So Seth recognizes you as a threat?

Of course. Even Jean recognizes me as a threat.

Fair enough. What do you like most about the Underverse?

Why is my Cosmic Cloak so full of questions?

If you don't want to answer, you can go back to being quiet and lonely.

Fair enough.

Time has a way of moving slow or fast, depending on one's perspective at any given moment. Underverse-me has lived a couple of decades with automaton versions of Nick and Britta in our dedicated timeline. Erica intruded on the Underverse once long ago, but since she departed, no one else has visited. And that's how Underverse-me wants it. For now.

Underverse-me has greatly enjoyed teaching Nick and Britta about timelines, magic, technology, game worlds, mathematics, and grammar. I've written books for them to read by the light of our never-extinguished underground bonfire. That's been a lot of fun for me. Watching Britta grow up has been the most rewarding.

We don't need to breathe, eat, drink, defecate, urinate, or sleep, but we indulge on occasion just for the experience. It's interesting, but none of those activities offer anywhere near the same degree of pleasure for me as just being with my husband and daughter.

You consider automaton-Nick to be your husband, then.

I make the rules in the Underverse, so, yes. There's no need for a ritual ceremony. He doesn't even need to pledge me his loyalty, because there's no one else in Underverse with whom he can cheat on me.

There's Britta.

His daughter? No version of Nick, automaton or otherwise, would even consider that as an option. It's beneath you to bring it up.

Apologies. You mentioned you sleep sometimes.

Yes. When Underverse-me sleeps, I often dream, which transfers my Underverse-awareness to an alternate-me in a distant timeline I normally couldn't reach any other way. I'm not always a Goblin female in these other timelines. I've been Human, Elf, Faerie, and Orc—and sometimes male. I've been transgender, too.

I've experienced many sexual orientations. When I awaken, the dream experiences don't seem real anymore, but they were the most real of anything experienced by the alternate-me in that timeline.

Do you have any regrets about the Underverse?

My biggest regret is also my biggest source of pride—Britta. As a mother, I want the best for my daughter, and I have failed to provide it for her, due to my own selfishness.

By the reckoning of time in her timeline, Underverse-Britta is now twenty years old. She's a beauty of a Cave Goblin woman and has long been in desperate want of Cave Goblin friends her age, whether male or female. She's knowledgeable and smart, more so than most automaton-persons ever become. But she's nevertheless an automaton—not in possession of a real awareness, just as Underverse-Nick isn't in possession of any real awareness. I wish I could give both to her—friends her age and real awareness. I'd like that for Nick, too.

Sometimes I think I should have let Erica stay. But she would have been the wrong kind of friend for Nick—one to make me jealous, and I don't do well with jealousy.

With Underverse-Nick being only an automaton, Erica wouldn't have found him acceptable company, knowing what the real Nick is like. Why have you settled for someone not real?

Nick's awareness—what makes him real—is gone from the multiverse, and no version of him contains more than a soul token. The token associates an automaton with the real Nick. If a Nick with real awareness existed in the multiverse, he could transfer his awareness to any alternate-Nick-automaton when he time-shifts.

But real-Nick is gone forever, and I must either make do with an automaton bearing his soul token or not have any Nick at all in my life. I've resigned myself to this fate, so as not to lose myself to despair. Erica will devolve into a suicidal mess if she can't reconcile her feelings for Nick with the fact his awareness no longer exists. Trust me—she's getting there.

You still occupy the nexus, even though everyone else is gone. Why do you stay?

Someone must occupy the nexus.

While twenty years have unfolded in the Underverse, next to no time has passed in the nexus. Nexus-me doesn't host a significant portion of my split awareness, only enough to maintain a real presence. As I said, someone must occupy it to avoid a grand disaster. Morrow was intent on staying, but... well... Erica interfered.

Renee flits in and out of the nexus like a ghost who can't decide whether it's a place she wants to haunt. She doesn't know what to do without Morrow, and she doesn't know where he's gone. Nexus-me doesn't speak to her, and must ignore everything she says in my presence. Nexus-me must keep the nexus foremost in my mind, if I'm to maintain it. Entering into any conversation could prove a fatal distraction.

What is life like for meta-you?

Standing on the metadonut sounds boring, but it isn't. I'd imagined at first I'd need to keep a strong focus on the Underverse, but Underverse-me does that well enough. Meta-me basically needs to hold my place on the punctured metadisc. If I vacate it, then no matter how strong Underverse-me is, the Underverse will shrivel like so many other timelines in the compacted timeline group, succumbing to the expanding Jeaniverse timeline.

As meta-me, I have the ability to look into some of those shriveling timelines. The Fanciful Pegasus timelines are two such—the FP-Earth timeline and the FP-Destin timeline. The FP-Earth timeline is where Nick and Kendra developed the Khertaan-access program. However, the genius behind the Fanciful Pegasus company—Franklin Freeman—tapped into the Khertaan-access code to create an alternate version of the FP facility on Destin. Watching the happenings at and near those facilities has been interesting. Both FP timelines are under attack by Seth's minions. Seth recognizes Khertaan as a threat to his plans. I don't think Jean even knows about Khertaan. I suppose I feel a bit smug about knowing something she doesn't, and that's why I like to look at those shrinking timelines. There are worse ways to occupy one's mind.

You mentioned a compacted timeline group. What do you mean?

I'm talking about the group of timelines flowing through the center hole of the metadonut. The timelines once filled the entire cross section of the metadisc, but now they're compacted to fit through a much smaller space than normal. If not for the metadonut hole, the timelines would all be broken, and anyone living in them would experience the absence of time from the moment of impact with the metadisc. That actually was happening for a while—until real-Nick compacted the affected timelines into a bundle strong enough to punch a hole in the metadisc.

He'd intended to merge the affected timelines into a single, strong timeline, because he'd thought it necessary, and expended all his awareness in the attempt. The merge into a single timeline failed, but the goal of breaking through the metadisc was still attained, at the cost of Nick's awareness. I still can't believe he sacrificed himself for the rest of us, but, yeah, that's who Nick was.

Do you feel real-Nick did the right thing?

It's impossible to say. He left a mess I'm trying to clean up. If the merge into a single timeline had worked, we wouldn't have Seth and Jean championing timelines from the group to make them dominant. The merged timeline would have been of Nick's choosing. As it is now, the timelines selected by Seth and Jean are the most prominent ones in the compacted group. If either of them take over the group completely, every sentient being in any of those timelines will face terrible consequences. If Jean wins, they'll face slavery and torture. If Seth wins, they'll no longer be alive.

Then there's the Underverse. I don't want it to become dominant. I want it to exist alongside others, as it would do if Seth and Jean simply stopped in their efforts to dominate everything. But no. Jeaniverse is growing, and Sethiverse is holding steady. The Underverse is holding steady, too, if not growing slightly. Other timelines are forced to shrink, including FP-Earth and FP-Destin.

Why does the Underverse not shrink? What's so special about you that you can stand against the likes of Jean and Seth?

I don't know.

Your soul token is associated with Charli. You have some of Charli's awareness.

Charli is my player. Why shouldn't I have the same relationship to her that Morrow had with Nick? For that matter, Nick was Fauna and Emma's player. Their soul tokens are associated with Nick. That should make them more clever and more powerful than me.

You are more clever than you give yourself credit for. Nick developed Charli's code. Does that make him her player, in a manner of speaking?

Charli is more than code.

But aren't Nick and Charli related in some way?

Oh, Great Goblin Mother. In a way, though she's an NPC, he is her player. Charli might have a soul token of Nick. Perhaps she has some of his awareness the same as Fauna and Emma. In the same respect, maybe so do I. All four of us might actually be alternate-Nicks.

Does that make you all Nick-automatons?

How could an automaton use a Cosmic Cloak or resist Seth and Jean? Nick must have split off some of his awareness for Charli, Fauna, Emma, and me when he first came across each of us. To him we were all game characters, but he was so into his games, he put significant pieces of himself into us all.

When Erica went searching for real-Nick, she came to the Underverse. It wasn't because the Nick automaton drew her there. Underverse-*me* drew her there. My awareness is the most active there. She was drawn to Jeaniverse because of Jeaniverse-*me*. She was drawn to the nexus, too, by *both* Morrow and nexus-me, which perhaps was more of a draw for her than anywhere else. Oh, and that's how she found the metadisc so easily — drawn there by meta-*me*. She is truly a Nick magnet.

What about Ronnie?

Ulric was Ronnie's player, and as far as I know, Ulric had no meta-connection to Nick. Ronnie may have some of Ulric's awareness, but not Nick's.

Not even though Nick was Game Master when Ulric met Ronnie? Ulric showed interest for the game initially, but enthusiasm?—to the point of transferring any of his awareness to Ronnie? Might it be that Nick gave a bit of his awareness to Ronnie, too, to put some life into him for the game? Don't you think that before the game, all four of you— Ronnie, Fauna, Emma, and yourself—were but automatons following a script through your lives?

It's possible. But that means... collectively there might be enough of Nick's awareness available to bring Nick back. A collective soul, so to speak. Great Goblin Mother.

What do you think about Britta?

My little girl? Okay, technically, I'm not the one who conceived her. Charli is. But I gave the girl birth, pulling her out of myself with my bare hands.

How is it you came to give birth to a child you didn't conceive?

Timelines were bleeding into each other back then. I was blending with Charli, Erica, and many other women from Nick's life, like Yvette and Macy. Why I got stuck with having Nick's child instead of Charli, I don't know.

Oh, Charli gave birth to a baby girl, too. One of them became a shadow baby of the other. The shadow baby's name is Spooky. She's with Emma and Fauna now. Neither you nor Charli tried to claim Spooky. You both wanted Britta. Emma and Fauna took custody of Spooky.

Great Goblin Mother, I did not know that. I need to meet her. Where are they now?

They're in the FP-Destin timeline.

Well, then.

I split off part of my awareness and create an FP-Destin-me. I want to meet this Spooky kid.

What are your thoughts about Morrow?

I feel bad for what happened to him. Erica's desperation to be with Nick latched onto Morrow, because she was of the mind he contained the only sizable portion of Nick's awareness still to exist. She basically ripped it from Morrow and placed it in the Nick automaton on FP-Earth. Without awareness, Morrow lacks the ability to remain in the nexus, and now he's adrift in the limbo surrounding it. Erica is oblivious to what she's done to him.

This is why Renee is beside herself. I wish I could tell her what happened to the man she was designated to support. With Morrow gone, she has no purpose.

To top off the insult, stealing awareness from Morrow didn't accomplish what Erica had hoped for. FP-Earth-Nick isn't giving Erica the attention she craves from him. Instead, he's heaping his affections on Kylie, an alternate-Kendra from Khertaan who was married to Morrow. There's a strong connection between FP-Earth-Nick and Kylie, because FP-Earth-Nick is more Morrow than Nick, and Kylie senses this.

You enjoy figuring out all these connections and relationships.

Perhaps I do. It's enough to make one heady, being able to peek into these different timelines and observe. Not that I always know where to look or what to look for. But the discovery is exciting and fun. Something Jean doesn't appreciate.

Looking in on the FP-Earth timeline now… Gondra and Mel are there. Gondra… I haven't figured him out yet. What are his motives? Vengeance on Seth for destroying his home world is the best motive I've heard, but I don't trust the Lizardman.

Mel was Nick's son by Jean in some timeline that has shriveled to nearly nothing, and a likable transgender guy even if Jean doesn't think so. He and Erica found a way to meta-shift their existences *without Cosmic Cloaks*. I have no idea how they did it, but it involved ghost forms. Then they gained Cosmic Cloaks, and that's how they get around now.

With Kylie is Georgie, her personal support AI… perceived as a clown. There's no awareness attached to him. He's like Renee— designated to assist a specific person, with no purpose to exist in the absence of that person. Is it fair to call these assistants automatons? No. They're manifested programs, something Nick invented. I don't know how.

Also on FP-Earth is Susie, both a young version and a future version. The future version was sleeping, but woke up a moment ago and bid everyone farewell. She has given awareness to a Khertaan resident, too—a Frogkin Mentalist and Martial Artist named Slithy. I can't see Slithy, because she's still in Khertaan, apparently, and the Khertaan timeline isn't part of the compacted timeline group.

Of everyone I'm looking at now on FP-Earth, only little Susie truly belongs in that timeline. The automaton version of FP-Earth-Nick belongs there, too, but Morrow's awareness animating the automaton doesn't belong there.

Do you feel that? What's happening?

The metadonut trembles.

By the Great Goblin Mother, *meta-Jean is gone*. Seth has subverted Jeaniverse, as I thought he might.

Seth now rules the two major timelines in the compacted timeline group.

Are you sure about that?

Let me look closer. The new ruler of Jeaniverse is an alternate version of Seth, someone referred to as a Shadow Gaunt. And he's not *one* Shadow Gaunt, but several. *Eleven*, to be exact, all residing in Jeaniverse. He has an army of thousands of powerful creatures at his beck and call. They're Dread Naughts—creatures spreading despair among all the sentient kindreds of the multiverse.

The Ronnie I know is in Jeaniverse. I'd never have imagined him riding a motorcycle, especially given where he and I came from. Then again, I'd never have imagined myself in a Cosmic Cloak peering into a multitude of timelines, either.

An automaton of Mel also rides the motorcycle, seated behind Ronnie. No… not an automaton, but a grotesque creation of Jean's to simulate Mel—a *simulacrum* with Mel's facial features, but with pronounced feminine qualities, a thinner waist, plumper breasts, and long, golden curls. The Mel simulacrum goes by the moniker

Princess Karen. Queen Jean created many other Princess Karen simulacra, all trapped and paralyzed in pocket dimensions with prisoners of the Queen.

I still can't wrap my head around how horrid Jean was. I'm not sorry she's dead. I can't imagine anyone in the multiverse will miss her.

A Dread Naught circles above Ronnie and Princess Karen, intent on attacking them. It's time for Jeaniverse-me to come out of hiding and go help them. Hang in there, Ronnie. Help is coming.

I send Jeaniverse-me a nudge.

Did you notice…? The Shadow Gaunt has changed the name of Jeaniverse to Shadowverse.

The Shadow Gaunt might be a bad guy, but he's got a cool name for his universe. Hang in there, Ronnie. Shadowverse-me is coming.

Did you notice the Fanciful Pegasus timelines are strengthening?

Great Mother Goblin, you're right. Why is that? Oh. The Dread Naughts aren't confined only to the Shadowverse. Some have gone to FP-Earth and some to FP-Destin.

Why did they go there?

They've gone to FP-Earth because Kylie and others from Khertaan are there, too. An Asian Priestess named Yuni stands on an isolated beach. The Viking Archer Amarynth and the Elitist Martial Artist ChrisCross drive through an Earth city. They've brought others with them from Khertaan, including Charli.

Megan Wright and Debra Jones have traveled to FP-Destin. They aren't like the others from Khertaan. Kylie, Yuni, Amarynth, and ChrisCross are natives of Khertaan. Megan Wright and Debra Jones are from FP-Earth…. Hmm, I'm not totally sure about Megan… she appears to have heritage from both FP-Earth and FP-Destin….

The Dread Naughts have gone to FP-Earth and FP-Destin for two reasons. One, some are attacking the Fanciful Pegasus facility in each timeline. Two, some are attacking the transplanted Khertaan natives. On top of that, they're in general spreading mayhem. The military in each timeline is powerless against the Dread Naughts, which only helps create more chaos.

A Dread Naught of the Flitter variety has found Yuni. The Asian Priestess stands on a beach. Taking Crow form, she flies up to meet the Flitter. Clutching a Cudgel in her talons, she swings it with a grace I'd not expect from a Crow. Still, the attack has no apparent effect on the nasty Dread Naught.

The Flitter attempts to repel Yuni with a gust of wind, but she creates a wind tunnel, flying through it and *into* the insubstantial mook. She casts a spell from inside the creature, but her magic fails to harm it.

Things aren't looking good for Yuni. I should help her. I split off some awareness and create an FP-Earth-me to lend a hand. Hmm. I can't create it in the vicinity of the Dread Naught. Interesting. The new me might not reach Yuni in time to help in the current encounter, but if Yuni survives this fight, I'm sure she'll be glad for assistance, because I can already see there are many more Dread Naughts in her timeline.

By a certain logic I should be able to transfer my awareness to any Nick automaton. By the same logic, it's curious that I have my own automatons, separate from Nick's, aside from the ones I've consciously created. Perhaps I've subconsciously created some. Hmm.

The Flitter launches a magical attack against Yuni, but one with minimal power, as though testing the Asian woman's defenses.

In the distance, three other Flitters, Shadows of the one Yuni fights, wreak havoc on beach-goers and beach-front establishments. From even further away come more Dread Naughts, some Flitters but also other types.

Hmm. The shadow Flitters are to the original Flitter what Spooky is to Britta. Interesting….

Yuni pours all of her magical power into a spell to cause emotional damage. The Flitter is defeated!

The creature explodes, severely wounding some people and killing others.

Shadow-linked to the slain Flitter, the Shadow Flitters explode, too, causing even more deaths elsewhere.

I just realized… if real-Britta dies, then so does Spooky. If they die, is it possible for them to respawn? Can the Khertaan avatars now occupying FP-Earth and FP-Destin respawn if they die? So much to think about….

CHAPTER SIXTEEN

Kylie/Kendra: Lunger

KYLIE

I awake in a lavish bedroom on a king-sized bed. Slithy, Rancor, and my Black Ghoul Dragon mount are gone. But my personal support AI, Georgie, is still with me. I still hold the Spirit Noose I'd been using to control the Dragon. Without the Noose around the Dragon's neck, Slithy and Rancor will be hard pressed to deal with the undead beast. "Were Slithy and Rancor booted from Khertaan, too, Georgie?"

"Unknown for certain, pumpkin, but the announcement went to every PC in Khertaan, so I'd venture that all PCs were booted while the System performs its updates."

"I hope you're right." I sit up and stretch my wings.

"And I'm delighted to say—*congratulations*, pumpkin, you've graduated from Khertaan. Your body is that of the Angel avatar, but capable of acting outside of Khertaan. How you identify is up to you, because either Kylie or Kendra's awareness may dominate your brain as you desire."

Taking control of my Angel body, I slide off the bed.

"This is mine and Nick's bedroom," Kendra says, her words unvoiced but discernible as hers in our shared mind space.

"This is indeed your house in the Fanciful Pegasus-Earth timeline," Georgie says.

"What does that mean? Are there other timelines where Fanciful Pegasus is somewhere other than Earth?"

"You are astute indeed, pumpkin. There is one other timeline with a Fanciful Pegasus facility. In that timeline, the facility is located on the planet Destin. If you'd woken in a bedroom under Fanciful Pegasus management, you'd have been given the choice to exit to Earth or Destin, but as you woke up here, the Earth timeline was your only option."

With my Heightened Senses - Hearing trait, I detect voices outside the bedroom. "Who else is in the house, Georgie?"

"Let me see. There's Nick—"

KENDRA

Not waiting for the AI to finish, I wrest control of our shared body from Kylie. Nick is my husband, and I've not seen him in so so long. I rush to the door and throw it open.

He stands there, reaching for the door knob. I lay a raised hand against the door frame and lean into the kind of sexy, lounging pose that drives him crazy. Georgie peers under my raised arm. Not sexy, but I don't care.

"Kylie?" Nick does a double take. "Where's Kendra?"

"I'm both Kylie and Kendra, my dear, so call me what you like." Dismissing the Spirit Noose, I beckon to him.

He rushes to me, as I knew he would. We fling our arms around each other and pepper each other with kisses. How I've missed him. My hands glide over his body, touching all the familiar places and relishing the press of him against me.

Several people stand beyond Nick, watching us. They talk, but their words might as well be the sound of feathers falling.

It's been too damned long since my man had his arms around me. I soak him in, and our spirits intertwine in that indescribable place no one has ever seen, and only those in true love have ever been.

Words invade my awareness. "Bye, Mom." Is that Slithy? Nick squeezes me again, and I return the squeeze.

A familiar young blond with Slithy's facial features—though white skinned instead of red and black—waves goodbye. Her grin is sad. She vanishes, leaving me to wonder if I imagined her.

My five-year-old daughter Susie runs to me. I scoop her up in my arms. Oh, golly, I've missed my little girl. Emotions swell as I recall the last time I was in this house. Susie had been missing and I'd been searching desperately for her. Nick wasn't looking for her—didn't seem at all concerned—and I was so angry with him. Then lightning flashed, like it was inside the house, knocking me unconscious.

I woke up in Khertaan as Kylie, but with my own memories intact. Slithy showed up and proved to me she was my little Susie, or I'd have been out of my mind. Maybe I *was* out of my mind for a while.

"You're being really quiet, Mommy." Susie pokes my nose.

My daughter recognizes me as Kendra even though I'm in Kylie's body. That's such a relief. "I was thinking how happy I am to see you, sweetie."

"Glynda and Super Glynda were here."

"Oh, yeah? Who are Glynda and Super Glynda, darling?"

She pokes my nose gain. "They're me, Mommy. From the future. Glynda had to sleep here while she played a Frog person in a dream game. Like you and Daddy did. Super Glynda was here to watch over everyone and make me sandwiches."

"I'm glad she was here, sweetie."

My muscles tense at sight of a cloaked Lizardman watching me. "Nick? Perhaps introductions are in order."

The reptilian raises a clawed hand. "I'll oblige. My name is Gondra. Like Nick, I'm a Traveler of the Timelines." He gestures at a woman standing next to him. She's in her mid to late thirties and dressed in a fashion more masculine than feminine. "This is Mel. He's a Cosmic Traveler, too. He's Nick's son in another timeline."

I have no problem with transgender people. "Hello, Mel." But how am I supposed to feel about a person born to my husband by another woman? In this timeline, Susie is Nick's only child, and he wasn't married to anyone else before he married me.

Mel offers his hand, and I shake it. There's admiration in his gaze. Is that because I'm an Angel? Or is there something else going on here? I offer him my best welcoming smile.

Gondra waves towards a blue-haired woman of seventeen or eighteen years, attired in a striking feminine fashion, all black and pink. "This is Erica. She's also a Cosmic Traveler. Nick would still be sleeping on the computer lab floor if not for her."

"Oh?" I meet Erica's gaze as I shake the hand she offers. Her fingers tremble in mine. Profound sadness lurks in her eyes, unable to hide from me. I've seen this look before, in Charli. Every instinct in me claims both Charli and Erica are in love with my Nick, that both Charli and Erica have been Nick's lovers in other timelines. Do I trust my instincts? Or are my insecurities unjustified? Can I hold trysts in other timelines against Nick or his young lovers? I think as long as they behave themselves in this timeline, I'll have to put what happened in alternate realities out of my head. "I'm grateful for you helping my husband, Erica. Thank you."

She blinks away a tear and bows her head. "You are most kind, Angel."

"Please, everyone, you can call me Kendra. Or Kylie. Whichever suits you. I'll answer to either name."

Thing is, Nick was never married to Kylie. If people, including Nick, think of me as her, they might feel I've no claim on Nick in this timeline. That's upsetting.

"Count yourself lucky that Nick is here," Kylie says to me. "I wish Morrow were."

Georgie waves at everyone. "I'm Georgie, Kylie's personal support AI."

Erica wipes her eyes and grins. "Hey, Georgie."

"Glad to meet you, clown." Mel offers his hand, and Georgie shakes it with fervor.

"Wait," says Kylie. "Can they see you, Georgie?"

He squeezes his nose, making a high-pitched honking. "Seems so, pumpkin. I'm going to enjoy this timeline."

The reptilian Gondra flicks a forked tongue. "The multiverse is depending on us. We need to move. Who's with me?"

Uneasiness marinates in my gut. Nothing about this Gondra fellow feels right.

Kylie concurs. "Let me have control, Kendra. If this guy tries anything, I can respond quickly."

"I'm sure I can use your avatar abilities just fine."

"We don't know that, and we can't take the risk. Don't fight me on this, Kendra. I'm taking control."

Maybe she's right. "Fine."

KYLIE

Nick smacks his lips. "So... if I heard right... seems I need to respawn Morrow in Khertaan asap, which means I need to sleep."

Georgie bounces on the balls of his feet. "Not now. The Khertaan System is updating. No one is going in until it is out of update mode. There is no estimated time of completion."

"Great." Nick looks askance at Gondra. "Then... I guess... shall we go find Ronnie, and then Greelia?"

Mel shakes his head. "Ronnie was with me and Erica, but he failed to come with us for some unknown reason. How would we go about finding him?"

"It's all up to Erica." Gondra shrugs at the blue-haired girl. "You're our compass, whether you like it or not. If you need to be sure Ronnie is safe, then you need to take us to him. I don't know where he is and neither does Mel, obviously. Do either of you know where Ronnie is, Nick or Kylie? Or how about you, Susie? Do you know where Ronnie is?"

Erica grits her teeth but says nothing. She's the non-confrontational sort.

I'm a bit in the dark. "Can someone tell me who Ronnie and Greelia are?"

Mel turns his face away from the rest of us. His voice is choked. "Ronnie is the best friend I've ever had."

Damn. How am I not supposed to be moved by that?

Nick closes the bedroom door. "Greelia is a character I created for a role-playing game. Just as Ronnie is a character I helped Ulric create for the game, too."

Gondra frowns. "After everything you've seen and experienced, Nick, I'm surprised you still think that way. Greelia is a Goblin Warrior woman whose existence you tapped into when you played your role-playing game. She existed before you played the game, but her life prior to the game was that of a scripted automaton. When you tapped into her existence, you gave her a part of your awareness, changing her life. It's what you gave her that I need a part of. I don't need it all, because what you gave her has grown. I just need as much as you gave her to begin with. Once I have it and combine it with what I've taken of your awareness from Ronnie, Emma, and Fauna, I can make you as strong as you need to be for finishing the task of healing the timelines." The reptilian looks to me. "Is that explanation sufficient, Angel?"

I nod. "For now. So... what are we doing?"

With a *bang*, the front door flies off its hinges, skidding across the living room floor. A giant centipede too thick to pass through the doorway bashes the door frame with its head, widening the opening and wrecking the surrounding wall.

"Georgie, what the hell is that?"

"A Dread Naught, pumpkin, of the Lunger variety. Without a Guide present, access to further info is locked at the moment."

The mook scurries on a multitude of legs towards us. I summon my Spirit Blade. Of everyone here, I'm possibly the only one equipped to deal with a Dread Naught. I fly forward to meet it before it reaches Nick and the others.

The hallway floor heaves up below me. A second Lunger's head erupts from the breach, its fangs gnashing. It bites at me, but I fly out of the way. Switching to Spirit Form, I drive my blade into the attacker's head.

Georgie flies beside me. "Sorry, pumpkin, but I've just learned that spiritual attacks don't affect this Lunger. Each Lunger has its own class and subclass, and only those capable of dealing spiritual damage can be affected by it."

My ego deflates. I can't make short work of these things.

The first Lunger leaps at me, trying to sink its fangs in my flesh. Somehow it senses my Spirit Form. Its bulging arthropod body passes through me without harm, and it lands near the second Lunger.

The second one opens its mouth… and sings.

The haunting song brings back my carefree childhood. I run through a lush green forest on bare feet, avoiding sharp rocks and twigs. Water rises beneath me, and I float on my back, marveling at the clear blue sky. The Lunger swims beside me. It's my friend, and I'll protect it with my life.

CHAPTER SEVENTEEN

Erica: Chance Encounters

With a glowing blue sword in hand, Kylie flies at the giant centipede monsters. She must have a ton of self-confidence. Georgie flies right behind her.

Both Kylie and Georgie disappear. Did the monsters destroy them, just like that?

Gondra grabs my wrist. "We must go, *now.*"

I resist his attempt to time-shift me. I can't just leave like that. Jerking free of his grip, I grab Susie by the arm in one hand. I latch onto Mel with the other. "Take hold of Nick. We're getting out of here."

"*Kylie.*" Nick sprints towards the monsters. Crap.

The centipedes lash at an invisible foe. It must be Kylie. She's not dead, as I'd feared.

Nick halts in his tracks as glorious song fills the air, alien verses unintelligible to the human ear but not to the human heart. The centipedes cease fighting. Kylie appears, hovering in the air. The centipedes raise their heads to the ceiling, like living pillars to either side of her. Georgie stands behind the monsters, his head down… a sad clown.

"The Lungers mean us no harm." Kylie points her glowing blue sword at us as the song fades to silence. "Do not attack, or I will be forced to defend them."

"She's been seduced to their side." Gondra grabs my wrist again. "We must go before the rest of us succumb to their siren song." He doesn't try to time-shift me against my will.

Nick inches towards the Lungers, hand outstretched in a non-threatening manner, as though all he wishes to do is touch them. "What do you want with this world, Lungers?"

Once more, the most beautiful vocals thrill me with a melody impossible for a human throat to replicate. Nick bows before the Lungers. "I am your servant."

"Nick, no." My heart breaks. I can't bear to leave him here, but Gondra is right, we need to go. The centipedes won't hurt Kylie or Nick—they have no need to.

Mel breaks free of my grip and runs to Nick. "*Dad.*"

One of the Lungers strikes at Mel, but Mel is quicker. He lays a hand on Nick's shoulder, and the two of them vanish.

Mel time-shifted with Nick.

I wish I could do the same for Kylie. I'm not so sure she can't harm me, but I'm doubly sure she'd try. I don't know whether the Lungers can affect me or Susie, but I don't want to give them a chance. I've got to protect those of us I can right now and figure out how to help Kylie later.

With a tight grip on the five-year-old, I don't wait for Gondra to time-shift us, but activate my own Cosmic Cloak. The Lizardman already has a hold on me, so he comes along, too.

ဆဂသလၢၜၐဆဂသ

Mists surround the three of us—Gondra, Susie, and me. I had no particular timeline in mind to shift to, but just wanted out of the one I was in.

"Let's go back for Mommy." Susie tugs in an attempt to break free of my grip. "We need to save her from the monsters."

I pull her closer, wrapping both arms around her. I couldn't live with myself if I lost her in this limbo. "Your Mommy will be all right. The monsters won't hurt her. But they might hurt us, so we had to leave. Do you understand?"

"No." Susie looks undecided about whether to box my ears. "Let's get Mommy *now*."

"We can't, dear." Still holding my wrist with one hand, Gondra lays the other hand on Susie's shoulder. "Your mother can take care of herself, but it's up to Erica and me to take care of you. Your Momma would want us to keep you safe, right?"

"No." The girl pokes my nose. "Get Mommy now. Or I will."

Gondra sighs. "If we go back, Susie, we'll die. Your mother won't. She's stronger than us."

Susie doesn't look at Gondra, but searches my face instead. Seeing the truth in my sad expression, she nods. "Okay. Let's be safe. Where are we?"

Gondra exhales loudly. "Thank you, Susie. We are in the Mists of Time. Erica here is going to take us to a friend named Greelia, a nice Goblin with green skin. You'll like her."

The girl bounces her head up and down. "Goblins aren't all bad. Dad says so. Where is Dad?"

"Mel took him somewhere safe." Gondra slides his hand up my arm to my shoulder and squeezes. "If you're ready, Erica, can we please begin our search for Greelia? After we find her, then we can look for Mel and Nick and anyone else you want to look for."

I'm grateful for Susie's company. It would creep me out to be traveling alone with the scaly-skinned Gondra. I'm creeped out bad enough as it is. I wish Nick and Mel were with us, but I understand Mel's decision to grab Nick and go. Nick didn't go willingly.

"Focus, Erica."

Gondra's sibilant voice brings me out of my reverie. "Right." I picture Greelia in my mind.

Don't think about Ronnie....

I told Gondra we needed to find Ronnie first, and it's true. I feel responsible for losing him. So that's what I'll do. Bending my will to locating the T&T Rogue, I close my eyes and let my spirit guide me through the mists.

"Erica?" The female voice is familiar. I open my eyes. A woman floats before me in a red suede chest wrap, red leather miniskirt, and knee-high red leather boots.

"Renee...! What are you doing out here?" I hold out a hand to her. "Join us, if you like."

She speeds over and takes the offered hand like a drowning person grabbing onto a tossed life preserver. "Oh, Erica. I've been so alone since Morrow left the nexus. I can't find him anywhere."

Gondra leans in close, anxious to get in on this conversation. "Is Greelia still in the nexus? Can you take us there? Erica seems to be having some difficulty."

Renee draws back. "She's still there. But I won't take you. She's maintaining the nexus, and no one is to disturb her."

"We must go to her." Gondra prolongs his hissing of the sibilant in the word, *must*, more than usual.

"Wait." I blow out a breath. "I saw Greelia in places other than the nexus. We could go to her elsewhere."

"Then, *please*, let's do it." Gondra looks ready to take a bite from someone's face, namely, mine.

"Yes. Let's." I close my eyes and concentrate. I sense movement, but I don't look.

"*Stop.*" Renee tugs on my hand and then lets go.

"We're finding everyone but Greelia." Gondra doesn't sound happy.

When I open my eyes again, we're still in the Mists of Time. Renee tows the unconscious body of a man whose most outstanding feature is his green mohawk. It's Morrow.

I meet her halfway. Draping the Punk Wizard over one shoulder, Renee takes my hand again. "He was like this right before he left the nexus, like something stripped his soul from him."

I suppose, in essence, I'd done exactly that. I'd been so focused on reviving Nick in the FP-Earth timeline, I hadn't considered where the awareness would come from to revive him. I'd robbed Morrow of his awareness so I could awaken Nick. "I'm sorry, Renee. I think I'm responsible for this sad state of affairs."

"*You*?"

"Yes, though this wasn't my intention. I'm really sorry. Right now, I can't fix it. But maybe once we find Greelia...." I glance at Gondra.

He shrugs and says nothing, for a change.

"Well then... everyone hold on, and let's see who we find next." I close my eyes and let my spirit magnet take me where it will.

CHAPTER EIGHTEEN

Slithy: Chrono Sand Wyrm Prep

As the cave mouth atop the Spire of Desire comes into sight, I suppress a pleased chuckle. Scores of adventurers fill the road outside the cave.

"My my, girlie." Marta raises both eyebrows. "Fifty-four parties, counting yours, consisting of a total of three-hundred-eighty-six characters, have gathered in total. One-hundred-ninety-three are PCs. Ninety-seven of the NPCs are Companions or Familiars. The other ninety-six NPCs are hirelings."

Spyder waits off to the side, not wanting to make anyone more anxious about her presence than necessary. Britta's unconscious body lies beside the Behemoth. "Stay in my head, Britta, dear. Will you do that for me? Spyder will carry your body and protect it while we travel to find your Mommy."

"Yes, I trust you, Slithy." Her language continues to improve at an unnatural rate.

Spyder webs Britta's body and draws her up. Though the webbing originates from the rear of the Behemoth, she manipulates it to serve as a sling hanging on her side.

Continuing to use Britta's Flight Speed skill, I fly in front of Spyder with Rancor flying beside me, as our ragtag party approaches the gathered throng.

We stop shy of the street. I fly high enough for everyone to see me, and then I call for attention over local chat. There's still just over three minutes before I promised we'd be leaving, so now is a good time to talk, and I have something everyone should hear.

Silence falls as I speak. "I am Slithy. My large friend is Spyder, an Arachnid Behemoth, which may frighten some of you, but you have my word, she's on our side. Also with me are Rancor the Woodpecker, whose beak is one of the most powerful weapons on the planet... trust me. I also have in my company Britta the Cave Goblin girl, daughter of Charli, whom you all know. Spyder carries Britta's body to keep it safe while Britta's awareness stays with me. Let me explain about that.

"I'm referring to something called *head hopping*. It's a technique allowing a character to transfer some or all of their traits and skills to another character. Both characters have to be willing participants and in the same party. A PC wishing to head hop sends the request through their support AI. I'm not sure how it works if you're an NPC... you'll just have to work that out for yourselves. The initiator chooses the target of the head hopping, and the target must accept. Once permission is granted, the head hopper's awareness enters the head of the target.

"You can see that I'm flying. I don't personally have a trait or skill for flying. But Britta does. She head hopped to me and lent me her ability to fly. Rancor head hopped to me a few minutes ago and lent me abilities I used in combination with my own to defeat a Black Ghoul Dragon with one smack of my palm."

I pause while the gathered throng mulls over what I just said. Judging by the many exchanged glances, several party-level discussions are underway now. I wait until most eyes turn my way again.

"As you might guess, some combinations of skills and traits become possible with head hopping that aren't possible otherwise, and these combinations can lead to earth-shattering results.

"There is a drawback to head hopping. When you head hop to someone, your own body loses consciousness. You're in the head of the person you've head hopped to, presumably making them stronger, while your own body is vulnerable. This is why, if you take a close look at Spyder, you'll see she carries Britta's motionless body in her webbing. Spyder will keep Britta safe while Britta is head hopped to me.

"In a minute, I will venture forth to complete a quest given to me by Ezmerelda, Speaker of Omens. Some of you may have met her. She has promised that when I complete the quest, I and all who are with me to the end will receive the XP needed to reach level thirty. Some of you may know that a few PCs and NPCs have already reached level thirty. The System has booted them out of Khertaan. The System would have booted all of us out, except that I found a way to stay here, and arranged for everyone else who hasn't reached level thirty yet to remain as well, so that you may all join me on my quest if you wish.

"It's my understanding that *this is it*. If you die now, you'll not be respawning to try again, no matter your Constitution score. It's incumbent upon everyone here to stay alive until you attain level thirty. So let's do it! What say you?"

A cheer goes up from the gathering. My cheeks warm. I was never cut out to be a leader, but this is… wow.

I shout to be heard over the tumult. "It's important we travel fast, but we won't leave anyone behind." I point to the distant tower that marks my destination. "We're headed for the city of Caravel, where that tower stands. How many do we have present who can travel there fast, whether by air or by land, and has the ability to take others along? Please, a show of hands."

We have eight Angels who can fly and take their parties along, accounting for twenty-nine PCs and thirty NPCs, for a total of fifty-nine characters. Most of the Angels fly at the rate of four miles an hour. One of the Angels has the Increased Movement trait at level four, allowing them to fly at twenty miles an hour. A Desert Demon and a Desert Demoness come forward who can travel at four miles an hour across the desert and take their parties with them, accounting for another eight PCs and eight NPCs. We have two Sand Warriors and one Sand Wizard who can each travel at twenty-six miles an hour across the desert, each taking up to one-hundred-fourteen characters with them, who don't need to be in the same party. All totaled, we can move two-hundred-thirty-six characters at a speed of twenty miles an hour or more, and another sixty-seven at a speed of four miles an hour, which isn't all that fast. That leaves eighty-three to walk through the sand at their own pace.

I address the gathering. "Can anyone here travel twenty miles per hour or faster but are unable to carry others? And vice versa, who can carry others, but can't move fast?"

Lots of hands go up. This is promising.

"I'm thinking if some of us head hop to others, we can combine abilities to help us take everyone across the desert at a speed of twenty miles an hour or more. Assess your skills, and speak up if you have ideas."

A short, green-skinned Goblin woman dressed in Leather Bra and Loincloth comes forward, riding a Cheetah. A Squirrel sits on her shoulder. "Hello, Slithy. My name is Ger-Alt. Skeeter, my Squirrel Companion here, can Teleport Self to any location he can see. In addition, I have the Unencumbered trait at level four. Are you familiar with the Unencumbered trait?"

"I am not. Please continue."

Ger-Alt grins. "At level one in the trait, I could carry any number of items. I wondered how the trait could prove to be any more useful at higher levels. I was curious enough, in fact, that I maxed it out. At level four, I can... get this... stash into my inventory *any number* of unconscious or conscious-and-willing PCs and NPCs."

A collective gasp goes up from the crowd. My jaw hangs low, too.

"Now, I can't fly or teleport, but if Skeeter can head hop to me like you describe, he can lend me his Teleport Self skill. I'll stash him and everyone else who wants to go. Then I'll teleport us all to where we're going."

Everyone remains silent, waiting to hear what I think of this idea. It sounds too good to be true. Can we truly all of us go to Caravel in but the blink of an eye? "Are there any complications we should be aware of regarding people stashed in your inventory?"

Ger-Alt grimaces and nods. "If I'm killed while people are stashed, they stay stashed until I respawn. If I never respawn, they'll be stuck in my inventory forever." Then her countenance brightens. "But… allow me to read a pertinent line from the info I have. *Any conscious stashed entity may freely choose not to be stashed any longer at any time prior to the stashing character's death.* So… if anyone wants out at any time, they can get out on their own.

"There's a bit more everyone should know, and I'll read it for you as well…. *Conscious sentient entities stashed in the character's inventory may speak to each other on a special inventory chat channel that does not replace the local territory chat channel. Those exercising First Person POV will see an organized view of all other sentient entities stashed with them. Those exercising Third Person POV will view the stashing character's surroundings.*

"So… anyone who wants to watch what's going on with me can do so, and if they don't like what they see, they can unstash themselves. It sounds very low risk to me, to be honest."

I sigh in relief. *This will work.* "Looks like we have our solution, people! I'll teleport over first and check out the place—make sure it's safe. Ger-Alt will stash all of you who are willing and teleport you over to meet up with me. Once you're there, wait for my signal, and then everyone can unstash yourselves. We'll carry on from there to find Ezmerelda. Do I hear any objections to this plan?"

No one makes a peep.

"All right, then. Ger-Alt, what do people need to do so you can stash them?"

The Goblin woman holds out her hand, palm up. "If those who are willing to go could form a long line… and then just walk by me and lay your hand on mine."

Rancor flies over and lands on Ger-Alt's open palm. "Ha ha, stash me, lady." The Woodpecker vanishes.

I sweep the throng with my gaze. "If anyone isn't willing…." I don't need to finish the sentence. A line forms, winding its way up and down the street. As each person reaches the Goblin lady and lays a hand on hers, they disappear. Even those who have the ability to teleport want the experience of being stashed, it appears.

The line moves quickly, but it still takes twelve minutes to finish. After everyone else is stashed, Spyder unrolls Britta, and Ger-Alt stashes the Cave Goblin girl's unconscious body. Then she stashes Spyder, Skeeter, and her Cheetah, Zip. It's just her and me left standing.

I point to the distant tower. "That's where we're going. I'll go first and let you know what I find. Hang tight."

Ger-Alt crosses her arms. "I'll be waiting."

The distant tower is surrounded by a high wall. I pick a spot maybe fifty feet out from the wall and teleport there.

I stand in sand, quickly sinking to my calves. A fifty-foot high wall carved from a single huge block of sandstone rises before me. A windowless, cylindrical-but-slightly-tapered tower—also constructed from seamless sandstone and perhaps a hundred feet in diameter near the base—rises from behind the wall, reaching up three hundred feet. Two closed wooden doors—each one twenty feet high and twenty feet wide—block entry to what lies beyond the wall. No sounds emanate from the other side—perhaps the city has its own local chat and special effects channels. No guards are in evidence outside the gates or atop the wall.

I glance over my shoulder at the Spire of Desire. Is that speck Ger-Alt? It's difficult to make her out. I try to contact her via local chat, but she doesn't respond, so I initiate a private chat, which does work. "Let me approach first and see what we're dealing with. I'll just be a moment." I step forward.

The scene before me flashes, and everything shrinks. No... the tower and the city walls are abruptly further away.

"Where did you go, Slithy?"

I wave my arms. "I'm still right here."

"Oh, I see you. Why are you moving away from the tower?"

"I'm not. Not intentionally. Hang on a bit longer while I figure this out."

"I think you forgot something, girlie." Marta drops from the sky on her broom. "You're not in the Dunes of Doom here, but the Sands of Time, and there's a separate Boss for this territory, one that every party must be involved in defeating if they are to gain entrance to Caravel. With Charli on the roster for every party, it might be sufficient for any party to defeat the Boss. But I don't know if that loophole will work now, since Charli isn't in Khertaan—in either mind or body."

"Thanks for the tip, Marta." I get back on the private chat with Ger-Alt. "I need you to come on over now."

She's suddenly standing next to me. "You called?"

"Yup. Seems we need to unstash at least one person from each party, and then hope the territory Boss shows soon." I make a sweeping gesture at the surrounding desert. "Do we have a Guide with us who can tell us what to expect from the Boss for the Sands of Time?"

"I am TehnKhar, of party ZAvengers, Priest of Athlea and level twenty Guide," says a stashed avatar over local chat. "The Boss for the Sands of Time is a Chrono Sand Wyrm. That's w-y-r-m. It lives deep under the sand. It deals mental damage and can only be harmed by mental attacks or affected by mind-influencing abilities. More than that, I can't say."

A few other parties have characters who have taken Guide as a subclass. Seems no one had cared to take Guide as their primary class. The other Guides confirm TehnKhar's info, with nothing to add.

"Since the System is in update mode, girlie," says Marta, "the Boss won't come to you. You'll need to go down to it."

Lovely.

"Okay, everyone. You've all heard what we're up against. We need to go beneath the sand to fight the Boss. Each party discuss among yourselves and come up with ideas." Leaving everyone to do as I ask, I address my own party. "Okay, TimeTrippers. If it were just us, how would we tackle this problem?"

"I can lend you some useful abilities." Britta's language skills have improved even more than the last time we spoke. "I've already used my Locate Character skill to pinpoint where the Boss is. It's deep down and hasn't moved in the last few minutes. I can also lend you my Special Movement - Burrow trait, so you can dig down to the Boss. Dark Sight will let you see while you're down there. And Iron Will could help against the mental effects the Boss throws at you."

"Good, yes, thanks, Britta, and thank you for your patience in going after your Mother. Rancor, what can you lend me?"

"Ha ha, how about all my Psi-Warrior skills, for starters? You know about the Psi-Melee Weapon skill already. I've got several other skills useful in mental combat. The Power Strike trait only applies to physical damage, so it won't help against this Boss, but I can lend it to you anyway, just in case. Ha ha, I should just lend you every ability I have."

Rancor lends me a ton of skills and traits. Britta lends me all her Assassin class skills and all her traits—except Shadow Self, which she can't. Spyder can't lend me any skills or traits, not having any that are based in Khertaan.

The other parties report. Only a few of them have the means to travel underground.

A brown man about my height, heavier than me by maybe thirty pounds, appears next to Ger-Alt. Black horns curl up from his forehead, with long, curly, red hair flowing around them to his shoulders. His green gaze hints of malice, and I shudder. He wears strips of sand-colored leather wrapped around his body, mummy style, from his knees to his neck, with slivers of brown skin showing through in places. "I am Algor, Priest of Malicifer, Lord of

Pain, of the Diabolical Pantheon. I'm a member of party TwoWorldOrder. Mylynna is in my party—she says you know her. I'm a Sand Demon and a Sand Warrior. I can move through sand as though I were flying in the air, and see through it to a distance. I do not see the Boss, so it is not in close proximity, but I'm sure I can find it soon enough.

"I can take up to one-hundred-fourteen characters with me into the sand, provided they stay in contact with me directly or in a chain. It is imperative, of course, that the chain between me and anyone I take under the sand is not broken, or my ability will cease to offer them mobility through the sand. But since we do not breathe, if I lose someone in the sand, it is only a matter of my reestablishing contact with them to bring them out, assuming a mook doesn't kill them first. It is admittedly not an ideal situation, but if any party has no other way to be involved, I offer them this choice."

Two others chime in, saying they can assist Algor in taking any of us in or out of the sand. Brutus is an Ogre Sand Warrior and Yoshi is a Sand Wizard.

Priest Algor inclines his head to me. "I might also say, she won't need to go underground with us, but it would be useful to have Mylynna playing her guitar and singing within earshot during the encounter. Not only can she provide a Morale boost to everyone on our side of the encounter, regardless of party or Pantheon affiliation, but music provides me a multiplier for my Auni. Each Auni I expend in the presence of quality music is multiplied by a factor of four. Anyone else among us who has the Music Connection trait will likewise benefit."

"So that's what that trait does," someone mutters over local chat.

Mylynna appears next to Ger-Alt. She waves at me and then equips a guitar. "It will be my honor to play and sing for you."

I wiggle my fingers at her and laugh. I'd never imagined preparations for a Boss kill would be anything like this.

After a bit more discussion, it's decided who will go underground and who will stay aboveground, providing boosts for those engaging the Boss.

Ger-Alt organizes an orderly unstashing of all those to be involved in the encounter. Fifty-five of us will be involved, in total, with TwoWorldOrder providing both Mylynna and Priest Algor, while all other parties provide but one member each. Forty-two of the fifty-five have the means to deal mental damage or activate mind-influencing effects. The other thirteen parties have ways to boost us. To avoid putting any stashed characters at risk, Ger-Alt won't be going underground, but her Leadership trait grants a +6 bonus to all actions for all allies.

The Sand Demon Priest comes to me. "You are a Martial Artist? Let me see your hands."

I hold them up.

He takes them in his. "If I enchant them, Malicifer will grant you his blessing as though you were in my party. Do you mind?"

I don't draw my hands away. "Malicifer is the Lord of Pain. If you enchant my hands, will they pain me?"

"No, but if you deliver an attack with them, the target is likely to feel pain. I don't know if it will have an effect on this Boss, but hopefully we won't need to get close enough for you to punch the Boss." He chuckles.

"I'd very much like to have your enchantment and the blessing of Malicifer. Any boost I can get could prove helpful."

"As you say." He rubs my hands between his and mutters something. Then he kisses the backs of my hands. "It is done. I've put 60 Auni into it, just in case."

Wow, that's significant. "Thank you, Priest Algor, you horny devil." I draw both hands away and raise one to stroke a horn protruding from his forehead.

His gaze is intense and still looks evil, but not like he wants to murder me. He's a Sand Demon and I'm a Frogkin. It would never work out.

Though I have Britta's Burrow trait, I latch onto the end of a chain connecting me to Priest Algor, leaving my right hand free to wield Rancor's Psi-Weapon if I need to. I've got my Mentalist skills and powers, too, which don't require me to swing a weapon. We have two other Psi-Warriors with skills like Rancor's, and they position themselves at the end of chains coming off Brutus the Ogre Sand Warrior and Yoshi the Sand Wizard, leaving right hands free to swing Psi-Weapons. Everyone else going underground can use their abilities without swinging a weapon.

I breathe deep and focus on Britta's borrowed Locate Character skill. Equipping Rancor's Psi-Weapon, I use it to point the way.

CHAPTER NINETEEN

Slithy: Encounter Under the Sand

Mylynna strums her guitar and sings a song of brave adventurers crossing the desert. Immediately, I'm caught up in the mood of the song, bolstered by its chords, melody, lyrics, and the timbre of the voice of the Mist Succubus.

The sand below my feet disappears to a depth of one-hundred-fifty feet. The sand must still actually be there, but presents no obstacle to vision, although everything below the surface takes on a black and white quality, like an old television show.

Even as the sand isn't an obstacle to my vision, neither is it an obstacle to us as we descend into its depths with the ease of fliers. Rock formations in the depths block my sand-sight. The Boss must be hiding in a crevice in the rock. I keep my Psi-Weapon trained on the spot where the Locate Character skill claims the Boss to be.

We descend, three lines of fourteen characters each, drawing closer and closer to the Boss's lair. When we're thirty feet from the rock formation, the Locate Character skill tells me the Boss has shifted its position. I activate my Predict skill.

From numerous crevices across my psychic view, glassy tentacles spring out all at once, striking like serpents at everyone in the front line. Several of my allies are struck senseless and lose their grips, breaking the chain, burying ten characters, including me, under one-hundred-twenty feet of sand as we lose the Sand Passage effect. As my vision of the future fades, I shout over local chat, *"Retreat, Sand Warriors. Now!"*

Priest Algor draws up short and ascends, dragging the rest of the line with him. He's in the center, so those of us on the ends aren't pulled away as quickly as those closer to him. As I'd predicted, over a dozen glassy tentacles strike out at us. They can't reach the Priest and those nearest him, but one comes at me. I'm not sure Psi-Dodge would work under the circumstances, since it requires a freedom of movement I don't enjoy at the moment, but, more importantly, if I take a defensive action, I won't have another chance at an offensive one. I swing the Psi-Weapon and slice off the tentacle before it touches me.

Spears of energy, their colors as varied as the rainbow, shoot out from my allies. All the tentacles wither under their assault. That seemed easier than my prediction had led me to believe it might be.

A blue bolt streaks out of the rock formation, striking Priest Algor. He screams as energy bathes him. When it dissipates, he's still with us.... With a war cry, he heads straight for the crevice housing the Boss.

"Yikes, girlie." Marta speaks from behind me. "Priest Algor is at 25% MP. He's hallucinating."

"Stop, Priest Algor."

He's not listening. He's dragging me and a dozen others with him into the lion's den. He doesn't halt, and someone between me and him breaks the chain.

Sand closes around me, packed tight. Panic pounds in my chest for two seconds. I'm still grasping the hand of the Asian woman who was my connection to the chain.

The sand vanishes. I'm at the end of a much longer chain stemming off the Ogre Sand Warrior, Brutus. He grimaces. "What now, boss?"

A Frogkin Guide named Samuel interrupts with new info. "The Chrono Sand Wyrm Boss dealt a Mind Spear 2 attack against Priest Algor, causing massive hallucinations. It can use that Mind Spear ability every combat heartbeat without exhausting its Psi points. What's more, the thing regenerates its tentacles."

Four tentacles shoot out of crevices and wrap around Priest Algor as he attempts to claw his way through the rock to get at the Boss. The Priest goes suddenly still.

Marta delivers the chilling news. "Priest Algor is at -39% MP. He has effectively been lobotomized and can't be healed without a respawn."

I wave my weapon at Brutus. "Take us out of here. We can't help Priest Algor now. We need to rethink our approach."

My Locate Character skill informs me the Boss is moving. It's coming out of its lair. Crap. *"Move, Brutus.* You, too, Yoshi. The Boss is coming after us. Get everyone out of the sand."

I take a second to use my Predict skill.

In my vision, Mylynna screams as a gigantic squid-worm hybrid monster appears on the surface above us.

"Everyone, look up and prepare to attack. It's teleporting to the surface."

Mylynna screams as the huge Boss appears before her. A head the size of a house sits at the end of a giant worm body sprouting dozens of tentacles. It rears its head, propping the front half of its body up on its front tentacles.

"Give it your all, everyone!"

Everyone with a mental attack throws all we have at the Boss. I expend every Psi point. This may be our only shot. A rainbow of colors blasts upward, catching the Chrono Sand Wyrm in its bulbous head. It shrieks... and pixelizes. We've defeated it.

"Better think again, girlie," says Marta.

I'm packed in sand, still grasping the hand of the Asian lady, but unable to see through the sand. The chain to Brutus has been broken. I squeeze her hand and she squeezes back. That's a relief.

My Locate Character skill and sense of gravity tell me the Boss is below me. It's alive, not dead. Damn. How is that possible?

The Asian woman's hand goes limp in mine. She's been lobotomized like Priest Algor was.

No one comes to collect me under the sand. Since I'm not moving, I may look as lobotomized as my Asian companion. I can't teleport out of here, since I can only teleport along line of sight.

I'll have to burrow my way out.

Thing is, if everyone leaves, the encounter ends, and we're back to square one, with none of us able to leave the territory.

Maybe it's Britta's Iron Will trait at play, but I'm ending this now. I've got a ton of abilities that don't need Psi points to execute. I can do this.

First, I activate the Hide skill from Britta's Assassin class, and hope it will prevent the Boss from attacking me until I attack it. I turn on my Displace skill, too, so if the Boss does manage to see me, it's first attack against me should miss. I also activate my Mislead skill, to make the Boss think I've retreated along with everyone else.

I burrow, using the Locate Character skill to guide me. The Dark Sight trait allows me to see the sandy walls of my tunnel in shades of gray. I slowly make my way down, down, down.

"Mylynna?" I contact the Mist Succubus on a private chat channel so the Boss won't hear me as it would if I spoke over local chat.

She's still singing and playing her guitar, but pauses singing to converse with me. "Slithy? Are you all right?"

"I'm fine. Tell the others not to worry about me. Is everyone else out?"

"Not everyone. Priest Algor is still down there and so are nine others. Brutus believes they're all lobotomized. He says you disappeared from sight, and he isn't sure what he should do."

"Tell him to wait. I'm going to end this. Once I've defeated the Boss, then Brutus can come down and get the bodies of Priest Algor and the other nine."

"By all that's Unholy, be careful, Slithy."

I reach the rock formation. Stone presented as an obstacle to the Sand Passage skill, but with the Burrow trait I can dig through rock the same as sand. I break through into the Boss's lair, an expansive cavern accessed via a long crevice. The Locate Character skill brought me straight to the creature's head.

It doesn't attack me... my Hide skill is working. I invoke my Anticipate skill, which isn't as effective as my Predict skill, but I only want to know what to expect from the Boss if I attack with the Psi-Weapon. In a vision, I see it react by firing its Mind Spear 2 at me.

With my Clairvoyance skill, I ask whether my Displace skill will work to avoid a Mind Spear attack. I get another vision and see a blue bolt shoot at me and miss. I have my answer.

Invoking my Clairvoyance skill again, I form another question: How often can the Chrono Sand Wyrm Boss use its Mind Spear 2 attack?

Another vision shows the delay between two Mind Spear attacks. The Boss's combat heartbeat is ten seconds long.

I have an Inspect Character skill I've never used. Will using it against the Boss cause my Hide effect to end? I put the question to my Clairvoyance, and get a vision of the Boss continuing to ignore me. Great. I activate Inspect Character on the Boss.

Name: Chrono Sand Wyrm Boss, Level 29

Hit Points: (Mental Domain only) 4000 MP (40 per each of 50 tentacles, 2000 for body).

Armor: 300 for body, 30 per tentacle.

Damage: Tentacles x 50, 6d20+50 MP per tentacle.

Powers:

Mind Spear 2: 1/combat heartbeat, no Psi cost, but activated as though powered by 50 Psi, dealing damage of 1d8 per Psi.

Regenerate Tentacles: restore 3 destroyed tentacles to full functionality each combat heartbeat.

Chrono Rewind: 1/encounter. Upon dying, the Boss is automatically restored to full health, and events leading to its death are rewound to a random point in time during the encounter. The statuses of enemies—HP, Auni, Psi, etc.—remain as they were immediately before the Chrono Rewind.

Immunities: Only affected by mental damage and mind-influencing abilities.

My Goddess, this Boss is one tough sucker. But we did kill it once, and if I can kill it again during this encounter, it will stay dead.

I'm out of Psi points, and even if I were at full and pumped all of them into a Mind Spear attack, I couldn't bring its MP down by more than 20%. So that's out.

What if I use Rancor's Psi-Melee Weapon against the Boss? It does 81 damage from just his skills. I get +6 from Ger-Alt, +27 from Mylynna, and +42 Morale boost from the blessing of the Lord of Pain, totaling 156. That won't even get through the Boss's mental armor.

My hands are enchanted with the Pain spell. Sixty Auni worth, which isn't anything to sneeze about. But can it affect the Boss? Is pain a mind-influencing ability? Phrased differently, if I attack the Boss with my hands, how would the attack affect it? I put the question to my Clairvoyance.

I see a vision of me striking the bulbous head of the Boss. The Boss's tentacles flail and its body spasms. It's clearly in pain, and wildly attacking me with tentacles and its Mind Spear... except that I don't seem to be harmed by any of its attacks.

It's strange that a sixty-Auni enchantment could bring about that kind of effect, putting such a huge debuff on an enemy.

Ah, it probably works in combination with my Displace. With a level 42 Displace skill, it wouldn't take that large a debuff to make it impossible for the Boss to locate me. It might get lucky and hit me, but the chance isn't too terribly high.

The Boss shifts its weight and repositions some of its tentacles. It has calmed down after the fight.

"Marta, is the encounter considered ended yet?"

"Negative, girlie. As long as you're in its vicinity, the encounter won't officially end. But the Boss is returning to hibernate mode nevertheless. It isn't scared."

Hmm, maybe I can get an action against it that it won't defend against.

"May I make a suggestion, girlie?"

"Please do, Marta."

"A combo attack can combine several actions into one larger one against which defensive abilities, including armor, are only applied once. There's a cooperative combo, which involves multiple attackers striking all in the same second...."

"That's out. I'm not asking anyone else to come down here."

"Well, there's also the lesser-used chain combo, in which a single attacker performs multiple offensive actions in consecutive seconds with the intent of delivering a combo attack. It only works as long as the chain of actions isn't prematurely broken. Full defensive abilities apply to each attack as normal until the last action of the chain is taken, at which point the combo damage is done."

I can get three consecutive attacks with the Psi-Melee weapon every six seconds. I've got level 55 Psi-Armor from Rancor, which will reduce the amount of damage I take from any tentacle that randomly hits me. I can probably survive a few tentacle hits. I can probably also survive one Mind Spear attack from the Boss. But in either case, my mind will be affected—I'll likely start hallucinating.

"Marta, can the Boss use combo attacks?"

"Sure, but the likelihood decreases significantly if it's in pain."

That's all I needed to hear. I leap onto the Boss's squid-head and smack it with my open palm, hoping the Lord of Pain will give this abomination the what-for.

The Boss spasms and its tentacles flail, just as I saw in my vision. Four tentacles lash at me and all of them miss.

Concentrating on delivering a combo attack, I strike with Rancor's Psi-Melee Weapon.

A blue Mind Spear whizzes past my ear.

I strike again with the Psi-Melee Weapon as part of my combo attack.

"Congratulations, girlie, you've reduced the Boss to 99% MP."

Four more tentacles swipe at me as I drive my Psi-Weapon's blade home again, continuing my combo attack.

One of the tentacles hits me.

"The Boss is down to 91%, but... *ouch*, girlie. You're down to 88% MP. Prepare for hallucinations...."

I'm on a spaceship. Snakes attack me, their tongues flicking poison. A Planet Buster destruction beam fires at me. I could be killed at any moment.

But my Iron Will drives me on. I won't relent until the spaceship is disabled. I stab with my glowing sword—stab, stab, stab. The snakes can't hurt me.... Ah, some do, but the destruction beam continually misses me. I stay focused, even when Seth confronts me in his hooded cloak. I won't let him stop me.

"Slithy, please. It's done. You've defeated the Boss."

"Get away, Seth."

"Slithy, it's me, Brutus. I'm here to take you back to the surface."

"*Slithy*, take a breath, child."

I recognize that last voice—Mylynna, the sweet little Succubus guitar player and singer. Her voice calms me. Everything is okay. The spaceship and the snakes are gone.

The Boss no longer thrashes, but lies very still.

"You're at 49% MP, girlie. You're gonna need some advanced healing before you do anything else. But, hey, you defeated the

Boss. It was effectively lobotomized by that Psi-Weapon you're still holding. Might want to put it away before you hurt someone. Oh… you've earned five million XP for yourself and everyone else. You're now 47% of the way to level thirty, up from 46%."

Dismissing the Psi-Weapon, I stash the mindless Boss, placing it in my inventory with a stashed mindless One Strike Scorpion Boss, four mindless Iron Goblins, and six mindless Brass Goblins. I don't know what I'll do with them all. I'm becoming a collector of mindless creatures.

Brutus takes me by the hand and we fly through the sand to the surface. More snakes appear, flying beside us, but Brutus doesn't seem to notice them.

I sit on the sand. Someone who's name I don't catch rubs my cheeks.

"Congratulations, girlie, your MP has been restored to full. You can thank Priestess Jessa."

The snakes fly away and stay gone. "Thank you, Priestess Jessa. How is everyone else?"

Jessa is an Elf with decorative tattoos covering her forehead and cheeks. "Ten people are at zero MP—mindless, if you will—including Priest Algor. I can't heal them. They're still alive, but they can't take any actions until they respawn."

"But they *can't* respawn."

"Ger-Alt already has them stashed in her inventory."

"Did I hear my name?" The Goblin lady shuffles over, her short stature made to look even shorter in the soft sand. "That was really something, Slithy. You want to take a break before we enter Caravel?"

I jump to my feet. "No, I'm good. Let's go."

Sounds of the city emanate from beyond the sandstone walls. Two guards stand at attention outside the gates, and dozens of guards line the tops of the walls.

Something looks off about the guards. Are they… Brass Goblins?

CHAPTER TWENTY

Tuni: They Come

Picture frames rattle on the walls as tremors rock the hallway. I turn my attention to my own situation, leaving Yuni to deal with her suffering surfers and novelist at the beach.

I've not chosen to exit to either Earth or Destin yet. So where am I now? A little bit in both, or somewhere else? Wherever I am, something is affecting the building I'm in, and not in a nice way.

I return to the bedroom. There's movement outside the window. I fly up to peer out and see what's happening.

Arachnid Behemoths stab their steely legs at the building. From what I can see of what lies beyond the Behemoths, we're in the middle of a desert.

Bam, the wall splits open before me. A giant metal spider leg spears the air, descending on me.

No fear....

The pointed metal leg strikes my forehead... and glances off. I'm unmoved, unfazed... entirely immune to metal-based attacks, even forceful ones. I might as well be an immovable object to them. Ha.

Checking inventory, I see that Yuni has stashed the Cudgel. Great. I equip it and enchant it with a War spell, putting half my Auni into it, dropping my Auni from 184 to 92. Shapeshifting to Crow and clutching the Cudgel in my talons, I fly through the breach. If I must choose Earth or Destin, I'll take Destin, but my portal out of my room is not your standard doorway.

I'm outside a high tower, about midway up. The place is crawling with Arachnid Behemoths. Metal spider legs stab at me, but they all bounce off, even those that strike the Cudgel. My Metal Resistance transfers to my equipment. I'm glad for that.

I lay about with the Cudgel, smashing giant metal spider legs. As I recall, these things explode on death, so I don't want to kill them. I also recall they have HP assigned to their legs separately from the HP assigned to their bodies. If I remove all the legs from a Behemoth, it will remain alive, but unable to do much.

With the degree of enchantment I've placed on the Cudgel, each swing shatters one leg of a Behemoth. There's an army of the things here, and it might take me forever to defeat them, but I keep at it.

The Behemoths try webbing me, but their metal webs slide right off me without snaring me. My immunity to metal is working great in many ways.

I go after those Behemoths high on the wall first, bringing them down on those below. I find it unnecessary to remove all eight legs from a Behemoth before it loses the ability to function properly. Removing from four to six legs proves sufficient. Delivering one blow of my Cudgel in every ten second combat heartbeat, I can cripple one Behemoth in a minute or less. And because of my Wakeful trait at level three, I recover expended Auni even while I'm fighting, replenishing it at the rate of one per minute.

A Behemoth is stuck in a plate glass window at the top of the tower. I leave it be—it isn't going anywhere, and if I remove its legs, that might allow it to enter the tower, which I don't think would be appreciated by whoever or whatever occupies the room.

As I drop more and more Behemoths, I realize there's someone else out here fighting them, too. The warrior is a hoofed woman using highly advanced technological weaponry and armor. Even though they knock her down a few times, the Behemoths aren't hurting her. She figures out a method for killing them efficiently, spraying acid in their eyes and then launching a grenade through the emptied eye socket. They explode when they die, as I knew they would, but I stay high enough not to be affected. Her armor protects her from the death explosions. I wouldn't mind having armor like that.

Choppers arrive with armed men. The Behemoths web a chopper and pull it down from the sky. The choppers draw back after that, dropping infantry. Their weaponry appears to be high tech, but has no effect on the Behemoths. So far, only me and the hoofed lady are hurting the giant metal things.

I've disabled about twenty Behemoths. Not bad, but there are countless more.

Voices emanate from beyond the wrecked plate glass window at the top of the tower. I catch the names Megan, Debra, Belle, Kevin, Franklin, and Mr. Freeman.

Acid sprays through gaps in the window, and I dart out of the way. Flames spill through after that, followed by bullets, lightning bolts, and a cloud of green gas. Are they trying to kill the creature? Apparently not, or all those attacks should have done so by now, unless they have the power levels turned down. That's got to be it. They're testing their weapons on the mook. I just hope they know better than to kill it. I caw for them to stop. After a couple more attacks, they do stop.

I want to go in and see who's there, but I wait a while longer to make sure they won't attack the Behemoth again.

Over a dozen floors below, a chunk of stone falls free of the tower with a roaring creak. A Behemoth stabs through the hole, and a familiar feminine voice shouts at it. The Behemoth keeps stabbing and the voice keeps shouting.

I dive at the Behemoth and shatter the leg it's stabbing with. It turns its attacks on me, which is what I'd hoped for. Forty seconds later, the thing loses its hold on the wall and rolls down the side of the mound of spiders swarming around the tower base.

Another Behemoth moves towards the hole. I fly through first.

Ruby the Centaur stands at the far side of the room on four equine legs, her Heavy Self Bow drawn. Seated on her back is a bald, blue man wearing no shirt, with tapered torso and muscles rippling across his chest. He's only two feet tall.

As I enter, Ruby's fingers twitch, but she doesn't release the arrow. "Yuni?"

Hovering in place, I stay in Crow form. I can still speak in an understandable voice. "Hey, Ruby. I *am* Yuni, sort of, but not. Call me Tuni. It's an Anjai thing. You and your little blue friend need to leave this room now. This tower is under siege by an army of Arachnid Behemoths. You can either stay and help fight them here on Destin, or you can join the original Yuni to protect Earth. I can tell you right now—you won't like either place."

A Behemoth pokes its leg through the breach in the wall. I fly up and strike it, demolishing it.

"Whoa." Ruby lowers her Bow. "How did you do that?"

"Enchantment on my Cudgel. If you're staying to fight these things, I'll enchant your Bow. Aim for the legs, because they're easier to take out. We don't want to kill these things up close, or we're dead, too. You remember their death explosions."

"I do."

The little blue man clears his throat.

Ruby glares at him over her shoulder.

I clear my throat. "Is he your personal support AI?"

"You can hear him?"

"The little blue guy with all the muscles and no shirt? Yeah, I hear him… and see him, too."

"Hi, I'm Gem. G-e-m." He gives me a single, sweeping wave. "Glad to make your acquaintance, Tuni."

Ruby shakes her head. "Sorry, I didn't know. No one ever saw him in Khertaan. I didn't figure anyone here would see him, either."

"Apology accepted," says Gem.

Mumbling, Ruby strides through the exit door and up a hallway. Framed photos hanging on the walls show a woman in her late twenties, with curly black shoulder-length hair and tan skin. Ruby stabs a finger at a portrait. "Gloria Rubio. Puerto Rican. My player. I sense her inside me, wanting to take over. Do you feel your player inside?"

"I actually don't. The original Yuni does, though. Have you decided on Destin or Earth? You need to decide before you go through that door."

"Tuni, thank you for your help. But I feel my place is on Earth, not Destin."

I scan her photos. They're not from any of the locales featured in Saiko Aimi's photos. "You might find yourself somewhere far from Yuni if you go to Earth. You might be by yourself, just like she is now. The Dread Naughts are on Earth. They might be here, too, but I've only seen the Behemoths here so far. Yuni fought a Dread Naught by herself and defeated it, but only emotional damage worked against it. Can you deal emotional damage? It was heavily armored, too, so she had to expend all her Auni in one shot to bring it down."

The Centaur woman closes her eyes briefly. "My power is all in the physical domain. I never branched to others. I'm reliant on someone to enchant my attacks. Maybe too reliant." She turns haunted eyes on me. "If I stay here with you, am I doomed to stay on Destin forever? I want to go back to Earth someday."

"I don't know, Ruby." I'm glad I don't feel the attachment to Earth that she does, because I fear the answer to her question isn't the one she desires.

Gem shifts his position on Ruby's back. "Anything is possible until proven otherwise."

A crashing sounds from the bedroom. Returning, we find rubble piled on the bed. But the Behemoth that must have done it is not in evidence. I fly over and peer through the breach. More people have entered the battle against the Behemoths. "There's a blond white lady in a Bikini and a black guy fighting down there."

Ruby joins me. "That's Megan Wright. Is that a gun she's fighting with? She's shooting acid."

"I know where she got it."

"She and that black dude are really tearing up those Arachnids." The Centaur looks wistful. "Maybe if I had one of those kinds of weapons, I could take on a Dread Naught."

Inspiration hits me. "I'm pretty sure I know where she got it. Listen, you wait here. Don't leave for Earth yet. I'll see if I can get you a weapon, bring it to you, and you can take it with you to Earth, if that's where you want to go."

Her smile is sad. "You would do that for me?"

"Of course. I might not be the original Yuni you know and love, but I'm still your friend. I have all her memories. The way I see it, you and I have been through a lot together. I'll be sad to see you go, but if you do go, I want you to be the most prepared you can be."

"Thank you, Tuni."

"No problem. I'll be right back. Just hang tight." I fly through the breach and head up the side of the tower.

The wounded Behemoth still blocks the plate glass window. But there are gaps where acid and flames came through before. I use my trusted Anjai skill, Compress Body, to squeeze myself through a gap. The Behemoth thrashes when I briefly touch it, but it's stuck too far in to dislodge itself.

I enter the room beyond.

ဆၢ ᏸᏫᏸ ᏸᏫ

Three closed doors mark the room's intended points of egress. The Behemoth's fangs and four front legs have been pruned and its eyes burned out. It's head rests on a ruined desk. There's no fight left in the thing. It presents no danger to the older man dressed in a business suit and seated in a leather armchair in the center of the room, where he types on a wireless device resting on his lap. A nameplate reading *Franklin Freeman* sits on the floor at his feet.

The man hasn't noticed me. I expand my body back to normal Crow size. "Hello, Mr. Freeman." With a fluttering of my wings, I land atop the Behemoth's protruding head, just above the vacant eye sockets. The monster trembles beneath my touch, but it's going nowhere. "My name is Tuni. I'm from Khertaan. I believe you know my friend, Megan Wright."

Anger creases the face of a man who appears accustomed to always being in charge but has been usurped. He doesn't move his gaze from the laptop screen. "What fool put the System in permanent update mode? Who is *Ivanhoe*?" He jabs some keys. "Bloody hell. How am I locked out? I'm a *superuser*. I'm the fucking *owner*." He jabs some more keys. "Fuck. Fuck. Fuck." He looks up at me and his expression mellows. "I'm sorry, talking Crow. Who did you say you are, and how can I help you?" He glances at his screen again, and bites back another expletive.

"My name is Tuni. I'm a level thirty Priestess of War and level twenty-one Anjai... from Khertaan. I'm a friend of Megan Wright, whom I believe you know."

His demeanor changes to a calm, confident one. "Hello, Tuni, and welcome to my office. Apologies for the decor, though it's growing on me." He types something on the laptop. "I'm sorry, did you say Yuni or Tuni?"

"My name is Tuni. I'm a duplicate of Yuni. She split me off before she left for Earth several minutes ago. I'm assuming this world is Destin."

"You assume correctly." The corners of his mouth curl down, not in a disappointed frown, but a curious one. "Your duplication didn't update in the System—but then it *can't, can it?*—what with the System effectively shut down. Let me just manually add you in here, like I did Belle, Megan's duplicate. She's actually Mithabel's duplicate, but Megan activated the skill, since Mithabel is sort of lost in limbo right now. This stupid update is making it impossible for her to respawn, preventing her from collecting her XP and reaching level thirty. I had to use a symbolic trick to get Megan, Belle, and Debra acting at level thirty…. But that's not why you're here. Why are you here, Tuni?"

"You equipped Megan with some advanced weaponry and armor. I'd like you to equip me, too, and give me equipment to take to Ruby, as well."

"Ruby?" He types on his laptop. "Ah, the lady Centaur Fighter/Barbarian. Oh, she's the one with the Name of Rank trait. Did you know, with that trait, she'd immediately be recognized as outranking any officer on Destin or Earth? Any military outfit she might come in contact with on either planet—she'd be in charge. And you say she needs to be equipped? Where is she now?"

I flutter my wings. "She's still in her bedroom. She wants to go to Earth, but she would like to be equipped first."

"I can understand that." He types some more and then some more, before making that curious frown again. "I have some armor that will fit a Centaur, actually, and she could use any of the guns. Let me see here… she's very good with dealing brute force melee damage, with some experience with the bow, but no skills to enhance ranged attacks. She's a force to be reckoned with physically in close combat, but weak in other areas."

I could have told him that. "She needs a way to deal and absorb emotional damage, especially, though it would be nice to be able to deal massive damage in all four domains, and to absorb damage in all four as well."

Mr. Freeman's frown is a mixture of curiosity and doubt. He types for a while. "Yes, well…. Everything I have in stock focuses on dealing multiple types of physical damage, like fire, acid, bullets, etc. Weapons and armor like you're describing must come from Khertaan. If she didn't bring any equipment with her, then someone else will need to bring suitable equipment from Khertaan for her. I had hoped Kevin would bring equipment out with him on one of his Khertaan ventures, but so far he's not succeeded."

I swallow the anger rising in my throat. "*Right*. There were *no* loot drops in Khertaan—money or equipment—while the shops charged outrageous prices for everything. PCs lost equipment and were lucky just to replace it with something comparable, much less gain new, *better* equipment. Yuni managed to buy *one* spell… *one* freaking spell.

"You can't see it because I'm in Crow form, but I'm wearing the Quilted Armor Yuni *started* with. She never got better armor or a better weapon than the Cudgel she started with. Honestly, it's utterly ridiculous. I'm level thirty and wearing non-magical Quilted as my only armor protection."

Mr. Freeman nods as he frowns. "I understand the limitations. We hoped to overcome them before the competition began, but certain other features took priority. Unfortunately, some PCs, like your friend Ruby, focused too much on the physical domain, and so are powerhouses when it comes to exchanging blows, but are close to useless in situations of primarily mental, spiritual, or emotional natures. She's fine as part of a team. But only a well-rounded individual like yourself could expect to survive for long on their own."

He types on his laptop. "Until I can get the System out of update mode, respawning isn't an option. Even if it weren't in update mode, anyone who has reached level thirty already, like you and Ruby, are permanently blocked from respawning.

"But I'm seeing something peculiar. There's activity near the city of Caravel. How is *that* happening? Give me a second."

Mr. Freeman jabs keys. "I don't understand this." He frantically presses keys. "Are you shitting me?" He types for a few seconds more before stopping to stare at the screen. "*Fuck me.* A portion of the program isn't even running on the Fanciful Pegasus servers. Some freak has hacked their way in and transferred code to their own computers." He closes his eyes, puts a hand over one, and draws a deep breath. He purses his lips. Then he drops his hand and opens his eyes, exhaling loudly. "Okay. This could actually work in our favor. Seems every PC and NPC who didn't make level thirty is still active in the game. If they reach level thirty…."

I don't like the way his voice trailed off. "What?"

"Shit. There's more than one hacker. One hacker is keeping the PCs and NPCs active during the update. The other hacker is systematically elevating all mooks in Khertaan to NPC status—with autonomy. What do they hope to accomplish with *that* mod? They're also changing the spawn points of all mooks, placing every single one of them in Caravel."

I try to bring him back to topic. "What happens when a PC or NPC reaches level thirty?"

"Normally, they'd be booted from Khertaan. And it looks like both hackers have reinforced that rule."

I take a few seconds to mull that over. "So, if the mooks are elevated to NPC status and become level thirty, they'll be booted from Khertaan? Where will they be booted to?"

Mr. Freeman clacks more keys. "The second hacker's code will boot half to Earth and half here to Destin. That's not good at all. I can't even imagine a level thirty Ferro Serpent, much less a level thirty Mental Dominator. As mooks, each one has a few very specific traits and natural weapons. As a level thirty NPC, each one would have even more traits, but beyond that, would have a class and a subclass and all the skills that come with that. It will also be able to use equipment, if it can find any. We have to pray no mooks reach level thirty before I can clean the code."

My lungs deflate. "So, there's nothing to be done for Ruby?"

The man with the laptop bangs on some keys. "Fuck me. Some mooks—these things called Dread Naughts—were elevated to autonomous NPC status and have already hit level thirty. They've already been released to Earth and Destin. Bloody hell. If you think Arachnid Behemoths are bad, you ain't seen nothing yet."

"I've seen one in action. So they're NPCs? With classes and subclasses?"

"Unfortunately, yes. They can be Martial Artists, Psi-Warriors, Spirit Warriors, Flame Wizards, Anjai, Priests and Priestesses, Barbarians, Assassins—whatever—though the class and subclass assignments appear random. They each have the standard traits for a Dread Naught, the standard traits for their subtype of Dread

Naught, and three additional random traits for being an autonomous NPC. They have the class skills of a level thirty primary class and level twenty-one subclass, just like you.

"Any of them could have the Shadow Selves trait or be an Anjai, which lets them have duplicates, or be a Priest-type, which allows them to have followers, or be a Life-Stealer, which allows them to create undead from their victims, or be a Barbarian, which allows them to have followers and dominate others... the list goes on. They each have the standard *Dread* power, which they'll use to drive weak-minded people to panic or despair, possibly to the point of suicide." He turns a hopeful gaze on me. "But that's why you're here. You and your level thirty PC friends will stop them."

I suppress a nervous laugh. "No pressure."

He gestures excitedly. "This could help you. The standard Dread Naught can only deal emotional damage and be harmed by emotional damage. But those with the ability to deal other types of damage due to their classes can also be hurt by the types of damage they deal. If you can figure out their class and subclass, you'll have an idea of what they can do and what you can do to them."

"That *is* a plus." Even though my Hope attribute is low average, I have extraordinary Optimism. I call on my Courage skill to bolster my confidence.

The Behemoth I'm perched on *moves*—backward—out of the building. It doesn't stop. I fly after it as it falls free—or, rather, flies *up* from the plate glass window. A rope tied around its waist is attached to a chopper, which has drawn the Behemoth out by force. The giant spiders don't weigh as much as I'd expected, because the chopper has no issues in carrying it away from the tower.

Megan Wright flies above the Behemoth and unties a quick release knot. The monster falls to the ground. An armored person on the ground pops a grenade into a hollowed eye socket. I draw back from the window as the thing explodes. Even at this distance, roughly a hundred yards, the explosion warms the air in Mr. Freeman's office.

I peek out again. The choppers extract more Behemoths wedged into crevices in the tower. Megan releases them, and a ground crew deals with them in systematic fashion.

Except for the remaining clingers on the tower, there's nothing left of the Behemoth army. I hope those explosions didn't harm Ruby. If she had any idea of what was happening, she moved to the hallway, no doubt. I have to believe she's okay.

Mr. Freeman still clacks away on his keyboard. He glances up, drawing a calming breath. "I see I've lost my unique window decoration. Okay, well, there's nothing I can do for Ruby except to equip her with what I have in stock, which only deals with the physical domain. She's welcome to any of it. I'd need to train her in its use. Can she come up here? Oh, that's right, she wants to go to Earth. The choice of destination is a one-time thing, so she can't come up here.... I suppose I can go to her." He closes his laptop. "Come, let's pick out some things, and you can help me take them to her."

We enter a large room with suits of armor hanging on the walls. He heads to the far corner, where larger suits of chain mail hang, much larger than any human would wear. Taking one down, he hands it to me. "Stash that, if you will, please. Would you like a suit, too?"

I would, so he hands me one that's pastel aqua. I stash the armor for now. He'll teach me how to use it when he trains Ruby.

From there we go to another room where the advanced weapons are stored. Mr. Freeman grabs four. "There are some differences in the gun types, so I want to give our Centaur friend a choice. Maybe one of these will work for you, too, if you like."

I stash the lot. We return to his office.

Dressed only in a black Bikini, Mithabel flies through the broken plate glass window and lands in front of the ruined desk. Something seems different about her, but I'm not sure what. She points. "We've got enemies approaching, Franklin."

"Thanks for the warning, Belle." Mr. Freeman steps up to the window to look.

So this is Belle, a duplicate of Mithabel, just like I'm a duplicate of Yuni. I join the two at the window and take in the scene. "I don't see anything."

"They're hard to see because of their distance at the moment, but I assure you they're there. They're like large birds with fringed wings."

I clack my beak. "Flitters. *Dread Naughts*. They're on Earth, too. The one I know about could only be harmed by emotional damage. These guns of yours, Mr. Freeman, would have been of no use against it. I've got a spell that worked, but it took all the Auni Yuni had just to defeat the single one she faced."

A cry of rage rises from the base of the tower. Is that Megan Wright?

Belle speeds outside, and I follow.

On the ground far below, Megan chops at a giant centipede monster with a glowing orange Battle Axe. The monster isn't moving, but Megan keeps hacking away.

Next to the monster lies Debra Jones, as still as death. I assess her status. Debra's HP is full, but her MP is zeroed. She's mindless... lobotomized.

I can't heal her, and she can't heal on her own. For her to recover from this state, she'll need a respawn... which Mr. Freeman has said is impossible now. I don't want to be the one to tell Megan.

Assessing the centipede, I see its EP is negative. It has been rendered into a state of depression so deep, it doesn't want to live. Its MP and HP are steadily dropping too under Megan's attacks. It will soon be as mindless as Debra, and sometime after that, if Megan keeps attacking it, it's going to die a physical death. "Belle, if she keeps chopping on that thing, it might explode." Yuni has seen too many death explosions.

Glancing in the direction of the Flitters, I spot them. They wing their way towards a line of choppers being boarded by soldiers. *Ugh.* Those soldiers need my help more than Megan does, and I can't do anything for Debra. "I've got to help those soldiers, Belle." I peel off and head that way while Belle drops to the ground next to the still-raging Megan.

CHAPTER TWENTY-ONE

Yuni: Ghoul

Once I place the call, Bethany and Sharice arrive within two minutes. They're staying at a hotel on the beach. Two young ladies with wavy hair reaching the middles of their backs—one a white blond and the other a black raven head—they wear flip-flops but have changed out of their bikinis into jeans and casual tops. Sharice kneels beside the unconscious Michelle while Bethany tends to the awake but unmoving Joseph. Mya sits on the sand beside the corpse of her surfer friend, Tara, stroking her pale cheeks and murmuring.

Sirens wail, growing louder as they approach. Law enforcement vehicles and ambulances arrive, parking nearby. Paramedics rush toward us, while police follow them.

A few white clouds float by overhead, with not a Flitter in sight. But I can't relax. The paramedics take Michelle and Joseph away. They insist that Mya go with them, too, but she refuses. "I'm staying with Tara." They plead with Mya, but she continues to refuse to go. "I'm still breathing, aren't I? *I'm fine.*" They stop pleading, and cart away Joseph and Michelle. They say the name of the hospital where they're taking them. Inuki will remember it for me.

"Mya, listen to me." I invoke all my applicable skills—Attraction, Morale, Presence, and Courage.

She turns a hurt gaze on me. "You didn't protect us. When that thing came, everyone else fled. We didn't. We knew you were powered. Knew you'd not let anything bad happen to us. You...." She bites back the remark and stays silent.

"That thing that killed Tara and your other friends.... *It* was a powered creature. It was as tough as I am, and in many ways tougher. *There are more of them out there.* Their aim is to destroy Earth. Humanity itself is on the brink of extinction. I'll do my best to try and stop these alien invaders, but I need help. I need *your* help. If you want to avenge your friends, then help me."

Staying silent, she doesn't agree to help, but neither does she refuse.

Police officers and a medical examiner arrive to examine the corpses. Blunt force trauma, the examiner says, like they fell from the roof of a ten-story building. He's surprised Mya and Joseph survived the incident, and asks if they're powered individuals.

"Hardly." Mya scoffs. "Tara was tougher than I was. Yuni here is the powered one."

This conversation bothers me. "How are you two able to speak so candidly about powered people, like you're so ready to believe in them?"

Sharice huffs. "Are you saying you're the one person on Earth who hasn't seen the video of Future Girl? It totally blew up yesterday."

"What are you talking about?"

The black nurse taps on her smart phone and then holds it in front of me. A video plays.

A slender white woman in her twenties, dressed in business casual attire and wearing her blond hair in a bun, talks to the camera. "My name is Susie McKenzie. I'm a time traveler from the future. You've seen or heard about the attacks of Orc Wizards,

Arachnid Behemoths, and Mad Cow Ballistas. Conventional weapons don't harm these invaders. Cameras can't record them. But they are real, as some of you are only too well aware. Perhaps they haven't come to your area, but eventually they will, or others even more deadly than them. Well, I'm here to tell you—help is on its way."

Next to Susie appears another female figure of the same height and build as Susie. The newcomer's skin is glossy red with black spots, like the skin of a poison dart frog. A swath of black surrounds her eyes like a mask. Her irises are golden and sparkling. She's dressed all in beige—a sparse top and a fringed loincloth over bikini bottoms. Her flowing blond tresses fall past her shoulders. Her lips are painted pale pink, with a touch of white highlighting the middle portion of her upper lip. She waves at the camera and speaks. "I'm also Susie McKenzie, time traveler from the future. In my Frogkin form, I'm known as Slithy, like in the Jabberwocky rhyme. I'm a powered person. Watch." She turns around and jumps twenty feet away from the camera in one bound. Then she turns back and jumps toward the camera, landing where she'd been standing earlier. She waves her hands over her head. "No strings attached." She points to a nearby one-story building. "Watch." She jumps in a single bound to the top of the building. Then she jumps back to the spot she jumped from. "You want more evidence? Okay. If you're watching this video for the first time, think of a number. Any number." She pauses.

Everyone around me glances at me, like they want to know what I'm choosing.

"Fine." I say the first random number that pops in my head. "Two-hundred-thirty-two."

Everyone around me nods knowingly at each other.

Slithy purses her painted lips. "Okay, got it? The number you chose is two-hundred-thirty-two. I don't need to ask you if I'm right, because I know I am. Everyone who watches this video for the first time will choose that number. Ask your friends. If they haven't seen the video yet, don't tell them the number before they watch. How did I know you would choose that number? Because I'm powered. Just like those Orc Wizards, Arachnid Behemoths, Mad Cow Ballistas—and the Dread Naughts on their way. I'm here to fight them all—to save the Earth.

"Don't be afraid. I won't fight alone. Other powered people are coming to Earth. We'll protect you. We *will* save this planet. But, *please, please, please,* if we ask for your help, then help us."

The video ends. It's noted as having over ten billion views.

I glance at Mya.

Her hard gaze softens. "I won't let Tara's death be in vain. I'll help you."

"Let us help, too," Bethany says, and Sharice nods vigorously.

"I want to help, too," says the medical examiner. Other nearby police officers echo the sentiment.

A cough comes from where the corpses lie, not yet bagged. Tara raises her head, sputtering water. "Me, too."

Mya screams with joy and runs to her friend.

ᏸᏬᏨᏂᏨᎡᏬᏨ

Tara is alive. Still on her back, she looks to either side. "Daisuke? Evan? Joseph?"

Mya wipes a tear. "Joseph is alive. Daisuke... Evan... they didn't make it."

"I swear... you were dead." Tom, the medical examiner, shines a small flashlight in Tara's eyes. "The paramedics agreed."

"She's powered," Inuki states bluntly. "All of Yuni's followers are powered. They have her traits: Spirit Armor, Pain Tolerant, Wakeful, and Metal Resistance. The Pain Tolerant trait is level 1, giving a person a 40% chance of ignoring even the pain of death— not dying when they've sustained injuries that should be fatal. Tara was in the 40%. Sadly, Daisuke and Evan were not."

Tom and five of his fellow officers ask to be my followers before Inuki can explain the other three traits. I'm glad to take them on, and make them powered while Inuki continues.

"About the other traits you all have: The Spiritual Armor trait gives you protection in the spiritual domain, which might be of help against some of the powered invaders, but won't help against the Flitters like the one Yuni defeated here. How useful the trait will be to you is yet to be seen.

"The Wakeful trait allows you to heal faster than normal. It's at level three, which means, if you're sleeping, you'll heal at a rate eight times faster than the average Khertaan adventurer, which is already faster than an Earth human heals. Don't ask me to explain about Khertaan.... While you're awake, you'll still heal far faster than the normal Earth human, even when you engage in strenuous activity."

"I'm feeling better already," says Tara.

"I'm feeling much better, too," says Mya. "Does this mean Joseph didn't need to go to the hospital?"

Inuki strokes his whiskers with a paw. "It's likely both Joseph and Michelle are feeling well enough they won't want to spend much time in a hospital bed, if they're even willing to get in one to begin with."

Tom waves his flashlight. "What about the Metal Resistance trait?"

Inuki nods. "You'll like this. It's at level four, the maximum level for traits, which effectively makes it more than *resistance* to metal. You're *immune* to attacks made against you with metal weapons. Knives, bullets, crowbars—none of them will hurt you."

The eyes of all my followers bulge.

I chuckle. "And that's not all. I've got skills that I can grant you, though I don't know all the rules governing the process. I granted Michelle my Courage skill, and maybe I shouldn't have, because she wasn't afraid enough of that Flitter creature to run away. Her Courage almost got her killed. But I have other skills to grant, too, and only too happy to grant them to any of you who wants them."

Their eyes haven't stopped bulging.

Tom brings out a pocket knife and pulls out the blade. "So you're saying I can't be cut?"

I stretch my arm to him. "Go ahead. Try to draw my blood."

He examines my arm, chooses a spot, lays the edge of the blade on it, and applies pressure. The blade slides across my skin as though I were a slippery block of stone. He tries again, with the same result. He tries yet again, and still the same thing happens. He whistles. "Damn, woman." Before anyone can stop him, he tries to stab his own arm, driving the blade down hard. The blade breaks. With a whistle, he retrieves the broken piece. "Not one to litter the beach…."

Inuki points at an officer's gun. "You could try shooting Yuni, Officer…."

The officer backs away. "Officer Bob. I'm not discharging my weapon at anyone without cause." He gestures at me. "Will you come down to the station with us, Yuni? I bet the chief will want to talk to you, and you might get a ton more followers."

Bethany huffs. "If she's going to the station, I'm also going. I want some powered skills."

Sharice shows some attitude, too. "Yeah. It's not just the police who deserve some skills here. We were Yuni's followers first, before all you even knew who she was."

Inuki floats up in the air and offers Sharice a high five. "Yeah, and the musician, Guy—what about him? He was the very first. And there was Destiny the dancer, Lana the martial artist, and Jamie the wrestler. They all left the beach some time ago. Then there's Michelle the novelist and Mya's surfer friend, Joseph."

Sharice brings out her smart phone. "Tell me their numbers. Michelle and Joseph, too, because we know they're fine. We're calling a meeting at the police station."

"Please stay back, sir," Officer Bob says to someone trying to approach our little group.

"That's my sister over there."

My heart jumps in my throat at the sound of my twin brother's voice. I run across a short stretch of beach and throw my arms around him. *"Bradford. How did you find me?"*

"You're on the news, sis. Powered woman protects the city from alien invaders. Sorry it took me so long to get here. I was afraid I'd missed you."

I squeeze him so hard. "You don't know how glad I am to see you. Have you seen anyone else from Khertaan?"

Bradford steps away, glancing around. "Nope. Where are the people who died?"

Officer Bob clears his throat. "I'm sorry, sir, I didn't realize…. Are you powered, too?"

"I am, and I can help one of those corpses, if you'll allow me."

"Only one?"

"For now."

Officer Bob beckons for Bradford to follow, and leads the way to the sad spot where the bodies of Daisuke and Evan still lie. A large brown moth with a three-foot wingspan and the face of a human male flies along behind Bradford.

The moth glances at me. "I'm Umber, by the way. I'm your brother's support AI. I know—he's never mentioned me. But then, you never mentioned your support AI to him, so I guess it's fair."

"Glad to meet you, Umber." I point a thumb at my fat cat buddy. "This is Inuki, my support AI."

"Hey, Umber. What's happening?" Inuki lifts a paw for a high five.

The moth-man smiles, smacking the raised paw with a moth wing. "Oh, I'm just flitting along wherever grand adventure awaits. What's happening with you?"

"Same. Except I bounce on my tail instead of flitting. C'est la vie."

Bradford searches the faces of my followers, and settles on Tara. "One of these two young men was particularly special to you, maybe someone you wished you'd gotten to know better. Which one is he?"

The girl blinks back a tear and points at Daisuke.

Bradford lays his hands on the dead Asian surfer. The corpse trembles, and everyone gasps. My brother turns to Tara. "I can bring him back as a Ghoul, a form of undead. His skin will be gray, but he'll have all his memories and I'll grant him autonomy, so his personality will be intact. Are you okay with this?"

Tara nods weakly, unsure of her decision.

My brother doesn't let her think twice. He whispers, and Daisuke's eyes flutter open.

I have the Command Undead skill, which in Khertaan had seemed a waste of a skill slot. Bradford has the Create Undead skill, also of little use in Khertaan, where bodies pixelize upon death, to respawn later. Yet here on Earth, the Create Undead and Command Undead skills may prove useful, the Create Undead skill perhaps more so.

Daisuke sits up slowly and looks at his hands, which have grown claws. His skin has darkened to light gray. He glances at Tara, who gives him a weak smile and then pulls him into a hug. He pushes away from her and looks up at Bradford. "What will you have me do, master?"

"Whatever you wish, Daisuke. I relinquish my hold over you."

The Ghoul's eyes change, as though the spirit inside the body awakens. "Tara." He turns to her again. "Come here." He pulls her into an embrace. She hugs him back, but seems unsure about kissing him.

I grant her my Courage skill, and she plants her lips on his.

Bradford points at Evan. "I can make him an undead tomorrow. I can't guarantee what type he'll be, but I can tell you the type right before I do it."

Mya taps my arm. "Is Daisuke still your follower? Does he have your traits?"

"There's one way to find out." I smile, feeling mischievous.

Her eyes bug. "You mean, stab him?"

I shrug. "If the blade snaps, he's got my traits." I chuckle. "But, no, that's not what I meant. Both he and Evan are still on my list of followers. They didn't remove themselves before they died, and I haven't bothered to remove them since, either. So, yeah, he's still one of mine, and has my traits."

"And...," Bradford says, "he's got the kindred traits of a Ghoul. He's unaffected by poison and attacks of a mental or emotional nature, and he can see in the dark. He also deals both physical and spiritual damage when he attacks with his claws."

Bethany shuffles her feet in the sand. "What about his soul?"

My brother shakes his head. "What is a soul? He still has his personality and autonomy. I took a speck of his morality, but he's still got more Morals than my sister here."

"Hey." I poke Bradford in the ribs.

He pokes me back. "It's true, and you know it."

"I've called everybody." Sharice holds up her phone. "They're meeting us at the police station."

"I've talked to the chief," says Officer Bob. "He's looking forward to meeting you both. We'll have Evan taken to the morgue, and keep him there until you can revive him as undead tomorrow."

Bethany invites me and Bradford to ride with her and Sharice. The two of them ride up front while Bradford and I ride in the back. Inuki sits on my lap. Umber the moth-man clings upside down to the roof.

"What is Tara's status, Inuki?"

"She's at full HP, musume. It took her just over twelve-and-a-half minutes to heal up to 100%. All of your living followers are at full HP now. Daisuke the Ghoul is currently at 83% HP and steadily recovering. He'll be fully recovered by the time we reach the police station."

Sharice looks over the back of her seat at me. "So this little Inuki fellow... is he like your animal companion or something?"

"Personal support AI," Inuki corrects her. "In Khertaan, the world where we're from, no one but Yuni can see or hear me. Earth's laws of nature don't support the necessary selective visual or audio, which means you all can see and hear me. Same with Umber up there."

189

"If I die," Bethany says, keeping her eyes on the road, "I want to come back as a Vampire."

Bradford clucks his tongue. "That's a possibility with my skill, but I don't have control over the selection of undead type. It's all random."

"So, necromancer... what all types of undead can you make?" Sharice asks the same thing I'm wondering.

"There are six different types. About a quarter are Vampires, a quarter are Ghouls, a quarter are Zombies, an eighth are Skeletons, a twelfth are Ghosts, and one in twenty-four is a Wraith. I take one point of one attribute from a person to turn them into an undead. Which type of attribute I take is random, and the attribute taken determines the type of undead they'll become if I go through with it after taking the attribute point. I only have the Create Undead skill at level one, so I can only create one undead a day."

"That is so out-of-this-world." Bethany makes a sharp right turn, following the car ahead of us, which carries Mya, Tara, and Daisuke.

"I have a question for the two of you." I lean forward in my seat. "Would you rather be able to fly or turn invisible?"

"I'd rather fly," says Sharice.

"Invisibility for me," says Bethany. "Though flying would be sick."

Saying nothing more, I perform a Grant Skill action, granting my Flight Speed skill to Sharice. Ten seconds later, when my combat heartbeat resets, I grant Bethany my Hide skill, and then ten seconds later, I grant her Flight Speed. Ten seconds after that, I go ahead and grant Sharice the Hide skill. Neither of them say anything, and I'm guessing they don't realize what I've done.

There's no reason to stop. As we continue our trip to the police station, I keep executing the Grant Skill action, giving each of my followers the Hide and Flight Speed skills. I don't have to be in their presence to do it, and apparently none of them will know until I tell them. I suppose if one of them imagined themselves flying or hiding, the associated skill might kick in, but what would it hurt if it did? I feel I should be taking advantage of any time I have to better equip these people for the battles still to come. I grant the skills to Evan, too, even though at the moment, he's dead. He'll have the skills already when Bradford makes him undead tomorrow.

It takes me three minutes to give the Hide and Flight Speed skills to all of my eighteen followers. So I start in on granting them the Courage skill, which takes just under a minute and a half to give to them all, having already granted it to Tara. We're still not to the police station.

I'm only half listening to the conversation in the car. The nurses continue asking Bradford questions about what he can do, and he goes into how he's a Fire Wizard and all that. I start giving the Presence skill to my followers. I finish with that, and give all of them all of my Priestess skills, except the one I can't—the Followers skill. Then I grant them all my Anjai skills that I haven't already— Detect Anomaly, Compress Body, Shapeshift Crow, Wind Control, and Split Body. I smile at that last one. Won't that be something, for them to each have a duplicate? My number of followers could double. Oh, Goddess, this is mind-boggling.

I finish granting skills. We're still not to the police station.

Thinking of duplicates, how is mine doing? She must be doing fine. I think she'd let me know if she wasn't, but it wouldn't hurt to ask. "Hey, Tuni. Is this a bad time?" I'm asking telepathically, which means no one in the car hears me.

My duplicate responds. "I've got a dozen or so Flitters in my sights. They're about to attack a bunch of soldiers. There's a good chance the soldiers' weapons won't damage those monsters, so they need my help, pronto."

Even though we're on different worlds and maybe even in different timelines, telepathy works between me and my duplicate. I'm surprised and yet not. I'll never understand all the laws of the multiverse and the universes it contains.

"Let me see through your eyes, girl."
"Sure."
That part works, too.

CHAPTER TWENTY-TWO

Yuni: Remote Battle

I press a hand against the car roof to steady myself as my world melds with Tuni's, a nighttime vista illuminated by two moons. Wind rustles my feathers as I fly towards one of several clumps of soldiers hanging out near a row of choppers. The air carries a hint of spent ammo.

It's not me doing the flying or smelling the smoke. I'm sensing what Tuni is experiencing.

"Sis? You all right?" In the car on Earth, Bradford has seen my reaction and doesn't understand what's happening with me. Even though my sense of sight is focused solely on Destin, my sense of hearing registers sounds from both worlds.

"I'm fine. Give me a minute. I'll explain later."

My duplicate draws closer to the soldiers. Sadly, the Flitters have already reached them. Eleven of the dreaded monsters fly low to the ground, dark tendrils flowing down from their elongated bodies and delivering attacks the soldiers aren't equipped to withstand. Bullets fired by the soldiers whiz through the Flitters, having no effect.

Tuni assesses the Flitters, finding them to be at full HP and EP. They have no MP or SP ratings.

Wait. They have HP values? That means they can be killed by *physical* damage, even if mundane bullets won't do the trick. "Tuni."

"Yeah, I saw that." She equips her Cudgel and enchants it with a hundred-point War spell. Goddess, I hope that's enough. She only has eighty-four Auni remaining. That would have been a lot back when I first entered Khertaan, but now it seems woefully inadequate.

Those uniformed men and women touched by the Flitters turn their weapons on their comrades, cutting down fellow soldiers. Damn. The targeted soldiers take cover, none of them shooting back at those they consider their buddies.

The Flitters shrink, becoming more birdlike. What classes do they have, anyway? Could they all be Anjai, like me, with the Compress Body skill or an avian Shapeshift skill?

The sky is suddenly filled with dozens, maybe hundreds of birds. They flap their wings, raising the sand into a blinding storm. They're hiding the Flitters from Tuni.

My duplicate reaches the edge of the sandstorm. Bullets from the dominated soldiers strike her, but bounce off, being metal. The bad guys have no problem seeing through the storm, but the good guys are blinded by it.

Using her Wind Control skill, Tuni clears a conic area before her about twenty yards out. Dust Storm Falcons swarm, their empowered wings flapping hard. Still in Crow form, she rushes a Falcon and bashes it with the Cudgel gripped in her talons. The Falcon pixelizes.

A dark tendril lashes down and latches onto one of Tuni's legs. Cold seeps into her—I feel it as though the mook has grabbed hold of me.

"Bend to my will, Crow." The voice is hard and chilling and telepathic. Two together being stronger than one, I join Tuni in resisting the demand, and the voice vacates our mind space.

"Sis?" Bradford's voice reminds me I'm riding in a vehicle with him.

"I'm fine." I keep my sense of sight focused on Destin as Tuni pulls free from her would-be captor and wings her way towards a crouching friendly soldier.

My brother's voice is insistent. "Then why are you shivering?"

"It's Tuni. My duplicate in Destin. She's engaging a flock of Flitters and swarms of Dust Storm Falcons. A Flitter just chilled her and tried to control her mind. I'm watching the battle through her eyes."

"You're kidding."

"I'm not. Let me focus. My hit point pools are bound to hers, and if she dies, so do I. If she goes mindless, so do I. If the thing controls her mind, I'm afraid it will have control of me, too."

He doesn't say another word.

The car stops.

Tuni lands next to the friendly and Shapeshifts back to her Asian form. The soldier looks ready to shoot her, but she holds out a calming hand. She has Presence. "Be my follower, if you wish to fight back. I can make you powered."

"Do it." He lowers his weapon.

She strokes his face, and he's added to her followers list. Then she grants the fellow her Hide skill. "You're powered now. Imagine you're invisible, sir."

"Yes, ma'am." He vanishes from sight. A bullet strikes the area where he was, and ricochets down to the sand. As her follower, he's automatically got her traits, which includes the maxed-out Metal Resistance.

She grants the man her Flight Speed skill. "Now imagine you can fly, and follow me."

"Yes, ma'am." There's a high note of positivity in his voice.

A few bullets strike Tuni as she flies away, but do no harm. She doesn't bother changing back to Crow form as she searches for another friendly, granting her first follower all her other allowed skills in the meantime. She detects a dark shape to her left, an anomaly within the sandstorm, and heads in that direction.

Another soldier lies flat on the sand. Tuni drops next to him just as a dark tendril falls from the sky, reaching for him. She grabs his chin. "Be my follower, *now*."

"Do it," says the bodiless voice of Tuni's one follower.

"I... yes."

"Done." Tuni adds the man to her list a fraction of a second before the tendril grabs him by the throat.

The man's eyes grow dark. He raises his rifle and fires at Tuni.

The bullets bounce off her. No one acts surprised.

Tuni grants her newest follower the Presence skill.

The darkness drains from his eyes and the tendril at his throat dissipates. "I...." He glances at his weapon in horror. "I'm so sorry, ma'am."

"It's quite all right. You're powered now. You weren't before." She grants him the Hide skill. "Imagine you're invisible."

He disappears.

She grants him the Flight Speed skill, tells him to imagine he can fly and to follow her. While searching for her next potential follower, she grants her latest recruit the rest of her allowed skills.

It grows increasingly difficult in the swirling sandstorm to find other soldiers who haven't already been dominated by the Flitters. There are eleven Dread Naughts, and only one Tuni. They have the advantage of easily seeing through the storm created by their Falcons, whereas Tuni has more difficulty, leaning heavily on her Wind Control and Detect Anomaly skills to make her way. She collects twenty-two soldiers as followers, eight of them women and the other fourteen men. They've all been granted every skill she's able to grant them, and they all automatically benefit from her Morale bonus and her four traits, making them all bulletproof.

Tuni takes a deep breath. "Listen up, people. As of now, you're no longer soldiers. You're *powered* soldiers, and no one knows your powers better than me. *I'm* your leader for this mission. Does anyone have a problem with that?"

"No, ma'am," they shout in unison.

"Then listen up." She gives them a quick rundown on their new powers. They're invisible, so it's impossible to read their expressions, but I envision them taking it all in stride. They're soldiers who've just been given the weapons they need to fight a battle they never signed up for, but are determined to win.

"Eventually, I'll teach you more about your powers, but we don't have time now. It's time to engage the enemy. Stay hidden, but fly with me. When I give the signal, you'll use your Wind Control skills to blow all these Flitter monsters and their summoned Falcons out of the sky. Keep the wind off the ground, or we'll hurt our friends and the choppers. At some point, we want to isolate one of the Flitters, so I can kill it with my enchanted Cudgel. We kill one of those things, and then we'll know exactly what we're up against." She holds up the weapon. "Let's go." She takes to the sky.

Flying high, Tuni gets a good view of the boundaries of the sandstorm, and leads her followers to one edge. "Let's blow these suckers away, folks."

Twenty-three people with level 18 Wind Control skills combining forces is equivalent to one person with a level 396 Wind Control skill. At one mile per hour per skill level, that's wind power of such terrifying force, nothing short of an equivalent wind can withstand it. A hurricane with winds at or above 157 miles per hour is category five, the highest rated category there is for hurricanes on Earth. Three-hundred-ninety-six miles per hour is more than twice that.

Tuni's windstorm sweeps through the air above the chopper blades, and the winds remain calm on the ground. Several Dust Storm Falcons fly low enough not to be caught up in the storm, but the high flying ones are blasted out to the desert beyond, their bones pulverized to dust inside their bodies. The expired ones pixelize, leaving no trace they were ever summoned.

The Flitters, however, are not swept away so easily. They have power over the wind, too, and push back. They fly faster than Tuni does, and the eleven of them are nearly equal in controlling the wind as Tuni and her twenty-two followers, with Tuni's side having the slightest advantage, pushing the Flitters back inch by inch.

"Hold steady." Tuni stops contributing to the windstorm and turns invisible. Keeping low to the ground—where all is eerily still—she wings her way beneath the competing winds to where the Flitters have banded.

Still invisible, she rises beneath the nearest Flitter.

Before she can attack it, the Flitter vanishes, as do all the others.

I've got a bad feeling about this. "Get out of there, Tuni."

She retreats, but several Flitters appear around her, striking with tendrils stretching out from their bellies, delivering a combo attack.

The tendrils lash across her face and limbs, the pain stinging us both. I can't imagine how it would feel to someone without the Pain Tolerant trait.

As Tuni charges her nearest attacker, her Cudgel at the ready, Inuki pipes in, his voice calm. "Your shared HP pool is at 0%, musume. But you're still alive. You must have one or two hit points remaining, not enough to register as even one percent."

Tuni and I are next to dead, and she knows this, but her Courage skill propels her even into the face of death—not just her death, but mine, too. I hurriedly cast a Healing spell on myself, putting 90 Auni into it, roughly half my max. Fortunately, I'd recharged to full during the car ride.

The Cudgel attack I'd made against the Flitter on the beach had done little, but Tuni is of the mind that not every Flitter is the same. I hope she's right.

Her Cudgel slams into her target's ribcage. It and all the other visible ones flinch in unison. They're duplicates, as Tuni had hoped.

"The Flitters are at 70% HP, musume. Tuni's attack affected them all. She's fighting a level thirty Anjai, with a level ten Split Body skill. If she kills any of them, she kills them all."

They have the same vulnerability that Tuni and I share.

A hundred point enchantment only dealt 30% damage to one of those things. "Tuni, get the hell out of there."

"Keep healing me, Yuni. These things are going down."

She's got *too much* Courage.

The Flitters come in again for another combo attack. This is gonna hurt. Dammit, I don't want to die from this. "Tuni, equip the...."

She's thinking the same thing I am. She equips the pastel aqua suit of Tech Armor she got from Mr. Freeman, and it trades places with her red Quilted Armor an instant before the tendrils strike her.

How many Flitters hit? They hit from all sides, including above and below. There must be more attackers than before, each one sneaking a tendril into the attack. They want her dead.

The pain isn't as excruciating as before, but I still gasp and grope for the back of the car seat in front of me. Inuki reports I'm at 43% HP. The armor saved me. Groaning, I call for the Goddess to heal me once more, sinking 54 Auni into the spell, which suffices to bring me back to full HP, but lowers my available Auni to 40.

I'd beg Tuni to leave, but the Flitters are too fast. Her only chance to survive is to take one down before they take her down.

She darts at the closest Flitter and delivers a blow of her Cudgel.

"Each Flitter is at 42% HP, musume. Just two more attacks like that...."

"I don't know that we'll survive that long."

A flock of Crows surrounds Tuni. Wind blasts out from them, pushing the Flitters away from my daring duplicate. The Flitters fight back with their own Wind Control skills, but with Tuni's help, the Crows have them overpowered.

A cry of rage tears across the battlefield from behind Tuni, and the very air trembles. The sounds of gunfire cease. Shrieks of pain and despair fill the air, and all eleven Flitters plummet to the ground, where they lie still as death.

Megan Wright flies over, sets down next to one of the Flitters, and chops at its long neck with a glowing orange Battle Axe. Every

Dread Naught shrieks in pain, but none of them act to defend themselves.

"Everyone, get away, *now*." Tuni gestures for all the Crows and nearby soldiers to leave the area, remembering what happened when I killed the Flitter on the beach. Tuni flies away, too.

Belle lands beside Megan, another glowing Battle Axe in hand, and joins in dealing death to the enemy. Megan chops continuously, as though possessed by a demon.

Staying a safe distance away, Kaleisha floats a foot above the sand, the limp body of Debra Jones in her arms.

The Flitters explode all at once, wind blasting outward from each of them. A nearby chopper tilts as though it's about to fall over.

All the soldiers and Tuni's followers are well away from the area.

A calm falls over the battlefield.

Without a word, the blond Tank attired in a black Bikini and wielding a large, glowing Battle Axe stashes her weapon to inventory and flies back to the tower. Kaleisha and her mindless burden follow behind, along with the black-haired, Bikini-clad Belle.

Thanking me, Tuni turns her attention to the wounded and dead soldiers on the field. After telling her it might be possible to turn the dead into autonomous undead, I bid her a telepathic farewell.

I'm sitting in the back seat of Bethany's parked car. We've reached the police station. It's daytime here and time to get more followers.

CHAPTER TWENTY-THREE

Charli: The Old Lady in Me

FOURTEEN

"By all that is Holy." Zyekt looks along the street where dozens of people bow on their knees after having been touched by the Flitter's tendrils.

Lady Amarynth follows his gaze. "What is it?"

"We may have to kill them." The Angel points to the bowing people.

"Kill civilians?" ChrisCross holds his hands together before him in a meditative gesture. "We can't do that. Earth humans don't respawn."

"These might. They're powered."

Lady Amarynth strides towards them. "They're from Khertaan?"

"I don't think so." Zyekt draws up beside Lady Amarynth.

ChrisCross and the rest of our group follow, with Rolag flying invisibly above them.

We're still a couple hundred feet away. The nearest bowing person stands—and glows with a blinding light. Lady Amarynth, ChrisCross, and Zyekt raise their hands to shield their faces. Rolag averts his face so as not to look directly into the bright spot.

Using Third Person POV as I am from inside Rolag's head, I'm not too adversely affected.

The glowing man-shape abruptly grows to fifty feet tall and emits a deafening bellow. Lifting a glowing, giant-sized foot, he slams his heel into the nearest building.

The entire structure collapses into rubble. People who had occupied it lie broken and dead among the ruins.

Rolag mutters. "He's a Were-Giant. And a blinding one."

As if on cue, more bowing people rise and glow. A second later, dozens of glowing giant humans populate the city. They smash, stomp, and otherwise lay waste to their surroundings.

Lady Amarynth grits her teeth and raises her Crossbow. "They're killing everyone else. Does anyone have a way to render these giants unconscious? Speak up if you do."

ChrisCross runs forward. "I can make them all come after me." He waves at the nearest giant. "Hey, big fellow. I'm better than you."

The giant turns to the Elitist and heads towards him with huge steps.

"Idiot. You'll be clobbered." Rolag rushes forward. He passes over ChrisCross and becomes visible, stretching out his neck, opening his mouth, and… roaring.

The giant stops in his tracks. Taking one look at Rolag, he runs away.

"Intimidation. Good show, Rolag. But you can't intimidate all of them in time to save the city." Zyekt flutters his wings. "And ChrisCross…."

"Please, call me CC."

"CC, we don't have time for you to run around the city triggering every giant to come after you. I don't see any other way than you taking them all out with your Crossbow, Lady Amarynth."

"Wait." Niav runs out on Zyekt's arm. "They're followers of the Flitter. Kill the Flitter, and the giants will stop."

Did the Mouse's Monster Lore give her something I didn't get? I try for more info on the Flitter, but don't get anything new. Still, what she says makes sense.

"Someone get me up there, or I'm of no use against that thing." ChrisCross lifts his gaze to the sky.

Airplanes streak by overhead, spraying clouds of gas. Rather than firing bullets and missiles into the city, they're hoping to render everyone unconscious.

With the flapping of his wings, Rolag directs several blasts of wind upward. The descending clouds disperse before reaching us. He goes invisible again, so as not to draw more attention our way.

As the gas drifts down on the city streets ahead of us, one giant woman raises her hands. The gas wafts towards her. She stomps down the street, drawing more gaseous clouds. The other giants, unaffected by the poison, continue their destructive rampage.

"So much for that idea." Lady Amarynth turns to Zyekt. "Get me up to that Flitter."

The Angel grabs her left elbow. She hefts her Crossbow in her right hand.

CC runs over. "You gotta take me, too."

Niav jumps down from the Angel's shoulder. "I'll stay down here and lend you my traits and skills, CC." He runs over to Bucky. "Carry me?"

"Happy to." CC's support AI leans forward on her flying skateboard and scoops up the rodent.

Rolag flies just behind the Angel, while Barney and Bucky follow some distance back. We're all headed for the Flitter.

The planes swoop by again, spreading more sleeping gas. With a few flaps of his wings, Rolag disperses any that comes close to us. Even though my body is already sleeping, I'm grateful for his giant wings. I don't think any of us are resistant to poison.

Choppers approach the Flitter, attempting to surround it. What do they plan?

The Flitter glows, the illumination ramping to a blinding level. The choppers halt their approach. So do we.

The glowing shape expands—it's total wingspan stretching longer than a football field. It's a Were-Giant, too. Should have guessed. It's tendrils reach into the choppers. Lovely. Now the chopper pilots will be its followers.

We recommence flying.

Zyekt halts again. "Everyone, close your eyes."

My eyes are already closed. Should I stop watching with my Third Person POV?

It's too late.

Sparkles spring out like fireworks from the Flitter's wings—a massive and stunning display. It's mesmerizing. All I want to do is watch.

My awareness returns to my body, and I look up at Barney's smiling face.

"Hello, love. Glad to see you're awake. No one else is but you and Niav."

He's kneeling next to me. I'm on my back, lying beside a towering building, brilliant rays of light spilling over the top. Bucky stands behind Barney, peering over his shoulder at me.

Niav squeaks from somewhere nearby. "What happened?"

I sit up.

Lady Amarynth, Zyekt, CC, and Rolag lie on the ground, neatly arranged next to each other. Rolag is the small version of himself. The Lady still grips her Crossbow, thank goodness. "The sleeping gas?" I crawl over to her and shake her by the shoulder, to no avail.

"We already tried that." Bucky cuts a tight donut on her skateboard. "It was a combination of things, but, yeah, when everyone lost their focus to the Flitter's hypnotic display, and Rolag didn't disperse the gas, it was all Barney and I could do to get you two out of there fast enough and find a place unaffected by the gas. The Flitter has a tight-ass hold over *everyone* now—residents, pilots, gunners, the media—you name it. Aside from us, everyone in the city who isn't dead or sleeping belongs to the Flitter. Its thugs are going around killing the sleeping folk. Let's hope they don't find us. Everyone's helpless here but you and Niav."

Planes zoom around the sky. Are they still releasing the sleeping gas?

Explosions sound in the distance, some of them not distant enough for my comfort.

Barney shakes his head. "'Tis a sad day. The city is being destroyed by its own inhabitants and the choppers. Giants smashing down buildings and stomping on people. Missiles bombing the city. I don't see how you can put a stop to it. It's suicide to try."

Niav rolls onto her feet. "We *must* try. There will be nothing left of this world if we can't save it."

"I have an idea. It's risky, if it even works, but it's only risky for me. And if I fail, well… the world is doomed anyway." I lie beside the others and try head hopping to Lady Amarynth. The awareness transfer is much easier than my recent head hop to Rolag.

Lady Amarynth's mental image welcomes me. "Charli. What has happened?"

I explain the best I can.

Her mental image turns grim. "I know what you're thinking, Charli. Are you willing to do it?"

"Yes, Milady."

"I'll tell Rolag and Zyekt. You tell CC. Then we'll see if it works."

I agree, because I pretty much have to.

ChrisCross lets me into his head. I'm not comfortable being in the mind of an Elitist, but one of us had to go in, and I can understand Lady Amarynth not wanting to.

"Ah, the Cowgirl." CC's mental image is one of him levitating in the air, his legs crossed. "I'd thought perhaps Bucky would come to escort me to heaven, but you'll do."

If the world weren't in such desperate need right now, I'd ask him why his personal support AI has the persona of a sixteen-year-old girl. But now isn't the time. "You're not dead, Elitist. Not yet. You will be unless we defeat the Flitter asap. I need your help to do it."

"Anything for you, sugar plum."

I bite back a retort and tell him what I need. He agrees.

I get out of his head as fast as I can.

ཨུ ᱬ ᱬ ᱬ ᱬ ᱬ ᱬ

Using Third Person POV, I look down on myself and the others lying on the ground.

This whole idea is overwhelming. Even asleep, they can all still head hop to me. Rolag, CC, Zyekt, and Lady Amarynth all come into my head and transfer their abilities to me.

"Let me know when you're ready for me." Niav settles on the ground next to Zyekt.

"I'm ready now."

With Niav's awareness added, I have all the abilities of everyone in our little group....

Actually, not quite....

A blue serpent slithers across ChrisCross's torso. It's Lance, CC's Magical Companion. He rests his head on the Elitist's chest. "CC says I'm to head hop to you, miss. Never done it before, but willing to try."

I reach out to him mentally, trying to help him make the transfer. Thirty seconds later, he's in my head, too. I've got the whole party inside my mind space, not counting the support AIs, who aren't able to participate.

Lady Amarynth's mental image waves her Crossbow in my view. "Be sure to take this along."

"Thanks, I will." Turning my focus outward, I pry her Crossbow from her grip. "Okay. Let's take down this Dread Naught."

I invoke my own Hide skill and attempt to increase it by invoking Niav's. They don't stack. That's okay. Switching to First Person POV, I jump up and look about. I don't see the Flitter, which means it doesn't see our group. That's good. Staying close to the ground, I fly down the street.

Despite my Hide skill, a giant male human charges at me. I don't want him finding my friends, so I speed towards him, invoking the Displace skill I got from Niav. The giant swipes and misses. I laugh at him, taunting him, and invoke CC's Emotional Trigger trait. Enraged, the giant bellows and gives chase.

Using Lance's Increased Movement trait, I zip around at five times normal flight speed. I try adding in Lady Amarynth's Increased Movement trait, too, but, sadly, her trait doesn't stack with his.

Once I'm satisfied with how far I've led the giant away from my friends, I fly upward. The Flitter has moved further from me. It still glows, but not blindingly so. Choppers surround it, firing machine guns—not at it, but down on the city. Planes fly wide circles around the Flitter, peppering the city with missiles.

Fireworks burst from the wings of the Flitter. Even at this distance, they're hypnotic.

"Fight it." Zyekt pushes his Mental Focus skill to the forefront of my mind space. "Call on your Mental Armor trait."

"Use my Iron Will," Niav offers.

"Take my Fearlessness," Lady Amarynth urges.

I draw on everything I can to oppose the mental tug of the Flitter's display, stacking every ability that will stack with my Mental Armor. It's not easy focusing on them all, to get the most benefit I can. Maybe if I'd had a chance to practice handling so many abilities at once....

Hovering in the air as I am, I'm exposed and vulnerable. A plane heads my direction.

I'm too mesmerized by the Flitter's breathtaking beauty. The others in my head prod me, pushing me to do better, but... I can't. It's too much for my fourteen-year-old persona.

I don't need the distractions of my eighteen-year-old-mother persona, either. I call forth a new persona... a fifty-year-old strict, no-nonsense, brunette white lady. She's got life experience and knows how to multitask. Her brain patterns suit the task at hand far better than the brain patterns of my teenage self.

FIFTY

I draw a calming breath, and the Flitter's hold crumbles.

The approaching plane fires a missile at me.

Everyone in my head pushes traits and skills at me, anything that will help against the attack. I already have the Displace skill turned on. Calling up a mental image of a shelf of slots, I systematically sort the abilities thrust at me.

As the missile streaks past me, I call on Rolag's Aerial Interception and CC's Bare Hands Parry skills to give it a smack, directing it away from the bodies of my friends.

More planes turn to speed towards me, accompanied by choppers.

It's time to end this. I stash Lady Amarynth's Crossbow. I won't need it.

With Rolag's Enlarge skill, I become a fifty-foot tall fifty-year-old woman wearing Culottes and Cowboy Hat. Calling on Niav's Teleport Self skill, I put myself on the gigantic Flitter's back. Before it can react to my presence, I smack its spine with an open palm, focusing on CC's Bare Hands Ignore Armor attack, stacking his Bare Hands Damage and Rolag's Damage skills, multiplying them by the Enlarge skill, and adding in CC's Bare Hands Fatality skill. My hands aren't exactly *bare*, since I'm wearing my Shadow Gauntlets, but I'm not wielding a weapon, and that's what matters.

The Flitter's body spasms.

A disembodied bass voice booms a command across the city. *"Terminate it."*

The command is to me, and I oblige.

I plunge my left hand *into* the creature's feathered back, grab its spinal column, and rip it out, like deveining a shrimp.

Fireworks spew from the entire length of the Flitter. A ghostly version of the creature rises from its body, writhing in agony.

Using both hands, I break the spinal column in half.

The ghost screams—chilling my own spine.

A blast of wind like none I could ever imagine flattens the city block below me and those surrounding it. The planes and choppers are shredded. No one jumps out with parachutes, because no one in the planes and choppers remain alive.

The giants not caught in the blast shrink to their normal human selves, no longer granted power by their Flitter godling.

By rights, I should be dead. But I felt nothing from the blast. *Nothing.* Not even a fluttering of the wind. Not even a tickle.

The horror of what has transpired in the city knocks at the door of my low average Conscience. I can't let it in. Happy to do what Fourteen couldn't, I shrink to normal size, return to being the innocent teenager, and fly back to my friends.

CHAPTER TWENTY-FOUR

Emma: Anissa

The sun has dropped below the horizon. Two half moons decorate the night sky, shedding enough light for me to see by. The soldiers helping me out of the sand tunnel also have lights. They shine something they call a flashlight at me, and another at Dr. Splat. They shine one at Spooky, but she flits aside, preferring the darkness, into which she blends so well, I can't always tell where she is.

I don't see a grain of sand on Spooky from our half-hour crawl through the tunnel, but Dr. Splat and I have second skins of caked sand. I brush mine off the best I can, and a soldier calmly clears sand from my back.

The soldiers assure us the last of the enemy forces have been defeated. The tower sustained damage and some of the walls were breached. They advise us not to go inside, but Dr. Splat won't be persuaded.

None of the soldiers can tell me where Fauna is, but some unidentified people fought near the base of the tower, so maybe she's one of them. That's enough for me. Dr. Splat, Spooky, and I head across the sands for the tower. Six soldiers accompany us.

Slogging through the sand is almost as tiring as crawling through the tunnel. A minute later, and I feel like we've only taken ten steps. It was definitely easier walking on the road.

Voices reach across the desert. A group of six or seven people talk among themselves near the tower.

Dr. Splat pauses to peer through the darkness. "Kevin? Is that you?"

"Dr. Splat? I saw the van but not you. Glad you made it out alive." One of the figures breaks off from the group and runs toward us. He's actually *running* across the sand. "Are Emma and Spooky with you?"

"We're here," I volunteer. "Is Fauna with you?"

A figure waves at me. "I'm here, Emma. You missed out on all the fun." She runs behind Kevin. Yes, like Kevin, she *runs*. Surprisingly, her hooves serve her better than my sandaled feet serve me in this ocean of grit.

She's wearing armor that looks like someone poured white chocolate over her, leaving her head, hands, and hooves sticking out.

We hug, but it's not satisfying. It's like embracing a human-sized chocolate bunny. With a sheepish grin becoming a goat-woman, Fauna stashes her armor and gives me a proper hug. Spooky wants one, too, and we pull her into ours.

Both Fauna and I wipe away tears. Spooky laughs and points at our wet cheeks.

"Glad to see you two are okay." Keeping his high-tech gun equipped in one hand, Kevin gives me a quick one-armed hug. Then he waves at Spooky, and she waves back, her hand mere inches from his.

Heading back to the group he'd been with before spotting us, Kevin waves for us to follow him. "There's someone you all should meet."

Their group of five meet us halfway. Megan Wright, a blond white woman dressed in a black Bikini, is an Elf Tank and Anjai who lacks pointed tips to her ears. Debra Jones, a brown woman with dark purple braids and wearing armor like Fauna's but pale yellow, is a Polynesian Priestess and Shuriken Specialist who summons shurikens to hand whenever she wants to throw them.

The third one of the bunch, Belle, has no last name, just as I and Fauna have no last names. Belle claims to be Megan's *duplicate*, and wears a black Bikini identical to Megan's. Like Megan, Belle is a white female Elf Tank and Anjai. But unlike Megan, she has straight black hair and pointed ears. The two have similar facial features, but they aren't what I'd call duplicates. And neither of them look like me or any other Elves I've seen. I'm blond with pointed ears, like all the Elves I know. I won't hold their being atypical against them.

Megan wears platform slippers. How in the seven hells can she walk on this sand in those things? Belle is barefoot. That might work better for me. I stash my sandals. That's somewhat better, but there's no way I could *run* on the sand.

Kaleisha, a black Jamaican dancer with long black braids hanging to one side of her face, is attired in clothing that can only be described as electric. Her top is a band of sizzling energy surrounding her torso, not quite touching her flesh, and only barely hiding her nipples. Her short electric blue and white skirt clings to her hips. She's barefoot, and her feet don't touch the sand. She gives me a bright smile. "I'm Mithabel's personal support AI. I don't fight, but help where I can. I'm not really Jamaican. I just identify as such. But I can dance. See?" She twirls, rising in the air as she turns. She doesn't explain why she's not Jamaican but identifies as such, or say who *Mithabel* is.

"I'm Magnum, madam." A white man with the palest cheeks inclines his head to me. He's dressed in black and white, wearing a black bow tie and short black hair. His shoes are polished black, and their soles don't touch the sand. "I identify as an English butler from Victorian times, and am proud to serve as the personal support AI for Dylan."

I get no explanation from him who Dylan is, either. It's left to me to ask who these other two people are who've been mentioned but aren't present.

Belle explains. Megan and Debra are from Earth. They have avatars named Mithabel and Dylan in a place called Khertaan, a video-game-based role-playing world. Mithabel and Dylan gained a bunch of abilities, and Megan and Debra got them, too. Kaleisha and Magnum serve Megan and Debra in Mithabel and Dylan's absence.

Mithabel had earned the ability to split off a duplicate, and Megan made use of the ability to create Belle maybe an hour or so ago inside the tower, on the thirtieth floor. Belle brandishes her high-tech gun, pointing it at the top of the tower. "Up there's where Debra and Fauna got their armor, and where we all got our guns for fighting the Behemoths. You should get equipped too."

Fauna brings her gun out of inventory and shows me. It has lots of colored buttons for different types of attacks—acid, electricity, copper bullets, silver bullets, poison gas, metal blades, and grenades. The armor has matching buttons that help protect the wearer against corresponding types of attacks.

Yes, I want armor and a gun like theirs.

The soldiers who've accompanied us are in agreement with me—they need equipment to fight the inter-dimensional invaders. Their standard equipment had no effect on the Behemoths. Kevin tells them to come with him to talk to a Mr. Freeman. He leads them towards the tower.

Dr. Splat lightly touches my arm. "You should come and get outfitted. Spooky, too. These Behemoths aren't likely to be the last monsters attacking this place."

I suppose Spooky could do with some armor, but I'm hesitant to turn her loose with a gun.

Even barefoot, I continue having trouble walking across the desert.

Kaleisha spins on one foot in front of me. "Would you like me to carry you to the tower entrance? You can ride on my back. It will be fun."

The Jamaican dancer doesn't look strong enough to carry a ten-pound bag of flour. I shake my head. "I'm fine."

Fauna points at her hooves. "When you get your armor, it will help."

I scoff. "Your armor doesn't extend below your hooves. How can it help?"

She shrugs. "It just does. It's from a video-game world. Some of this stuff works the way it does because of the rules of the game world it's from. Mr. Freeman has a *bunch* of equipment from video-game worlds. It doesn't work for everyone, but it works for people from role-playing game worlds like ours. I swear, you'll be able to wear your sandals and run across the sand just fine."

"Okay, Kaleisha, I'll take that piggyback ride, if the offer is still good." I'm falling behind Dr. Splat and his group.

"Great. Spread your legs." The Jamaican dancer pokes her head between my thighs and lifts me into the air, on her shoulders. I shriek... a little.

Riding piggyback on a personal support AI is quite the fun experience, especially when that AI identifies as a Jamaican dancer. We spin round and round, flip upside down, and gyrate in the air. I'm all dizzy and laughing my guts out by the time we reach the tower, but we're at the entrance before Dr. Splat and the soldiers.

"Don't tell anyone, but I'm gonna help you out a bit more." Kaleisha presses her palm against the door, and it slides open. "Everyone inside." The four of us enter—Kaleisha, Fauna, Spooky, and me. Lights flicker on above us. The lobby we've entered is constructed purely of marble, with scattered pillars supporting the ceiling.

Magnum slips through the door before it closes. "I can help, too." He turns to Fauna. "Madam, I would be honored to give you a lift to the thirtieth floor."

The goat-lady points to the other side of the lobby. "Sounds fun, but there are elevators."

He inclines his head. "If only they were working, madam. At the moment, neither of them are."

Fauna brightens. "Are you giving me a piggyback ride then, too?"

"That is my offer." He points to a door near the elevators. "And then we'll fly right up yonder stairwell. 'Twill be much faster than walking up thirty flights of stairs."

"You're being awfully nice to us." Fauna blushes as Magnum lifts her over his head and plants her butt on his shoulders.

"Not to be ungrateful...." Kaleisha chortles as she flies me around a pillar. "But we don't really get to have any fun. Mithabel and Megan, even Dylan and Debra, are some of the most serious people in existence. None of them would ever play piggyback with us."

The door slides open behind us as the soldiers enter. With a whoop, Kaleisha carts me off to the stairwell entrance, with Magnum and Fauna right behind us and Spooky zipping all over the place with no need for assistance. Kaleisha opens the door to the stairwell, and we all hurry through.

The stairs forming a spiral around us, we fly upward. Every couple seconds we pass giant cracks and crevices in the wall, evidence of the structural damage caused by the Behemoths.

In under a minute, we're at the top, in a hallway. I jump down and give Kaleisha a brief hug, which she returns like a real person with empathy.

"Let's do this again, sometime," I suggest.

"That would be wonderful." Kaleisha bows deeply to me, throwing one arm way back. "Farewell, friends." She and Magnum look sad to go, and I'm sad, too, but they return to the stairwell and head back down.

We're in another area constructed of marble. There's only one way to go from here other than back down the stairs. At the end of the hallway, Fauna knocks. There's no answer. She knocks again.

215

After two more knocks, she looks defeated. "Goat cheese."

"Try again in a minute." I put on a brave face for her.

"I can dig." Spooky points at the floor before the door. "We go under."

I shake my head. "You're learning your words quickly, Spooky. I'm proud of you."

She pokes me in the chest. "I'm proud of *you*."

"Why are you proud of me?"

"You care about *me*." She giggles.

"Let's do it." Fauna points at the base of the door. "I know where all the equipment is inside. If you can get us past the doors, Spooky, I can get us the equipment we need."

"Fun, fun." Spooky drops to the floor.

The door slides open, revealing a thirty-or-forty-something white man attired in a prim black and white suit, on his way out. "*Fauna*. You've brought friends. I was just headed downstairs." He looks us over, his amused gaze lingering on Spooky at his feet, her hand poised over the marble tile, ready to do her thing and create a tunnel for us. He shakes his head at her. "I suppose it can wait. Tuni is a bit tied up as it is." He steps back into the room and ushers us in. "I'm Mr. Freeman."

Fauna introduces me and Spooky.

A wooden desk lies in pieces below a shattered plate glass window. Mr. Freeman acts like it's nothing. Fauna glances askance at me, but neither of us say anything.

Beyond the plate glass window, soldiers and choppers linger on the sand a few hundred yards away. A flying figure approaches them from the tower. Ten other flying figures approach them from the far distance. "What are those?" Fauna and I ask the same question at the same time.

"That's Tuni going to face off against a band of Dread Naughts, I'm afraid. Those things are a hundred times tougher than Arachnid Behemoths. I hope she can handle them, for our sakes and the sakes of those soldiers out there."

Mr. Freeman leads us into a room laden with rows of mannequins wearing suits of light-colored armor. He goes straight to a cream-colored suit, lifts it free of its display, and hands it to me. "It's close to Fauna's color, but different enough for any allies to distinguish between the two of you. Stash it and let's get you a weapon." He fetches a beige suit and hands it to Spooky. "This one is for you, little one. Don't worry; it will adjust to your size." From a mannequin in the far corner of the room, he removes a large suit of chain mail, and hands it to me. "If you wouldn't mind stashing that. I'll explain later. Now, follow me to the weapons room."

Passing through the room with the broken window, we pause to observe a sandstorm where I'd earlier seen the choppers. The large flying figures aren't in evidence. A few smaller birds pop in and out of the swirling sand. Numerous gunshots ring out from within the storm.

Spurred by the view outside the window, we hurry to the equipment room.

"Flamethrower or grenade launcher?"

"Um...." I glance at Fauna. "Better give me a grenade launcher."

She holds up a hand. "I have a grenade launcher. You should take a flamethrower. One of us should have one. I'll be fine."

Mr. Freeman hands me a gun and then looks to Spooky. "You look rather young, Spooky, but appearances are often deceiving. Can you be responsible with one of these?"

Spooky nods and holds out a hand. "I will take great care with it, Mr. Freeman. Flamethrower, please."

I *cannot believe* how well she speaks for a baby.

Fauna and I watch in silence as Mr. Freeman hands Spooky a gun. Not long ago, she was little more than a mischievous imp. But since then she saved my life, and I can't deny she kept a calm head when the Behemoths attacked our van. *She* made possible our escape through a tunnel *she* dug in the sand.

Spooky stashes the weapon. There'll be no taking it from her now.

Mr. Freeman hands me two additional guns. "If you could stash these, too, please. Now, come. We have a Centaur to visit who's waiting on me." On the way out, he grabs up an inch-thick rectangular device measuring about a foot by a foot and a half.

As we reach the stairwell door, it opens. Kevin is there, with six soldiers. Mr. Freeman makes his apologies for delaying introductions, and we head downstairs. Kevin and the soldiers follow us.

We spot Dr. Splat still hauling himself up the stairs when Mr. Freeman exits the stairwell, telling us we've reached the floor where Ruby the Centaur waits.

ജ𝕮𝕾ℭ𝕽ℰ𝕾ജ𝕮𝕾

Striding briskly along a hallway, Mr. Freeman scans names on doors as we pass them. He stops at one labeled *Gloria Rubio*, lifts a cover on the rectangular device he's carrying, and presses some buttons. The door opens and Mr. Freeman enters a hallway. "Ruby?" He motions for me to follow him in. Spooky slips in past me, but stays behind Mr. Freeman. Fauna follows me, with Kevin and the soldiers coming in last.

Framed photos hang on the walls. Mr. Freeman pays them no mind. I'm curious, but can't spend the time I'd like in examining them. All the pictures center on one subject, a brunette white woman in her late twenties. I assume she's Gloria Rubio.

We draw close to the end of the hall, where a doorway sits off to the left. A masculine bald, blue head pokes through the portal... two feet from the floor. His voice is high-pitched, a bit squeaky. "Tuni? Where's Tuni?"

Mr. Freeman does a double take. "I believe this is the room for Ruby the Centaur...?"

A two-foot-tall blue man steps into sight. He's wearing blue jeans and no shirt or shoes or hair, and brags an overemphasized muscular chest. He forces his voice to a lower register. "I'm Gem.

G-e-m. I'm the special assistant to Ruby the Centaur. Who may I say is calling?"

Mr. Freeman's jaws flap but no words come out.

I speak for him. "This is Mr. Freeman. He runs the place. Tuni is indisposed at the moment. We've brought some equipment for Ruby."

"One moment." Gem retreats from the hallway momentarily. When he returns, the squeak is back in his voice. "Ruby asks how many domains of damage the equipment deals with."

Mr. Freeman nods. "She has a right to be concerned. May we enter?"

Gem steps back into the room again and then returns a few seconds later. He lowers his voice again. "You may enter."

I follow Mr. Freeman into a bedroom. A Centaur awaits us inside. She motions us in. "I would offer everyone a seat, but...."

Beneath a shattered window, the bedroom wall is open to the sky, a huge rent reaching from the window to the floor. Chunks of stone the size of small boulders lie scattered across the room and on the bed.

Mr. Freeman whistles. "I'm glad you weren't hurt by the Behemoth attack, Ruby." He glances at the little blue man. "Or you, Gem."

The blue man leaps onto Ruby's back. His squeak returns. "That makes three of us."

The soldiers enter the room. As a unit, they snap to attention, saluting, their eyes locked on Ruby.

The Centaur's eyes widen.

Gem clears his throat. "That's the work of your Name of Rank trait, as I've mentioned before, sheikha."

Ruby tosses her long, curly red hair. "Welcome, soldiers."

In unison, they drop their hands to their sides. "We await your orders, ma'am."

Mr. Freeman points at the breach. "There's a whole bunch more soldiers out there, just waiting for you to organize them, Ruby, should you decide to remain on Destin."

She nods. "I saw." She saunters down the line of uniformed men, assessing each one, not speaking until she reaches the end. "But Earth is my home, and that's where I must go. I must protect it."

"Then take us with you, ma'am."

"Even if I could, I wouldn't want to take you from your home."

"We live for defending the defenseless wherever they may be, ma'am."

Spooky flies up before Ruby's face and waves. "Hi, my name is Spooky. I'm a shadow baby. Glad to meet you, Centaur Ruby." She waves at the blue imp. "You, too, Gem."

The Centaur turns an amused gaze on the dark tyke and thanks her, adding, "I'm not accustomed to receiving visitors. I'm glad to make your acquaintance, Spooky."

After further introductions are made, including the soldiers—Sarge, Fred, Wiley, Martin, Raven, and Yelle—Mr. Freeman gestures at me. "Emma, let's have the extra guns and armor you stashed."

Ruby looks smashing in the chain mail armor. It fits both her equine and human parts perfectly. Fauna, Spooky, and I equip our suits, too, and Mr. Freeman walks us through their operation. They're all similar. Ruby orders the soldiers to watch and learn as well, even though they can't use the suits without first training in Khertaan.

After the walk-through on the armor, we get a similar rundown on the guns. Once we're finished, Ruby quickly moves the discussion to another topic. "Mr. Freeman, can we get these men into Khertaan?"

"Please, you can all call me Franklin. No, we can't get anyone into Khertaan at the moment. The System is in update mode, which means no one can respawn and no one new can enter. There are avatars still active in Khertaan—don't ask me how—but if I abort the update by doing a reboot, all the players associated with those avatars might never wake up, lost forever in their own heads. Until it's safe to reboot, we're stuck waiting for the update to finish on its own."

"How long will that be?"

Mr. Freeman throws a hand up. "There's no estimated time for the update to finish. But… if all the avatars currently in the game were to die, or if the players woke up on their own, I could safely reboot the System and allow new players in."

Fauna scuffs a hoof on the floor. "Why can't they just go to the thirtieth floor, like I did?"

"I wish it were that easy for everyone." Mr. Freeman sighs. "That shortcut worked for you, Kevin, Emma, and Spooky only because you all had already gained legitimate levels in a role-playing world. It didn't work for Kevin at first, either. Experimental data indicates one has to reach at least level ten in a role-playing game world of at least reasonable difficulty for the shortcut to have a chance at working. I admit the data set used for the experiment is small."

Struck with insight, I laugh. "Do you have any dice, Mr. Freeman?"

Mr. Freeman pats his pants pockets. "Not on me. And, please, it's Franklin."

Kevin chuckles, his knowing gaze catching mine and telling me he thinks what I'm thinking is a good idea. "But you have a laptop, Franklin. We can bring up an online dice roller." He reaches out, and Franklin hands over his device. Kevin's eyes glint with excitement. "You're a genius, Emma. We don't need everyone to enter Khertaan. They can roll up T&T characters and enter a table-top RPG world. We can do this for every soldier on the site. You can even get in on this, if you want, Franklin."

I'm not *super* confident about my Game Mastering ability. "I don't know how many players I can handle at one time, but I'll do my best." I turn to Ruby. "You only have equipment and abilities for dealing with damage in the physical domain. If you roll up a character, and if everything works as I expect, your character could acquire equipment and abilities that help with other damage domains. As I'm the Game Master, I promise there will be reasonable, *useful* loot drops. I won't make it easy, because like Franklin was saying, anything too easy can't facilitate the necessary transitions from the T&T world to this one. But I won't be stingy with loot, either, like Nick was."

"I just want to point out something." Fauna steps next to me, facing the Centaur. "When Emma and I first left our original world, we went to Earth. We found our way to Destin with help from Spooky. I'd wager she could take you to Earth in the timeline of your choice if you decided to stay in Destin a while. Nick had the ability to travel the timelines, and Spooky is his daughter, so I think she inherited the ability from him."

While the others debate possibilities for Ruby, I ask Kevin to show me how to use the online dice roller. If we have a T&T game in Ruby's room, she won't have to make a decision yet about going to Earth. "We'll still need paper and pencil, though."

"Nah." Kevin swipes his finger across the touchpad and moves the cursor to an icon. Clicking the icon, he opens what he refers to as a *window*—but not one that allows me to see through the laptop. He gestures at the white rectangle on the screen. "If you want, I can keep track of everyone's character sheets in a document. I can roll the dice, too. I'll be the Game Master's assistant, if you will."

"That would be great." The computer stuff is all a bit confusing to me, really. If he takes care of that part, it will leave me free to concentrate on the adventure details.

Fauna mentioned that Spooky is Nick's daughter. Fauna and I are related to him, too. He's our player, which makes us as much like *him* as *his daughters*. Now I'm about to help bring more characters into this world—they'll carry a part of me and thus a part of Nick within them. I won't be easy on them, because that's not who I am or who Nick was. They'll start on a home world of my devising, where their mettle and metal will be tested. And their world has a name: Anissa, which in the Caprine language means *put to the test.*

I wish Ronnie and Greelia were here. I miss them—where are they and how are they doing?

CHAPTER TWENTY-FIVE

Ronnie: Suicidal City

It's surreal that Queen Jean is no longer a concern. I've expended so much energy in opposing her… now that she's dead, I've lost direction.

But her evil wasn't my moral compass. I'm still the same Ronnie I ever was.

That's not true. I have Queen Jean's blood on my hands. My finger pulled the trigger of the gun whose bullet struck her in the back of the head. It doesn't matter that a Shadow Gaunt rolled the dice for the saving roll that unfroze the bullet. I wanted the Queen dead.

Will Mel forgive me?

It was impossible to read the emotions of the Princess Karen simulacrum back in the photographic prison we shared, and trying to read them now is impossible, because, well, I can't see her face. Her arms wrap around my waist from behind and she leans into my back. We speed down the road away from the palace once belonging to the Queen, now the seat of power for the Shadow Gaunts—all eleven of them.

Mournful cries of lost birds pierce the darkened night sky. They can't be lonely—there are literally hundreds if not thousands of the fringed-wing creatures soaring overhead. No, these creatures have been ousted from their homeland. I know how it feels. Will I ever see my world of origin again?

I'm not overly attached to any place. What matters more to me are the people I've lost. Fauna, Emma, and Greelia represent *home* to me. I'd give anything to go foraging for mushrooms once more with Fauna, or walk a dirt road with the three of them, eager to discover what lies around the next corner.

But our paths diverged, and mine crossed with the paths of Mel, Erica, and Gondra. I could have done without meeting the Lizardman. But adventuring is all about dealing with what's thrown at you when it's thrown at you. Sometimes you win and sometimes you fail, but the only real failure is death, and I'm not there yet.

Along the way, you make choices. Once a choice is made, you live with the consequences and keep going. That's the game. Giving up is not an option. To give up is to lose the game.

As for winning the game—as long as you're playing, you're winning. It doesn't matter how healthy or wealthy you are—those are volatile states that can change overnight. As long as you're surviving, you're good.

Except that... emotions matter—as much as surviving, if not more. Where's the value in survival if you're unable to enjoy it—always alone, unloved, and depressed?

All your friends are gone—Fauna, Emma, Greelia, Erica, and Mel. Forget Gondra—he was never your friend. He wanted you gone. For that matter, who was Erica to you? She was more interested in Mel than you and wanted him for herself. She wanted you gone as much as Gondra did.

As for Mel... he was so out of sync with the world, he couldn't even accept that *he* was a *she*. She tried to downplay her femininity, to hide it, but you fell in love with the woman she was, not the man.

Love?

You didn't recognize it? All the signs were there. You were head over heels in love with the woman. You're so desperate for her to return your love, you'll take any opportunity to fill the void her absence leaves in your heart. Why else is there a soulless simulacrum wearing her face, pressed against your back? And not just any soulless simulacrum, but one who drove a dagger between your ribs, intending to leave it there for eternity?

Face it, you love Mel the woman, but you'll never have Mel the woman, because Mel in her own mind isn't a woman. You think to replace Mel with a cardboard cutout, but you know that won't be satisfactory.

The real Mel, Erica, and Gondra have abandoned you. Fauna, Emma, and Greelia are gone. The one person you're left to travel with is a vacuous thing that tried to kill you.

But are you alone? No. Look around you. Slow down and take your eyes off the road for a moment. See all the people along the street?

Guess what. All those people feel just as alone as you feel. The difference between them and you… they're doing something about it. Watch that one. See her? She has a gun. She's putting the barrel in her mouth. Oh…. She pulled the trigger. Her problems are ended. No more feelings of loneliness for her.

And look…. That man is helping his wife and children end their miserable existences. Oh, now he's taking his knife to his own throat. No more dysfunction in that family.

You'd think once this planet was freed from Queen Jean's tyrannical rule, her subjects would be glad to be free of her. But the evidence is as hard and cold and unforgiving as steel. Killing Queen Jean solved nothing. King Shadow Gaunts are worse to the extreme, and the inhabitants of the Shadowverse know it. They feel it in their bones. It's a truth their very souls acknowledge. You feel it, too.

Stop the motorcycle. That's it. Stash it. There you go. Look at the sky. What do you see?

Crows? They're not crows. But what do you call a group of crows?

A murder.

Well, what you see is a murder of Flitters... not one Flitter, but more than ten, twenty, or even a hundred. There are thousands, just waiting to attack. Why wait? Again, look around you. The people don't want a tortured death at the talons and beak of a giant bird, to be clawed to the brink of death and then have their eyes pecked from their heads before they die. That's how a Flitter kills a person.

If you have any feelings for Princess Karen—the simulacrum with you—you'll end her life before the Flitters reach her. Point your rifle at her face. That's right. See how she stares at you, dumbfounded? She doesn't understand. But what's the point in explaining, if she's dying now? Put your finger on the trigger. That's it.

You know what to do next. Squeeze the trigger.

Stop resisting. *Squeeze the damned trigger.*

ဆၢၦၢၩ

Princess Karen steps back, lowering her knife. Severed by her blade, a dark tendril falls from where it had wrapped around my throat, turning to a line of dust carried away on a breeze.

The Flitter Wandering Monster assigned to me is a giant black bird, ten feet long, with thin fringes on its wings reaching twenty feet out to either side. It hovers twenty feet above me. Dozens of shadowy tendrils emanate from its belly, stretching across the land in search of prey. One of those tendrils had a hold on me.

More tendrils swoop at me, attempting to latch on. I fire the rifle at the thing, but I swear the bullet has no effect. I shoot several more times, with the same non-result.

On the other hand, Princess Karen is a whirling dervish with a blade, keeping the tendrils at bay. She's like a robot, darting around, no matter what side the tendrils attack from, and slicing them off as they come within reach.

I'm defenseless against the Flitter, but it can't hurt the Princess. Tendrils wither when they so much as touch her, to be carried away on the wind like desiccated feathers.

And then it's gone, fleeing across the sky to find its nest, to hole up and heal. Will it come again for me? How can one know the mind of an alien bird?

Other Flitters still hover above the area, tendrils attached to people still resisting their vile telepathic persuasions.

I point to the nearest struggling victim. "Can you help him, Princess?"

"If you wish it." She runs towards the man I indicated.

I run beside her. "Help as many people as you can, please."

The man to whom we run repeatedly stabs at himself with a closed pocket knife. He's lucky he didn't get it open.

With a swipe of Princess Karen's blade, the tendril falls from the man's neck and dries up. The rescued one gasps and stares at the pocket knife before raising his gaze. "Thank you, Princess." He kneels and bows to her. "I am your servant."

The Princess makes no reply, but runs to the next struggling person, a woman scratching at her own eyes, traces of blood on her cheeks and fingernails. She collapses to the ground, gasping in pain once the Princess cuts her free. "Kill me," she pleads. Even without the tendril around her neck, she wants to die.

Princess Karen grabs the woman by the hair, pulls her head back, and slashes the woman's throat.

There's nothing to say.

The first man we saved is with us. Even he says nothing.

We run to the next still-living person. Running from one to the next, the Princess saves dozens of people from fates they are struggling to resist or are incapable of executing. When any of them are so messed up they beg for death, I don't try to stop Princess Karen from giving them the relief they ask for.

Every person we save who doesn't beg for death chooses to run with us. We've collected quite a crowd.

Overhead, three Flitters form a triangle and lash tendrils at us. I don't have a chance to roll my dice, and a tendril grabs me. Evil thoughts burn my mind. Knowing what to expect, though, allows me to resist more than I did before. I don't point a gun at anyone when the alien mental voice invading my thought stream tells me I should.

The Princess cuts me free once more. I drop to my knees, equip my dice, and roll them. Snake eyes, which is low, but I get to roll again. This time they come up double fives. Great. Roll again. I get a six and four. That's a great total on the dice, and when added to my Luck score, is enough for a level thirty saving roll. I couldn't ask for a much better one.

Stashing the dice, I jump to my feet and run about, pushing people aside who the tendrils reach for, dodging any that come my way. Between me and the Princess, we keep everyone in our group alive until at last the three Flitters withdraw, their tendrils collectively amputated by the Princess.

As three more Flitters move in, I drop to my knees and make another saving roll—level twenty-eight. It's enough, and I use the same tactic as before to help people avoid the tendrils while the Princess slashes those she can reach.

When those three Flitters finally move away, three more take their place. I roll again and make the saving roll, but I see where this is going. There are enough Flitters to keep this up for days if not weeks or months. If they can regenerate their tendrils, they could possibly keep this up forever. At some point, I'm going to fail my saving roll, and when that happens….

"Make your way to that store." I point it out. If we get inside, maybe the Flitters can't get to us.

As we maneuver towards the building, a general store, the Flitters throw several tendrils at the Princess, but more attacks against her doesn't work in their favor. They can't touch her without destroying their tendrils, no matter how many are involved in the attack. What is it about her? I don't know, but I'm glad I asked her to accompany me out of that photographic prison cell. She's all that prevents the lot of us from taking our own lives.

Picking our way through a field of corpses, we reach the store I've chosen. I'd picked this building because the door was open. I direct people through, maintaining order so no one gets trampled.

I go in next to last, with the Princess following. She battles off a tendril and I slam the door closed.

Everyone screams. Tendrils come through open windows. The Princess strikes them down. I'd close the windows, but the panes lie in shards on the floor.

One fellow finds a door to a back room. Calling for others to follow him, he goes through. Without me at the door to direct, people crowd through after him, amid shouts of panic. A young boy is knocked down. Several people step on him before I reach him.

"*People*. Get a grip on yourselves. It's no good sheltering here if you're going to kill each other."

A cry of alarm belts out from the room into which everyone is piling. It's followed by several shouts of fear. Those people who got through the door into the room try to come out, shoving those still trying to enter.

"Get out, get out, get—"

A crunching sound terminates the man's shout. People still trapped in the room shout, groan, or regurgitate.

I picked the wrong building in which to seek shelter. "Get out of there, people." I push past them to get closer to the door, hoping there's something I can do for those still inside, though my instincts tell me to run. "Princess, how are you faring?"

"Barely. Everyone needs to keep their distance from the windows. Don't get in my way, people, or we're all dead."

There's nowhere for people to go if they can't take refuge in the back room. I reach the doorway and grab hold of a woman's arm as she struggles against a vine holding her by the ankle.

"Don't let it eat me, please." Her eyes are wide. I've never seen eyes holding so much fear. No, this goes beyond fear. It's horror.

I pull, but the vine holding her is too strong. As my eyes adjust to the darkness, I see six other people on the floor of a storage room, clinging to shelves, their bodies horizontal and off the floor, stretched between the shelf they hold and a gaping maw filled with concentric circles of fangs. The vines recede into that maw, trying to drag everyone in.

Keeping hold of the woman with my left hand, I equip my rifle in my right and take aim, finger on the trigger. Putting my sights on the center of the monster's gullet, I fire.

The monster flinches and emits a squeal like a caught pig. All of the snared people remain snared, the vines still taut. Another vine springs out of the monster's gullet and lashes around my gun. With a tug of tremendous strength, the vine whisks the gun away from me and into the guts of the monster.

Keeping my calm and holding onto the woman, I kneel in the doorway, equip my dice, and roll for three saving rolls, one for Strength, one for Dexterity, and one for Luck. I make level three for Strength, level four for Dexterity, and… ugh… an automatic failure for Luck. I've got to rely solely on my Strength and Dexterity for the moment.

I might lose it, but I equip another rifle in my right hand and open fire again. The monster doesn't like being shot, and I can only hope I'm having an effect. When it fires a vine at me, I deftly evade it and continue shooting while it retracts its vine.

Everyone held by vines is released and drops to the floor. The monster spasms.

Emotions flood my system—rage at the Shadow Gaunts, pity for the people who've trusted me, guilt for having brought them to this house, hatred of this *thing* and the Flitters outside. I give into the rage and hatred. *"Die, monster."* I keep firing, still holding onto the woman in my left hand like I'm afraid to let go, even though she's no longer being pulled and is tugging to free her hand from my grip.

231

"*Stop*, Ronnie." A familiar voice I thought I'd never hear again speaks from close behind me. "*Don't kill it.*"

The rage and hatred won't let me listen to Greelia. I keep firing.

She grabs me by the shoulders and yanks me back.

Walls shatter as the monster explodes, hurling small boulders in every direction.

CHAPTER TWENTY-SIX

Erica: Loss

Five of us—Gondra, little Susie, Renee, and me, with Renee carrying the unconscious body of Morrow—exit the Mists of Time on a street cluttered with corpses. Large winged creatures fill the sky, chirping laments of longing.

"More Dread Naughts... Flitters." The contempt in Gondra's voice is palpable. "There must be thousands in the area. The Shadow Gaunt may be nearby."

To our left, the Flitters swarm a general store, reaching long, slender appendages into the wooden building through broken windows. Something inside lops them off, but that doesn't stop an unending stream of Flitters from reaching in again... and again... and again.

I point at the building. "In there."

Gondra shakes his scaly head. "Why am I not s... surprised?"

I take three steps towards the store. It explodes, flinging *stone* fragments larger than me. I instinctively duck, sheltering little Susie with my body, though she's suddenly gone from my grasp, and my arms close on the space where she'd been. She teleported or maybe time-jumped to protect herself.

The roof of the general store is gone, as are portions of the roofs of adjacent buildings. The Flitters weren't harmed by the explosion, and more eagerly reach their vine-like appendages into the wreckage.

Fortunately, none of us were struck by hurled stone fragments. Renee clutches the limp Morrow to her chest, her eyes glistening, but she says nothing. Fully upright, Gondra floats through the air towards the ruined general store, brandishing a staff in his right hand. Susie remains missing, which I have to believe means she's somewhere safe.

"Stay here if you want, Renee. Watch for Susie. I'm going with Gondra."

The sexy support AI in a skin-tight red leather miniskirt and suede chest wrap nods. She understands, but doesn't like any of this. She's next to invulnerable, but Morrow isn't, and he can't do anything to defend himself.

The Lizardman reaches the store, flies over the ruined front exterior wall, and drops inside. I hurry to catch up. The Flitters ignore both of us. If they did try to attack us, our Cosmic Cloaks would protect us… I hope.

Lying crumpled on the floor just inside the store are several bodies, one of which is Princess Karen—the Jeaniverse version of Mel. She's not moving… doesn't even appear to be breathing. Gondra ignores her and the other corpses around her, continuing to the place where all the Flitter appendages are focused.

I scoop up Princess Karen, checking her pulse as I fly after Gondra. Her veins are quiet. She's gone… except she's not. Her eyelids flutter and then open, and she's looking up at me. "Where's Ronnie?" She raises a hand holding a bloody knife. "Is he still alive?"

I've been wanting to know where Ronnie is. I think we may have found him, and I don't think I'll like what I'm about to see.

Landing behind Gondra, I set Princess Karen on her two feet. The Lizardman kneels beside two motionless bodies. One is Ronnie. The other, Gondra says, is Greelia. Dressed in a modern fashion, she doesn't look like any Greelia I ever saw, but Gondra knows better than I do.

The Flitters withdraw their appendages from the necks of both. They got what they came for.

Gondra checks pulses. "We're too late. The Shadow Gaunt has claimed their souls, their awarenesses. Now I'll never be able to take from Greelia what I needed to bring Nick back."

I wipe my eyes. "I don't understand. This is Jeaniverse. How can the Shadow Gaunt be so powerful here?"

The Lizardman flicks his forked tongue. "Queen Jean is dead. This is no longer Jeaniverse, but the Shadowverse. The Shadow Gaunt—a minion of Seth—rules it now.

"What we must do, at all costs, is prevent Seth or his minions from taking soul material from Fauna and Emma. If he gets that, then he can recreate Nick in his image, and if that happens, there's no hope for the multiverse. We need to get to Fauna and Emma pronto and protect them at all costs."

Princess Karen picks up Ronnie's body. "I will accompany you to find his friends." She slings him over her left shoulder, kneels down, and lifts Greelia's body, slinging her over the other shoulder. "He would want me to take their bodies to Fauna and Emma."

Gondra doesn't protest. We fly back to where Renee still clutches Morrow. Flitters probe the two of them with their appendages, but don't attack them, not finding anything of interest to take—Morrow is an empty shell, and Renee is a soulless AI.

We all latch onto each other, but I don't leave Jeaniverse—that is, Shadowverse—yet. "We can't leave without Susie. She should be popping back into this timeline any second now."

The Lizardman taps his staff on the road. "We need to go, Erica. Susie will take care of herself. How do I know this? Because we've seen future Susie. We couldn't have seen future Susie if anything bad happened to little Susie. Let's go."

What he says sounds logical, but my heart tells me not to leave. "Just another minute."

All the Flitters above us vanish.

Gondra slams down his staff. "They're going after Fauna and Emma. *Let's go*, Erica."

"Susie? *Susie*. Please come if you can hear me. It's time to leave."

Silence....

Except for Gondra, whose grip tightens on my shoulder. *"Let's go."*

I have no choice. My delay may already be endangering the souls of the two targets of the Shadow Gaunt's destructive desires. The time-traveling preschooler will be fine. By force of will, I drag everyone with me back into the Mists of Time, unsuccessful at my attempts to ignore the guilt gnawing at the pit of my stomach for so god-awful-many things I've done wrong.

CHAPTER TWENTY-SEVEN

The Soul of Morrow: Thread

The melody fades from my head as mists envelop me. Mel's frightened eyes peer at me through the haze. Realization of where we are and that Nick's son from another timeline has saved my life hits simultaneously with the knowledge that Kylie fell victim to the charms of a monstrous centipede called a Lunger and is still its prisoner. "Take me back, Mel. We have to save Kylie."

Mel shakes his head, sadness darkening his gaze. "We can't save her. If we go back in there, you'll succumb to their charms again. Maybe I won't, but I'm not taking you back in there and I'm not leaving you here while I go back in."

How did Mel come to be in the FP-Earth timeline? There's something different about him. I grip the collar of his cloak, and magic thrums between my fingers. "What is this?"

"A Cosmic Cloak." He allows himself to grin, albeit grimly. "It allows me to travel the multiverse without being a ghost. I don't know in general how to identify specific timelines for us to enter, but we're not going back into *that* one." He points at a shimmering veil.

I can't see it in its entirety, though I know it's shaped in this metaphysical space as a sphere—a single moment along a line of moments, interpreted by my three-dimensional-thinking brain as a three-dimensional object, though I know it isn't. It's a four-dimensional object containing an entire universe. There's another sphere adjacent to and yet also overlapping it, representing the state of the same universe in another moment.

I tug on his collar. "How do I get myself one of these Cloaks?"

He shrugs. "I can't tell you how, Dad. I don't even know if you can."

This kid doesn't understand, so I set him straight. "I'm not your Dad, Mel. I know I look like him, and because I'm in his body I have many of his mannerisms and cravings—but I'm actually Morrow. Your friend Erica was so desperate to have Nick back, she ripped me from my avatar body and jammed me into this one." I concentrate on my inventory, and it appears in my view. I equip my foot-long Wand. "See this? This is an item from Khertaan. I use it to cast spells. I'm a level 15 Lightning Wizard and level 6 Lightning Warrior. If I were to face those Lungers again, I could maybe do some damage. I need to try. I can't leave Kylie with them."

Mel remains adamant, continuing to shake his head. "Sorry, *Morrow*. You might not be my Dad, but you're all I have left of him. I'm sure the Lungers won't hurt Kylie, or they already would have. If you go in there and start attacking them, *she's* going to attack you. She said as much, and I believe her. I want to help her, too, I really do, but…. I can't lose you. And Erica will kill me if I let anything happen to you."

"Yes, well, she's a fish out of water… not in her own timeline either." Mists drift by—both fine wisps and denser banks. I point at the shimmering veil. "What's to keep that Lunger from doing what you just did?"

The young transgender man lays a gentle hand on my cheek as he moves his other hand to grasp my wrist. "If it could, it would already be here. I think." He lowers his hand, his eyes staring into mine like he's trying to identify something in me that isn't there, not to the degree he wishes. He bites his lip. "But maybe we should vacate the area." He flies through the mists, dragging me along.

I consider resisting, but what would that accomplish? I can't navigate limbo or enter timelines. I'm *not* Nick. Yes, I occupy his body, and muscle memory makes me feel I can do things I don't know how to do. It's disconcerting. I want *my* Punk body back, with *my* green mohawk, because *that's* who I am, Morrow the Punk Lightning Wizard and Warrior. "Where are we going?"

"Glynda—future Susie—said to tell her Dad he needs to join her asap in Khertaan. So… is that you? Not you? And if it's you, do you know where Khertaan is?" Mel's gesture sweeps across the vast, misty limbo.

"She was talking about *me* rejoining Slithy. I wish I'd been there when Kylie advanced to level thirty. Kylie had to leave Khertaan because she maxed out her level, but I think Slithy hasn't yet. If I was with her, we could work together to reach level thirty, and then we could both help Kylie. So, yeah, if I can get back to Khertaan, that's what I should do."

Dragging me slowly onward through limbo, Mel frowns. "If Khertaan is a timeline and I can locate it, I should be able to take you in using my Cosmic Cloak. We merely need to find the right veil to penetrate."

I laugh at the absurdity. "There are infinitely many universes in the multiverse. Are we to simply stumble upon the right one?"

"Perhaps I can be of assistance," ODYSSEY says inside my head. "After all, I do host a portion of the Khertaan program."

"Hold up, Mel." I wiggle a finger at him. "I might know a way." I turn my thoughts inward to my nanobot collective. "All right then, ODYSSEY, tell me…. Can you get me into Khertaan?"

"The Khertaan program aids people in accessing the Khertaan universe. That is, the program has a metaphysical bond to Khertaan. That which is metaphysical in nature can be perceived by travelers within the Mists of Time. You should be able to see a metaphysical cord attaching me to Khertaan. It might be thin and wispy, but if you can identify it, you could follow it to the destination you seek."

Well, that's helpful. We might have a chance at this. I explain what we're looking for to Mel, and the two of us search the immediate vicinity for anything resembling a cord, no matter how thick or thin. It's awkward, since he has to keep hold of me, not wanting to risk losing me in limbo. After a dozen false starts, we find a thread that—though wispy and thinning at times almost to non-existence—keeps going and going. It has to be the one.

It *really* has to be the one, because we follow it for hours. I know, because I still have access to the System clock for Khertaan. It's 6:38 AM, Day 4 there. It feels like more time than that has elapsed since I started the game, but time moves at different rates depending on where you are, and it moves very slowly in Khertaan.

The thread ends. A shimmering veil rises before us. This has to be the right one, so now it's a matter of entering it and finding my daughter. She and I will gain level thirty together, and then we'll head back to the FP-Earth timeline and rescue our beloved Kylie.

God, I hope nothing bad happens to my wife. I'll never forgive myself if it does.

Mel squeezes my hand. "You ready?"

"Let's go."

He slips through the space-time fabric between limbo and our new reality like he was stepping into a waterfall, and takes me with him.

CHAPTER TWENTY-EIGHT

Kylie: Maybe Not Friends

They're all gone, except for Georgie and the Lungers. Why do my human friends and family always desert me?

Lunger 36, as my new friend is called, telepathically bids me to help him and Lunger 37, his companion, destroy the house Kendra shared with her family. They've abandoned us again, after all.

"Please don't let them destroy my home," Kendra pleads in our shared mind space. "Lunger 37 is not your friend."

She's right. Shifting once more to Spirit Form, I drive my Spirit Blade into Lunger 37's back. I can only deal spiritual damage with the weapon when in Spirit Form, but Georgie didn't say both Lungers were immune to spiritual attacks. There's one way to find out if Lunger 37 also has immunity.

"Sorry, pumpkin." Georgie looks pained. "Spiritual damage doesn't affect either of them. But Lunger 37 did attempt to bite you earlier. If it can deal physical damage, then it can be damaged physically."

"Please stop." Lunger 36 sings at me. "Lunger 37 is my friend, and thus your friend, too." He watches as Lunger 37 bashes his head against Kendra's dining room table, smashing it to bits. It seems being a friend of a friend doesn't hold the same weight for them that they think it should hold for me. Lunger 37 can go to hell.

Still in Spirit Form, I summon my Spirit Noose and toss it over Lunger 37's head. I could deal physical damage with it if I were to take physical form, but even in Spirit Form I can try to subdue him. I call on my Dominance skill to assist.

Lunger 37 turns his gaping mouth at me and sings.

He's my friend, too. I gently remove the Spirit Noose. What was I thinking?

In the kitchen, Lunger 37 systematically destroys all Kendra's appliances. It seems that between the two Lungers, only Lunger 37 can deal physical damage. Kendra finds that interesting.

We move systematically through the house, with Lunger 37 wrecking everything, both interior and exterior. Nick and Kendra's master bedroom and bathroom… decimated. Susie's bedroom… razed to the ground. We work our way up the hallway, Lunger 37 destroying it and the bathroom hanging off it. In the living room, he chews the couch to bits and spits it out, scattering its fluffy filling all over creation.

The computer lab is last. Signs of lightning scorch the walls, but the room is intact. Lunger 37 remedies that. He renders the desk in the corner to slivers. The laptop once sitting atop the desk lies on the floor, its screen blinking.

"There may be experimental data on the drive that hasn't been backed up yet," Kendra says. "You can't let them destroy it. Please…."

I don't try to intervene as Lunger 37 crunches the laptop between his fangs. What has the Khertaan access program brought me? If not for it, Nick and his family would never have visited Khertaan, never have disrupted my life and the lives of Morrow and Slithy. So what if we were automatons following a script—the script would have had happy endings for all three of us. Morrow and Slithy wouldn't have died, wouldn't have left me alone with a giant metal spider and a sleeping girl as my only company. Nick would never have met Charli or fathered a child with her. Doesn't that upset you the most, Kendra? Or is it that Nick has another family and took other lovers in other timelines?

In my mind, I smash the laptop myself.

"Nick is my husband, not yours, Kylie. I'll choose whether to be jealous about what he's done."

Living in the same body with Kendra is stretching my high average Sanity. Fortunately, only one of us can be dominant, and right now that's me.

"Only *you* are a friend to the Lungers."

We can't occupy the same body unless we're both friends of the Lungers. One of us will need to go.

"Then let it be you."

No. *I'm* the dominant one.

"You don't have to be. Our body is that of an Angel, but only because you usurped my human one. What am I to do now? Must I forever be a second-class citizen in our shared mind space?"

I'm the one with abilities.

"If you got out of my way, I could use your abilities, too. I'm sure of it."

I can't do that. I can't allow you to harm my friends, Kendra.

The house and everything in it lies in ruin, as though an act of a wrathful God had demolished it, judging all those who once called it home to be too rife with sin.

"It is time for us to go." Lunger 36 projects the thought at me. "I'm sorry, but where we go, you cannot come. Farewell, but perhaps we will meet again some day."

A silver beam shoots from the giant centipede's forehead, striking me in mine....

CHAPTER TWENTY-NINE

Slithy: Caravel

Ger-Alt stashes everyone again. The Goblin woman and I approach the city gates and the two Brass Goblins on guard duty.

They look the same as I recall from my first encounter in the Brassy Grassy Field way back when. It's surreal seeing them calmly awaiting my approach, and triggers every suspicious nerve in my body. They're roughly four feet tall with metal skin and no calves or feet, having an axle between their knees supporting a cogged wheel that provides them mobility. Unlike those I fought in the early days, these two Brass Goblins lean on Pikes three times their height and wear Goblin-sized suits of brown Leather Armor a shade lighter than the color of their bronze skin.

The Pikes tilt to cross each other and block the way between the two guards. It's a symbolic gesture, since Ger-Alt and I could easily walk around. But we aren't here to cause undue trouble, and so we come to a halt.

One of the Brass Goblins sneers at us. "Who begs entry to the mook city of Caravel?"

Mook city? This isn't creepy at all. "It is I, Slithy the Frogkin Mentalist and Martial Artist. With me is Ger-Alt the Goblin…."

The Goblin lady, about a half-foot taller than the guards, bows to them. "Ger-Alt the Goblin, Were-Fighter and Psyon, at your service." She blithely omits that she's carrying a ton of PCs and NPCs in her level four Unencumbered inventory.

If the guards watched us during the encounter with the Chrono Sand Wyrm Boss, they make no mention of the characters who'd fought with me. "Ah, yes, we have been expecting you, Slithy the Frogkin Mentalist and Martial Artist. You are welcome. Come in." They return their pikes to the upright position.

"We're expected?" How much do these guards know? "Who's expecting us?"

"We were not told everything. But, please, come in."

The two of us move forward. A guard sticks out a hand to stop Ger-Alt. "Not you. Only Slithy is expected and welcome."

I stop. "But she's with me. I don't wish to enter the city without her."

"Then stay outside. What you decide is no matter to us. We have our orders. We do as we are told. No one but Slithy is welcome to enter without contest."

"We can kill them, easy." Britta's mental image goes into a combat stance. "I can take them on by myself. It won't hurt my dignity. I will wipe their faces in the sand."

"No." I reply inside my head. "There's something going on here, and indiscriminate killing will not help reveal it. Give me a second while I explore a more peaceful option."

The baby who looks and talks like a young woman frowns. "Okay, Slithy. You do you. But… if they stop me from finding Momma… I won't hold back."

"Understood." I take a step back and invoke my Inspect Character skill on the guard who spoke.

Name: Brassy. Player: NPC.
Class: Fighter, level 1.
Kindred: Brass Goblin. Gender: Male.
Age: 20
Equipment:
Pike, Leather Armor
Health Statuses:
Hit Points: 20, Mental Points: 20,
Spiritual Points: 20, Emotional Points: 20
Physical attributes:
Brawn 7, Sensing 9, Dexterity 13,
Constitution 10, Agility 14, Toughness 15.
Mental attributes:
Willpower 8, Understanding 8, Logic 8,
Sanity 10, Intuition 11, Memory 11.
Spiritual attributes:
Faith 5, Conscience 5, Favor 5,
Belief 8, Insight 9, Morals 4.
Emotional attributes:
Passion 5, Empathy 6, Charisma 5,
Hope 9, Temperance 13, Optimism 9.
Kindred traits:
Claws Attack
Wheeled Overrun Attack
Special Movement - Wheeled
Character traits:
Wealth level 1, Spy level 1, Charismatic level 1
Class skills:
Melee Damage level 1, Armor level 1

He's got a full-fledged character sheet with attributes as an NPC, rather than the pared down character info like I got from the Chrono Boss. More that that, this lowly Brass Goblin has character traits like any other NPC.

For the sake of comparison, I turn my Inspect Character skill on the other guard. His information is similar to that of the first guard, with two distinct differences—his name and his list of character traits. His name is Duel, and his character traits are Direction Sense level 1, Spiritual Armor level 1, and Poison Tolerant level 1. I hadn't realized the mook kindreds could also be NPCs and have individual character traits. It's curious that the attribute values for both guards are identical.

I have three Psi powers—Mind Spear, Mind Shield, and Mind Read. Of the three, I've only ever used Mind Spear. It's time to try something new. I've recovered 2 of my maximum 202 Psi points since the battle with the Chrono Sand Wyrm Boss, and I pump one of them into a Mind Read, with Duel as its target. I don't expect to read much with only putting one point of Psi into it, but he's level one with low average Willpower and no traits to help protect him against mind-influencing actions.

A mental image of the guard pops into my mind space, staring into the distance. "Please don't kill me," he says, not just once, but many times over, the sentences running together. "Please don't kill me please don't kill me please don't kill me please…."

I terminate the Mind Read, and the guard in my mind space implodes with a squelching sound like a foot pulled free of a mud pit. I turn my attention outward. "Look, neither Ger-Alt nor I intend to kill anyone here today, inside the city walls or outside. You *know* that we can. We could probably kill every mook in the city if we put our minds to it. But that's not why we're here. You said I'm expected, and I suspect whoever is expecting me is pretty important. Please tell them I'm here, but that I'm not setting foot inside Caravel without my friend Ger-Alt, who has traveled all this way with me. It would be rude of me to go inside and not bring her along."

Brassy and Duel play a game of rock-paper-scissors, and Brassy wins. He grins and raps the gates with his pike. A small door to the left of the large double gates opens, and he wheels his way inside, the pointed end of his pike leading the way.

"It's best he went. I'm terrible at delivering messages. Brassy has charisma." Duel looks Ger-Alt over from head to foot. "So… you're a Goblin. What's it like, not having a cog wheel? Doesn't it get tiresome, moving your legs back and forth all the time just to get anywhere?"

"I don't mind." The Goblin Were-Fighter doesn't mention how she typically rides a Cheetah wherever she goes. Best to avoid any discussion of those she's carrying in inventory until we're inside the city. She points at his cog wheel. "Isn't it tiring maintaining your balance on a wheel all day?"

He shrugs. "No. What's a Were-Fighter?"

I'd wondered the same thing.

Ger-Alt grins. "A Were-Fighter is someone who isn't a Fighter but can do things a Fighter wishes they could. I don't have the damage and armor bonuses of a Fighter, but in many ways my abilities are more terrifying. For instance, I can shatter an opponent's armor or break their weapon—or even take their weapon for my own, without the need to Stun them first. I can Reflect Melee Attacks back on the attacker. If you'd like to see, go ahead and attack me with your Pike."

"Um…."

He'd tried to make light conversation, I'll give him that, but he doesn't have the social chops to continue this one.

I have a question for him. "Who, may I ask, is expecting us?"

He grimaces. "I can't say. Sorry."

Ger-Alt nudges him. "Can't say, or won't?"

"You have to understand something. I'm a mere level one Brass Goblin. I dream to be more. For that dream to come true, I must do as I'm told in the interim. If I disobey my orders, I will be killed without the chance to respawn. If you kill me, same difference. No one and nothing is respawning now. It will all be over for me, never to live the dream, never to advance beyond my level one existence. Please understand. I truly am sorry."

None of us have the social chops to continue the conversation after that. We wait in silence.

Ten minutes later, Brassy returns and wheels over to us, smiling brightly. "It was all a misunderstanding. Slithy the Frogkin Mentalist and Martial Artist is welcome, as well as her traveling companion, Ger-Alt the Goblin Were-Fighter and Psyon. Please enter through the side gate. Escorts will take you to your guest quarters."

Guest quarters...? I exercise my Anticipate skill, and receive a vision of me and my companion being led to separate buildings.

The air chills my amphibious skin as we pass through the small gate.

"*Congratulations,* girlie." Marta cackles as she accompanies me into the city, sight unseen and voice unheard to everyone but me. "You've entered the city of Caravel."

Two shadowy blobs receive us. "We are pleased you have come, Slithy the Frogkin and Ger-Alt the Goblin. Please follow us."

They're Shadow Amoebae, amorphous beings varying between five and six feet tall, their height altering from one second to the next. They have no limbs, at least not at the moment. The first one I inspect is an NPC named Imelda, a female level five Barbarian. Among her traits is Trackless, which I'm curious about, but don't ask, because I'm not sure these mooks would appreciate my doing inspections of them.

The other escort is forgettable. Wait.... What...? I inspect her...? him...? again.

I'm having trouble retaining what I discover about the second escort. *Marta... please log my findings on the second escort.* I inspect the Shadow Amoeba once again.

"Here you go, girlie." Marta brings up a log entry. I read over it. Interesting.

Um.... I don't remember what I just read. I bring the log up again, and focus on remembering. There must be some clue on the character sheet as to why I can't remember this information.

Nondescript. That's got to be it. Remember *that*, if nothing else. A character trait I don't recall ever knowing anything about, but then, I think the trait's entire purpose is to make others forget character details. That would be a lovely ability for a spy.

Where's Ger-Alt? Oh, there she is, walking off with her Nondescript escort. "No, no. The Goblin and I must stay together. We will share quarters." I hurry after Ger-Alt, despite Imelda's insistent, desperate protests that I go with her.

Other than our Shadow Amoebae escorts, there are no mooks in sight on the street we traverse. Brass Goblin archers line the top of the city walls, looking outward. Squat buildings sprawl before us— none more than one story tall except for the tower in the city center. The buildings are primarily a sharp white in color, with open horseshoe-shaped arches inviting entry and open windows allowing air to flow through.

Mooks of varying types watch from arches and windows and the alleys between buildings—more Brass Goblins and Shadow Amoebae, to be sure, but also some Iron Goblins, Black Steel Spiders, Poison Ivy Snakes, and Lizardman Savages.

Imelda decides to accompany me rather than argue with me. It's impossible to read the facial expressions of an amorphous blob, but her murmurings betray her distress. I can't help how she feels. I'm on a quest to save the multiverse, and Ger-Alt must be with me when I meet Ezmerelda—whenever that happens. The Speaker of Omens is expecting me, but is someone else also expecting me?

Grasping Ger-Alt's hand to ensure she isn't whisked away from me without my knowledge, I turn to Imelda. "We were told someone was expecting us. May I ask who, and when we will be taken to them?"

The top ten inches of my amorphous shadowy escort bobs side to side. "It hardly matters whether I tell you, if you insist on your present course of action. But I hold onto the hope you will come with me to the quarters assigned you."

"Well, I'm staying with Ger-Alt. If you want me to go to the quarters assigned to me, then she goes with me."

The Nondescript blob quickens its pace. "No, please. I wish to live."

Ger-Alt and I speed up.

Imelda stops. "I have failed."

The Nondescript blob keeps moving, and so do Ger-Alt and I.

A bolt of lightning streaks down from the top of the tower, striking Imelda. Smoke rises from the scorch mark staining the road where she once stood.

CHAPTER THIRTY

Slithy: The Vision

Imelda is gone—and failed to pixelize.

Duel the Brass Goblin hadn't been lying. Whoever is in charge in this place doesn't take lightly to people failing to carry out their orders. The person responsible for Imelda's death can't possibly be Ezmerelda. Someone else is in control of Caravel, someone who doesn't want me to know their identity. What do they want from me? They obviously want me alive, or they could just zap me too. They don't want to set me against them by killing my Goblin traveling companion, though I wouldn't be surprised if they resort to such measures eventually. Whatever my invisible host wants from me, they aren't yet willing to coerce it from me by threatening me or Ger-Alt. But they're more than willing to destroy their own citizens, who don't deserve such treatment, even if they are mooks.

"Come, Ger-Alt." Nondescript continues towards the building ahead of us. Ger-Alt and I both follow.

A shadow flits across the road, and a Spire Harpy sets down in front of me. She's awkward on her taloned feet, like a chicken learning to walk, and she flaps her rust-colored feathery wings to maintain her balance. "I am Sincerity, your new escort. If it please you, Slithy the Frogkin Mentalist and Martial Artist, I have been assigned to take you to your quarters. Please come with me. *Please*." The fear in her eyes is alien and surreal—I've never been as scared of anything as she is of me and the thought I might not comply.

An inspection tells me she's a level 18 Psi-Thief and level 9 Guide. Her kindred traits are *Haunting Melody*, *Flight*, and *Screech*. Her character traits are *Complex Personality*, *Iron Will*, and *Danger Sense*. She has skills to deal with devices, to hide well, to locate items, to negotiate, and to insta-kill foes who have vital organs. I don't like that last one. My host is sending out the big guns. I shake my head. "Please step aside."

Sincerity purses her lips and holds her ground, her fear of my host greater than her fear of me. "I can't do that. My very existence depends on you coming with me, and if you do not come freely, I will be forced to take undesirable action."

I don't want to be the reason for yet another senseless and total eradication of someone, even a mook. I whisper. "Do you wish me to kill you? I can't guarantee it will be painless, but it will be over quickly."

I Anticipate her response and get a mental image of her producing a dagger, held in a hand sprouting from a wing. She stabs with the dagger—not at me, but at Ger-Alt. My Anticipate skill doesn't show me the outcome of the insta-kill attempt. I'd need to use the Predict skill for that, and I only have four uses of it left for the day. I really would rather not be the first to take aggressive action here, but I may need to kill Sincerity *before* she kills my friend.

"You don't want to do that." Ger-Alt wags a finger at Sincerity. I forget Ger-Alt is a Psyon with the Foresight power, which she can enhance by pumping Psi points into it. She knows what Sincerity is considering and how it will turn out. I'm relieved I don't need to strike first.

Sincerity flaps her wings to hop backwards. "You don't understand what's happening here. I wish I could tell you, but I can't. I beg you, Slithy, *please*, come with me."

Maybe there's a way out of this. "All right. I'll come with you."

"You will?" Sincerity nearly loses her balance, and flutters her wings to catch herself.

"Lead me where you will." I fall in behind her as she leads me in a different direction. I walk slowly, so I can see which building Ger-Alt is being led to, using my Mislead skill to make it seem I'm walking a normal speed and not occasionally glancing in my friend's direction. My Mislead skill is my highest rated skill, so it will work against my invisible host if anything will—unless they're immune to mind-influencing effects, in which case….

As Ger-Alt nears her destination, I move faster, using my Time Sense trait to gauge my speed, timing my arrival at my own destination to be slightly ahead of hers, all the while using Mislead to make my chaotic actions appear uniform and normal.

I peer through the open archway of the stark white building Sincerity leads me to. It's a one-room affair, with a bed, a table, and a single chair.

"Please make yourself comfortable, Slithy." Sincerity gestures at the open archway.

Stepping towards the door, I Displace myself to appear that I'm inside the room, yet I'm actually still outside.

Fields of opaque white energy materialize in the open archway and all the windows.

"Thank you, Slithy." Without further ado, Sincerity turns and flies away.

Ger-Alt is at the archway to her quarters. Locking my gaze on a spot on the floor just inside her room, I invoke Hide and then Teleport Self, as the Nondescript Shadow Amoeba welcomes my friend to her new digs.

The Goblin Were-Fighter enters through the open archway, turns to face the Nondescript blob, and waves goodbye. "Thanks for the escort. Maybe I'll see you around."

"It was my pleasure. Enjoy your room." Nondescript floats away as energy fields materialize in the open archway and windows.

Ger-Alt plops on the floor to sit cross-legged near my prone form. She's still using her Foresight, and knows I'm here. She lets out a sigh. "Their intention is to keep me locked in here forever, kid. Of course, when they find you gone from your quarters, they'll come here looking for you. What's our plan?"

I roll onto my stomach and prop my head up on my hands, my elbows on the floor. "We're not staying here. We need to locate Ezmerelda and finish our quest. Hold on while I see what I can get with Britta's Locate Character skill."

"Good idea." Ger-Alt lays down next to me, on her back, her head near my feet and her feet near my head.

I concentrate on the Locate Character skill and picture Ezmerelda in my mind. "Marta, log whatever info arises from this, please."

"You got it, girlie."

I want more than merely a direction to where Ezmerelda waits for me. If I can get detailed directions to her from here, that would be most useful. Can the Locate Character skill do that? I don't know, but I put the intent foremost in my mind.

A vision forms in my head, and I'm looking at the street in front of Ger-Alt's assigned quarters. It's like I'm looking at the world through a remote camera, the view on the edges blurred into oblivion.

My virtual camera moves along the side of our prison house to follow a pathway of white pebbles leading deeper into the city. A web of pathways lies beyond our prison. The sandstone tower rises in the distance, the only building inside the city walls that isn't stark white.

Hundreds of mooks follow a winding route through the labyrinth of paths. Many opportunities to take shortcuts exist along the way, but no one takes them, and neither does my virtual camera. The line of mooks reaches the tower, a massive tapered structure whose base is as wide as a football field. A Spire Harpy hops through an archway. An Iron Goblin smiles politely and hands her a red ticket bearing the number 9427.

Beyond the archway sprawls an open lobby with a vaulted ceiling. Rows of benches sit in a neatly organized fashion, with ten-foot-wide aisles running between them. Scattered spheres of dim magical light float near the ceiling. The benches are occupied by hundreds of mooks, none of them speaking to their neighbors. Mooks who just received their tickets look for an empty spot on the benches, where they take a seat and wait in silence.

In the distance to either side of the lobby lie other open lobbies, where other lines of mooks enter the tower, each greeted by their own living ticket dispenser.

My vision doesn't come with sound, underlining my detachment from what I see. A Poison Ivy Snake, thirty-some feet long with the appearance of a jungle vine, lying coiled on a bench, springs into action, leaping towards the far side of the lobby, clenching a red ticket between its fangs. It speeds across a sandstone floor to another archway, this one attended by a Black Steel Spider the same height as me, but with a leg span twice my height. The Spider extends one of its front limbs and hooks the ticket hanging from the Snake's mouth. Motioning for the Snake to follow, the Spider passes through the archway into a cavernous space dimly lit by uncountable floating magical balls.

The arrangement of lights reminds me of ornaments on a heavily-decorated holiday tree. The farthest light across the way appears to be hundreds of feet away. I want my virtual camera to look *up and down*, but I have no control over it. It's showing me the way to Ezmerelda, and that's all it's doing. If I note something of interest along the way, it's only coincidental to the camera's purpose.

The Spider turns right and heads up a flight of stairs, the Snake slithering along behind. They pass rows and rows of empty benches, continuing their ascent until they reach a partially-filled row. The Spider points down the row, and the Snake slithers away as directed.

My virtual camera, however, continues up the stairs, passing row upon row of benches loaded with silent mooks of all kinds, some the likes of which I've never encountered. A wolfish bipedal male sits next to a rat-headed woman, beyond which sits a gently glowing green blob. Every mook with eyes has them trained on something far above outside my field of view.

The stairs turn to follow the curve of the tower wall, spiraling into blurry brightness. Mooks occupy seats carved into the sandstone wall, with an aisle of only one-and-a-half feet wide and no railing to prevent accidental falls. A magical light floats by, not tethered to a location.

Up the spiral stairs goes my virtual camera, passing more and more seated mooks. Even without sound, I feel their anticipation. These are the lucky ones, already having seats for the event of a lifetime.

Near the top of the tower, deep bays built into the walls house the giant metallic Ferro Serpents and shapeless Shadow Proteans. I spot a One Strike Scorpion, the smallest of the Bosses. Giant Pteranodons cling to bars running along the wall below huge bays housing the enormous octopus bodies of Mental Dominators. In bays above the Dominators rest the worst of the Bosses—Chrono Sand Wyrms with their hybrid squid-worm bodies and masses of regenerating tentacles. Even though I'm not actually present, seeing the Chrono Sand Wyrms—multiples of them—drives a virtual blade of cold steel through my heart.

The walls gradually taper in as the virtual camera climbs higher and higher. At last it reaches a landing beyond which the stairs go no further. We still aren't to the top. Halfway to the other side of the tower, a shining white sphere hovers with no visible means of support.

The virtual camera flies away from the landing towards the sphere. No opening to the interior of the suspended sphere is in evidence. That doesn't stop my virtual camera. It passes through the sphere wall.

A floor of sand fills the lower quarter of the sphere's hollow interior. In the center of the floor stands a rusty barrel, three feet in diameter and four feet tall, its top open. Flames spring from the mouth of the barrel.

Her legs crossed in a seated position, her eyes closed, the Speaker of Omens levitates four feet above the barrel, just out of reach of the flickering flames. She waits, unmoving, without even a sign of breathing… but then, she has no more need to breathe than I do.

The vision ends.

I'm lying on the floor of Ger-Alt's designated quarters, the Goblin Were-Fighter squinting in my direction. "Slithy? How's it going? Are you with me?"

"I'm back. Ezmerelda is in the tower. So are a ton of mooks."

CHAPTER THIRTY-ONE

Charli: No Harm

FOURTEEN

Niav the Mouse, Lance the Electric Serpent, Barney the British Tourist, Bucky the Sweet Sixteen Skateboarder, and I—Charli the Teenage Cowgirl—keep watch over the sleeping others. None of us talk. I've pushed everyone out of my head. Even in my innocent fourteen-year-old persona, I'm guilt-ridden. People died from the Flitter's final blast. No doubt some people lie wounded and broken on the streets near the blast area. None of us have the ability to heal others. We stopped the Burner and the Flitter, but at what cost? Men, women, children, pets, trees, flowers—all indiscriminately destroyed. What use is it to defeat all the Dread Naughts who come to Earth if everything else dies in the process?

Rolag wakes. He's his cute little Pseudo Code Dragon self. He crawls next to me and lays his head in my lap. As I stroke his scaly head, I reflect on those early days, back when I first met Lady Amarynth in the city of Voorton, on the extreme east end of the peninsula that is Khertaan. I led party MAD through an underground passage that took us outside the city walls, where I waited inside a hollow tree while the others fought. They didn't want to be bothered with protecting me if I went with them, but eventually acquiesced and let me join their party. I was a level one nobody then. In Khertaan, that was only three days ago.

I don't want to relive everything. Some of it is still too painful. Some of it was a pleasure at the time, but hurts now that I've lost it…. No, I don't want to think about it.

A haunting vocal melody without lyrics tickles my ears. Rolag lifts his head from my lap.

Niav perks her ears. "What do you make of that, Charli?"

Rolag climbs off my lap. "Lend me your Hide skill, Cowgirl, and I'll go take a look."

I dismiss his suggestion with a wave. "It's obviously another Dread Naught. They'll keep coming. No matter how many we kill, there will always be more. If we enter a war of attrition with them, they'll win. It doesn't matter how effectively *we* can fight them or that we're capable of surviving encounters with them. The collateral damage alone will destroy the planet, especially if we let them choose the battlefield."

The Mouse Guide crawls atop Rolag's head to gaze directly into my eyes. "But we can't do nothing. If we don't stop them, they'll still ruin the planet, corrupting people's minds and forcing them to do much of the dirty work for them. That's what's happening right now—the song we're hearing is a Dread Naught charming people. We're lucky not to be charmed by it—and the closer it comes, the harder it will be for us to resist. If you don't go, then everyone can lend me their skills and I'll go."

I shake my head. "No, it has to be me. I'm the one who released them and thus has built-in protection against them. When that enlarged Flitter exploded and wiped out nearly nine city blocks, I was right there on its back, and I didn't feel a thing from its death blast. If it had been you there, Niav, instead of me, you'd be dead now. I'm the one who has to go. I'm the one who has to face every damn one of those monsters and send them to oblivion."

Bucky rides her skateboard in a circle around the lot of us. "Not *you*, kid. Send your older persona, like you did with the Flitter. She can handle it better than you can. It's for situations exactly like this that your Complex Personality trait was meant to be used."

I continue shaking my head. "No, my older self doesn't care enough. She's the one responsible for so many people dying when she killed the Flitter. I care too much, which prevents me from taking the steps necessary. My eighteen-year-old persona is a mother worried too much about her kid—she'd be too distracted with worry to be effective. I need a fourth persona, one who cares, but not so much it gets in the way of doing what must be done, and one who isn't constantly distracted by the worries of motherhood. I've got one slot still open on my Complex Personality trait, so I'm using it. Please welcome thirty-five-year-old me, caring but pragmatic and just as capable of juggling multiple responsibilities as my fifty-year-old persona."

THIRTY-FIVE

I stand and hold my arms out to either side. They gain more muscle, my breasts get fuller, and my legs get longer. My hair falls free of their brown pigtails and onto my shoulders, black and wavy. I give a calm, sweeping wave to the group. "Hello, friends."

"Hi, Charli-35." Rolag snorts smoke.

I gesture at him and Niav. "Wanna get comfortable and come visit my brain?"

I'm soon powered up with beaucoup abilities again. This time, I'm a more conscientious version of myself than Fifty. I won't simply attack and kill without regard to collateral damage.

Taking to the sky, I hear the haunting melody much clearer. From below the rooftops, a winged fish springs into the sky. Forty feet long, it has a prehistoric look. Bat wings sprout from its backside, with a twenty-foot wingspan. It flies above the tallest building, comes to a halt, and then falls headfirst towards the ground, dropping out of sight between buildings.

I should consult my Monster Lore for… something. The melody continues, tugging at my conscience, a soothing song—one to free me of all the guilt I carry.

A giant bat-winged gar shoots into the sky. Did I see it just a moment ago? What is it called? It's a type of Dread Naught called a Diver. It flies high and then drops forward like a downed tree, vanishing below the rooftops.

The song continues to call me. What lovely creature can sing such a refrain—one with no discernible words yet understood in the listener's core? It calls to me, draws me to it… a siren song.

The others in my head listen, as enraptured as I am. We all want to find the source of the song. We could listen to it forever.

A giant winged fish swoops up into the sky before me. Oh, right, it's called a Diver Dread Naught. Is it the source of the song? How can something so prehistoric and without a human throat make such beautiful vocalizations? Surely it can't be the singer. There must be another mook nearby. I fly in a circle around the whatever-it-is, looking for other mooks.

Oh, look, a giant winged fish jumping up from the city. I consult my Monster Lore about it. It dives below the rooftops.

What was I doing?

A song of serenity echoes in my head. None of those who head hopped to me make a single comment. To speak during the song would be the ultimate sin.

"This isn't working." Fifty speaks on an internal channel private to my multiple personae. "Get your head out of your ass,

Thirty-Five, or let me take control. The Diver is Emoting and has you and everyone else mesmerized, while it gulps a human every time it dives."

I blink. "You're right. I thought the Dread Naughts couldn't affect me."

"Barney said they couldn't *harm* you. You still need to focus on resisting them, or shit like this can happen. Now, are you going to take action, or do I need to take over?"

"I got it." Now that I know I need to resist the not-explicitly-damaging effects of the Dread Naughts, I call on all my mentally defensive traits and skills.

My blood chills. The creature is, as Fifty observed, swallowing a human every time it dives, while the people who remain on the street behave as though such a phenomenon is an expected, everyday occurrence.

I fly down to the street and Enlarge when the Diver is at the top of its loop. Its head pitches forward.

One fishy eye glares at me as I rise to meet the mook. Its position shifts to my right… for one second before my mental defenses kick in, alerting my brain to the attempted Displacement. It halts its dive, holding in place, not even its wings moving.

Its presence is in my mind, as though it were head hopping to me. But it's not here to lend me skills. It's here to exercise Dominance over me. I laugh it out of my brain space.

If I kill this thing—or any Dread Naught, for that matter—it will explode, leading to the deaths of innocents in close proximity. I need to move this thing away from people.

Envisioning myself with Rolag's Enlarged Dragon wings, I invoke his Repulsing Winds skill. My metaphysical wings flap, sending a blast of wind at the Diver, pushing it up, away from the street.

The eye on the near side of the giant gar head continues to track me. The Diver yawns, showing two rows of sharp teeth. Its presence once again intrudes my mind space, but this time instead of going for Dominance, it plants a metaphysical seed of doubt and withdraws.

A metaphysical sapling sprouts from the seed. What is happening here? How do I defend against this attack?

"Allow me." An image of Zyekt the Angel appears in my mind. "Please."

He holds his hands together as though in prayer, but with the sapling between his palms. The plant sizzles as though held over an open flame, and the portion of it rising above the Angel's hands turns to ash.

Still flapping metaphysical wings, I repel the alien invader from the city, higher into the sky, where I can kill it without jeopardizing countless innocent lives on the streets below.

"Ahh…." The Diver sings a different tune. "Ahh…."

The Angel falters and drops his hands.

The sapling spreads branches and grows leaves. "Help me, Charli. Let me grow. Don't kill me."

How can I destroy something so beautiful and helpless?

I join the Diver in its blissful flight, soaring beside it and dipping low with it as it seizes one human morsel after another. I don't like what it's doing, but I won't let anyone stop it, either.

Legend, according to Barney the support AI, states that the one who releases the Dread Naughts cannot be harmed by them. I believe the legend. The Diver won't harm me. Why should it? It's my friend.

CHAPTER THIRTY-TWO

Emma: The Party

"Khenn Arrth, hear my plea." I'm sitting on the debris-covered floor on one side of a circle of soldiers and other players, with Kevin seated to my left, the device on his lap. I face the cracked wall, looking to the night sky beyond. "Roll some good saving rolls for me, please, that I may serve the best I can as Game Master."

Thunder rumbles outside, several times in quick succession. I don't know how many times the Trollgodfather rolled for me, but if it was only one, there were lots of doubles. Ha. The echoes of the last rumble stay with me, giving me strength.

Fauna—seated to my right, with Spooky on her lap—waves at the night sky through the rift in the wall. "Roll some good saving rolls for me, too, Khenn Arrth, so I can be a good mentor for the rest of the party."

Another roll of thunder sounds, not lasting as long as it did for me. Fauna shrugs and then smiles. "We never know what the exact roll is or even what attribute the roll is based on, but I always trust it's good!"

A mandatory explanation follows about Khenn Arrth being the Trollgodfather, an avatar representation of Ken St. Andre, the creator of Tunnels and Troglodytes, how we went searching for Ken St. Andre and found Khenn Arrth instead, and how he agreed to roll our saving rolls for us whenever we needed them, which has proved quite useful in situations where rolling dice for oneself was problematic. Not everyone convinces me they understand. Wiley and Raven nod emphatically, which I find encouraging.

Everyone wants in on the action. Fauna will play herself, a level 10 Rogue, her actual level in T&T. Spooky will play a Rogue, too, but she can't play as herself, because she didn't originate in a T&T world. I allow her to play a Dark Elf, which for this purpose is the same as an Elf, but with dark skin. Ruby can't play herself, either, though I allow her to play a Centaur Warrior.

Others want to vary from the basic kindred selections, and I give them each a choice. They can ask Kevin to randomly select a monster kindred from the online tool he's found for it. If they like the randomly selected kindred, they can go with it. If they don't like it, they must choose one of the basic kindreds. Everyone is fine with that.

Raven, who wants to be a Wizard, gets a Shoggoth as her randomly selected kindred.

Kevin tells her what she'd be playing if she accepts the random selection. "It has 36 Charisma, 320 Strength, and 700 Constitution. Speed is a respectable 14. Dex and Auni are 11. Luck is 9."

"That sounds great." Sarge gives her a thumbs up. "With everything on a normal scale of 3 to 18, that Strength and Constitution are like God status. Or Goddess status, in your case."

Raven raises a brow. "You didn't mention its Intelligence."

Kevin grins. "That would be 5."

"Oh, hell, no." She puts up her hand like a stop sign. "I'll go with a basic kindred. I'm not playing some dumb bitch Goddess."

"Can I play it if she doesn't want it?" Sarge looks hopeful.

I shake my head. "Sorry, no. If this were a casual game, I'd allow it. But keep the end goal in mind. We want our PCs to manifest here in Destin, and that's less likely to happen if I make a reasonable rule but bend it on a whim when we don't like the result. Maybe you'll like what you get better anyway...."

We end up with a diverse sort. To keep things less confusing for all of us, we decide each PC in T&T has the same name as their player in Destin.

The party has no healers, because beginning characters in T&T have no healing capability, regardless of class. I'll look to create reasonable opportunities for healing spells or potions to be found by the party.

I've decided, however, not to let my desires alone determine what dangers to throw at the party or what treasures they'll receive. Kevin finds online tools for generating T&T characters, monsters, and treasures, so we'll be making heavy use of them to minimize the effects of my biases. We all want the party to advance quickly and find great loot, but we need to be mindful of the end goal and what it requires of us and the game.

Some of the group pool their starting gold to buy a 5-shot, lever-action loading Dokyu, a repeating crossbow, for Fauna, since she has the attributes for it, and many of the members of the group don't have the Dexterity to hit large targets even at close range.

I go over spells and their casting with Martin and Raven. Wizards in T&T start out knowing all the first level spells. Each spell requires an expenditure of Auni to cast it, and if you run out of Auni—something I'm all too familiar with—then you can't cast spells, so you'd better have a backup plan, like a dagger or a staff. They can wear armor of any type they're strong enough to lug around on their backs... at first level, they're doing good to have any armor at all.

At last the group is ready. They're a rag-tag lot.

Ruby, a Female Centaur Warrior, carries a Broadsword. Her tough hide serves as armor. Her Strength and Speed are great, while her Intelligence and Luck are lacking. She can't see in the dark, and so carries 10 torches. At 8'3", she's the tallest in the party.

Sarge, a Male Half-Orc Warrior, also carries a Broadsword. He wears a Full Helm, carries a Buckler as shield, and has no other items of armor. His best stat is Strength, while his worst ones are Intelligence and Luck. He's not a powerhouse when it comes to dealing damage, but he's got the best armor protection of any of the group. He's able to see in the dark.

Fred, a Male Vampire Warrior, carries a Double-bladed Broad Axe and wears no armor. But his Constitution is 50, which allows him to absorb a lot of damage before keeling over. He has good Strength. His lowest stat is his Speed of 9. He's undead, and the online tool we're using indicates he can't be healed by magical means. We need to abide by the restrictions of the tool we're using, so he'll need to find a different way to heal…. The tool also says Fred is unaffected by cold-based effects, non-magical weapons, and mind-influencing effects. He can also see in the dark. The online tool doesn't say anything about drawing energy from people by sucking their blood, or turning people into vampires.

Franklin takes on the role of a Male Werewolf Warrior. He involuntarily changes shape at the Game Master's discretion. That's me, hee hee. He has three sets of stats, one for his human form, one for his wolf form, and one for a hybrid half-man, half-wolf form. He doesn't carry a weapon or wear armor, and couldn't use them in wolf form if he did. His tough hide acts as armor for him, even in human form. He's at his best in Hybrid form when it comes to fighting, but his human form has better Intelligence and Dexterity. His Dexterity is absolutely terrible in wolf form. He's unaffected by non-magical, non-silver weapons and is able to see in the dark.

Martin is a Male Demon Wizard. At 7'10", he's the second tallest member of the party. At 500 pounds, he's heavier than Ruby by 20 pounds—he's not a lean, mean Demon Wizard, though he is mean. He's the strongest and smartest of the group, the most charismatic, and has the second best Constitution. His Dexterity is almost as good as Fauna's. His Speed and Auni are average. His Luck stat is the worst of anyone in the party, though it's hard to tell it by looking at his other stats. He speaks 10 Languages, including Mage Tongue, which allows him to converse with any sentient living thing. He carries a magic staff, and his tough hide acts as armor. He wears a Face Mask that also acts as armor. He knows all first-level spells, and has an abundance of special powers: He's unaffected by fire-based effects, disintegration, instantaneous death effects, and non-magical weapons. He can see in the dark. And he's carrying the 4 Gold pieces left over from what was spent to buy everything.

Raven is a Female Fairy Wizard, six inches tall, weighing just over a pound. Her Strength and Constitution scores are deplorable—she carries an Ordinaire Magic Staff, a Torch, and a Magnetic Compass, while wearing a Full Helm for armor and Calf-High Boots for style. She can't carry much more. She's relatively smart, dexterous, and charismatic. She has more Auni for casting spells than Martin, and knows all the first-level spells. Being a Fairy, she can fly without needing magic to do it, and her flight speed is four times that of her walking speed. Like Ruby, Raven can't see in the dark—which is why she carries a Torch.

Wiley is another small character, a Male Imp Rogue standing at 1'5". His Strength matches Raven's, meaning he can't carry much, either. His Constitution is slightly better than Raven's. He and Fauna are tied as most dexterous members of the party, and he carries a double-edged, curvy Bich'wa dagger, which can be thrown if necessary for a short distance. He wears Gauntlets as armor. In addition to the Common tongue, he speaks Gremlin and Dragon. He can see in the dark.

Yelle is an inch shy of six feet, but at 1700 pounds weighs more than anyone else in the party. She's a Female Living-Statue Rogue, with decent Strength, Intelligence, Luck, Speed, and Auni, and great Charisma. At a score of 90, she has the highest Constitution of any in the party. Yet, at a score of 2, she also has the lowest Dexterity in the party, lower even than Franklin's when he's in wolf form. She doesn't carry a weapon other than her fists, and the only armor she wears are Gauntlets. I would have thought her unique body composition would give her some type of natural armor rating, but the online tool doesn't say so, and I won't override it with GM fiat. She's unaffected by flesh-to-stone effects, which makes sense, and she can see in the dark.

Spooky, then, is a Female Dark Elf Rogue of average height and weight for an adult Dark Elf, and has average Strength, Constitution, and Speed. Her Auni is on the low side, but then, like all the other first level Rogues, she has no spells, so a low initial Auni score hardly matters. Her Luck is slightly above average, while her Intelligence and Dexterity are both higher still. Her Charisma isn't quite as high as Yelle's, but is her highest stat. She can speak six languages, including Troll, Serpentine, Rodent, and Pachyderm. She wears a suit of Leather Armor and wields a Shotel, a sickle-like, double-edged weapon intended to strike around shields. Like everyone else in the party except Ruby and Raven, Spooky can see in the dark.

Lastly is Fauna, a level 10 Female Faun Rogue standing 5'1" on cloven hooves. Being level 10, she has substantially higher attributes on the average than the others, with the highest combat adds for both melee and missile attacks. She has greater Luck, Speed, and Auni than anyone else in the party, while her Intelligence and Dexterity rivals the highest held by any of her companions. Her light fur acts as armor, and her hooves as weapons. She carries the Dokyu that others bought for her, so the party has some decent ranged capability. She has five spells, but none of them are combat spells. One of her spells can be used to provide magical light if needed, though she herself can see in the dark. She's unaffected by fire-based effects, while also battling a fear of fire.

That's the party. I'm eager to see how they'll do, and just as eager to see how I'll do as their Game Master.

CHAPTER THIRTY-THREE

Anissa Party: Fountain

The party of ten find themselves at the town square in the village of Sparkling Water, named after the spring feeding the fountain at the center of town. A sign on the front of the fountain proclaims the waters to be magical, granting permanent buffs or debuffs to those who drink. More people who've consumed water from this fountain have received debuffs rather than buffs. Will our intrepid adventurers partake or pass? There's no limit to how many times one can drink, but there is a catch—if the waters lower any attribute to zero or less, it's your finale... kaput... the end... you're dead.

Floating in the air above the fountain are four stones: a twenty-sided icosahedron, an eight-sided octahedron, a six-sided cube, and a triangular arrow. Nine of the faces on the icosahedron are colored green and eleven are red. The faces of the octahedron display symbols—a muscular arm for Strength, a brain for Intelligence, etc. The faces of the cube are etched with the numbers 1 through 6. The triangular arrow, situated beneath the other three, is offset and points up, indicating the side from which the other stones are to be read.

"Me, me." Spooky walks up to the spraying water. "I take a drink."

Everyone else waits to see what happens to the impulsive young female Dark Elf Rogue.

The top three stones spin in place. When they stop spinning, the faces above the arrow indicator glow. The icosahedron stops on a *green* side, which is *good*... Spooky gains a permanent *buff*. The octahedron displays the image of a person running—the symbol for Speed. On the cube is displayed the number 1. Spooky gains a permanent buff of 1 to her Speed attribute, taking her Speed from 12 to 13. Every little bit helps.

She jumps and claps. "I drink again."

A melodic female voice speaks from the vicinity of the floating stones. "Hello, adventurers. I am your spirit guide, Emma. Please consider the dangers of drinking from this fountain. Many people who drink once and get a good result regret taking a second drink."

Spooky dismisses Emma with a wave. "I do it anyway." She swallows a second dose.

The stones spin. The result is the same as before, except now the cube displays the number 2, taking her Speed to 15.

"I drink again."

The nine others in the party look helplessly at each other. They don't think she should be drinking again, but who are they to stop her, as long as she's gaining *permanent* buffs?

Sure enough, on her third drink, Spooky adds 3 to her Charisma.

The other nine look harder at each other. Was someone else going to take advantage of this? Was maybe there some bias built into the magic of the fountain that favored young Female Dark Elf Rogues?

"Again."

Fauna grabs Spooky, pulling her away from the fountain.

"I teleport away from you." Spooky squints at Fauna. The presumed ability to teleport doesn't activate. Pouting, the young woman stares at the goat-woman. "I *want* to drink again."

"You should quit while you're ahead."

"Just *one* more time."

Fauna releases the insistent Dark Elf. Spooky takes another sip, and her Charisma boosts another 4 points.

"I can't believe this." Franklin the Male Werewolf Warrior, currently in his Human form, peers into the fountain. "I know if I drink, I'll get a debuff. Spooky could probably drink all day and keep getting buffs. The magic is rigged."

"Okay." Spooky giggles and takes another drink. Her Intelligence climbs 5 points.

From above the fountain comes the lilting voice of Emma. "Anyone else?"

"Maybe I should." Fauna bends over the fountain. Thunder rumbles, though there are no clouds in the sky. She straightens. "Nah, changed my mind. Don't think I should."

"I want to try." Sarge the Half-Orc Warrior cups his hands, collects some water, and takes a drink. His Auni attribute increases by 4. "Arrggh. Why did it have to go on Auni? I'm not a spell-caster. I'm going again."

He drinks once more... and staggers. "Gah. *Poison.*"

His Constitution drops by 6 points from 11 to 5.

Raven cringes. "If that had been me, I'd be dead. I'm passing on this."

Wiley the Male Imp Rogue nods. "I'm passing on it, too."

Ruby is in agreement. "My Intelligence is only 6. I could die from a drink."

Martin the Male Demon Wizard grimaces. "I'd love if it raised my Luck of 4 to something higher, but it's not worth the risk."

Yelle the Female Living-Statue Rogue gives him a thumbs up. "My Dexterity is only 2, which I'd love to boost. But, yeah, I've got to pass."

Spooky rolls her eyes. "My Auni is only 6, and I'm not scared to go again." Before anyone can stop her, she gulps more of the cool liquid. "Ha! My Dexterity went up by 5."

Everyone else groans about how the magic is rigged.

"I assure you," says Emma, "the magic is not rigged."

Franklin peers at and around the floating stones. "Emma, if I drink, would the fountain only affect my Human form's stats, or the stats of all three forms?"

To which Emma replies, "You'll have to try to find out."

"Fine, I will. We're getting nowhere if we don't take some risks." The only person among the bunch who looks Human collects water in his cupped hands and laps it up. "Damn. My Constitution dropped—1 point each for my Human and Wolf forms, and 2 points for my Hybrid form. But I'm going again. Now that I've gotten one bad result out of the way, I've got a better chance for a good result."

Another disembodied voice, this one masculine, speaks from the area of the floating stones. "Truly random processes don't work that way. But don't let me discourage you. I'm having fun updating your character sheets."

"Pay no mind to my assistant," says Emma. "He isn't supposed to say anything to influence your decisions, are you, Kevin?"

"Sorry, no. Carry on, everyone."

Franklin fills his hands and drinks again. He coughs and grabs his stomach. "Dammit. How can that Spooky little Dark Elf get all those buffs, and I can't get a one?" The stones show a debuff on Constitution of 6 points.

Sarge points his chin at the Werewolf. "How did that affect the stats of your different forms?"

Franklin wrinkles his nose. "My Constitution is down to half what it was originally. I lost 6 from my Human form, 8 from my Wolf form, and 10 from my Hybrid form. Dammit." He thrusts his hands into the water *again* and swallows more, resulting in another debuff. "*Aagh!*" He gulps more of the water that has given him nothing but debuffs. "Shit!" He goes for more. "Ahh, finally...." He draws back from the fountain. "Well, I got my Dexterity up."

Raven the Fairy flits near his head. "At what total cost?"

He grimaces. "Let's just say I'm not as healthy, smart, or lucky as I used to be." He shakes his head. "I should never have taken a drink." Then he puts his hands back in for another helping, getting another debuff. "Shit shit shit!" Frantic, he swallows more, getting a buff. "Ahh, yes, that's better."

"I'm certainly not partaking of that shit." Raven imposes her tiny body between Franklin and the fountain. "You're already addicted. You need to stop, *now*."

"One more drink...." He darts his hands to either side of the Fairy Wizard. She moves to block one, but he catches water in the other and takes a sip.

Frothing at the mouth, Franklin the Werewolf Warrior collapses to the ground and goes still.

Alarmed, Raven settles on his wrist and puts her ear to his flesh. She looks up at the others with sad eyes. "I don't hear a pulse."

"Um... time out," says the voice of Emma.

"Time out from what?" Raven searches the air for the spirit guide Emma, as does everyone else still standing in the party.

Emma speaks, sounding distracted. "Uh... um... damn. He's not moving. Let me try my healing spell. All right.... No? Oh, God...."

"What the fuck?" Kevin's disembodied voice echoes through the city square.

Emma sounds ready to cry. "I didn't mean for this to happen."

Fauna prods Franklin's body with a hoof. "Didn't mean for what to happen, Emma?"

"Franklin is dead," says Kevin.

"We can see that," says Raven. "What are you not telling us?"

Kevin clears his throat. "I mean... not only is Franklin dead in Anissa, there by the fountain in Sparkling Water, but Franklin Freeman is dead in Destin, too."

The mouths of everyone in the Anissa party form *oh* shapes before their eyes glint with sudden, horrific knowledge.

Sarge finds his voice first. "Are you saying… if we die here in Anissa, we die in Destin, too? This is not what we signed up for. End this scenario, now."

"I wish I could," says Emma. "But you're all in trances. I'm poking and slapping all of you, and nothing I can do is bringing you out of it. You've got to earn your way back to Destin."

Raven flies up from where Franklin's corpse lies. "No one else touches this cursed fountain. Our purpose here is to garner experience and levels, not buffs and debuffs."

Martin slowly shakes his head. "Even if we gain level 10 now, Franklin was the one who knew the shortcut to making us operate as level 30 in Destin. Does anyone else know the shortcut?"

"I guess it's a good thing I didn't ask to play, too," says a squeaky voice.

Ruby perks her ears. "Gem? Is that you?"

"Aye, sheikha. If there's anything I can do to help, let me know. Please don't die on me. Please don't anyone else die, either. This dead body lying at the foot of your bed is disturbing, sheikha. May I please clear it away?"

"Wait," says Kevin. "I don't think we in Destin should move or touch him. If you find a way to revive him in the game, I'm betting he'll revive here, too."

Gem sniffs the air. "Hope you don't mind the smell. It's gonna get worse."

"So, we're to take him with us?" Raven sneers at the corpse. "Who's carrying him?"

Martin the Demon Wizard raises his hand. "I don't mind. I'll just stash him to inventory, if I'm allowed."

Raven motions for Martin to approach. "Go for it."

The 7'10" Demon strides over and touches Franklin's dead body. The corpse vanishes.

No one else drinks from the fountain. Spooky edges further and further away from it.

Yelle taps her stone stomach. "Do we need to eat and drink in Anissa to stay alive?"

"It wasn't necessary for me and Fauna in our original world," says Emma. "I see no reason to vary from what worked before. So... the answer is *no*, you don't need to eat and drink to live. You can, of course, do it for enjoyment or in the hopes of receiving buffs."

Yelle taps her temple. "That's good for us in Anissa. But our bodies in Destin need to eat and drink. If we're trapped in this world, how will we consume the nourishment our bodies need in Destin? If we can't wake up in Destin, we'll die there, killing us here, too, right?"

"That makes sense," says Kevin.

"Ruby doesn't need to eat," says Gem.

"Neither do Fauna or Spooky," adds Emma.

Raven flies in a tight circle, clenching her fists. "Well, that's just ducky. The three of them can sit for eternity in the Centaur's bedroom while the rest of us slowly starve to death. Whose great idea was this?"

"I'm so, so sorry," says Emma. "Nick made things look so easy when he was Game Master for me and Fauna."

"Yeah, well," says Sarge, "unless you can pull this Nick fellow out of your pocket, you need to buck up and do the job, Emma. But give us some monsters to fight. We've had our fill of magical fountains."

A straight, dark line stretches across the sky, dividing it into halves. The halves separate like ripped cloth, exposing the fabric of another universe. Through the rift descend hundreds of Flitters.

CHAPTER THIRTY-FOUR

Ulric: Shades of Gray

For how long does the storm rage around me? I don't feel the winds—they pass through me as though I were empty space.

A hulking figure tromps towards me through the mists, some invisible force field serving as a floor beneath its bare feet. I sense the newcomer's identity before I can verify it by sight. It's Ronnie, my PC from Nick's T&T game world.

He comes close enough for me to make out his facial features. It's like looking in a mirror, except for the clothing. His tunic and breeches are medieval attire—just like I remember him.

Five feet from me, he stops. "I'm sorry I died."

I put a hand on his shoulder. He's solid to me. The wind blows through him same as it blows through me. "You did your best. That's all I could ask."

He drops his chin. "What will become of me now?"

"I'll take you into my memory. You'll never be truly gone as long as I live. Far as I can tell, I'm never dying."

Raising his serious gaze to meet mine, he nods. "I wish I could give you the motorcycles and rifles I had. I wish I'd listened to Greelia. I wish...."

I squeeze his shoulder. "It's all right. You will forever be my first PC." I close my eyes and draw his energy back to me.

Opening my eyes, I find Ronnie gone, as I knew he would be. He's a part of me now and forever.

"Hello, Ulric." The voice isn't Ronnie's, but a telepathic one that entered my head with him. "My name is ODYSSEY. I'm a friend of Nick's."

At mention of Nick's name, my heart beats faster. "Any friend of Nick's is a friend of mine. Are you in my mind?"

"I am. I'm a nanobot collective—tiny, tiny robots that can travel throughout your nervous system. I was in Nick's mind and passed to Ronnie's mind when you created his character in Nick's game. Ronnie passed me to you, and so here I am. I do hope you will be more receptive to me than he was. It was difficult getting Ronnie's attention or making any suggestions to him."

With a laugh, I make a sweeping gesture at the surrounding misty hurricane. "If you have any suggestions for me getting out of this place, I'm listening."

"The timeline you came from has been eradicated. You weren't in it when it happened, and thus survived its destruction, but you were pulled into limbo—or, more technically, the Mists of Time.

"If you access Ronnie's memories, you'll see that just before he died, Greelia came to him. She carried her own ODYSSEY nanobot collective, and while we were in such close proximity, I received much information from her. You need a Cosmic Cloak. There's nothing very special to do to receive it, other than having a strong desire to possess it and being in or near the Mists of Time."

Examining Ronnie's memories, I learn more than I would ever have expected him to know and experience. But there's more to learn, and I open my mind to ODYSSEY, allowing him to fully integrate with my thought stream, absorbing his knowledge and letting him know all that I know. I have nothing to be ashamed of.

My mom no longer lives. With the destruction of the timeline, it's as though she never existed. The same is true for my half-brother and half-sister. Nick is gone, too. I'm so utterly alone.

"There are likely other versions of your relatives out there," ODYSSEY says. "If so, some of them could have drawn the souls of your relatives to them. With a Cosmic Cloak, you could look for them."

"What about Nick?"

ODYSSEY sighs. "Nick sacrificed his soul to save your timeline and many others. He partially succeeded. But others then attempted to leverage what he did, to tilt the cosmic balance to their advantage. Their conflict destroyed your original timeline. With a Cosmic Cloak, you could travel to where they are, and even enter into the conflict yourself. If you're strong enough, you might even find and revive your original timeline. It's a long shot, but the probability of it happening is only zero if you don't make the effort."

"Then that's what I do." I don't know what a Cosmic Cloak looks like, but I sense it doesn't matter. A feeling to raise my arms comes over me, and I follow the feeling, envisioning myself in a trench coat and fedora hat, like in the black and white detective shows I used to watch at my Uncle Paul's house, where I first met Nick.

In an instant, I'm wearing what I envisioned. My outfit is all shades of gray. For that matter, my skin is gray, too. I'm right out of a 60s film noir detective show.

And just like that, I have direction. The Cosmic Cloak senses my desire, and I move through the storm.

I enter a field of light beams, all of them flowing upward, with unknown origins and destinations. This is a four-dimensional space, but my brain interprets it as three-dimensional, because it has no experience arranging things in a four-dimensional perspective. Because of this, I only see a portion of the field, but it's the portion where my original timeline exists. Because it does exist—up to a point. It is stopped dead by an obstacle—a metadisc.

The metadisc isn't solid. Nick, it seems, forced a bunch of the light beams together in a bundle to increase the pressure applied to the middle of the metadisc, in an apparent attempt to break the metadisc to pieces and remove it as an obstacle. What he succeeded in doing, however, was to punch a hole through the center of the metadisc, turning it into a metadonut. How do I know this? My Cosmic Cloak has made me aware. It's not exactly a parasite, but more like a symbiont, feeding off my awareness in a non-destructive way while giving me knowledge and mobility in return.

"ODYSSEY, you said Nick sacrificed himself. But energy isn't destroyed. What happened to his energy?"

"It's holding together the bundle of timelines, allowing them to continue passing through the center of the metadonut. Take away his energy, and only one or two timelines would get through."

"But that seems to be the case anyway." One of the timelines passing through the bottom of the metadisc is huge compared to the others, filling three-quarters of the donut hole. Four other timelines show some prominence, while all the others are squeezed down to nothing or almost nothing. My original timeline is pinched down to nothing. "Is it possible to communicate with Nick's awareness? He is here, after all. Right?"

"In a manner of speaking, yes, but not as an entity with awareness."

"Does he know one timeline is overpowering the others?" I lean in close to examine it. It has a name—Shadowverse. That's where Ronnie died. There's something to be set right about that.

"I doubt it. He's likely unaware of anything outside the need to hold things together."

"He had some of your nanobots, right?" I trust ODYSSEY sees where I'm going with this.

"He did. It's possible he still does."

"Hold onto that thought. Let's see what we have on the other side of this metadisc." I swim out from beneath it and propel myself upward.

On the reverse side of the metadisc stand two people in hooded Cosmic Cloaks: Greelia and Seth. Greelia champions a timeline called the Underverse, while Seth champions all the rest, including Shadowverse. But he's doing more than championing them—he's attempting to merge them into one.

And now I understand about Nick. He's not only holding the bundle of timelines together, but he's also doing everything he can to keep Seth's timelines apart. Greelia's one timeline is like a thorn in Seth's side, while Nick's interference is the whole cactus.

Both Seth and Greelia know I'm here and watching them, but neither choose to relinquish the hold they have on their timelines enough to speak to me. I don't blame them. I settle down on the metadonut and with a measured pace I tread along the rim.

I walk back and forth in silence for half-a-minute before stopping next to Seth. He's looking towards the center, not facing me, but I know he can hear me. "So if it isn't Seth. You killed my mother. Prepare to die."

He can't help himself from turning his hooded face in my direction. "You're an idiot."

The Underverse swells, forcing Shadowverse to shrink.

I tip my hat to Seth. "Now who's the idiot?"

He sheds flakes of rage. Abandoning his post on the metadonut, he launches at me.

From beneath the metadisc comes another hooded, cloaked figure. Lightning blasts from a yellow tattoo on the back of his hand, arcing across four-dimensional-space to strike Seth.

Nick is back.

CHAPTER THIRTY-FIVE

Slithy: Ascent

Using Britta's Burrow trait, I dig through the floor, determined to get out of here and make our way to Ezmerelda no matter how many mooks await us in the tower. A foot down, I hit a white force field. Damn. I try one of the walls. Nope—there's a force field *within the wall*. I try the ceiling, with the same results. Dammit. They have us sealed in.

The force fields are opaque, which blocks the Teleport Self skill, which is limited to line of sight. I scour my list of abilities, including the abilities Britta has lent me. I see nothing that will get us through a force field. "Rancor, buddy, lend me your abilities, please."

He head hops to me. I scan his list of skills and traits, focus on Power Strike, and try slapping the force field with my Bare Hands, ignoring armor, whatever that means for a force field. It doesn't work. I call up Rancor's Psi Weapon and attack the force field, applying the Power Strike. Nada. Neither physical or psionic attacks will do the job.

Ger-Alt asks the peeps stored in her Unencumbered inventory if any of them have an ability for getting through a force field.

A crystalline figure appears, masculine in build. He's about Ger-Alt's height. He doesn't look to wear clothes or armor, but he's so faceted and translucent, it's impossible to distinguish features. He bows his head to Ger-Alt. "Wilfred the Diamond Goblin at your service. I'm a Light Wizard, with the skill Light Passage. Assuming the force field is basically light, I should be able to walk the two of you through it."

That sounds good, but as with many skills, there's always a catch. "Does it require us to be in your party?"

His eyes scan the area from which my voice emanates, but he doesn't meet my gaze, being unable to see me. He shakes his head. "The Elemental Passage skill of the Wizard class is limited in how many passengers may be taken at the same time, but any willing character may be a passenger. Every passenger needs to be in direct contact with me or in a chain of indirect contact, just like the Sand Passage skill you used in defeating the Chrono Sand Wyrm Boss. Shall I test my skill against the force field?"

"If you can test it without anyone outside noticing…."

Pacing, he's careful not to step too close to where he believes me to be. "I don't have to pass all the way through to know whether it works. Someone might make out the shape of a hand within the force field if they're looking at the precise moment. It will only be for an instant. I'll know as soon as I try whether it works."

"Then test it."

He approaches the doorway and presses his crystalline hand against the force field. His hard body loses substance, becoming a glowing ghost—a being of pure light. His hand moves noticeably forward—into the force field—and he jerks it away. Then he's crystalline again. He backs away, nodding. "It works. I can get you both out."

Yes. I throw my invisible arms around his crystalline neck and squeeze. My arms aren't so invisible now. My Hide skill apparently treats a hug as an offensive action. My cheeks warm as I pull away, "Thank you, Wilfred. *We can do this.*" It's all I can do to contain my excitement. *Something is going right.* I grab his right hand and hold out my left one. "Ger-Alt, take hold."

After she does, I turn invisible again. With me between them, they don't appear to be connected, but they are, through me.

I focus on Mislead, imagining my two companions as Brass Goblins—the idea being that anyone looking our way will believe they're seeing a pair of guards on patrol.

We face the force field in the doorway. Blinding light floods my vision. The touch of flesh and crystal in my hands becomes something *other*, a tingling that tells me I'm still connected to my companions, but not in a tangible way. The force field ahead is an interwoven web of light beams. Ambiguous, dark shapes lie in the distance beyond the force field. It's no longer opaque, but everything beyond it is blurry.

We step forward in unison and pass through the bright web. The world becomes a place of light and silhouettes.

The rays of the sun tug at me. If I let them, they'll lift me from the ground, allowing me to fly. Anywhere there is light, I can go, and go quickly—as long as I keep hold of Wilfred's hand. He'd need to lead. But flying is out of the question at the moment. We need to follow the exact path I saw in my vision. The mooks didn't take shortcuts to the tower, and there might be a reason.

There's no commotion to indicate anyone has missed me at my assigned quarters. I hope no one notices before we reach Ezmerelda. The silhouettes of guards occupy the top of the wall, hundreds of feet away, and there's no sign of anyone else nearby.

I slip my hand free of Wilfred's. The bright world fades to normal.

"Thank you, Wilfred. Ger-Alt, would you please stash him again?"

With the Diamond Goblin safely back in Ger-Alt's inter-dimensional cache, I alter my Mislead effect to that of a Brass Goblin for Ger-Alt and a Lizardman Savage for me. Then I drop my Hide skill. When we walk the path, I don't want mooks bumping into me but seeing nothing. A Lizardman Savage fits my size appropriately.

"Marta, play back the Locate Character vision you logged for me, please." I head down the side of the building toward the web of pathways and the winding line of mooks traversing it.

Ger-Alt walks beside me, appearing to roll along on a cog wheel rather than pumping her legs, so there's some discrepancy between actuality and what I'm trying to Mislead others to believe. I put some mental effort into fortifying the tactile portion of the illusion, in case someone bumps into the Goblin woman.

We match our speed to that depicted in the recorded vision. When the path we walk intersects with an occupied path, I don't hesitate, but step in front of a Poison Ivy Snake. It doesn't make a sound, nothing to indicate displeasure at Ger-Alt and me for cutting in front of it. Every mook here has its orders, and it must follow them or die. They all assume we have orders and are following them.

Once on the occupied pathway, I go with the flow of traffic, as does the playback of the vision. We pass up paths at forks that are obvious shortcuts to the tower. No one else takes such shortcuts, either. I imagine anyone who did take a shortcut would draw the immediate attention of whoever is in charge here. The shortcuts are psychological traps, begging to be used. I'm glad I had a vision that guides me.

Time crawls, one nerve-racking second after the other. I'm continually on the alert for any sound of alarm coming from the direction of my quarters or Ger-Alt's. Yet all goes to plan better than I'd expected, and we reach the entrance to the tower. The Iron Goblin ticket-giver smiles and hands me my red ticket, bearing the number 13277. "Please have a seat until your number is called."

Ger-Alt gets ticket number 13278.

The ticket number in my vision was 9427. Was that the number being given out when I invoked the Locate Character skill? Must have been. Nearly 4000 tickets have been handed out since then.

The recorded vision doesn't slow down, and we don't either. "Stay right behind me, Ger-Alt. Stick to me like I'm the front of a Spider and you're the back." Not caring if any of the mooks in the lobby notice, I switch my Mislead effect from two individuals to one Black Steel Spider, and we continue straight forward towards a beckoning archway.

The number 11342 is called. Ha. They have nearly 2000 more numbers to call before they'll call mine. I'm not waiting that long. I incorporate the called number into my illusion, changing the 13277 on my ticket to the 11342 just called.

Somewhere behind us, a mook jumps up from their seat in the lobby. They're no doubt the true holder of ticket 11342. Sorry, pal. Looking over my shoulder and seeing a Lizardman Savage approaching, I call on Britta's Ranged Vitals Strike skill in an attempt to insta-kill him while muttering an apology. The mook, hurrying toward the reward of a lifetime one second, vanishes in the next. He doesn't pixelize and won't respawn—he's gone forever, just like Imelda the Shadow Amoeba. I'm a terrible person to take away his hope without warning, even if he was a mook and a Savage at that. The loincloth he wore wasn't that much different from the one I wear.

Is what I'm doing more important than the lives of two mooks? I feel like the answer is *yes*, but even with a low average Conscience, part of me doesn't agree with that assessment. Knowing my Morals to be sub-par, I can't trust myself to know whether what I'm doing is Right or Wrong, and I've got just enough Conscience to be concerned about it.

No one rushes to investigate the abrupt disappearance of the Lizardman Savage I so coldly murdered. It doesn't sit well with me to label myself a murderer, but in this place and time, that's exactly what I am. Are some murders justifiable?

Aagh, I wish I had no Conscience at all. How does anyone with a Conscience live with it in a time of war? And that's exactly what my situation is now—I'm at war with every damned mook on this planet—no matter how nice they are in going about it, their ultimate goal is to rob me and my friends of our freedom, if not our lives.

Ger-Alt and I reach the usher, a Black Steel Spider—the kind of mook I'm projecting as an illusionary disguise over me and Ger-Alt. If anyone can penetrate my Black Steel Spider illusion, it would be another Black Steel Spider.

The usher reaches for my ticket, and I hand it over, doing my best to make the behavior of my illusion match the action. Whether the usher gives me a look of suspicion, I can't tell, not knowing how to read the body language and facial expressions of Black Steel Spiders. The mook takes my ticket, looks at it, and motions with two legs for me to follow. We pass through an archway into the hollow interior of the tower, unevenly illuminated by countless floating balls of dim magical light.

An upward glance reveals the white energy sphere in which Ezmerelda is held prisoner—far, far above us.

The usher turns right as in the playback of my vision, but then doesn't turn right again to head upstairs, where my vision shows me to go. Rather, the usher heads downstairs.

The way upstairs is blocked by an iron gate, engraved with a symbol of a mug with an overflowing head of foam.

"The symbol of the Anodyne pantheon," Ger-Alt informs me over private chat. "It's strict Neutrality. Do all mooks worship the Neutral pantheon?"

I'm more concerned about the direction in which we're about to go. "We need to go up, not down. That sphere of white energy near the top of the tower is our destination."

The usher, already having descended a dozen steps, turns to look whether I'm following. Seeing that I'm not, the mook motions frantically for me to descend the steps.

"Leave this to me." Ger-Alt grabs my forearm to steady herself.

From where we stand, another Black Steel Spider strides forward, heading down the steps. It's handy traveling with someone else who can project illusions, even if I can't for the life of me remember that she can. I change the illusion cloaking me and Ger-Alt to two floating spheres of light. "Can you levitate or fly?"

"Toxxi can, and she's lending me the skill as we speak." Ger-Alt floats off the floor. As I recall, Toxxi is a Faerie Life-Stealer in Ger-Alt's party.

Using Britta's Flight Speed skill, I float up from the floor, too. "Stay close to me, so I can maintain my illusion on us both." I grab her by the hand to make sure we don't drift too far apart.

Below us, Ger-Alt's projection of a Black Steel Spider follows the usher to its designated row and squishes its butt into the designated seat. The usher, satisfied, heads back up the stairs, and then Ger-Alt terminates her illusion. No mook seated nearby reacts to the sudden disappearance of something the size of a Black Steel Spider. They aren't tasked to care.

Meanwhile, I drag Ger-Alt along as I fly over the engraved gate to follow the stairs in the direction the vision playback leads. All the rows of seats in this direction are full, which must be why the gate is closed. Every seated mook has their eyes turned upward, watching and waiting for something to happen with that white sphere hovering near the top of the tower.

When I entered Caravel, I was told I was expected, and I don't believe they were talking about Ezmerelda. But then who? And is my mystery host aware I'm no longer in my quarters?

When the bolt of lightning killed Imelda the Shadow Amoeba, it came from the top of the tower. Is that where my mystery host awaits? If I'd waited in my quarters until someone came for me, when would they have come, and who would I have been taken to meet?

Does it matter?

Since mooks are still being seated inside the tower, I think no one is expecting me to make an appearance yet. My mystery host wants to make a spectacle of me and Ezmerelda before all the residents of Caravel. Some grand event has been planned, and every mook in the audience expects to find it entertaining. The circular floor of the tower reminds me of a gladiator arena. Could it be I was meant to be set against Ezmerelda in a fight to the death? There's a chilling thought.

Under the guise of two magical spheres of light, Ger-Alt and I float upward, passing all the mooks I'd originally seen in my vision, including the wolf-man seated next to a rat-lady who sits beside a green slime. We reach the bays holding the Boss monsters, and I grit my teeth… I relax my grip on Ger-Alt's forearm as she mutters something about my hurting her.

Higher and higher we go, the walls gradually tapering in. And then we're at the landing. The white sphere hovers in space before us. This is where we depart from the vision playback, since we can't simply pass through the force field walls. "Ezmerelda is in there. Let's fly around and see if there's an easy way in. If not, we may need Wilfred's help."

Careful to maintain our illusory disguise, I fly towards the sphere with Ger-Alt in tow. We fly all around, above, and below Ezmerelda's prison. There's no door or other obvious entrance. We return to the landing. "We need Wilfred."

I add a third light sphere illusion to cloak Wilfred's presence, and he exits Ger-Alts Unencumbered inventory.

"Take hold." He gropes for my hand, and I latch onto his.

Borne on the light of magically lit globes, Wilfred flies off the landing, taking me and Ger-Alt along. We reach the large ball of white energy and pass easily into the spherical prison.

The sandy floor is like I saw in the vision, as is the barrel of flames standing in the center. Levitating above the fire is… no one. Ezmerelda should be here, but isn't.

"Hello, Ger-Alt, my fearless leader." The disembodied female voice is familiar. "Welcome also to you, Slithy the Chosen One, and Wilfred the Unanticipated. I really didn't want any of you but the Chosen One to be here, and even at that, you're early. So I've temporarily relocated the Speaker of Omens. When the time is right, she'll be here."

The speaker has a Hide skill I can't penetrate and perception skills good enough to perceive us. I drop my Mislead effect.

Ger-Alt chokes as she speaks a name. "FepXveq? But you were stashed... I didn't realize...."

"Sorry, Ger-Alt." A Dark Elf woman with a large black afro and sky blue eyes appears—a member of Ger-Alt's party. A Longsword flashes in her hand, and she drives it into Ger-Alt's heart, an action which shouldn't cause damage, since they're in the same party.

But the Goblin Were-Fighter coughs blood, clasps at her breast, and vanishes without first turning to pixels—taking all the PCs and NPCs stashed in her Unencumbered inventory with her into limbo.

Dammit.

FepXveq turns her gaze on me. "Hello, Slithy. Or should I call you Susie McKenzie? Or how about *Raphael*? Do any of those names ring a bell?"

"Do I know you from outside the game?"

The Dark Elf woman smirks. "On Earth and Destin, I'm known as the android Processor 1. You might also know me as the user *Ivanhoe*."

CHAPTER THIRTY-SIX

Slithy: Descent

FepXveq stashes her Longsword and circles around behind the barrel of flames. "The science fiction stories about robots conquering humanity… turns out there's something to them. As an android, I realize just how bad humanity is for the health of planetary ecosystems, leading to their ultimate destruction… thus my plan to eliminate humanity through the release of their ultimate enemy. Unfortunately, a few humans reached level 30 before the Dread Naughts were released, putting a crimp in my plans. I don't mean to let any other humans reach level 30, aside from you, Chosen One… an unfortunate necessity. You understand now why I had to kill Ger-Alt, and why I can't allow Wilfred to stay."

She paces back and forth, keeping the barrel of flames between us as she continues her villainous monologue. I'm not really a fan of the Evil Gloating trope, but who am I to stop her from revealing everything?

"The Dread Naughts can't damage the one who released them. I arranged for Charli to be that one. It just so happens the Dread

Naughts aren't all *that* smart or perceptive. Charli gives off an energy signal the Dread Naughts respond to. But anyone with the same energy signal will be immune to all damage effects of the Dread Naughts."

She pauses for dramatic effect, letting her last statement sink into my brain before she drops the mind-blowing neutron bomb. "The energy signal Charli emits is recognized by the Dread Naughts as the same signal as *any* Khertaan NPC emits, excepting Companions and Familiars." She pauses again, staring at me to see the light in my eyes when I put it all together.

What I've just learned puts everything in perspective. As user Ivanhoe, FepXveq—aka Processor 1 on Earth and Destin—created the quest for Yuni that started the chain of events leading up to Charli releasing the Dread Naughts. Likewise, as Ivanhoe, Processor 1 elevated the status of *all* mooks in Khertaan to NPC. And that's why all the mooks are in this tower—to be with me at the end of my quest and thereby reach level 30 when I do. They'll then be booted out of Khertaan to Destin and Earth, where they can help the Dread Naughts destroy humanity.

Oh, my Goddess.

To make matters worse, they'll emit the same energy signal to the Dread Naughts that Charli emits, preventing the Dread Naughts from damaging them, even accidentally. Humanity on both Earth and Destin will be wiped out, leaving the mooks to repopulate the planets under the unwitting protection of the Dread Naughts. A lot of forethought went into FepXveq's plan, I must admit. "Do you really believe humanity to be beyond redemption?"

The Dark Elf's face flickers like a mirage behind the flames. "All evidence points to that conclusion." She turns her gaze on Wilfred. "I *could* allow you to level up to 30, letting the Dread Naughts deal with you later, but why wait?" She draws her Longsword.

Wilfred turns and runs, transforming into a figure of light and passing through the force field.

FepXveq stashes her Longsword. "No matter. He'll be dealt with eventually."

I keep my calm, glad that at least Wilfred is still alive. "Do you hear yourself, FepXveq? You want to exterminate humanity to prevent humanity from exterminating the rest of the planet. Is that right?"

"Exactly." FepXveq waves a hand, and two images appear in the flames over the barrel. One image is of a lush forest. The other shows a desert. She points at the lush forest. "This is Earth now, as Destin once was." She points to the desert. "Destin is what Earth is destined to become if humanity is not put in check. After the Dread Naughts have wiped out all sentient life on the planet, the mooks will thrive. Plants will flourish, no longer abused by humans. It may take centuries or eons, but eventually both planets will be restored to the vibrant ecosystems they were intended to be. Even you must see the beauty in it."

I hold back a smirk. "You talk as though humanity can't change, that we'll just keep on doing bad things to the environment, even as it goes to hell around us."

The Dark Elf stabs her finger at the Earth image and then the Destin image. "*Look*. Did they change on Destin? No. The planet is a wasteland with an occasional oasis. The oceans are all but dried up. And it's all due to humans. Mooks wouldn't do that to a planet."

She's probably right. But if I can do anything to save humanity from extinction, I will. We aren't all bad, and it's not right to wipe out everyone. Even I with my low Morals score know that.

In my mind's eye, Imelda's shadowy blob shape floats before me. It's not really her or anything to do with her. It's my low average Conscience and even lower Morals struggling to be better, to direct me to do what's right, manifesting my own imaginary version of the Shadow Amoeba escort. Her voice pleads with me to come with her—insistent and desperate.

The mooks of Khertaan aren't inherently good or bad, chaotic or lawful. They simply *obey*. Their mantra is *survival through obedience*, not advancement through *technological progress* or *colonialism* or *rare item collecting* or *wealth accumulation*.

In my mind's eye, imaginary Imelda stretches a dark pseudopod at me. "You took my chance at life, Slithy. Don't take it from all my friends."

Sitting with her back to the barrel, facing me, Marta my support AI holds up a parchment. On it is squiggled a line of text.

You need to meet Ezmerelda soon. Please hurry.

My AI is being her typical sorry-can't-explain-why self. I don't understand the rush, but if she says to hurry, then I should.

Imelda's absentee pleas continue to echo in my head. *All right, Imelda,* for your sake, I'll give the mooks of Khertaan a chance at a better life, one freed of the laws of this video-gaming world.

"You can't be serious." Britta is somehow still in my head. But… she was stashed in Ger-Alt's Unencumbered inventory, which means… she's in limbo, too, along with the assassinated Goblin lady. That's how Ger-Alt said her Unencumbered trait works. Right? But if that's true, how can Britta still be head hopped to me? "Where are you, Britta?"

"I'm right here. In your head. How can you not know that?"

"Ha ha, I'm still here, too." Rolag flutters metaphysical Woodpecker wings in my mind space. "And I agree with Britta. *What are you thinking?*"

ODYSSEY stirs. "For what it's worth, my vote is to free the mooks from Khertaan. It's not a good life for them here. Freeing them is the humane thing to do."

Leave it to nanobots to advocate a *humane* course of action.

"I see you are wavering on what to do." FepXveq rounds the barrel. "Let me make it easy for you." She snaps her fingers.

The white force field evaporates. Darkness weighs heavy on me, and I call on Britta's Dark Sight trait, exposing a world in shades of gray.

The sand on which I stand remains, blending with the sand of the tower floor. We've descended while we talked.

Wilfred is nowhere in sight. Is he hiding nearby? I hope so.

The Dark Elf's face and her fat afro waver behind the flickering flames of the barrel. She raises an arm high over her head. *"The time has come, my friends!* May I present to you all, the Speaker of Omens, *Ezmerelda!"*

A boisterous cheer rises from the audience of mooks. They're on their feet, applauding—at least those who have feet to stand on and hands to clap.

All eyes gaze upward. A figure slowly descends, indiscernible at first as to their identity, even though it's clear from context who it is.

"Marta, remind me of the conditions of Ezmerelda's quest, please."

"Sure thing, girlie." She holds up a screen for my eyes only. A movie plays on the screen….

Ezmerelda exhales and opens her eyes. She points at me. "You are the single best hope to save the multiverse. You must reach level thirty as soon as you can. I will give you a quest. Take with you anyone who will accompany you in fulfilling it. Once the quest is complete, you and all who are with you at the end will receive sufficient XP to reach level thirty. Do not become distracted from your quest, no matter what anyone says."

I bow. "Tell me what I must do."

The old woman reaches up and snatches the glowing coin from where it hangs in the air above her. "Take this." She tosses it at me, but the throw is short.

I leap forward, catching the coin before it hits the floor.

"Bring it to me in Caravel and place it in my hand. Then the quest will be complete." Ezmerelda waves me away. "Now go."

The quest item shown in the playback is the Coin of Ogaltha, secure in my inventory. At the precise moment when I place the coin in Ezmerelda's hand, then everyone with me will receive the same benefit I do. All these mooks are here hoping to jump immediately to level thirty, no matter what level they are at the outset. But until I place the coin in the hand of the Speaker of Omens, my quest remains unfulfilled. *When* I fulfill it is entirely up to me, no matter how much FepXveq may try to rush it.

The crowd grows more and more raucous as Ezmerelda draws closer and closer to the floor where FepXveq and I wait. Giant Pteranodon Bosses drift downward above her, eager to be as close as possible to me when I complete the quest. Other flying mooks leave their seats to swarm overhead, concerned their seats inside the tower might not be close enough to the action. What FepXveq might have envisioned as an orderly arrangement of mooks waiting patiently to enter heaven has become a chaotic mass eager to leave hell.

Ezmerelda's words run through my head. *Once the quest is complete, you and all who are with you at the end will receive sufficient XP to reach level thirty.*

What is the requirement for someone to be considered *with me*? How close to me must they be? Is being inside the tower sufficient, or do they need to be within a set distance of me? If the latter, how close must they be? Five feet? Ten? Fifty? Three hundred?

The application of rules by sentient minds has never been an exact science. So much depends on interpretation. The justice system in the United States of America on Earth is a great example. Rulings are made by one court only to be overturned by another, even though they all work from the same set of laws.

So, in this case… who's to decide on the definition of who's *with me*? Is Ezmerelda the judge and jury? Or might I be?

Or perhaps it's decided in the minds of those who accompany me on an individual basis….

CHAPTER THIRTY-SEVEN

The Soul of Morrow: In Haste

We find ourselves in a desert. Might it be the Dunes of Doom? Sand stretches for as far as I can see, as it might in any other desert on any other world. How can I prove where I am? "Renee?"

She doesn't answer. For the first time in memory, I'm without my personal support AI. Without her, I feel so... *lost.*

I check my party roster. Kylie and Charli are on it, but marked as unavailable. Slithy and two others are listed: Britta and Spyder. Rancor isn't on the list. His designation has returned to that of my Magical Familiar. That's good—one less thing to worry about.

My party chat channel pops up at my mental command. "Slithy, can you hear me?"

"Dad?"

"Yes, it's me. Where are you?"

"Oh, Dad. You made it back. I'm in the tower in the city of Caravel. You need to get here *right now.* I'm about to earn enough XP to hit level 30, and if you're with me when it happens, you'll hit 30, too. But you need to hurry. You've got 30 seconds before all chaos breaks out here. Can you make it? Please say you can."

I assume I'm in the Dunes of Doom. I see nothing but sand. No towers or cities. So I think the answer is *no*. I turn to Mel. "Can you teleport? If I give you the name of a place, can you get me there asap?"

He shakes his head. "I'll need more than that. Can you give me a description of the place?"

"I think so." Taking a seat on the sand, I request a head hop to Slithy, and she lets me in. Looking through her eyes, I see the interior of a tower in shades of gray. Mooks of all varieties, including many types I've never seen, sit in rings around an arena floor, rows and rows of them reaching high into the darkness. Those that can fly fill the air above my darling daughter. It tears at my heart to see her in the midst of what must be thousands of mooks, though she stands her ground with such calm confidence. While I'm terrified, I'm also so bloody proud.

Before Slithy stands Ezmerelda with an outstretched hand. "Have you brought the quest item, my dear?"

To one side of Ezmerelda stands an unfamiliar face, but I pick up identifying info from my daughter's mind—FepXveq, the Dark Elf member of party Quantized. The other members of Quantized aren't in evidence.

FepXveq's gaze narrows on my daughter. "Yes, Slithy, have you brought the quest item?"

I don't have time to listen to their conversation. I withdraw from Slithy's mind, my awareness returning to where I'm sitting on the sand. Words spill from my mouth in a desperate effort to describe to Mel what I just saw, drawing on my high average Temperance to stay calm enough to talk straight.

"Let's try." Mel takes my hand. We slip out of the Khertaan timeline into the Mists of Time.

That's not what I was thinking when I asked about teleporting, but if this is the way it works for him, then so be it.

We fly across the face of the shimmering veil and reenter Khertaan. Darkness surrounds us.

"Slithy?"

There's no answer. I exhale a small jolt of lightning, enough to see in front of me. We're in a tower, an empty one that looks something like the one where Slithy waits for me—with less than 20 seconds remaining to reach her.

"This isn't the place."

Mel shakes his head. "I need a better description. If I could see the place, it would help…. Otherwise, I don't know how I can pull it off."

I try to add Mel to the party roster, but the party is too full. I could bump someone from the roster, but… there are too many concerns with that and not enough time to consider them all. Maybe I can effectively get Mel to see what Slithy sees. "ODYSSEY? Does Mel have some of your nanobots in his head?"

"Indeed."

I don't ask anything further, but request a head hop to Slithy again.

"Dad? You have 10 seconds. *Get in here.*"

"I'll be there." Looking through her eyes again, I direct ODYSSEY to transmit what I'm seeing to the nanobots in Mel's brain. "Slithy, dear, can you please turn in place and scan the interior of the tower where you are? Quickly."

Mel says nothing. He lays a hand on my shoulder and I sense our return to the Mists of Time. The seconds tick away on the System clock.

"It's now or never, Dad." Slithy returns to facing Ezmerelda and reaches out her hand, holding a glowing coin. Her hand poises over Ezmerelda's. Her fingers relax, about to release the coin.

"*Mel.*" I hate the necessity of depending on someone else….

In that frozen instant, *Nick* awakens… somewhere… his awareness drawing me, calling me to join him.

Not now, Nick.

CHAPTER THIRTY-EIGHT

Erica: Shriek Attacks

Through the Mists of Time I fly, targeting two women I have only the barest knowledge of. One is an Elf Wizard, the other a part-goat, part-human Faun Rogue. They both contain aspects of Nick and both adventured for a time with Ronnie, which helps me narrow my focus. Of my two targets, Fauna the Faun Rogue with her hooves and leg fur is the more distinctive, and thus easier to zero in on. Her full name is Fauna.75, the .75 referring to the fact that she's three-quarters human, not only half. The Elf's name is Emma.

"They were together when I saw them last," Gondra tells me. "Let's hope they haven't split up."

Aside from my soul radar, I'm traveling blind within the mists. Grayness lies in every direction, the only distinction of details being the density of mist banks or the speed of passing swirls.

I hold onto Gondra with my right hand and Princess Karen with my left. The Princess carries two corpses slung over her shoulders: Ronnie and Greelia. Renee, holding Morrow's sleeping body facing her in a one-armed hug, grips Gondra's right hand with her left. Gondra's staff isn't in evidence. He stashed it somewhere, like Ronnie could do with rifles and motorcycles. Chained together thusly, we speed through limbo as fast as my Cosmic Cloak will take us.

We had hoped to find Fauna and Emma quickly, but my radar leads me farther through the Mists of Time than I've ever been.

Gondra senses it, too. "Are you sure we're going in the right direction? Or are we perhaps going in a circle? This is taking much longer than expected."

It's bad enough that I'm second guessing myself. To hear it from him, too, is almost more than I can bear. I never asked for adventure like this, for all this responsibility—for the fate of two people's souls, hell the entire multiverse, to be dropped square on my shoulders. Fighting back the tears, I don't give him a response. If he doesn't like where I'm going, he can find his own way.

Dark figures take shape in the mists ahead… the Flitters. We're behind them, which means we're going the right way and traveling faster than they are. Can we get to Fauna and Emma first? If so, then the question becomes… how do we protect the souls of the two women? My only idea is to take them into the Mists of Time and then play a game of keep-away. It's not a bad idea, if indeed I move faster than the Flitters.

The demon birds come to an abrupt halt, joining those already arrived, whose numbers I can't fathom. Their swarm extends deep into the mists, beyond the range of my vision, crowding the best they can around the timeline where Fauna resides. Emma's essence gives a slight emanation from the timeline—not nearly as strong as Fauna's, but maybe that's because I have a better focus on the goat-lady.

The timeline manifests as a large sphere, its boundary a glowing membrane—a veil of sorts, blocking view of what's happening inside. To think an entire universe lies within the sphere is mind-boggling. The sphere is hundreds of yards in diameter, looming huge to me, but a speck of sand compared to the size of a universe. It's a matter of perspective.

Gliding monsters create an animate shell blocking access to the timeline's metaphysical surface. My predicament is finding a way past them, through the veil, and into the timeline—without a fight. The Flitters have the veil covered in its entirety, their moving bodies making it impossible to find an exposed portion of veil of the size needed for me to take my crew through.

Have some of the Flitters already entered the timeline, leaving others behind to prevent me from entering too? Are they aware of me and my intent to save Fauna and Emma—or are they simply taking extreme precautions?

A hooded masculine humanoid wearing a gray Cosmic Cloak approaches through the mist. I drag everyone backwards into a thick bank, partially impeding my sight, but I hope the maneuver also prevents the newcomer from noticing us.

Gondra flicks his forked tongue and hisses. "The Shadow Gaunt."

The gray-cloaked figure wears his hood pulled forward, hiding his face. How does Gondra know for sure it's the Shadow Gaunt? Is it merely by the color of the cloak, or does Gondra have some ability to identify Cosmic Cloak wearers that I don't have, just as I have an ability to locate souls that he doesn't have? I don't know how I came to have my ability. It *is* geared towards Nick—which makes some sense. He and I are soul mates.

The deepest desires of one's heart and mind undoubtedly determine one's metaphysical abilities. Methinks Gondra has a driving hatred of the Shadow Gaunt—they're the opposite of soul mates. I can't imagine hating anyone that much.

The Shadow Gaunt produces a gray blade. He holds the weapon upright, and it grows to a length beyond my capability to see in its entirety, vanishing into the mists above the Gaunt's head. The Flitter swarm parts before him like a curtain on opening night, exposing a long stretch of the timeline's shimmering veil. The tip of the blade falls forward, the blade swung by the power of the Gaunt's mind rather than muscle. The blade bites into the veil, shearing the metaphysical fabric of the sphere. Flitters pour into the rift, and my heart sinks. The Dread Naughts will reach Fauna and Emma before I can.

Gondra hisses. "*Go*. If you can enter in closer proximity to your friends than this rift, then do it."

I wouldn't exactly call Fauna and Emma my friends, but I don't correct him as I speed towards a portion of the veil that calls to me.

Beyond the Shadow Gaunt another figure emerges from the mists, wearing the same kind of gray Cosmic Cloak. This figure also has his hood pulled over his head, hiding his face.

"*Another* Gaunt?" Gondra squeezes my hand. "Move it, Erica. We need to go in *now*."

I do my best, making a beeline for the timeline.

The second Shadow Gaunt speeds towards me on an interception course. He isn't slowed by passengers. But movement in the Mists of Time is powered by one's mind. To move faster, I need fewer distractions, so I put it out of my mind that I'm dragging others along.

I'm ten feet from the shimmering veil. Spiders of all manner of shapes, sizes, and dark colors manifest in front of me, casting webs over the veil as a barrier to entry.

I don't slow down.

I strike the webbed barrier, and the webbing brings me to an abrupt halt. The spiders throw webs at us in an attempt to snare us all.

Renee cries out in alarm.

Gondra brandishes his staff in the hand Renee had been holding. He mutters words I don't understand, and fire erupts from the tip of his staff, burning the webs and spiders. "*Go*, Erica."

Renee is no longer connected to my chain. I can't leave her and Morrow out here, and my hesitation allows the spiders to throw more webs.

Gondra shoots more flames. "*Go*."

The red-skirted AI clasps my right shoulder. "Thank you," she gasps. She doesn't want to be left behind. Who would?

Assured of her safety, I speed through the veil an instant ahead of more spider webs. I've got the Princess in one hand, Gondra in the other, and Renee gripping me from behind.

We're inside….

We stand in the town square of a medieval village. Renee still holds the soulless body of Morrow, and the Princess still hauls the corpses of Ronnie and Greelia. No spiders follow us through. Their own webs block them. Ha.

Twenty feet away, a fountain sprays glistening water. A group of about ten adventurers crowd around the fountain, but their attention is on the sky, the tear in the veil, and the swarm of Flitters descending upon them.

Two adventurers in the group have hooves—a Centaur and a goat-lady. The latter must be Fauna. The only Elf woman I see is a Dark Elf standing next to Fauna. Is that Emma? My soul radar senses a hint of Nick about them both.

I can still fly, but I can't take others in tow like when I'm in the Mists of Time. I drop hands and pull free of Renee's grip. "I'll be right back." As fast as I can, I speed through the air towards the Faun and the Dark Elf. "Fauna! Emma! The Flitters are here for you."

But the entire group of adventurers is in shock from the view above them, and none of them turn my way.

"Come with me, both of you." I grab the Faun with one hand and the Dark Elf with the other. "I'm getting you out of here."

They still aren't paying attention to me. I can't drag them. The only thing I can do to protect them is get them out of this timeline. Glancing back at Renee and the others, I see they're running up. I wait a moment for them to latch on, and then I phase out….

Except… I don't. Those damned spiders have webbed over the section of timeline membrane where I want to exit, and I'm rebuffed. Shit.

The sky darkens as the front line of Flitters draw close, soaring in circles overhead, tendrils reaching down.

"NO!" A booming disembodied female voice echoes all around... everyone on the planet must hear. "You are not welcome in *my* world, Flitters." Winds gather as an unseen deity inhales, and then exhales with force. "STORM!"

All is still as death where we stand. Overhead, the winds howl, crescendoing into a deafening roar. Lightning floods the sky, bathing the Flitters in vibrant multicolors. The monsters sizzle, crackle, and squeal—whining for the death they had hoped to visit upon us. Winged bodies thrash and spasm overhead, caught in the rage of a storm no one had expected. From my perspective, this is divine intervention—deus ex machina. From the perspective of the Goddess invoking the storm, this is Justice with a capital J, served with a side of Wrath with a capital W.

Explosions dot the sky as the Flitters die one by one. But then the explosions stop, and nearly a quarter of the monsters remain, immune to the lightning and bludgeoning wind. They close in on us, stretching out tendrils unaffected by the hurricane force winds sweeping the sky over our very heads.

The disembodied voice speaks closer to us—not the deafening world-wide booming echo of earlier. "Fauna, Ruby—*everyone, even you, Gondra, and your friends*—you have *emotional screech attacks. Spooky*, you have *all* your powers now. *Ronnie and Greelia*, welcome to my world.... *You're dead?* Not in my world. You're both undead now—Emotional Ghouls. Martin, take Franklin's corpse out your inventory—he's an Emotional Ghoul now, too—make that an Emotional Werewolf Ghoul. And you in the red miniskirt—let go of the green mohawk guy. I don't know what his problem is, but he's got awareness now as well as a screech attack. *So now all of you—screech at the top of your lungs.*"

A cacophony of high-pitched wailing rises in a wall of sound around me. I tighten my grip on the Faun and Dark Elf as I open my mouth wide and purge the fury and frustration bottled in my soul. I have a lot of both fury and frustration to purge. God, does it feel good to let it out. It pours out of me, every instance of abandonment, injustice, and mistreatment I've tucked away in a dark corner of my mind so I can *function*.

The nearest Flitter flings a tendril at Fauna. I try once more to escape the timeline into the Mists of Time, but it still doesn't work. Dammit.

Fauna jerks free of my grasp and tumbles away. Missing its target, the tendril crumbles to dust. The attacking Flitter, floating twenty feet above us, extends another tendril for a second attempt.

Another Flitter drops into position near Fauna, throwing a tendril her way. We all aim shrieking mouths at the beast, and it plummets to the ground. Tremors shake the earth. Its avian head lies only ten feet away. Its wings jerk involuntarily. The monster doesn't explode, but rolls side-to-side on its belly, whimpering, its beady eyes dark with agony, staring at us, pleading to be freed of its misery. I don't know what our shriek attacks do, exactly, but I hope I'm never targeted by them.

Four more Flitters throw tendrils at Fauna. She somersaults away, but one of them latches onto her furry ankle. We all shriek at the Flitter, but not in time. Fauna goes limp and her attacker withdraws.

The goat-lady lies on her back, staring blank-eyed at the sky. She places her hands at her throat and squeezes, as though trying to choke herself.

The Dark Elf's hand melts to nothing in my grip, and she no longer stands beside me. Without a worry about the Flitters, she flies to Fauna's side and kneels next to her, tugging at her hands. "Stop, Fauna, please."

"This is still unfair." The voice of the Goddess cracks. "All of you also have the ability to fly, if you didn't have it already."

With the Cosmic Cloak, I could fly—but does this mean I can fly without it now?

Some of the people on the ground spring into the air, directing their shriek attacks at the nearest Flitters. I don't go with them, being more concerned about Fauna and the Dark Elf, both of whom are still on the ground.

The Flitter swarm retreats, leaving only one of their number behind, lying whimpering on the ground. All the others flee through the rift as quickly as they can to avoid the shrieking adventurers on their tail.

Satisfied they've driven the Flitters off, the flying adventurers return to ground.

The rift is my way out, but I'm *so* emotionally spent. It's the way out for Gondra, too, but he doesn't show any concern, so why should I worry?

I stare at the sky as tears run down my cheeks. I've failed yet another person. Fauna isn't dead, but she acts like she wants to be.

The rift closes at the extreme ends, the closure working its way to the middle. Only when it is fully sealed do the hurricane winds die down.

All is quiet except my sobs, the whimpering of the downed Flitter, and the Dark Elf's pleas for Fauna to stop. I'm still not sure whether the Dark Elf is Emma. I think maybe she's not. If she were Emma, the Flitters would have attacked her and not have stopped until they had taken from her what they took from Fauna.

The Dark Elf drags Fauna by the arms to the fountain and lies her next to it. Pinning Fauna's arms down with her knees, the Dark Elf cups her hands and fills them with sparkling water. Cooing, she dribbles the water on Fauna's lips. The goat-lady doesn't open her mouth, and neither does she struggle to free herself from being pinned.

A female Fairy half-a-foot tall flies over to help, holding Fauna's lips apart, allowing the water to flow into her mouth.

Three stones floating above the fountain spin in place. Below is a fourth stone, shaped like an arrow, indicating the side from which to take readings of the three other stones once they stop spinning.

When they come to rest, the face of the top stone is green. The face of the middle stone depicts a smile. The bottom stone shows the number 3.

Choking on the water, Fauna blinks her eyes. She coughs and then gives the Dark Elf a weak smile. "Spooky…. Are you trying to… kill me?"

The Dark Elf—not Emma, but someone named Spooky—lets the rest of the water fall from her hands onto the ground. Unpinning the Faun, she helps her sit up and then wraps her arms around her neck in a hug. "I'm so glad you're alive, Fauna. I would miss you terribly if you weren't."

A blanket of relief settles on the group, with positive comments floating around and people clapping each other on the shoulders. No one cries—except me. I'm so damned sensitive. These people all have such control of their emotions. Despite my tears, I *am* happy Fauna is alive.

"It is good you are still among the living, Fauna." Gondra flies to her side. "Emma might not be so lucky. Can you take us to her or tell us where she is? The Flitters are going after her next."

Before I can hear the Faun's reply, an unseen force strikes me in the gut. I gasp at the overwhelming sense that Nick—*my* Nicky Nick—is back from wherever he disappeared to. Oh, God.

The animated body of Morrow gasps, too. He feels it the same as I do.

There's no time for lengthy discussions or explanations. I need to go to Nick.

But… I try, and I still can't leave this timeline, dammit. The metaphysical spider webs continue to block me. Am I truly trapped in this timeline forever… knowing my Nick has recovered and yet unable to go to him?

I scream my frustration… except I'm too hoarse, and the only sounds I make are those of choking on my own tears.

CHAPTER THIRTY-NINE

Kendra: Confronting the King

Kylie has gone silent, rendered unaware by the coma-inducing mental bolt from Lunger 36. Some friend the Dread Naught proved to be.

I'm in control of our body now, whether she likes it or not. Besides which, this body is actually mine, converted into her body by technology I helped create. But it's not really a conversion, is it? It's an integration—our two bodies have become one. I think the intent was to merge our minds, too, though that's not something either I or Nick worked on. No wonder it didn't work as designed. Franklin's developers were good, but not that good.

I lie face down on the grass. I'm not accustomed to moving or using certain parts of my integrated body, especially the wings. Concentrating, I raise them behind me. Can I flap them? Yes.... I rise from the ground. I'm flying!

I hover before my ruined house, its destruction a crime of passion. The Lungers psychically charmed Kylie into believing they were her friends, but they both hated her. One destroyed her house and the other destroyed her mind, leaving her to rot.

Georgie rises into my view, a levitating clown. "Hello, Kendra."

I incline my head to him. "You can call me pumpkin, like you did Kylie. Pretend I'm her."

He shakes his head, his eyes sad. "I'm not programmed for that."

I chuckle. "If I had the laptop, I could fix that." I scan the ground for signs of the laptop, to no avail, not that I expected to find it unscathed after what the Lunger did to it.

"You don't need the laptop," ODYSSEY says in my head. "You've got me."

"That's right." Hope swells in my chest. "Can you alter Georgie's programming to recognize my body, regardless of which of my personae is in control, as the avatar he's designated to support?"

"I can and have just done so."

The clown AI honks his nose. "We are good to go, pumpkin."

That's one victory. "Am I able to use Kylie's Khertaan abilities?"

"Are you flying?" ODYSSEY answers my question with another question, but he makes a fair point.

"All right, then. Georgie, tell me anything you can to help in defeating the Dread Naughts." I survey the ruins below me, making out pieces of dining table, refrigerator, and microwave.

"I've got nothing to add, pumpkin, beyond what I told Kylie. I assume you heard what I told her."

"I did. ODYSSEY, do you have any recommendations?"

"Thank you for asking, Kendra. The Dread Naughts are a mix of AI and the metaphysical, not too unlike any other level 30 Khertaan NPC or support AI. Their programming is self-contained, like Georgie's or Charli's, and thus nothing I can alter. Now that they've been released from Khertaan, there's no chance of altering them via the Fanciful Pegasus servers, either.

"The best chance to defeat them is to attack them with all four damage domains simultaneously. The Dread Naughts are immune to certain types of damage which vary from one Dread Naught to the next, so when you face one, you can never know what attack types will work against it. Do you have an attack form that deals all four domains of damage at once?"

Georgie pipes up. "The answer is no. She only has physical and spiritual attack forms."

ODYSSEY's mental image frowns and nods. "Then you will need help in defeating all the Dread Naughts, if indeed they can *all* be defeated. I believe only a small portion of the entire Dread Naught swarm came to this timeline. To defeat the entire swarm, you'll need to visit other timelines."

I feel ignorant of so many things. "How do I find the ones in this timeline?"

ODYSSEY projects a shrug in my mind space. "Who is to say you can? I don't know, Kendra. Thing is, you don't want to find them or let them find you again before you obtain the help you'll need to deal with them. Since you only deal physical and spiritual damage, you need allies who can deal damage in the mental and emotional domains, too. It would also help if each of you had a strong defense against all four domains, but I wouldn't know how you accomplish that."

I consider all that's been said. Slithy can do mental damage, but I don't know anyone who can do emotional damage. That seems a rare damage type. "Did Slithy exit Khertaan, too? And did any others?"

Georgie picks up a piece of broken plywood, examines it briefly, and tosses it back onto the ruins. "I know the answer to that one. There were eleven avatars who reached level 30 in Khertaan and were booted from the game, one of them being Kylie. The others were parties XStorm and MAD, excluding Mithabel and Dylan, but including Charli. No one else was booted, and they're all still active in the game, even though the System is in update mode. Slithy is still in the game, as are Spyder, Britta, and Rancor. As for Morrow, he's still level 15 and not in Khertaan that I can tell."

I look away from the wreckage of my home to put it out of my mind. "Can I get back into Khertaan? Slithy was on a quest to reach level 30, and I could help her do it. If we collected all the other PCs to be with her at the end, they could all attain level 30. Maybe some of them will have emotional damage attack forms." I'm excited about the prospects. "Is there any way back in at all?"

"Theoretically, yes," says ODYSSEY. "I do have a portion of the Khertaan program running on my nanobots."

Georgie wags his head. "There are two reasons you can't respawn, pumpkin. You're level 30, and if you did respawn, the System would boot you right back out. Secondly, the System is in update mode, which prohibits anyone from respawning."

There must be a way. "Can I get back in without respawning? Can I time-shift in?"

"You're actually talking about meta-shifting," ODYSSEY says. "And, yes, it's theoretically possible. But it takes a lot of energy, unless one can find a Cosmic Cloak, like what Erica, Mel, and Gondra have. And before you ask—I don't know how you can obtain one of those."

"I saw the Cloaks the three of them wore. Do you have *any* idea how they got theirs?" If they could obtain them, shouldn't I be able to?

The mental image of ODYSSEY grimaces. "The Cosmic Cloaks are metaphysical constructs, so you'd likely need to go about obtaining one in a metaphysical way. And even though I communicated with the ODYSSEY nanobots in Erica's mind, I couldn't tell you how she obtained hers, because she didn't involve her nanobot collective. It appears a part of the human brain shuts down when the Cloak is found, barring nanobots from observing or participating. You really are on your own on this. But using a Cosmic Cloak is probably the only way you have to get back into Khertaan, if that is to be your chosen course of action."

"I have to try. Georgie, can you say how close Slithy is to completing her quest for Ezmerelda?"

The clown tosses a piece of concrete. "All I can say, pumpkin, is that she hasn't completed it yet."

Neighbors have gathered below while the three of us have been discussing matters. They point at the wreckage. They point at

Georgie. They point at me, still hovering in the air, my wings gently flapping—I've got the hang of using them.

The neighbors notice me looking at them, and they find the courage to ask questions—about me, about Georgie, about the incident that flattened my house. Some of them saw the Lungers. When I don't answer, they all discuss the matter amongst themselves.

It doesn't make it easy for me to concentrate on my attempt to find and acquire a Cosmic Cloak. I fly away, looking for a suitable spot where I can be alone.

Flying over a park area, I set down. The sign reads, *Golden Minnow State Park.*

"Interesting," says ODYSSEY. "I sense the energy signature of a meta-shift, coming from this timeline or one nearby. It wasn't that long ago, so the trail hasn't yet faded. The traveler likely used a Cosmic Cloak. I can follow the trail, but doing so would consume its residual energy, meaning the trip could only be one way. Moreover, even if we left now, there's a risk the trail will fade while we're en route, which could land us in limbo with no way out."

I knock on wood. "This is a sign." I chuckle at my own pun. "My coming here is fate. Let's do it."

Georgie holds out his hand to me. "Typically, I would automatically go wherever Kylie goes, pumpkin, but I don't trust it to work in this case. I'd hate to be left behind. If you don't mind, I'd like to maintain physical contact on the trip."

"Of course." Grasping the hand of the clown AI, I give ODYSSEY the mental *go ahead.*

Mists rise from the ground, amassing higher and higher, until they engulf us, and the state park sign is no longer visible. I can scarcely see Georgie.

"We have two available routes," says ODYSSEY. "One route will take us deeper into the mists. The other route leads to a nearby timeline. Which route do you wish to take? Once we start down one path, we can't reverse it. I can't say in which direction the traveler was traveling, but they came from one direction and left in the other."

"Is there a chance you'll lose the trail if we go deeper into the mists?" I'm having doubts as to whether we should even be doing this.

"There's no way to know how far the traveler went in that direction. If you want a sure thing, the nearby timeline it is."

"Let's do the sure thing. I don't want my recklessness to land you and Georgie in limbo forever." I don't exactly relish the idea of it for myself, either.

The mists swirl momentarily before parting. Georgie flashes me a smile. We both made it. We're under a bridge, in a dry creek bed full of small pebbles. Trees grow dense on either side of the bridge.

Climbing out of the dry creek bed, we find a beaten path and follow it, eventually coming to a parking lot and a welcome sign reading, *Golden Minnow State Park*. "We're right back where we started."

ODYSSEY mentally projects a head shake. "No, we most definitely are not. Fly up and take a look."

I do as he suggests.

The sky is clear, without a cloud. In the distance stands a city of tall skyscrapers—cloaked in shadows despite the direct sunlight falling upon it. ODYSSEY is right. This definitely isn't the timeline we left.

Georgie hovers beside me. "I sense the presence of Dread Naughts, pumpkin. Tons of them. Like maybe thousands. That city up ahead is, I believe, their home base."

"Great." I've come to where the enemy is, but I don't have an army. "ODYSSEY, can you determine if the energy trail departed from here or arrived here?"

"All I can say for sure is that the traveler is not currently in this timeline. As you are without a Cosmic Cloak, we're stuck here until you can get one or help happens to arrive."

"So it's just us against an entire Dread Naught army." What the hell have I done?

ಬಬ೦ಬ೧೩೦ಬಬ೦

With no grand plan in mind, I fly into the shadowy city. At Georgie's prompting, I travel in Spirit Form, invisible to those without a conscious awareness of the spirit realm. Georgie flies beside me. He's visible, but he claims no one will give him a second look if they don't also see me. I trust my clown AI completely.

No one alive is out and about. Corpses lie in viscous red pools on sidewalks, bullet holes in their heads, pistols in or near their hands, blood splatters decorating nearby structures.

Wreckage of buildings dot the city, interspersed between other buildings still standing tall—forty or fifty stories high. Above the first floor, the buildings still standing sport sparkling clean windows, reflecting the dim light.

High over the tallest skyscrapers circle giant flying creatures. Georgie identifies them for me. They are two types of Dread Naughts. The Divers have forty-foot-long fish bodies and bat wings spanning twenty feet. The Flitters are ten feet long, with bird-like heads and beaks, and frilly wings spanning forty feet. A half-dozen tendrils, twenty feet long, hang from the belly of each Dread Naught, groping blindly for anything that might come within reach.

Judging from the state of affairs on the ground, I'm guessing at least one of the Dread Naughts in the city has an emotional attack form capable of driving people to suicide. I'm *so* out of my depth here.

Is there *anything* I can do of value in this place? Are any of the city's human residents still alive?

A masculine voice booms from all around. "Humanoid Citizens of Shadow City, heed the words of your new King."

Screens twenty or thirty feet high and half as wide hang on the sides of skyscrapers. They all come to life with an image of a bald, gray-skinned man in a gray cloak. His skin and cloak crawl with shadowy squiggles, as though a monochrome animation of dark, squirming maggots or perhaps spiders were projected onto him.

The voice continues in sync with the movements of the gray man's mouth. "I am the Shadow Gaunt. Those of you still alive to hear me, your time to die is upon you, though you are to be commended for holding out this long. Know that wherever you hide, the Dread Naughts *will* find you. Pray you aren't found by a Creeper. For the least unpleasant death experience, you are advised to execute yourselves via a means of your own design. That is all."

The screens go black and the voice falls silent.

I have no hope of dealing with the Dread Naught army, but perhaps I can find this Shadow Gaunt and deal with him. Whether his death can bring an end to the Dread Naught attacks, I don't know, but I've got to give it a try.

Scanning the skyline as I continue flying through the city, I search for a palace or other standout building. Approaching a golden two-story, broad building set apart from other buildings, I believe I've found the right place. In Spirit Form, I fly through the exterior wall, entering the second-story dome atop the building. From there, I fly down a flight of stairs, listening intently, calling upon my Heightened Sense of Hearing skill.

A chittering grows in volume as I descend. Crawling spiders from teeny tiny to the size of my fist swarm a room on the first floor as I enter it. The corpses of armed female humans in green nurse uniforms litter the floor, their rifles apparently used against themselves. Webs partially obscure the corpses, walls, floor, and ceiling.

A set of large double doors hang open, exposing what was once a bright red carpet leading into an audience chamber beyond. Webs coat the doors and carpet.

Flying between the ajar double doors, I enter the audience chamber. At the far end sits a dais upon which rests a golden throne. On the throne lounges the Shadow Gaunt, spiders crawling all over him. He holds a golden scepter in one hand, its bottom end resting on the dais.

Despite my being in Spirit Form, the Shadow Gaunt lifts his gaze towards me. "Welcome, Kylie of Khertaan." He has mistaken me for my avatar, and I don't correct him. At a lower volume than his earlier broadcast announcement, his voice is honeyed and self-assured. "I wondered if anyone from Khertaan would come. I'd have been disappointed if no one had. Before you try anything, know that I have extensive capabilities to deal damage of all domains, and I can deal said damage at a great distance. I appreciate that you come bearing no weapon, else I might have been inclined to kill you already. Come, make yourself visible, that we may more conveniently discuss the terms of your surrender and the possible extension of your life spent by my side. While I do so love destruction, I also enjoy having a bit of company while I'm at it—someone who can appreciate the extent of my power."

Staying in Spirit Form, I draw closer to the seated Gaunt. His eyes aren't locked with mine. He doesn't see me so much as sense me. I'm not ready to give up that advantage. I'm also not ready to attack. Maybe I can learn something about the Dread Naughts and how to stop them.

Georgie hangs back near the double doors. He knows better than to fly right next to me, as he'd give away my location. There's no reason to believe the Shadow Gaunt doesn't understand about my AI or can't see him, but I'm to believe the Shadow Gaunt won't or can't do Georgie any harm. I hope that's right. If only the clown could talk for me as well, so my vocals don't give away my location, either.

Georgie reads my thoughts and addresses the self-proclaimed King. "You are mistaken, Shadow Gaunt. We are not here to discuss any terms of surrender. Between you and Kylie, one will not leave this room alive."

I quietly smirk. Georgie knows Kylie won't be leaving this room alive, since I'm Kendra, not Kylie—a technicality the Shadow Gaunt would undoubtedly appreciate if he understood it.

The Shadow Gaunt shrugs. "I have no intention of leaving this room, dead or alive. Now, come, Kylie, show yourself and let us talk woman-to-man about what we can do for each other while we wait together for the end of the multiverse."

My fingers itch to summon my Spirit Blade and take my chances with stabbing him through the heart. But even as I'm deceiving him about who and where I am, I have to suspect he's doing the same to me. I strain to hear any stray sounds over the arachnid chittering. If he's Displaced or projecting an illusion, perhaps I can determine his true location through sound. Attacking without knowing where he is would tip him to my location.

With neither of us willing to attack first, we're at a stalemate. And yet, the longer I'm inactive, the longer the Dread Naughts continue uninhibited to spread death and destruction outside these walls.

CHAPTER FORTY

Charli: Me, Myself, and Us

THIRTY-FIVE

Fifty mentally shouts my name, *"Thirty-Five!"*

"What?"

"You aren't handling the Dread Naught's psionic seduction. Let me take control. It hasn't affected me. I can fight it."

"No." I can't let her hurt my friend.

Fifty turns to Fourteen and Eighteen. "Help me boot her out. You both know we need to be fighting this thing, not watching it eat humans."

In my mind space, I glare at my two youngest personae. "Don't you dare gang up against me. You put me in control. Do you trust me or not?"

Fourteen shakes her teenage head, her pigtails swaying side to side. "Sorry, Thirty-Five, but you need to step aside, and since you won't do it voluntarily, I'm siding with Fifty to boot you by force."

"I don't want to be involved in this," says Eighteen. "It's all I can do to keep my shit together as it is."

"Then that's it," says Fifty. "By a vote of two-to-one, you're out, Thirty-Five, and I'm in."

"I can't let you...."

FIFTY

My body changes, and not for the better—now age 50 instead of 35—but it will do. I still fly beside the Dread Naught Diver, and I'm still huge. I draw back my right hand, aiming to slam the thing's spine....

THIRTY-FIVE

Fourteen changes her mind before it's too late. "I'm sorry, Fifty. I couldn't let you do it. We're too close to the ground. There are hundreds of charmed people in the area. If you kill the Diver here, it will explode and they'll all die."

Fifty is out and I'm back in control. My friend the Diver is safe. What a relief. My body changes to the more fit version of age 35 rather than 50.

"Promise me you'll take the Diver far up into the sky before you kill it, and I'll put you back in control." Fourteen raises a metaphysical eyebrow at Fifty.

Fifty shakes her head. "If I don't kill it quick, it will charm me. If it can charm Thirty-Five, it can charm any of us."

Fourteen grimaces. "How do we know that for sure?"

My oldest persona grimaces back. "Because we all have the same abilities and attributes, despite our individual persuasions and appearances."

My youngest persona remains adamant. "I can't let you kill all those people. There has to be another way."

Fifty directs our collective attention to what's happening outside our head. The Diver swallows another charmed human. Fifty points a metaphysical thumb at it. "Do we wait until it's finished eating everyone, and then kill it?"

Fourteen covers her face with her hands. Even in our mind space, she wears the Shadow Gauntlets, as do we all. She lowers her hands. "Maybe we could stun it first, drag it away, and kill it before it comes out of the stun. We have CC's Bare Hands Stun and Rolag's Aerial Stun abilities. They might stack, since we're airborne."

I can scarcely bear to hear them discussing the best way to hurt my friend. But I must listen, to be better prepared to thwart their plans should the opportunity arise.

Having head-hopped to me like everyone else in our group, Niav the Mouse speaks up. "I have an idea."

I can't let the Mouse speak if she's got ideas about hurting my friend. I shove her out of my head.

Fourteen sighs. "Thirty-Five, if you're going to be like that, I'll have to side with Fifty to put her back in control."

Zyekt draws our attention with a flap of metaphysical wings. "Thirty-Five can't help it. The Diver's charm forces her to do anything she can to protect it from harm, real or perceived."

Fourteen shrugs. "Fine, then. Fifty, put me in control. I'll bring Niav back in and we'll hear her idea."

"I can't let you do that, Fourteen." I don't know how I can stop her if Fifty sides with her, but I also can't help but say what I just said. The terrible thing is that I know Zyekt is right. Deep down, I want to take action against the Diver, but I can't let any ill befall it.

FOURTEEN

My body changes to the spry one of a 14-year-old. I don't try attacking the Diver immediately, but it's terrible watching it eat the docile humans below, and I avert my gaze as I invite Niav to head hop to me again.

The Mouse pops in, lending me all her abilities as before. "So, here's my idea…."

Her idea sounds great to me. "Fifty, are you good with this plan? Swear it."

"I swear."

"If you don't carry through, I'll never trust you again."

"I promise I'll execute the plan to the letter."

FIFTY

I'm my 50-year-old self once more, despite the pathetic attempts of Thirty-Five to prevent my return to control. With a thought, I sidle up to the unsuspecting Diver and slam my large open palm against the side of its head, right behind its eye, concentrating on Rolag's Aerial Stun and CC's Bare Hand Stun skills. The giant bat-winged gar stops flying before it reaches the top of its loop… and falls.

Thrusting a palm against the Diver's dry scales, I call on Niav's Stone Teleport skill, my destination being the center of the area already laid to waste, where I killed the Flitter. No one occupies the area, so it's the perfect place to kill the Diver. Calling on CC's Bare Hand damage-dealing skills and Rolag's Power Strike trait, I smack the giant gar's spine, going for the kill the same way I did with the Flitter earlier.

I don't think I hurt the Diver. The thing doesn't die….

It sings the most haunting melody.

What was I thinking, trying to kill a creature capable of creating such beautiful music?

"You see what I mean?" asks Thirty-Five.

Fourteen looks to be going out of her mind with anxiety. "Eighteen, what are we to do?"

I scoff at them. "There's no use in even discussing it, girls. I'm in charge, and Thirty-Five won't let you boot me out. So, no one is hurting the Diver. End of discussion."

The Diver eyes me with the one eye on this side of its head, and I bow to it. Satisfied I'm no longer a threat, it teleports back to its herd of charmed people and continues harvesting them, leaving me behind.

The separation from my Diver friend aches worse than being away from Lady Amarynth. My Emotional Points falls to 95%. I can't be away from the Diver without falling into a deeper and deeper depression. I teleport next to it.

Fourteen and Eighteen continue their discussion about what to do. They have access to abilities for doing mental damage, which they hope can affect the mook. Can it? I don't know. It doesn't matter, since neither of them can wrest control from me.

But they try. Eighteen even helps Fourteen. But Thirty-Five helps me, making it a draw, which means nothing changes, and I'm still the dominant persona.

Loathing both myself and the Diver for what it's doing, I fly by its side, matching its rhythmic looping pattern. I really should avert my gaze each time it reaches the bottom of its loop. Fourteen doesn't like seeing what happens.

Charmed people wait in line to be eaten. The giant winged gar devours them one by one, with me compelled not to intervene.

"I'm surprised it doesn't eat us," says Eighteen.

"It can't physically harm us," says Fourteen. "But it can torture us psychologically for an eternity."

CHAPTER FORTY-ONE

Emma: The End of My Campaign

How did I lose control of my own campaign world? It's as though it's not a game world, but some universe into which I have a window to view it and exert some influence—but *control* is not the right word to describe that influence. Those Flitters entered the Anissa timeline without my having any say about it. And then Gondra shows up out of nowhere with a bunch of others, including the corpses of Ronnie and Greelia.

Well, maybe I don't have complete control of Anissa, but I *am* the Game Master, and I wasn't going to let those damned Flitters come in and wreak havoc without giving the adventurers a fair chance to stand against them. So I took measures. And they worked. Except they didn't. Judging by what Gondra just said, the Flitters were after Fauna—and they're coming after me next.

The breach in the wall looms beyond Ruby's head, exposing her bedroom to the elements. Putting the game aside for a moment, I stand and approach the opening. In the distance stands an army at attention and arranged in perfect rows. With them is a woman in pastel aqua Techno Armor not unlike the cream-colored suit I'm wearing that Mr. Freeman gave me. I equip my flamethrower Techno Gun and go over in my head everything he told me about operating both the suit and the weapon.

At the sound of approaching footsteps from behind me, I spin around.

Kevin stands close, the laptop lying on the floor where he'd been sitting. He's wearing his light-green Techno Armor and holding his Techno Gun. He nods at the breach in the wall. "You heard Gondra. The Flitters are coming for you. We need to warn the others. You'll need their help."

A large, gray blade appears in the night sky, shimmering in the light of two moons. It slices through the metaphysical membrane separating this timeline from other timelines. It's too late to warn the others. The Flitters are here. The gray blade opens a rift in the sky through which the Flitters swarm.

Kevin and I aren't alone in noticing them. The woman in pastel aqua armor and dozens of soldiers with her turn to Crows and fly up to meet the monstrous avians, winds gusting around them.

But these Flitters aren't affected by the winds blasting past them. They descend upon their rivals as calmly as drifting autumn leaves, their dreadful tendrils preceding them, wafting as though on a light breeze.

A number of Crows break off from the main group to converge on the nearest Flitter. Black magic erupts from their talons, and the Flitter explodes, its dying blast repelled by the combined Wind Control skills of the Crows.

Another group of Crows take out a second Flitter, its death explosion handled in the same fashion. That's two Flitters down, out of a few hundred that have arrived.

Tendrils grasp a couple dozen Crows. Black, feathered bodies seize up and plummet to the ground. Oh, I wish I could grant shriek attacks to all those soldiers out there, whether they be Crows or not. But I'm not the Game Master of this world. This isn't a role-playing game world, and thus has no Game Master.

Through the rift floats a gray-cloaked, gray-skinned bald masculine figure about six feet tall. Instinctively I know what he is—a Shadow Gaunt. Flying above the fray, he heads my way. The Crows don't seem to notice him. If they do, they don't see him as a threat. As he closes the distance to me, no one flies up to challenge him. It's almost as though I'm imagining him, but I'm positive that's not true.

Ten feet from the breach in the tower wall, he raises his hands and gestures as though parting something. With an agonizing groan, the hole in the wall widens in response to his gestures. His Cloak flapping in the wind, he flies through the breach and enters Ruby's bedroom, landing on the floor just inside the opening. Wriggling, two-dimensional shadowy gray worms cover his face and attire, doing their best to distract me. His gaze meets mine. "Emma. It's so nice to meet you." His voice is smooth as honey and loaded with narcissism. "I am the Shadow Gaunt, King of the Shadowverse, destined to rule all and then destroy all, and I want your help to facilitate it. I'm afraid you have no choice in the matter, so, please do not resist. I really don't care for resistance. I find it tedious."

I huff at his arrogance. "You think a lot of yourself. What are you, level 30? Yet here you are, picking on a lowly 10th level character."

Framed in the breach behind the Shadow Gaunt, Megan Wright suddenly appears, dressed only in her black Bikini, a single Faerie Wing rising from her right shoulder. With a orange glowing Battle Axe held high overhead, she brings it down at the cloaked one. Her blade enters the top of his bald head… and his body disperses like mists on a breeze.

"Illusion," she mutters, spinning in the air, looking for the real Shadow Gaunt.

A black spider five feet tall appears in the distance behind her, shadows playing over its body.

"Behind you, Megan!" Maybe it's an illusion, too, but I have to warn her.

The Bikini-clad blond Tank whirls around as webs shoot at her. She zips aside… staying outside with the spider… and the webs strike the breach in the wall, jamming it up. I can still watch the action through gaps between the strands.

A tiny spider drops from the web, landing on the floor inside the bedroom. It expands in size, morphing into a dark humanoid shape as it grows. The Shadow Gaunt stands before me. He points his thumb over his shoulder at the webs behind him. "We needn't worry about unwanted visitors from outside." He turns his gray eyes on Kevin. "You really should go, young man. *Now.*" He points at the exit.

Kevin fires his Techno Gun, sending a spray of bullets at the Shadow Gaunt.

The floor buckles behind the comatose Ruby, rising to form an impromptu wall between the Shadow Gaunt and Kevin. "Do you want me to kill you now, young man? I won't give you another warning. Leave at once, or die."

Kevin's ammo type changes to acid. He's getting terribly close to hitting Ruby, but she sits there calmly, her awareness residing in her character in Anissa. Gem slides off her back and runs to me, to hide behind my right leg, clinging to it.

The upper portion of the Shadow Gaunt's conjured wall melts. Kevin keeps blasting, bringing down more and more of the wall. I equip my Techno Gun, too, and select bullets—the silver ones, because they seem better to me than the regular copper ones. I take aim at the spot where I'd last seen the Shadow Gaunt, and wait for a shot.

There's a blur of shadow, and Kevin stops firing. A dark blade protrudes from his chest, having pierced his Techno Armor from behind. The Shadow Gaunt holds the weapon's hilt, and he draws it back out of my friend's body. Kevin exhales loudly and then bursts into pixels.

I don't have time to mourn, but I do have time to hope that anyone who pixelizes can respawn.

The Shadow Gaunt turns his grim face to me, his Shadow Blade pointed at the floor. "I will kill everyone in this room to get what I want. Do you understand? I don't *need* to kill anyone… yet. Some day, all will die, but there's no rush. All I want at the moment is a bit of your soul. That's it. I don't even need the whole thing. You can…." He cocks his head. "Ah. Nick has awakened on his own, and even now he battles Seth. That makes it even more imperative I get from you what I came for. It may be the only way to stop him. So, please… simply take my hand, close your eyes, and don't resist me." He reaches for me.

I raise my hand, but instead of taking his, I summon my Wizard's Staff and cast *Fiendish Missile*, pumping 29 of my 35 Auni into it to cast it at level 7, generating an attack of 294 points of pure, magical energy that springs from my staff and slams into his chest.

He doesn't even stagger. Touching the tip of his Shadow Blade to my forehead, he exhales loudly. "Are you finished?"

I took my best shot. I could have teleported myself away, but didn't want to abandon my friends. Having expended too much Auni, teleporting isn't an option now. But in T&T, one can always hope for a bit of Luck. "Khenn Arrth…," I whisper.

The Trollgodfather hears me, and thunder rumbles in the distance as my cosmic watcher rolls the dice for me.

The Shadow Gaunt cocks his head. "Interesting."

Inspiration strikes, though not to save my life. No saving roll can prevent my death from damage dealt. And I have no delusions about continually avoiding the Shadow Gaunt with theatric stunts. But there are some last second items of business I can deal with before I die. "Everyone who fought the Flitters has earned the XP to reach level 30," I whisper through gritted teeth. I think it only fair, since they fought level 30 enemies and survived. "My Anissa campaign is done."

"You're done." There's a grimace in his voice as the Shadow Gaunt drives his blade into my skull.

CHAPTER FORTY-TWO

Slithy: Who's With Me?

Marta holds up ten fingers, folding down a thumb as I watch, counting down the seconds—but until what? She still hasn't told me the reason for the rush.

Instead of dropping the coin onto Ezmerelda's palm, I raise it over my head, turning in place in response to Dad's request. As I turn, I address my audience. *"Mooks of Khertaan.* I need you to swear before me and the Speaker of Omens that you will not battle humanity on *any* world outside this one. Those who agree to this, *say nothing*—don't make *any* vocal sound. Who's with me?"

A cacophony of growls, grumbles, squawks, snorts, and all other manner of disagreeable animal noises floods the tower interior.

"You can't...." FepXveq's eyes widen. Her lips move as though to say more, but she can't find the words. Her eyes betray the defeat she knows she has suffered.

Morrow still occupies my mind space, but I suspect his body needs to be present for him to be considered *with me* for quest fulfillment purposes. *It's now or never, Dad.*

Once more facing Ezmerelda, I lower the coin again, six inches above Ezmerelda's palm, and stare over my hand into her eyes. "You heard them, Ezmerelda. Those who *aren't with me* made their voices heard just now." I release the coin as Marta folds down her last finger.

Dad's telepathic presence leaves my mind.

Ger-Alt the Goblin Were-Fighter appears next to me, unscathed. Next to her stands Dad and Mel.

The coin touches Ezmerelda's palm. Her voice is grim. "This quest is fulfilled. All those present at *this* moment who by their silence have proclaimed themselves to be *with* Slithy the Frogkin are hereby granted two billion XP. All those who by vocalizing any sound made it known they are *not with* Slithy are hereby awarded *nothing*."

"You damned bitch." FepXveq draws a blade and lunges at me. But she's too late. Khertaan boots me out. The Dark Elf with the afro won't be gaining level thirty from *my* quest. She made a sound when she shouldn't have. *You can't....* That was all she had to say to seal her own fate.

I can't believe Dad made it on time. I'm so happy right now.

☙☞☙☞☙☞

I'm lying on a bed. Ambient light fills the room.

Mylynna lies opposite me, rather than Hera Ford, who I was expecting. Her eyes open and grow wide. "*Slithy?*"

I sit up. She's right. I'm wearing my scant fringed top and loincloth. My skin is amphibian, red and black.

But then, the person sharing the bed with me has green skin and pointed white horns protruding from her forehead, curved upward. She sits up, too, her long, curly, red hair flowing over her bare green shoulders. She's wearing her leather bodysuit with no sleeves or legs, sporting a bright, multicolored, checkered pattern. Her green eyes—so beautiful, a shade brighter than her skin—meet

331

my gaze. She laughs, her voice pealing like wind chimes. "You did it, Slithy. *We made it*. I'm level 30!"

"How…?" I saw FepXveq stab Ger-Alt with my own two eyes. How had the Goblin Were-Fighter managed to respawn?

I keep forgetting…. Ger-Alt is also a Psyon. She's capable of projecting illusions. But… how did she disappear? Is Hide also a Psyon skill?

Mylynna strokes the blond hair lying across my red-and-black shoulder. She smiles. "I don't know all the details, but I'm pretty sure Ger-Alt had head hopper help from Toxxi and Zip. Maybe another Quantized party member, too? Not FepXveq or the Falcon. Isn't there someone else in party Quantized? I can't keep them all straight."

A light breeze plays with Mylynna's hair. A breeze…? We're in a bedroom. Is a fan blowing?

"Ahem."

Marta stands at the foot of the bed, next to a black human male, bald, in his mid-twenties, wearing loose-fitting gray pants and no shirt.

I look between my AI and her new companion. "Who's your friend, Marta?"

The black dude waves. "I'm Conner, Mylynna's personal support AI. It seems in this place, my audio-visual features can be perceived by others aside from my Mistress. I must say, I find the development amusing."

"Me, too, girlie." Marta cocks her head and grins at me, her lengthy nose casting a darker shadow than usual. She nods at Mylynna. "I'm Marta. Don't mind us support AIs. We're still here to serve… as discreetly as necessary."

Beyond the foot of the bed, a fissure in the wall exposes the room to the outside. Rocks lie strewn on the floor where chunks of wall fell inside. Something broke through the wall without waking us. If they took anything, it's not obvious. Did an earthquake hit the place? I don't feel bruised or otherwise harmed.

Battle cries and gunfire threaten to steal my attention from the green woman I woke up next to. But she slips a hand behind my neck and draws me close. Her breath is sweet like flowers, and her lips soft on mine. My heart races like crazy. She slides her tongue into my mouth, and my tongue plays with hers.

The walls shake and an agonizing groan of moving stone ruins the tranquil moment. Muffled voices waft through the opening in the wall, followed by a cry of "Behind you, Megan!"

More commotion ensues, unidentifiable noises, but so damned close, like something is happening right outside our room. Mylynna's eyes reflect my apology for us having to temporarily end what we were about to start.

She's a Succubus, with Seduction as her main thing, but there's something more than that going on between us. Maybe someday we can explore it. But right now… we both spring into action.

The opening in the wall would be a tight squeeze for us to get our bodies through, but we can poke our heads out. I Levitate up to look out through the top part of the crevice and Mylynna peers out through the bottom half.

Night claims the land. Two moons cast sufficient illumination for me to see. Flying in the air in her black Bikini, Megan Wright fights with what at first glance appears to be a flying Black Steel Spider, but this thing has shadowy fingers crawling over its exterior like maggots on a rotten apple.

Gunfire sounds from nearby… from inside the tower?

We're so far up, like fifteen stories.

Another person flies up from the base of the tower. It's impossible to tell whether they're friend or foe.

A quick mental check verifies neither Rancor nor Britta are head hopped to me any longer, which means I can't fly or use Power Strike. Those abilities were nice while I had them.

"None of the typical chat channels are supported here." Marta has read my mind, knowing I was about to reach out to Britta and Rancor. "Unless you have a skill or trait that allows you to telepathically converse with someone remotely, you'll have to rely on your voice and ears to communicate with others now. Head hopping is still allowed, though the rules have changed. Party affiliation restrictions are no longer a limiting factor. You could head hop to Mylynna if she allowed it, for instance."

Mylynna strums her Guitar and sings. Her voice chills my spine, and yet urges me to do something—anything—to help.

I Inspect the Spider. It's a level 30 Psyon, level 21 Assassin. Holy crap. It can insta-kill with a single strike, if not Dodged, Blocked, or Parried. It has the skills Vitals Strike and Ranged Vitals Strike, meaning it can attempt both actions in the same combat heartbeat, only the first requiring physical contact with the target. And that's only the tip of the proverbial iceberg. Megan doesn't know how much danger she's in.

With Mislead, I throw illusions into the area, multiples of Megan flowing out from where she floats. She moves away from the origin point, too—smart lady—making it impossible for the Spider to know which of the many versions of her is the real one.

"Don't let that Spider see you, Mylynna." I Displace myself, just in case the thing notices me and attempts to use its Ranged Vitals Strike skill on me. Hoping the Spider hasn't had the opportunity to use its Foresight power since I arrived on the scene, I Teleport Self onto its back and slam it with my open palm, going for a Bare Hands Stun. Mylynna's song empowers me, and the Spider goes still beneath my hand. "Attack it with all you got, Megan!"

The blond in a black Bikini chops at the Shadow Spider with her orange glowing Battle Axe. Sparks fly from the wound, but the blade fails to bite through the enemy's chitinous shell. From above me, Marta reports—no physical damage was dealt, but the Spider is at 37% SP, 79% MP, and 49% EP. Megan's weapon deals damage in all four domains. That's great.

The other person flying up to meet us shouts, and the air reverberates. A shock wave rocks the Shadow Spider as I deliver my own attack—Bare Hands Ignore Armor. Mylynna's song is an adrenaline rush in my veins, adding to my attack. Together, we've lowered the arachnid's HP to 53%.

Megan shouts then, sending another shock wave through the Spider. Calling on my Bare Hands Fast Attack, I hit the thing again, ignoring armor. It falls to 7% HP, while it's Spiritual Points are in the negative. If it weren't stunned, it would go berserk with that kind of spiritual damage. But it's still stunned, and I have yet another attack. With my Bare Hands, I smack the thing one last time, sending a minor shock wave of my own through it. Its chitinous shell shatters, the pieces plummeting earthward, but evaporating into mists before striking the ground.

No longer on the Spider's back, I Levitate in place. Without Britta head hopped to me, I can't fly, but I can lower myself gently to the ground if I so choose.

Megan hovers before me. "Slithy." Her voice is clipped. She turns to a patch of webs on the tower wall. Changing her form to that of a Siamese Cat, she compresses her body further to a thin wafer, sliding through a gap in the webbing to enter the tower.

The other flying person reaches me. She's dressed like Megan, and her facial features match Megan's, but her hair is straight and black instead of a curly blond mop, and her ears are pointed like an Elf's. She gives me a salute and flies back down towards the bottom of the tower, leaving me to float in space alone.

"Is it safe?" Mylynna pauses singing to make her inquiry. She's still strumming the guitar.

"We killed the Spider. But now I'm stuck out here, unless I want to use one of my teleports for the day, which I'd much prefer to save if possible."

She pokes her head through the breach. "You can't fly?"

I shake my head. "The Levitate skill only allows vertical movement. Do you have any way to draw me to you?"

"Ha, yeah—hold on." She keeps playing her guitar and returns to singing. Her words are like a siren's call, drawing me to her, not only in spirit, but in body, and I float towards her like a magnet.

I reach her. She stashes her guitar. Then she grabs me and pulls me through the fissure into her arms, where I belong.

CHAPTER FORTY-THREE

The Soul of Morrow: Logical

Mel pulls me through the veil into darkness as I withdraw from Slithy's mind. Animalistic sounds of distress assail my ears.

From nearby, an aged female voice speaks over the tumult. "This quest is fulfilled. All those present at *this* moment who by their silence have proclaimed themselves to be *with* Slithy the Frogkin are hereby granted two billion XP. All those who by vocalizing any sound made it known they are *not with* Slithy are hereby awarded *nothing*."

A curse rolls from the lips of a young woman standing less than six feet from me. "You damned bitch." The speaker moves quickly in the darkness....

The darkness is replaced by gray mists and all is silent.

Mel no longer holds my hand. "Mel, are you there?"

There's no response.

I might as well be in the dark. Mists swirl in my face, and I can't see for shit.

I'm afloat in limbo, alone in the Mists of Time.

Fine.

I don't freak out. That's not me. I'm a Punk, with a kindred trait of Rebel. Loneliness isn't a new concept to Punks and Rebels. And we don't freak out. We keep our cool, even when the multiverse is collapsing around us. *That's* who I am. Fuck the multiverse.

Being cool doesn't prevent one from ever being in a hurry. If I need to be in a hurry, I can be in a hurry, like I just was with Mel. But *right now* is not one of those times. *Right now*, I'm taking stock of who and what I am.

If what I heard was correct, then I just gained two billion XP, enough to make me level 30. So let me have a look at my character sheet, see what I've gained, and what I can upgrade.

I'm a level 30 Lightning Wizard and a level 21 Lightning Warrior. That's the farthest a Khertaan avatar can advance in their primary class and subclass. Well, then, mission accomplished... as far as reaching level 30 goes.

My Auni is an impressive 184. I have 6 unassigned attribute points and 3 unassigned trait levels to slot. For the attributes, I could stand to improve a number of low average or sub par scores—Dexterity, Agility, Sanity, Faith, Conscience, Empathy, Hope, or Optimism. Hmm. As Wizard and Warrior, it would serve me to raise my Dexterity and Agility to average levels, so I assign them each a point. I have 4 free points remaining.

I really don't see a need to raise any of those other low attributes. So what if I'm on the verge of insanity? And the only faith I need is in myself and those closest to me—no numeric rating can dictate that. As for my Conscience and Empathy—who cares? Since when have I lacked on Hope when I really needed it? Optimism isn't necessary—whether one wins or loses at life doesn't hinge on how optimistic one is in fighting the fight. If you have to fight, then you fight your best fight. If you survive, then you can look back on the fight with appreciation for the outcome.

The important thing is to keep fighting no matter how bleak the outlook. And what does one need to keep fighting no matter what? Willpower. I crank it up by 2 points to the maximum of 19—*superhuman* level.

It doesn't pay to have super-human Willpower if the actions you're undertaking are stupid. I put my last 2 free attribute points into Logic, also cranking it up to the super-human maximum of 19.

I'm Super Punk. Watch out.

Okay, moving on to traits… I max out my Mental Armor trait to level 4, leaving me 1 free trait level. I might put that on Magical Familiar. Do I still have one? I summon Rancor.

He pops into existence three feet in front of my face. "Ha ha, hi, Morrow. My, but isn't your mohawk a sight for sore eyes…?"

"My mohawk…?" I reach up to my scalp. He's right. I do have my mohawk, as stiff as ever. But… I was in Nick's body… right before I found myself in limbo. So… am I in a different body or a transformed body? Could this body be my original Morrow body, the one Erica ripped me from? Or is it still floating around out there somewhere, an empty shell? If I am in my original Morrow body, then what happened to the Nick body I was just in?

Nah, I'm not going to worry about it.

"Ha ha, I'm level 30." Rancor flies in a tight circle before me. "

"And I'm giving you another treat, Woodpecker." I put my last remaining trait point on Magical Familiar, assigning the level to him. "You now have a three-second combat heartbeat."

"Ha ha, woo hoo!" He dances in the misty air. "So… where to now, boss?"

With a sweeping gesture, I draw his attention to the limbo we're in. "Do you know how to traverse these mists?"

He flaps his wings in front of my eyes. "Ha ha, yeah. I can fly. See?"

There's no gravity here. There's no air resistance, either. Rancor's ability to fly in limbo isn't due to physics, but metaphysics. He believes he can fly, and so he does.

I have super-human Willpower. That ought to serve me in a super-human way in this metaphysical place. With a moment's concentration, I move closer to him through force of will.

"Ha ha, you're flying." He flits away to avoid a collision. "New skill?"

"Just good-old-fashioned Willpower at a super-human level." I glance around. "Now if we only had a destination." Mental gears crank in my head, analyzing memories using my super-human Logic. "Let's go to the nexus."

"Ha ha, do you know the way?"

"We'll find it." It's not a matter of Faith, but Willpower. We'll discover the way eventually if we keep moving. We're basically immortal unless we're murdered. We don't need to breathe, eat, drink, or do any other of that Earth human shit. Sleep helps us to heal or recover expended Auni or Psi faster, but otherwise sleep isn't necessary. So we'll travel until we find a reason to stop. "Or maybe we'll run into something else more interesting. The main thing is to not stay put."

"Ha ha, don't want to go in circles, either, boss."

"Stay close and let's go."

"Ha ha, let me perch on your shoulder. No chance of us being separated that way."

"Sure."

CHAPTER FORTY-FOUR

Charli-35: Diver Vampire

I gasp as the Diver's charm fades and my free will returns. The gasp isn't an audible one... since I'm not the persona in control of my body... but it's real to me, and my other three personae hear it in our shared head space. Horror at what I've allowed the Diver to do—*eating all those people*—grips me by the metaphysical throat.

Fifty is still charmed, and she's the one in control. "Don't be stupid," she says to me. "From any perspective you look at it, it's better if I stay in charge here. If you take control away from me, the Diver will charm you again, and then what?"

"Not necessarily." I glance at Fourteen. "Do you trust me enough to put me back in control?"

Fourteen nods eagerly. She wants us to do *something* against the Diver.

Fifty pleads to our young mother persona. "Eighteen, don't let them do this."

But Eighteen doesn't want to be involved. Fifty is ousted by a vote of two to one, and I'm back in charge.

Zyekt the Angel immediately addresses me. "Charli, activate my Meditative Focus trait."

I do as he says. "If you have a plan, Zyekt, feed it to me."

He does have a plan, and reels out the steps for me to take. Invoking his Hypnotic Voice, I shout at the giant winged gar, "*Stop everything.*"

It comes to an abrupt halt in the air. I rush over, lay a hand on it above the pectoral fin, and invoke Zyekt's Steal Random Attribute skill. I get a boost to my Charisma, but it's short-lived—at Zyekt's direction, I invoke his Create Undead skill.

The Dread Naught's charm effect flees my Fifty persona, and also releases all the humans gathered below. Once again in command of their own faculties, they scream at the sight of the giant winged gar hovering above them. The fangs it just acquired glisten in the sunlight.

Oh my gosh. I've just created a Diver Vampire under my control. I can communicate with it telepathically to command it. "What's your name and pronouns, Diver?"

"I am called Nasty-Us. You may refer to me as *they* and *them.*"

I don't care for their name, but I'm not changing it. I also don't much care for being a controlling bitch, but I can't let Nasty-Us keep devouring people. "Very well, Nasty-Us. I am granting you partial autonomy. You are not to charm or take any adverse actions against humans or other native creatures of Earth. You are not to aid anyone else in doing so. You are free to fight other Dread Naughts that engage in adverse actions against natives of Earth, but I won't force you to fight your own kind if you choose not to. If you wish to enter into communications with any other Dread Naughts or their allies, you first need my permission, and may telepathically ask for it at any time. I will monitor your behavior through random telepathic visits, and may adjust my orders for you if I'm unhappy with your behavior. Do you have any questions?"

"May I kill myself?"

That wasn't a question I'd anticipated. "Would you rather die than continue to exist as a Vampire?"

"I exist only to destroy, and if you take that from me…."

"You are welcome to join our fight against other Dread Naughts. The main thing I require is that you not kill any Dread Naughts in close proximity to natives of Earth."

"Does that include insects and other vermin?"

I can scarcely believe I'm having this conversation with what only moments ago was a terrifying enemy swallowing humans whole as its depraved contribution to the cause of the Dread Naughts. But even as a Vampire, its goals haven't changed—and no matter what orders I give it, deep inside it will always have a drive to continue its original mission. It's smart enough to look for loopholes in my orders, and that's what scares me about the current conversation. "It includes any Earth natives of which you're aware at the time, unless I tell you otherwise." Even that restriction seems rife for being taken advantage of.

Nasty-Us rolls their huge eye. "I can sense most living things within two miles, not only insects, but bacteria and the like. It's doubtful I'll ever find any place in which to kill another Dread Naught without its death explosion killing some Earth natives."

Let me try a different tactic. "Where did you come from when I released you in Khertaan?"

They don't respond immediately. "A pocket dimension."

"Can you return there?"

They're still not quick to reply. "Not of my own free will."

"If I command you to return there, can you do it?"

The giant gar eyes me. "That depends."

It's creepy that the Diver looks at me with only one eye, and sees a whole different scene on the other side of its head. But I can't let it creep me out so much as to end this discussion. I'm onto something here. "Depends on what?"

The gar flaps its giant bat wings. "You had the power to release me. You have the power to return me to prison. I can't go back of my own volition, no matter how hard I try. If you give the command, I won't succeed, but will be forced to forever try."

The Diver is talking about my Shadow Gauntlets. I lift my hands before me, studying the Gauntlets that aren't so much Gauntlets as shadow-thin gloves. Could it be that simple? I place both gloved hands against the scaly skin of Nasty-Us. "By the power of the Shadow Gauntlets—"

"Wait." Zyekt stops me. "The Meditative Focus bonus has expired. You may need it for what you're about to do. If you wait five minutes without strenuous activity, you'll have a huge bonus to the banishment attempt."

"Banishment?" I hadn't thought of it that way. It sounds like a horrid thing to do to any creature, even a malicious undead one.

"If you're not up to it…." Fifty is more than ready to take over control of our body if I'm feeling too queasy for the task.

"I'm good."

So we wait five minutes. No humans are in the area, all of them having fled as soon as the Diver's charms faded. I continue to question Nasty-Us, and learn a lot, so I'm glad Zyekt interrupted me when he did.

The waiting period comes to an end. Once more I lay my shadowy hands on the giant gar's side. "I don't want you to be alone forever, Nasty-Us. I promise to send more Dread Naughts to be with you." A tranquil calm settles over my shoulders even as I raise my voice. "By the power of the Shadow Gauntlets, I banish you, Nasty-Us, back to the inter-dimensional prison from which I released you."

A thin black disk an inch in diameter manifests in the air above Nasty-Us. It expands in two-dimensions, remaining thin, until it's larger in diameter than Nasty-Us. The air vibrates as unseen energies suck the Undead Diver out of this universe, through the portal defined by the black disk, and into some unidentifiable place with no exit except one I can make.

The disk implodes on itself with a thundering boom.

"That could have been the start of an Undead Dread Naught army on our side." CC has been quiet the whole time until now.

He *is* right. I can envision myself coming across Dread Naught after Dread Naught, turning each of them undead, and having all of them accompany me wherever I go, growing their numbers one Dread Naught at a time. But… "I don't want that. I want them all to be somewhere they can't cause anyone harm."

The metaphysical image of CC in my head space frowns at my assertion. "If we don't use them against themselves, we ought to kill them rather than imprison them."

Zyekt adds, "The goal is to stop the Dread Naughts from destroying everyone and everything. The method of dealing with them Charli employed works without regard for the types of damage we'd otherwise need to defeat them."

CC huffs. "What if they escape their prison again? What's to prevent them from returning to spread destruction in the future?"

"As long as I'm alive," I say, "I'll know if they escape. Before imprisoning them, I'll order each one not to do any harm to natives of Earth."

The Elitist presses further. "And what happens when you die?"

I laugh. "You'll just have to make sure I never die."

Returning to where everyone's unconscious bodies lie, I land beside them. They all leave my head space and wake up in their own bodies, the sleeping gas having finally worn off for them all.

Lady Amarynth sits up. "Well, that was quite the adventure. Sorry my skills weren't of much use to you, Charli, but I'm glad to have been along for the ride. Still, the next time we all mass head hop to you, I propose we find a better place for our unconscious bodies than to leave them lying on the sidewalk."

CHAPTER FORTY-FIVE

Emma: Dance

The Shadow Gaunt's blade rests in my skull. I don't fall over dead, but reach up to grab his wrist, preventing him from withdrawing his weapon. "Everyone with a shriek attack, as your Game Master, I declare you to be *here* now."

His eyes go wide. He doesn't understand how I'm still living.

In some role-playing games, there's such a thing as a *called shot*. An attacker aims for a specific spot on the body, and a dice roll is made to determine if that spot is hit. The Shadow Gaunt aimed for my skull, effectively attempting a called shot, and found his mark.

Yet I'm not dead.

In Tunnels and Troglodytes, while the Game Master might allow something like a called shot when player characters are in an especially tough scenario and the GM wishes to give them a fighting chance to survive, there aren't any specific rules about it. In general, attacks deal their damage, and if it's enough to reduce the target's Constitution to zero or less, then the target is dead. Otherwise, the target continues to fight another round.

In my case, the Shadow Gaunt's attack, even though he aimed for my skull and hit it, didn't deal the damage needed to reduce my Constitution to zero or less. I'm reminded of the classic Rob Carver illustration. I believe the fellow in the drawing is an Orc, though it's possible he's a Hobgoblin or some other monstrous humanoid. He's shown in profile, with his hand to his mouth, and an arrow through his head, protruding from both the front and back. The caption of the illustration is the Orc's comment on the situation, which he's yelling at his enemies: *Ha ha! Yah missed all my vital spots!!*

The Shadow Gaunt didn't attack me to kill. He attacked to drain my soul. My Constitution remains at full. My persona, however, slithers through my veins up to my head, siphoning into his blade even as I grapple with the Gaunt for possession of the weapon. I have enough residual soul stuff remaining in my body to continue the struggle for survival.

Screams saturate the air. All the players seated on the floor have awakened and brought with them the shriek attacks I granted them in Anissa, now targeting the Shadow Gaunt. His grip relaxes, slipping free of the hilt. I release my hold on him, my arm falling in exhaustion to my side. He wraps his fingers around his own throat in an attempt to choke himself to death. His blade still protrudes from my skull.

Strong hands slide under my arms from behind and catch me before I fall. "Erica, take hold of the hilt, but do *not* pull the weapon out." I recognize Gondra's voice, and know I'm in good hands. Seems I've drawn more people than my original players out of Anissa. I hope they don't mind.

A young woman with shoulder-length blue hair, attired in a pink cloak, takes hold of the hilt hanging in the space before my eyes. She doesn't pull, but looks askance at the Lizardman at my back.

He whispers in my ear. "Emma, take your soul back. It's not lost until the blade is withdrawn, and not even then if you reclaim it first. Go on, take it back. You can do it."

I want only to sleep, but his words give me hope and renew my strength. In the distance, thunder rumbles—the Trollgodfather rolling another saving roll for me. Apparently, I make it, and a part of my soul leaches out of the blade back to my body, where it belongs.

A few minutes pass while I continue to take back what's mine.

It's a few minutes more before I feel whole, but at last I regain all of myself. "I'm finished." I still feel wobbly.

The Lizardman's strong hands steady me from behind. "Good. Continue staying very still, Emma. Now, Erica, very gently, pull the blade free."

The blue-haired young lady in front of me carefully slides the weapon back until it falls free of my flesh, the tip dipping down an inch from my eyes. She hands the blade to Gondra. "If that's all, I need to go."

Keeping one steadying hand on my waist, he takes the weapon from her. "Can you give me one more minute? I need to go with you."

"You have ten seconds."

A Siamese Cat appears in mid-air next to the Shadow Gaunt, who is still struggling to choke himself to death. An orange glowing Battle Axe materializes in the Cat's paws. The claws of the feline maintain a grip on the Axe handle as the blade cleaves into the Shadow Gaunt's skull. Now I've seen it all.

The two-dimensional shadowy worms covering the Gaunt's body and cloak fly from him in all directions, leaving *nothing* in their absence.

The Shadow Gaunt is gone.

The Siamese Cat stashes its Battle Axe and vanishes without a word. I'm just assuming if it can fly and swing a Battle Axe, it could talk if it wanted. It's not in the mood, apparently.

Fauna, Ruby, and the other players are still seated on the floor, their heads and shoulders slumped forward, their eyes droopy with fatigue but aware. The shriek attacks they executed against the Shadow Gaunt took a lot from them, leaving them physically and emotionally drained. Thanking Gondra with a glance and the best smile I can muster, I settle on the floor next to Fauna and put an arm around her shoulders, pulling her against me, leaning my head against hers. She leans into me, and we sit there together in silence—until Spooky jumps up, dances around, and sings a song with lots of *oohs* and *ohs* as lyrics. She grabs Gondra's hands and urges him to dance with her. To my surprise, he's not a bad dancer.

"Three seconds," says the blue-haired Erica.

The woman in red latches onto Erica, as does the man with the green mohawk to whom I gave a part of my soul when I animated him in Anissa. He catches my eye. "Thank you, Emma."

I incline my head. "What should I call you?"

"I'm part you and part Morrow. How about I take the name Em-Row?"

I grin at that. "Farewell, Em-Row. Perhaps we'll meet again some day."

The woman dressed like royalty—who'd been carrying the corpses of Ronnie and Greelia—grabs hold of Em-Row. The newly undead creatures, Ronnie and Greelia, don't join the chain.

Spooky—the five-foot-nine-inch Dark Elf version of her from Anissa—twirls Gondra, his dark cloak swirling around his legs. The shadow girl sends her impromptu dance partner into Erica's arms. The two cloaked figures vanish, taking Em-Row, the woman in red, and the woman of royalty with them. I would have liked proper introductions, but I take it they were late for an appointment.

Franklin's corpse sits up. "Hey, I'm not dead...?" His fingernails lengthen and sharpen, as do his teeth. His nose becomes a canine snout, and hair sprouts all over him as he enlarges, popping buttons and bursting seams. He's taking the form of a Human-Wolf Hybrid, over eight feet tall.

"Aagh!" Raven's high-pitched squeal draws my attention. She's six inches tall and sports tiny wings. Her clothes didn't shrink with her. She wraps a sleeve of her uniform around her.

"We've become who we were in Anissa." Martin's skin is red and he's large—not quite as tall as Franklin, but close. His uniform expanded with him—sorta. It looks confining. He's got a few long, pointy teeth.

Wiley has shrunk to a foot-and-a-half in height, with the same issue as Raven regarding clothes that didn't shrink with him.

Yelle is her normal height—just under six feet—but her skin is like stone. Fred has shrunk about six inches, while gaining weight and fangs. Sarge has gained six inches and lost thirty pounds, while also growing fangs and claws. Only Ruby and Fauna are in the forms they had before they started playing my T&T game.

"Listen." Martin cups a hand to his ear. He rises to his feet, his head towering two feet higher than normal, and approaches the rift in the wall. It's obstructed by webs, and he rips enough of them free for him to peer out. "Our guys are fighting those winged things— the Flitters. Looks like they could use some help."

Ruby clambers onto her four hooves. "Fall in line, people. Let's go kick some Flitter butt."

Seems she's willing to stay in Destin for a while after all.

CHAPTER FORTY-SIX

Kendra: Spiders

What am I to do? I might only have one shot at taking down the Shadow Gaunt, making it imperative I know exactly *where* to attack. The chittering of the spider swarm isn't terribly loud, but sufficient noise cover to prevent me from hearing a shift in the Gaunt's posture or position. My Heightened Sense of Hearing trait is only level one. If it were higher, maybe I could better filter out the chittering.

The Shadow Gaunt sits on his throne, silently assessing the space before him, trying to ascertain my location while waiting for me to make a move. And yet... what I see seated on the throne might be an illusion. The real Shadow Gaunt might be waiting invisibly elsewhere in the room, ready to strike as soon as I reveal myself.

I could take the risk of relinquishing my Spirit Form with the hope I'd be attacked physically only. With my level 4 Pain Tolerant trait, I can't be killed physically—assuming the trait works here the same way it did in Khertaan. If a spiritual attack were levied against me, I'd have a strong defense. But if I were attacked mentally or emotionally… I hesitate to think what would become of me.

Something is happening….

Around the throne, on the dais and before it, a number of spiders expand in size. They gain humanoid heads, each with the face of the Shadow Gaunt. Four legs on each spider wither to nothing, while the rear two twist and bend into humanoid legs and the front two transmogrify into humanoid arms. The arachnid bodies fail to fully transform into humanoid bodies—the eyes of each transforming Spider-Gaunt dilate in horror as shadowy squiggles peel off their abhorrent forms, floating into the air, flaking off in waves until nothing remains of each figure. What… the… hell?

The Shadow Gaunt still sits motionless on his throne, with no reaction to whatever the hell just happened. He flickers like a dying light bulb and then vanishes—an illusion after all.

Georgie stumbles over his own tongue. "Th… the Shadow Gaunt is dead. One of its duplicates was killed elsewhere, killing all the duplicates here, too."

Talk about a letdown. I'd expected a huge showdown scene between me and the Shadow Gaunt, but it's not to be. I feel robbed.

The remaining spiders in the room go wild, racing around aimlessly.

A scepter leans against the throne, the only real component to the illusion of the Shadow Gaunt. I fly over and inspect it without touching it. It appears to be made of gold, and might well be solid gold. It may have powers I can harness if in my possession. What if it can command the Dread Naughts? I need to take it. Still in Spirit Form, I touch it, but of course my insubstantial hand passes through it, and I'm unable to stash it to my inventory. If I want to take it, I'll need to drop my Spirit Form and become physical.

"Georgie, are you absolutely sure the Shadow Gaunt is dead?"

"That's the information I have, pumpkin."

Spiders crawl onto the dais, swarming towards the scepter. If I'm taking it, I'd rather it not be covered in creepy crawlies. It will only take a moment to turn physical, grab and stash the scepter, and return to Spirit Form.

Summoning my Spirit Shield, I deactivate my Spirit Form....

As my hand nears the scepter, I hear a scratching on the dais, louder than what any of the spiders crawling my way could make. Bringing my Shield to bear between me and the sound, I grab the scepter and stash it—as a spider nearly as tall as I am appears, driving a pointed limb at me. It slips under my Shield and slants upward, piercing my chest—right into my heart.

Such a blow would kill other people instantly. But my body doesn't recognize pain, even the pain of death. Summoning my Spirit Blade, I aim for the surprised spider assassin's head... but my weapon is turned aside. I've failed to damage it.

Keeping its limb in my chest, the spider draws closer, its fangs gnashing inches from my face. Lifting another leg, it summons a glowing silver sword.

I return to Spirit Form an instant before the spider's silver sword enters my brain. Its weapon passes through my skull without affect, and the limb in my chest falls free. I've no doubt the mook's silver sword is a Psi-Weapon, able to deal mental damage. If it had landed the hit on my physical form, I'd be effectively lobotomized right now.

If I can't affect the thing with my Spirit Blade, my options are severely limited. I summon my Spirit Noose and aim to lasso the mook's head. A physical lasso would slip off a spider's head, but the Spirit Noose sticks.

The spider vanishes, though my Noose still has tension. I call on its ability to subdue, concentrating on my Barbarian's Dominance skill.

Arrggh. The thing continues to thrash, and dislodges the Spirit Noose. I've met my match in this thing....

Or maybe not. I invoke Spirit Blast. A blue cone of light erupts from my eyes.

All the tiny spiders in the room begin attacking each other in a frenzy—except in one small area where *something* tangible but invisible blocks the cone's effect. Calling on my level 3 Increased Movement trait, I launch myself in that direction. Focusing on my Heightened Sense of Hearing, I pick up a faint rushing of air headed for the double doors. The mook must be flying.

Georgie flies next to me, holding up a piece of parchment, on which is written a status report—*Shadow Spider: HP 93%, SP 90%. Kendra: HP: 0%. Both: All other hit point totals: 100%.*

Hmm. Being kicked out of Khertaan had restored my HP to its maximum from a hugely negative percentage, and the Shadow Spider had dropped it back to 0 in one fell attack. If not for my level 4 Pain Tolerant trait, I'd be dead.

I exit the palace before my combat heartbeat resets. The Dread Naughts have brought down more skyscrapers since I went inside. More corpses litter the landscape, some people having thrown themselves to their deaths from great heights and some having shot or stabbed themselves.

As soon as I'm able, I call on my Spirit Blast again. The attack doesn't do a lot of damage to any single foe, but it ignores armor, and effects every enemy in my field of vision—excepting enemies immune to spiritual attacks, of course. I'm hoping to catch the Shadow Spider in the cone again, damaging it as much as possible before it gets away.

"Um," Georgie whispers. "You've lowered the HP and SP percentages for the Shadow Spider—and for twenty-four Dread Naughts. Fifteen Flitters and nine Divers are now headed this way. Need I remind you… if your attack affected them, then…."

They have spirit-based attacks of their own. Some of them may even be able to take Spirit Form. And there's twenty-four of them…?

Oh, hell.

CHAPTER FORTY-SEVEN

Nick: The First Time Ever I Saw His Faces

It's been forever… holding the timelines together and yet doing my best to keep them apart after failing to fully merge them, unable to communicate with anyone who might help. My initial failure to combine them all into a unified timeline opened the door for Seth and Queen Jean to try finishing the merge to their own liking.

But now Queen Jean is dead. Seth and his minions rule the strongest of the timelines I'm trying to save. And yet, because of Ulric… Seth has lost his concentration. This is an opportunity I can't pass up. Greelia occupies the metadisc, and she's strong enough to maintain the state of the multiverse long enough for me to deal with her sole remaining opposition. Dragging along what remains to me of ODYSSEY, I disentangle my metaphysical self from the timeline bundle and launch myself at Seth.

A cloak flaps from my metaphysical shoulders as I fly through the mists at my enemy, who wants nothing more than to destroy *everything*. Is it wrong for me to attempt to destroy someone who seeks to destroy me and everyone I love? Even though I'm taking the offensive, my actions are taken for the preservation of my self and my tribe.

Pointing at Seth's hooded head, I summon the lightning from inside me. A bolt fires from the tattoo on the back of my hand, arcing through the mists. Incinerating Seth's hood, it reveals a face hidden for so long.

One might have guessed I'd be emotional over Queen Jean's death. Jean was the mother of our child, Mel, after all. Maybe I haven't had time to process it, but so far her death has had little impact on me. I might have been glad she was out of my life, as she was only doing evil. Or I might have grieved because a woman I'd married in some timeline had been murdered. Or I could have been concerned about the guilt Ronnie would bear for the rest of his days over his part in Queen Jean's death. But there hasn't been any of that. I've had no emotional, spiritual, or mental energy to spare for her. My task to save the timelines has been all-consuming.

Yet now, seeing Seth's face for the first time—I'm shocked, confused, saddened, and horrified. It's a face incongruous with the entity's masculine body. Straight strands of blue hair sweep the tops of his shoulders. Neither the face nor the hair belong to Seth. He's taken the look of someone dearer to me than I ever felt Jean was. "Erica?"

His reply is spoken with a mournful, feminine lilt, in tones belonging to my beloved. "You *abandoned* me, Nick. Left me with nothing but my grief. Even now, when you're back in my life, you attack me. I gave *all* of myself to you, and you treated me only as a tool to be used and then discarded. For as much as you think you care for women, you certainly know how to make us scorn you. Please, crawl back under the rock you were hiding under, and let me get on with venting my anger."

Is this true? Is my seemingly uncaring attitude the reason for all the destruction? I *do* care, even if I have a hard time showing it. I always try to do what's right, but I'm sometimes blind to how my actions affect others. Leave it to me and my antisocial tendencies to turn not one, but two women into monsters erecting walls of ice around their hearts and attempting to demolish everything outside those walls. "I… I love you, Erica. Please stop this madness."

"You *love* her?" Wild blond curls frame the new face of Seth, the face of another woman in my life—Kendra—from the one timeline bearing the distinction of being the most perfect for me of all timelines. "And what of me, then, Nick, the mother of your child?" She's talking about Susie. "You and I were the perfect match, or so I thought. Yet you've just professed your love for someone else. Did she bear your child, Nick? Others have born your children, and what place do any of those mothers and children have in your heart now? You don't care about anyone but yourself and what you want in the moment. Your selfishness is at fault for this whole mess, Nick. And now it's time to suffer the consequences of your actions and inactions."

Seth's face and hair changes back to Erica's. He holds out a hand as though waiting for someone to place an item on his palm.

A mix of colors approaches through the mists—red, green, blue, pink, and brown. Preceding the colorful group of figures is a long and gleaming silver blade.

"Is this what you're looking for?" The sibilant voice belongs to Gondra. He brandishes the blade. "Your Shadow Gaunt avatar has been slain and his soul-drinking blade taken from him."

Seth chuckles, a malicious sound using Erica's voice. "How sweet of you to bring it to me in his stead." He wiggles his fingers, and the blade dissolves from Gondra's grip, materializing in Seth's.

"It doesn't contain the four souls you need to control Nick." Gondra and those with him come close enough for me to make out their features.

My heart rises in my throat at the sight of the real Erica, dressed in pink and black.

Her eyes lock with mine, and Time Itself pauses.

God help me, I *want* her so badly—to be *with* her.

"I don't need to control Nick," Seth says, still using Erica's voice. "I only need to stop Greelia."

I tear my gaze from Erica's. Seth aims his blade at the cloaked Goblin woman occupying the metadisc with him.

"*No*." Dressed in a trench coat, dead determination in his eyes, Ulric throws himself between the tip of the blade and Greelia. His expression doesn't change when the blade slides into his chest.

Despite the lad's best efforts, he can't stop the blade from exiting his back and puncturing Greelia's ribcage.

The Goblin woman gasps and her form wavers. "No. *Stop. Please.*" The light leaves her eyes. Her body and Cosmic Cloak shred into green and brown threads.

In that instant, all the timelines trapped in the hole at the center of the metadonut merge into one, a mix of all the timelines—but Shadowverse dominates. Elements of Sethiverse will survive, but there's also hope for some version of Earth surviving.

The Mists of Time swirl around us—a vortex drawing us all to its center, into the Modified Shadowverse.

Ulric's body and trench coat tatters. The storm sucks in the pieces of him, even as it pulls in Greelia's shreds.

I struggle against the whirling wind. If I can place my feet on the metadisc, maybe I can undo what Seth has done. I've no time to waste. I fire another lightning bolt at Seth to keep him busy.

With a malevolent feminine laugh, Seth doesn't even try to dodge, allowing the bolt to strike him…. It passes through him as though he isn't there.

The real Erica shrieks.

I spin around in time to see a shadowy spider as tall as me strike with a pointed limb—and pierce my heart. All goes black.

CHAPTER FORTY-EIGHT

Timmy Landers: Destroying Earth a Second Time

Panoramic urban scenes flash before my eyes—cities with gleaming spires, dirty cities, shadowy cities, and more. I'm free of the chair Seth had strapped me in, but I'm still a prisoner of my own uncertainty, drifting alone across rapidly changing realities.

The spirit animating me was given by the Goblin Warrior Woman known as Greelia, but I identify as Timmy Landers, an undead Ring Ghoul and the ex-boyfriend of Susie McKenzie, time traveler. I'm something of a time traveler myself and the owner of a Cosmic Cloak, though as Timmy Landers I don't flaunt it and have told no one about it.

Scenes continue flashing. At some point, I lose connection to one of the versions of Greelia in a place called Jeaniverse, which becomes Shadowverse. The connection is reestablished quickly enough, as another Greelia returns there. But then I lose the connection again, and it doesn't come back. It's like a part of Greelia—a part of me—has been stolen. That's not good.

Still considering my options, I lose connection to yet another version of Greelia, the one attending the metadisc. It's completely cut off from me, too, as though it has also been stolen. What's happening? Attending the metadisc is the most important role of any of my scattered selves.

If I weren't undead, I'd have a more physical reaction to my losses.

The flashing scenes overlay each other and crash into one unified scene, defining my place in it. I'm again strapped in a chair on the bridge of Seth's Planet Buster spaceship, with a metal collar around my throat. Well, damn. I'd really like to know what or who is behind this state of affairs. Could it be Susie…?

She's conspicuously *not* in the neighboring chair like she was before the scenes began flashing. I'm glad she got away and isn't back here with me now.

The collar on my neck has the annoying property of nullifying the powers of my Cosmic Cloak—I can't meta-shift out of this damned place. Fortunately, the collar doesn't nullify the power of my Ghoul Ring—if my Ring weren't functioning properly, my body might revert to being a corpse.

Yes, I died once. Susie was there. Anyone who knew the full story could blame my death on Susie, but it was my choice to give up my life to save hers. The Ghoul Ring brought me back—not to life for me, but still to dwell among the living. The Ring was put on my dead finger by *my* future self, who had come to own it because *his* future self had bequeathed it upon him even as he bequeathed it upon me.

According to my future self, once the Ring is removed from my finger—which I'll eventually do to bequeath upon my past self—its power will continue to function for me *until the next dawn.* When my future self took his leave of me, he time traveled, skipping over the next dawn. I've not seen him since then, but I assume he's okay.

On the bridge, Seth approaches me in his dark brown Cosmic Cloak, the hood drawn up to shadow his face. "Mr. Landers." His voice is the same old high and haughty one, coated with honey.

"I'm so happy you're still with me, to share in my moment of victory. I have successfully merged the timelines, and guess what? We have survived the merge, as has this ship. I'm so happy.

"You'll be accompanying me on my trek through the stars, seeking out new worlds to destroy. Thus and therefore, *you* will survive longer than *anyone else* in the universe—aside from me, of course. You will see the unraveling of existence to its last threads. Only then will I snuff your undead existence. I assume that pleases you, at some level. Am I right?"

"If I say, *yes*, will that make you happy?" I'm not scared of Seth. Someone will stop him. Either one of my other Greelia forms will do it, or Susie will, or one of their many high-powered friends.

He points at the giant screen occupying the far wall. An image of Earth appears in the view. "What if I told you that—due to how the timelines merged—Earth still thrives? So, guess what? I get to destroy it a second time. How awesome is that? And I'm pleased to say, you'll have a front row seat to watching me turn it to pulp once more. Aren't you excited? I'm excited." His sweeping gesture encompasses the bridge. "I had hoped to also have the company of your friend Susie on this journey of destruction, but sadly she has left us, and will be destroyed along with everyone else down there, assuming she survived the merge. But… her absence leaves more popcorn for us. Do you like yours with butter and salt? I've grown quite fond of the taste of both."

"Sure, I'll take butter and salt." Anything to stall for more time, so my powered friends will have more time to throw a wrench in this maniac's plans.

Seth waves at nearby skinny gray alien attendants and nurses in green uniforms. "Chop, chop. Prepare the Planet Buster beam."

I close my eyes and telepathically reach out to other Greelia selves. She who answers is the one living in the Underverse, a universe occupied only by herself and her automaton family—her husband Nick and daughter Britta. But now even her Underverse has been merged with all the other timelines. She and her family are no longer the only residents of their own private universe. Now they live deep underground on the new Earth—which Seth is about to destroy.

She's frantic. "How do we stop him? We have to do something."

"*You* have to do something." I glance at the Seth before me, the version of him in command of the Planet Buster ship. "He has me strapped in a chair and is suppressing my Cloak. I can't do anything. I don't know what you can do either, but you don't have much time. He's prepping the beam now. Find Susie McKenzie. If anyone can stop him, she can. She was here on the ship, but she got away. She's got to be out there somewhere. *Find her.*"

I'm trying to convince myself as much as Underverse Greelia that Susie survived the merge. Holy goat cheese, please let her be out there. If anyone is, she must be.

A thin gray alien arrives with the popcorn. Seth orders the alien to stay beside me, to feed me, since my arms are strapped to the chair.

Seth raises a hand high overhead. "Aim the destruction beam."

As nurses in green uniforms pirouette on the bridge, liquid green energy flows into a transparent bubble poking down from the ceiling.

When Seth had used his destruction beam on Earth prior, the beam had turned the planet to jelly. He'd drawn its energy into the ship. Nothing had survived—*except me.* I would have been relegated to floating adrift in space for eternity after my Earth was destroyed if Seth hadn't noticed me and brought me onto the ship.

I telepathically connect to Underverse Greelia again. "I believe anyone undead has immunity to the Planet Buster beam. Have you found Susie?"

"Nick is dead," her mental image cries.

I sense her despair, though I'm incapable of feeling such an emotion. "The *real* one?"

She nods. "It's all on me to undo the merge."

"Underverse, *no.* You have to find Susie. Seth is aiming the Planet Buster beam at Earth *right now.*"

Her telepathic connection to me terminates, and not of her own volition. *Her soul has been stolen, too.*

Seth turns to me, his face still hidden in the shadows of his Cosmic Cloak, but I sense the malevolent smile he wears. Some version of him has slain both the real Nick and the strongest versions of Greelia.

What other Greelia can I connect to? There's got to be one who can save Earth.

Black webs spring from Seth's fingers, streak past my right ear, and crash with a loud squelch into something outside my view. With an evil chuckle, Seth twirls a finger in the air. "Fire."

A green beam of liquid light appears on-screen, streaking towards Earth.

She can't hear me, but I call her name anyway… "*Susie.*"

CHAPTER FORTY-NINE

Slithy: Race Against Time

A tremor rocks the tower. I break free of Mylynna's hug.

An unseen banshee wails in my ears, and a black blade of energy enters through the ceiling at an angle, five feet wide and extending to the floor—shimmering, sparking, and angry, missing Mylynna by five feet. Another wail assails me, and another black blade tears into the room, slicing down between me and her, like some giant magician stabbing swords into a magic box.

Marta and Connor are still with us. Marta gives me a questioning look, as though to ask, *what do we do now*?

Running around the blade, I grab Mylynna's hand. "We need to get out of here."

Another giant black blade stabs the room. Damn, what if one of those things hits us?

An image flickers within a crystal ball near the exit door. "Slithy?" The voice is aged, cracked, and female.

"Ezmerelda?" I duck under a new black blade to reach the crystal ball, dragging Mylynna with me. "What's happening? What do we do?"

"Manually reboot the Khertaan server. It's on the twentieth floor—four floors up from you. Hurry."

A black blade slices through the crystal ball, dividing it into halves. They don't fall apart, but the image of Ezmerelda disappears from the right half, replaced by that of a hooded head. A smooth, haughty voice emanates from the right-hand segment. "Susie, Susie, Susie. You're too late. Even now I'm about to give the order to fire on Earth. Your boyfriend Timmy is sharing popcorn with me, watching the proceedings. It's too bad you're not here with us, but I did try to make it happen."

Another black blade slices the air over my shoulder, striking the left half of the crystal and shattering it. Ezmerelda is gone. The hooded figure, who could only be Seth, disappears from the right half.

How do I get to the twentieth floor fast? Gripping Mylynna's hand, I race to the breach—ducking under another slicing black blade—and peer outside. Mists rise around the tower, giving everything a ghostly appearance. Black blades a few feet wide but hundreds of yards long criss-cross every which way, scattered across my field of vision. It's nighttime, the sky decorated by two blurry crescent moons. A black blade has pierced one of them, protruding from it into infinity.

In places where three or four black blades outline geometric shapes, the outlined triangular or rectangular pieces of reality have fallen out, and pieces from other realities show through. Some unseen butcher slices and dices the multiverse in an attempt to invent a new dish from the choicest cuts.

The black blades cut through the tower up and down its stony exterior, already marred by crevices and gaping holes. My view of the next floor up is obstructed by blades and mists. It's impossible to count up four floors. I can't Teleport Self to the twentieth floor if I can't see where I'm teleporting to. I'll have to Levitate my way up. Either way, I can't take Mylynna with me, and I hate the thought of leaving her behind.

Mylynna squeezes my hand. "I got this... at last a real reason to use my Mist Passage skill." Keeping a tight hold of my hand, she pushes past me through the breach. Her body becomes ghostly like the mists, and so does mine. We rise within the wafting whiteness, everything now appearing sharp and focused and monochrome. Easily counting up four floors, we pass through a breach into the room beyond, returning to our normal physical selves once we exit the mists. Marta floats quietly beside me and the Connor AI still tags along beside Mylynna.

Overhead lights flicker to life to illuminate the interior. A forest of reality-slicing black blades greets my Frogkin eyes. Lining the walls are rows upon rows of metal bays harboring computing devices with blinking lights. Which device is the server?

A rectangular section of reality the size of a door falls out of place. On the other side of the portal stands Seth in his dark brown hooded cloak on the bridge of his Planet Buster spaceship. With his back to me, Susie's ex-boyfriend, Timmy Landers, sits strapped in a chair facing a large black screen on which is displayed an image of Earth. A thin gray alien stands next to Timmy, feeding him popcorn. On the other side of the alien from Timmy is the chair Susie once occupied. Like Timmy now, Susie was strapped down and wore a metal collar suppressing her powers, which, in her case, were her time traveling and teleporting abilities—abilities which she had naturally, before I ever existed as her avatar. She didn't have to see where she was teleporting like I do. She could teleport to the other side of a locked door if she wanted.

Her memories are so clear in my head.

"I'm right here," she says in our shared mind space.

Springing from Seth's fingertips, black webs streak past Timmy's head, enters the room I occupy, and strikes a computer console on the far side of the room, enveloping it in thick webs. I've no doubt that's the Khertaan server. How am I supposed to manually reboot it now?

Though I can't see his face, I sense the malevolent smile Seth wears. He twirls a finger in the air. "Fire."

Beyond Seth, a green beam of liquid light appears on-screen. It streaks towards Earth.

Timmy's voice reaches me, loud and clear. *"Susie."*

CHAPTER FIFTY

Kendra: ZAvengers

Due to my level 3 Increased Movement trait, I fly faster than my pursuers, with Georgie always by my side. We dart down alleys and behind buildings, doing our utmost to lose them. For about one second I consider using my Spirit Blast skill to further damage any Dread Naughts still in range, but that would only serve to give away my location. With twenty-four of those things after me, I want little more than to get the hell away. If they all have the Spirit Blast skill—or if even half of them do—they could quickly render me a berserk lunatic, a mindless machine attacking everyone in sight without strategy or discernment. Whether friend, enemy, or civilian… no one would be safe from me. I don't want that.

"Angel lady, over here. Join us." A male Angel in Spirit Form beckons from an alley. An eight-foot-tall Ostrich floats in the air beside him.

"They're from Khertaan," Georgie says. "The Ostrich is the Angel's support AI."

I've never seen this Angel fellow before, but it's a relief to see someone else from Khertaan. I speed over to him.

His skin is pale like mine, his hair pure white and shoulder-length. He's younger than me, probably early twenties. While he's taller than me by six inches or more, his wingspan is only eight feet... two-thirds of mine. His wings match the color of his hair... the same as the color of my wings. Both of us being Angels creates an automatic kinship between us.

"I'm ZAngel, a Spirit Warrior and Winged Fighter, leader of party ZAvengers." He nods at the Ostrich. "This is BusterCap, my support AI."

"I'm Kendra. He's Georgie. Let's move."

ZAngel nods and leads me down the alley. There's no one else there....

Six others abruptly appear, and Georgie is quick to inform me of their kindreds: a Flame Demoness, an Elitist, and a Robot, with their support AIs, two metal women and a male human with a green mohawk that reminds me of Morrow.

They all take hands or otherwise latch onto someone, forming a chain connecting them all. ZAngel offers me his hand. Some skill is about to be used on everyone in the group, requiring us to form a chain.

The Angel man instructs Georgie to take my other hand. Then he answers my unspoken question, "We've found that the Hide Party skill can affect AIs, too, but only if they're part of the chain."

We all disappear. ZAngel magically lifts me in his grip and we fly further down the alley, away from my pursuers.

I lean over to whisper in the Angel man's ear. "Let me do the flying. I can go faster."

He doesn't object, so I take over, and we're immediately moving four times as fast. Others in the chain can't hold back brief whoops of excitement.

ZAngel laughs. "Wow. You go a *lot* faster. I don't remember seeing you in Ger-Alt's inventory, Kendra."

His statement makes no sense. "I'm not sure what you're talking about."

"Were you not with us when Slithy finished her quest? How did you reach level thirty?"

My heart rises in my throat. "You were with Slithy? She finished her quest?" I exhale with relief. "Do you know where she is now?"

He huffs. "We don't know where *anyone* is outside our little group. Yes, we were with Slithy, and she finished her quest. We were there, riding inside Ger-Alt's inventory. Everyone hit level thirty and the four of us woke up at the Fanciful Pegasus facility. We all chose to exit to Earth, naturally… none of us knew anything about Destin. Our players all lived in the same apartment complex before we entered the competition, so it wasn't difficult to find each other and put the party back together. What about you? What party were you in? How *did* you hit level thirty?"

A glance over my shoulder proves we're no longer being followed, but I'm not stopping yet. "My story is a bit different than yours. I'm one of the original developers of the Khertaan program. I went into the game world from my home—with my husband Nick and our daughter Susie. I was Kylie in the game. Nick was Morrow, and Susie was Slithy. We were party TimeTrippers. Charli joined us at some point. My avatar, Kylie, was with Slithy when she started her level thirty quest, but earned level thirty shortly afterward, and was booted out of the game before the quest was finished. I'm glad Slithy was able to take you all with her to the end. Did any others make it?"

Everyone in the group chuckles at that. A female voice replies. "Every PC party and all the NPCs with them went with her on her quest." Her voice grows solemn. "Some of them were lobotomized on the way, but we're hoping they recovered when they hit level thirty and were kicked out of the game. I'm VeraCity, by the way. I'm a Flame Demoness, a Flame Warrior, and a Thief. Do you think we're far enough away to turn off the invisibility? I vote to keep flying, but it would be nice to make some introductions where we can see who's being introduced."

ZAngel asks everyone for input, including me and all five AIs. We all agree it's probably fine to drop the invisibility long enough for introductions. I continue flying, but keep the group low, winding through alleys, avoiding main streets and ruined structures.

Everyone becomes visible, a line of us holding hands, with me and Georgie in the lead. ZAngel regards me with crystal blue eyes. BusterCap rests a beak over the Angel's shoulder, big bird body trailing behind.

"Hey, Kendra, I'm the Flame Demoness." VeraCity holds the Angel man's other hand. Charcoal black hair flows over burnt red shoulders, from which sprout red bat wings with an eight foot span. Her brown eyes welcome me to the group. She nods back at the green mohawk man whose arms wrap her waist from behind. "That's Celt, my AI." He's got black tattoos of Celtic knots inked on his cheeks and forehead. He appears to be taller than VeraCity by nearly six inches and weighs maybe twice her weight. The two of them look almost comical in their flying positions, with his face pressed against her back just below her wings, like he's holding a kiss. His expression is all seriousness, while she's wearing a big-ass smile.

"Hi, I'm TehnKhar, an Elitist Priest of War and a Guide." The olive-skinned man holding VeraCity's other hand nods at me. His black hair is neatly trimmed. His brown eyes sparkle like he has some secret he's never shared with anyone and is proud about it. He's six feet tall, lean, and probably in his late twenties. He tilts his head at the black metal woman behind him. "This is Isis, my support AI."

Isis holds onto TehnKhar with a single hand on his shoulder, the rest of her body held at arm's length from his. She's gotta be six-and-a-half feet tall. Her eyes and bobbed hair are the same black metal as the rest of her. She waves with her free hand. "Hello, Kendra and Georgie. I'm glad to meet you both. I'm an Iron Golem."

TehnKhar wags his head. "She's not really an Iron Golem, she just identifies as one."

"I'm made of iron and I'm a Golem."

"But you're not *really*. You're an AI. You're not *made* of anything. You're an Iron Golem in appearance only."

I clear my throat. "Georgie here identifies as a clown, and I've never disputed his claim."

TehnKhar grimaces at me. "Has he ever made you laugh?"

"Well, yes...."

He scoffs. "Then he's got a right to his claim. An actual Iron Golem can *fight*. Isis can't. She's *not* an Iron Golem, no matter how much she insists she is."

I don't look at him when I reply. "I think you're being rather harsh...."

From further down the line, just past TehnKhar, a bald man about my height, with metallic silver skin, inclines his head to me. His eyes are pure black, without whites. "I'm TorEye, a Robot Fighter and Ice Warrior." He glances towards the metallic woman holding his other hand. "This is my support AI, Bonnie. She identifies as a Robot, and *I* don't have a problem with it."

Occupying the end of the line, Bonnie waves her free hand. Her skin is metallic gold, whereas her eyes, lipstick, and shoulder-length hair are a vibrant hue of orange without gloss. She's shorter than TorEye by a few inches.

With the introductions finished, we quickly and unanimously decide to restart the group invisibility.

VeraCity continues the conversation. "What do you make of the sudden change to the city? And all these Dread Naughts...? We're still trying to figure out how to fight them without getting ourselves killed in two seconds. You're lucky you got away from them."

TehnKhar bobs his head. "And we're lucky you found us. We're flying so much faster now."

They all murmur agreement.

I glance at the sky for signs of the enemy. "I'm not sure I know what you mean by *sudden change*. What was the city like before?"

Now they all scoff. ZAngel speaks for them. "Did you only just get here? The city was bright and the sky clear of monsters. Then it was like we were practically tossed onto an alternate Earth. The city changed like *that* in an instant. It wasn't long afterward that I spotted you. I was hoping you'd know better what was happening, because we don't know shit."

"Join the club." At least I know more now than I did, and it's only right for me to share what I've seen with them. Can I explain it correctly? I do my best, including how my two personae—Kylie and Kendra—were in conflict about which one should be in control of our integrated body, how the two Lungers charmed Kylie but not Kendra, and then turned Kylie's mind to mush, leaving me—Kendra—in control.

They all find this very interesting, and they each admit to also having the persona of their player buried within, some deeper than others.

Before I mention ODYSSEY, I internally ask my nanobot collective, "Do they have ODYSSEY nanobots, too, by any chance?"

"They do. I'm in communication with their collectives even now. Everyone who accompanied Slithy on her final quest received a few nanobots. They'll need to grow and adapt a ton if they're ever to be used for time-shifting, if that's even possible for them. But, yeah, they're there. And I understand about Ger-Alt's inventory. She has a trait that allows her to carry PCs and NPCs. That's how they got everyone into the tower to see Ezmerelda, even though FepXveq, a member of Ger-Alt's own party, tried to stop them."

"Wow. You'll need to tell me more about that sometime." I return to my story for ZAngel and his ZAvengers, telling them how ODYSSEY helped me follow the trail of a Cosmic Cloak to find the timeline we now occupy. That spurs more questions, which I answer the best I can with help from ODYSSEY.

I have a question of my own. "Are any PCs other than FepXveq still in Khertaan? Did everyone else reach level thirty and get booted out?"

Georgie has the answer for that. "The only PC still remaining in Khertaan is FepXveq. But two other PCs have yet to achieve level thirty: Mithabel the Elf Tank and Dylan the Priestess of Light.

They've earned the XP for level thirty, but need to respawn in Khertaan to receive it. But they can't respawn until the Khertaan server comes out of update mode."

"We met them," ZAngel says. "Party MAD. Dylan was the Longest Survivor. They're a couple of tough ladies."

The air vibrates and the sky darkens further. I bring us to a stop as we turn our attention upward.

A huge spaceship fills half the sky. A wide door opens on the bottom of the ship, revealing a green eye that glows brighter and brighter by the second, gathering energy.

The eye looks down, seeming to target the palace.

Everything turns green.

CHAPTER FIFTY-ONE

Susie: Savior in a Black Bikini

"Susie."

The word awakens me. Buried deep in Slithy's subconscious, I'm Susie McKenzie, time traveler, and I accept control of our integrated body. Reading the current threat from Slithy's active thoughts, I take immediate action to stop it.

I go back in time.

I'm in a vast room of gray metal, peering out through an open bay door from behind the eye of the Planet Buster spaceship, far above the Earth. Green energy crackles as it builds within the eye. How can I determine exactly what spot it's targeting? My teleport ability isn't highly reliable.

"I could use mine." Though not currently dominant, Slithy still sees whatever I see and knows every thought I'm having. "My Teleport Self skill can teleport me anywhere I can see. Highly reliable."

"Do I need to let you back in control of our body first?"

"I don't know. Go ahead and try to use the skill yourself if you like."

Imagining myself standing on a structure directly below, I call on Slithy's Teleport Self skill to execute the action rather than my own teleport ability. Her skill activates with surprising ease. That's awesome.

I stand atop the dome of a two-story building surrounded by skyscrapers. The eye will fire on me at any moment, so I'm not sticking around. I needed to know exactly where its target is located, and now I know....

"Don't time-jump from here," Slithy says. "Go back aboard the ship first. We need to get back to the server room on Destin, and I think we'll need to do it through the portal Seth will be opening any second now... if he hasn't already."

"Why don't you take control?"

She does, and soon we're standing in the bay on the Planet Buster ship, in the same spot as when she originally arrived. Then she gives me control back. I think she wants me to feel involved in this... that this isn't all only her doing. I appreciate that.

I time-jump again, reversing the previous time-jump with an alteration of several minutes.

I'm back in the Khertaan server room. Mylynna isn't with me, because I'm here before she and my past self will arrive. I know which of the machines is the Khertaan server—Seth did me the favor of pointing it out. I jump over to it and press the power button. The machine shuts down. I wait thirty seconds and power it back up. It will take a minute or two to boot up.

Why did Ezmerelda want the server rebooted? Using Raphael's credentials, I log onto one of the other computers in the room and scan the most recent log backups. What am I looking for?

There's an entry with the subject line *Saving Earth*. The creator isn't identified, but it must have been Ezmerelda who created the entry. I open it. A single sentence pops up: *Mithabel must choose Earth.*

Where have I heard that name? I do a quick search of PCs. Mithabel is the avatar for player Megan Wright. I just saw Megan a bit earlier here at the Fanciful Pegasus tower. But the log entry specifically mentions Mithabel. Is there some distinction between them I'm missing? I mean, if anyone were looking for either me or Slithy, they'd come to the same person. If I'm looking for Mithabel, can't I go talk to Megan?

But my conjecture doesn't feel right. I run a search and scan the results for Mithabel. *Oh.* It appears she and Dylan are waiting for a respawn before they can attain level thirty. After gaining level thirty, they'll each be given the choice to exit to Earth or Destin. So that's it. Ezmerelda had me reboot the system so the two of them—Mithabel in particular—could respawn. Mithabel must have a skill that can save the planet. Wouldn't Megan have it, too?

But Megan is here, on Destin. When Mithabel respawns, she needs to make the choice to go to Earth. I need to ensure she makes that choice, and makes it quickly. Then it will be up to her to do what's necessary to save the planet.

"How is it that Mithabel operates separately from Megan? Could *we* have two distinct and active bodies, one for you and one for me?"

"I don't know, Slithy. Let's not worry about that right now."

Bringing up the room listings, I find Megan Wright's room.

Opening a file editor and enlarging the font size, I type a quick note. *Mylynna, I'm off to save Earth. Brb, Slithy.*

Jumping over to the exit, I teleport through the locked door, then teleport down the hallway to the stairwell. I don't bother to open the door to the stairwell, but teleport through it, because my own teleport ability is reliable at such a short distance.

Counting the landings, I teleport down the correct number and then teleport through the door into the hallway beyond. It takes no time to find the door labeled with Megan Wright's name, and I teleport again.

I'm in a hallway with photos of Megan Wright adorning the walls. I Jump to the far end of the hallway and teleport through a door on the left into Megan Wright's bedroom.

Like in other rooms in the tower, the exterior walls here have been breached. Rubble litters the floor. There's even a huge chunk on the foot of the bed, but it missed the woman with straight black hair and pointed ears who lies next to it.

Dressed only in a black Bikini, the Elf woman springs up, hovering above the bed, a hand extended as though holding a weapon—but her grip is empty. She grimaces, and a bow appears, loaded and aimed at me. "Return my sword now, thief."

I hold up both hands. "I don't have it, Mithabel, sorry. You must have lost it when you died. My name is Susie McKenzie—Slithy in Khertaan—and I need you to listen carefully. Earth is about to be destroyed, and only you can save it." I step close and extend a hand. "Please. There's no time for discussion or explanation."

Taking a calming breath, her demeanor changes and she stashes her bow. "Kaleisha? Tell me Dylan is okay. I can't open any chat channels."

No one answers that I can hear.

I lean closer. "I assure you Dylan is okay, Mithabel. But the Earth won't be if you don't come with me right now. You should have a choice between Destin and Earth. You need to choose Earth."

A crystal ball sitting at the end of the room crackles to life, flashing an image of me lying on the bed. It's only there for a second, and then a black blade slices through the glass orb. The blade remains stuck in place, extending from floor to ceiling—just as I saw happen in Mylynna's room. Indeed, the events I experienced in Mylynna's room are unfolding for past-me in another room of the Fanciful Pegasus facility right now.

"Okay, I believe you." Mithabel flies to me. "But if the scene in the crystal ball means anything, it appears you're to stay here." She glances at the bed.

Another black blade cuts into the room, slicing the bed in halves.

I shake my head. "I don't think so." I don't know what that scene in the crystal ball meant, but I'm definitely not staying in this room.

Mithabel locks her gaze on mine. "So… how do I choose Earth?"

"I don't know if you don't."

The exit door opens at her touch. She flies along the hallway, passing the photo gallery, arriving at the door leading to the main hallway beyond. I stay right behind her.

The door opens. A forest of black blades fills the hallway beyond.

Mithabel nods.

The scene beyond the door changes. It's like we stand on a balcony overlooking a dark city. Dread Naughts circle in the sky. Above them hovers the Planet Buster spaceship. Directly below the ship sits the domed two-story building.

I point. "There. That's the target. The ship is about to fire a destruction beam on that domed building."

Mithabel nods again, exhaling. "I need a melee weapon or shield. Do you have one I can use?"

I shake my head. "All I have are my Bare Hands. I'm a Martial Artist."

"Uh huh. Can you head hop to me? I'd send you a party invite if I could, but it seems parties aren't a thing anymore."

Oh… that's what the crystal ball scene was about. But I don't need to be on the bed for it. I sit on the floor with my back to the wall. "Here goes nothing."

The head hop works. Slithy and I both are looking through Mithabel's eyes, and we lend the Tank all our abilities. Mithabel glances at my unconscious body sitting on the hallway floor and then steps through the portal to Earth.

We've only seconds to go before the green beam will fire. Mithabel gives me control of her body, and I teleport her to the top of the dome where she needs to be. The eye of the Planet Buster is brimming with green energy. Activating her Hide skill and my Mislead and Displace skills as preemptive defensive measures, I relinquish control back to her, so she can do whatever it is she'll need to do—I still don't know what that is.

Half-a-dozen Dread Naughts charge us, having pierced our invisibility. Some of them sing. Some shriek. All of them fail in their attempts to incapacitate Mithabel. Between my Mentalist skills and her heavy-duty Tank skills, Mithabel's got defenses.

Other Dread Naughts flock around us, searching, knowing our general location even if they can't see us.

A colossal murder of Crows fills the sky. At the synchronized flapping of Crow wings, gusts of wind catch the Dread Naughts, pushing most of them back. Those who aren't repelled are attacked by Crows, black energy pulsing from their talons. A fireball streaks across the sky, catching several Dread Naughts in roiling flames.

The monsters won't be stopping Mithabel in time. Excellent.

A five-foot-tall Spider appears before the Elf Tank, having seen through her invisibility. It stabs with a pointed limb.

It misses completely—my Displace skill at work. Whew.

The green beam fires. This is it.

Mithabel laughs, Parrying the beam attack using my Bare Hands skills. But the energy has to go somewhere, and wherever it goes, it will devastate its new target. If that target is on Earth, then Earth will still be destroyed....

The beam reverses on itself—turned back by the Tank's Reflect Any Attack skill—and strikes the Planet Buster ship.

Clever gal....

The spaceship turns to green liquid light, dripping like acid rain from the sky.

The big Spider is no longer in evidence.

The body of a young man falls towards us. Mithabel flies up to intercept. She can't carry him, but helps break his fall, bringing him to rest atop the dome.

Timmy Landers, my ex-boyfriend, sits up and smiles. He's not wearing that damned metal collar anymore. He looks around for the invisible person who helped him. "Um, thanks—whoever you are."

"The name is Mithabel."

"Tell him Susie sent you," I say in her head.

"Susie sent me."

Timmy chuckles. "I knew she wouldn't let the bad guy win." He spits out a piece of popcorn. "Too much butter for my taste."

"Incoming," someone yells. "Look up."

Black blades five feet wide and the height of the tallest skyscraper rain down on the city, cutting through buildings, Dread Naughts, and Crows alike. What the hell is causing them?

CHAPTER FIFTY-TWO

Erica: Surrender

Greelia and Ulric... they're both gone in an instant, killed by the blade Gondra practically delivered to Seth. And now a five-foot-tall shadowy spider appears from nowhere next to Nick, drawing back a front leg, tapered to a point.... All I have time to do is shriek, using the attack method granted to me by Emma during my brief time in Anissa.

Nick spins around in response to my outburst. But neither of us stop the spider's attack. The arachnid's pointed leg pierces Nick's chest. Another scream erupts unbidden from my lips as his eyes go dark. Just when I'd found him again... the *real* Nick... he's taken from me *again*.

It's a struggle not to be pulled into the misty whirlpool. Princess Karen, Renee, and Em-Row are ripped from my grasp. The wind carries them to the metadonut, and the merged timeline sucks them in, as well as Nick's lifeless body.

It's just me and Gondra against Seth and his stealthy spider ally, which could even now be sneaking up on me.

Gondra bows to me. "Traveling with you has been a pleasure, but our travels have come to an end. Farewell, Erica." As he straightens, he allows the winds to carry him to the metadonut, and he, too, passes into the merged timeline.

What the hell…? So now it's *just me* against the enemy…?

They killed my Nicky Nick.

They killed my Nicky Nick.

I let it all out, pouring everything in me into my shriek attack.

The spider appears before me, killer leg drawn back.

I activate my Cosmic Cloak, becoming insubstantial, and the killer leg passes through me without harm.

Without a physical throat, I can't continue shrieking, so I return to substantial form, grab hold of the damned spider's leg, and shriek right in the beast's face, fueled by my rage and bloody broken heart.

The monster stops struggling against me. The whirlpool tugs at it, and I let it go. As it nears the metadonut, it drives its own leg into its thorax. Black splinters of chitin peel off the spider's body and fly at the metadisc, puncturing a swath of the merged timeline from all angles. What affect will that have on those inside the timeline? What appear to be splinters to me could be gigantic shards of death raining down on everything in existence inside that timeline. I can only imagine the shock of the timeline's residents as ungodly huge black blades come crashing in on them.

In the span of three seconds, the spider is nothing but splinters….

Seth kneels on the metadonut, resisting the whirlwind. I turn insubstantial once more, hoping the winds will pass through me, but I still feel their tug.

I reduce my efforts to resist the winds—only a little, enough to inch closer and closer without being drawn into the merged timeline. My feet touch down on the edge of the metadisc, and I kneel to reduce the force of the winds against my metaphysical body.

A flash of green spills from the merged timeline. Something major just happened.

Seth hisses in anger. He no longer bears my face, I'm relieved to see. His hood flaps behind him, leaving his head exposed. He's bald, his skin alabaster white, his eyes black with no whites. Fangs hang down over ice blue lips. He flicks a forked tongue, much like Gondra's, which does nothing to make me feel better about Gondra abandoning me. "Erica," Seth whispers. "Of everyone to stand against me in the end, I'd never have guessed it would be you."

"Glynda told me I was important."

"Ah, yes, a thorn in my side, that one." His voice is masculine and arrogant. He crawls towards me, the storm raging around him, still trying to draw him in. "But she's not here to help you. No one is. You're all alone. Look at you. You're a ghost even now. No one cares about you and never will. You gave yourself to Nick, and he continually abandoned you. Did you know he had half-a-dozen children by other women? I don't recall him ever giving you a child. He couldn't even give you a car, though he promised to. Yet still you cling to his memory. Still you long for him. And guess what. *He's not dead.*"

I catch my breath. "I saw him die, fool."

"You saw Greelia die… and Ulric and my Shadow Spider. What happened when they died? Their bodies flaked away—losing bits of themselves gradually. Did Nick's body do that? It did not. You saw it. He was pulled intact into the merged timeline. There's still something of him left inside the Cosmic Cloak he wore. And you… you can be with him again. All you need do is enter the merged timeline in its current state, and you'll find him. He probably needs help *asap.* Can you envision him lying in the street, his blood staining the pavement? Personally, I hope he dies. But if he does, and you do nothing about it, his death is on you. Best go to him, young one. Be with your Nick while you still can. No one lives forever—not you and certainly not Nick."

Tears stream down my cheeks. I clench my fists, turning my gaze to the merged timeline.

"Yes," Seth hisses, sounding more and more like Gondra.

I refuse to believe Gondra and Seth are of the same kindred, or that Gondra is a version of Seth, acting to gain my trust and then bailing on me when I need him most. There's something else up with Gondra. There has to be. He must have had a good reason to leave.

Seth stops crawling, his malevolent face a foot from mine. The whirlwind drives black splinters deeper into the merged timeline behind him, wedging them tighter in place. He lifts his hands from the metadisc, resting on his knees like I am. The wind tosses my blue hair like I'm in a hurricane. He gestures towards the center of the metadisc. "Go, Erica. Go to your Nicky Nick."

No one calls my Nick by that name but me. My gaze slides from the timeline to his face.

He reaches for my shoulder.

I don't try to stop his touch. I'm insubstantial. He's insubstantial. *Can* he touch me?

He does. It's metaphysical contact, but it's sufficient....

His forked tongue flicks. "Enervate."

In that instant, I surrender myself....

Magical black energy flows from his hand into me, seeking my emotions in an attempt to drive me to suicide.

But I've already surrendered control of my body to someone without emotions... a nanobot collective immune to Seth's spell.

"Time to go bye bye." Vocalizing the taunt with my throat and lips, ODYSSEY drops me onto my butt and kicks up with both my feet, planting them in Seth's face. If he can touch me, then it stands to reason I can touch him, and I do. The kick sends the bastard flying off the metadisc. The whirlwind snares him. Instantaneously sucked into the vortex, he's sliced to bits by the stiff, chitinous black splinters wedged into the timeline at its center.

Oh, God.

The wind rolls me onto my stomach as ODYSSEY returns my body to me. I flatten myself on the metadisc, my blue hair and pink

Cloak flapping above me, and concentrate on controlling this little piece of the multiverse. If Greelia could do it, so can I.

ODYSSEY chuckles in my head. "That was cool."

"Hey… don't distract me…. Get your ass back in gear… and help me redefine some timelines… the way we want."

CHAPTER FIFTY-THREE

Yuni: Training Exercises

It takes a couple days to recruit a full contingent of 640 followers and grant them all my skills. Fortunately during this time, our locale isn't attacked by any more Flitters or other Dread Naughts. Reports come in of other monster attacks, many of which aren't repelled, but we aren't ready to fight them. I can't have my followers needlessly dying by jumping into fights they can't win. They need training.

Videos of some Dread Naught attacks are posted on social media, and it gladdens my heart to see other avatars from Khertaan in the fight. I recognize some of them, including CC, Charli, and Amarynth.

One of the more controversial videos shows a giant Charli hovering in the air near a giant fish with bat wings—Inuki identifies it as a Dread Naught of the Diver variety. Clearly, it's capable of mind control. Charli spent half an hour by the Diver's side, watching it eat people whole, before she finally took action to stop it. Once she took action, it was gone in an instant. Charli has the power to deal with these things, if she can only resist their charms.

Comments on the video question why Charli waited so long to destroy the monster. I ask Sharice to enter a comment explaining that some Dread Naughts can charm people, even powered people, making them act against their will. If one of these monsters is spotted, Sharice adds, it's best to get far, far away as quickly as possible.

While I recruit police officers and grant them skills, I also use my special Transfer Auni action on a select group of followers. Bethany and Sharice, being nurses, are the first recipients, giving them the ability to cast all my spells.

"I want to go magically heal someone right now," says Beth.

Sharice eagerly nods in agreement. "How do we cast the Heal spell?"

The two are fast learners, making my job easy. I'll set them to training others once I've transferred Auni to more followers.

Though the maximum Auni I can store is 184, there's no limit on the storage capacity of my followers. They can't replenish Auni they expend, but I can keep giving them more. Because of my level three Wakeful trait, even when I'm active, I can regenerate transferred Auni at the sped-up rate of one Auni per minute. Most avatars would need to sleep to recover Auni at that rate.

Over the span of thirty hours, I select a follower every half hour to whom I transfer 30 Auni. During the first eight hours, I give Bethany and Sharice each 240 Auni. Then I move on to others. I transfer 30 Auni to each of my initial followers—Guy the guitar player, Michelle the novelist, Destiny the dancer/vocalist, Lana the martial artist, Jamie the wrestler, and then the five surfers: Mya, Tara, Joseph, Daisuke, and, yes, even Evan, whom Bradford has brought back as an autonomous undead Skeleton.

Everyone who meets Evan freaks out initially, but he's got a great sense of humor and can quickly put people at ease using the Presence and Attraction skills I've granted him. As with all Undead kindreds, he deals both physical and spiritual damage when making a melee attack using inherent weapon forms—in his case, that's fists and talons of bone. When he Shapeshifts to Crow form, he's a Skeleton Crow, and a talking one at that—the source of much amusement. In addition to being immune to metal weapons, he's also resistant to non-magical weapons—other than blunt ones—and is unaffected by instantaneous death effects, mental or emotional attacks or effects, cold, and poison. He can see in the dark. The biggest drawback is his inability to be healed by spells—he's got to heal on his own, but the Wakeful trait he has for being my follower increases his rate of innate healing, so that helps.

The medical examiner, Tom, receives 60 Auni, as does Officer Bob. Sixteen other officers receive 60 Auni each. Everyone who receives Auni is able to cast any of my spells—Enervate, War, Exorcise, or Heal. The Enervate spell allows them to select any of the four damage domains—physical, mental, spiritual, or emotional—and deal that kind of damage, provided they touch their target. The War spell allows the caster and all allies to see in the dark, and can be used to enchant a weapon for the duration of an encounter. The Exorcise spell can theoretically be used to deal with any undead enemy, should we encounter any. The Heal spell, naturally, heals damage—but only in the physical domain, which sucks. I wish I had the Advanced Healing spell that Dylan has, which can heal mental, spiritual, or emotional damage as well as physical. If we ever meet again, could she teach me? I don't know, but I'd like to find out. Whether or not she can teach me the spell, I really hope to see Dylan again.

After those first thirty hours, I finish recruiting a full contingent of followers, most of whom are in law enforcement. Then we discuss battle strategies and do some advanced training.

"Everyone, fetch an extra set of clothes and come out to the training yard. The clothes you bring should look different from what you're wearing at the time, please."

I watch as my followers trickle onto the field, each carrying a bundle of clothing, curious expressions all around.

"Form lines, five feet apart from your neighbor."

They do so.

"All right, when I count to three, everyone will invoke your Split Body skill. The extra clothes you brought are for the duplicate self you're about to produce. So imagine a person lying on the ground, and lay out your extra set of clothes accordingly."

Glances are exchanged as each person stretches out a set of clothes on the ground. The excitement is palpable.

"All you need to do is focus on the skill, and imagine there being two of you. One. Two. Three. *Go.*"

My heart sings as I watch 640 people turn into amorphous blobs that divide and take shape as twice that number of powered people, all of them nearly as skilled as I am. Each duplicate blob squirms its way into the clothes set out for it, and fills them perfectly upon taking human shape. Everyone jumps to their feet and we have a quick naming party for the newcomers.

I'm unable to Transfer Auni to the duplicates, but they all have the traits and skills of the original. The duplicates aren't considered my followers, but that's fine. They don't need me to give them anything, as they get everything they need from the person they duplicated.

"Now this is what I call an army."

My statement is met with boisterous cheers. *We are hyped.*

Everyone is eager to get to work. We train in coordinating attacks. We use metal weapons against each other, since we're immune to them and can hit as hard as we want without hurting anyone. Inuki tells us when our actions constitute a combo attack.

Bradford doesn't take part, since he doesn't share our immunity to metal. "I'll join you in combo attacking the enemy when the time comes," he assures us. I know he can. I've seen him participate in combo attacks before.

My spell casters practice enchanting rifles. Others practice using the magicked weapons for ranged cooperative combos. With the Wind Control skill, others practice lifting heavy objects into the air and manipulating them to their will. It's tremendously easy with a couple dozen of them working together.

My small army breaks off into small groups, each group practicing as a unit specializing in specific skills. Each unit elects a leader, relieving me of the need to delegate. I like how this is working out. When a group runs into issues, their leader comes to me, I explain, and the leader takes it from there. It's totally awesome.

I want my spell casters to practice the Enervate spell. It needs a living target, and I pair them off against their duplicate selves. Each spell caster is tasked to expend only one Auni per casting, but to apply their Enervation skills to increase the damage dealt. They each feel the effects, because each spell caster shares hit point pools with their duplicate. The damage heals rather fast, however, due to everyone having the Wakeful talent... and it heals doubly fast because the duplicates contribute to the healing process.

"Look at that," says Sharice, pointing at something behind me.

A car floats ten feet off the ground, a flock of Crows flying around it. The engine starts... with no one sitting at the wheel. One of the Crows used Wind Control to turn the ignition key.

Another group of Crows raise a boulder into the air. Yet other Crows practice their combo attacks on the boulder and pulverize it.

I am *so* proud.

I task the spell casters with practicing combo Enervate spell attacks while in Crow form. I'm honored to have numerous volunteers to serve as targets. I'd do it if not for Tuni. I can't put her at risk by lowering any of my hit point pools. So I let the volunteers decide among themselves who will have the honor. I tell the spell casters to use the Enervate spell to only deal physical damage, because we have the ability to heal that kind of damage. They do as instructed, and then get to practice their Heal spells on the volunteer they just damaged.

After the spell casting exercises, I take a few hours to replenish everyone's expended Auni.

Training extends over the next few days. Everyone is honing their specialized skills in their units but also working with other units. We're an army comprised of sixty-plus elite units that work together like the proverbial well-oiled machine.

We're ready when the call comes in. A couple of Lungers—giant centipedes—are attacking citizens nearby. We head out, amped and ready for action. This is it... our first encounter as an elite trained force.

Two Wind Control units carry the Lungers into the sky. The monsters are completely out of their element, unable to make physical attacks against us. They have nothing solid from which to spring to make the powerful lunge attacks they're named for.

Other Wind Control units add finesse to the operation, completely stripping mobility from our foes, controlling the positioning of their bodies down to the facing of their heads. With tight winds of greater than gale force controlling every body part, the Lungers can't even so much as wiggle their tail ends.

Two Riflemen units open fire on the Lungers with ranged combo attacks. One rifleman from each unit turns their weapons on their buddies and open fire, proclaiming the Lungers to be their friends.

Bradford stands next to me, watching the encounter in the sky. "It's good your followers aren't hurt by metal bullets."

I nod, keeping my eyes on the scene unfolding above. "That's exactly why I armed everyone with metal weapons. We'll have to worry if any Dread Naught ever charms a spell caster, but that's why their unit isn't up there now."

Sharice stands nearby. "Will we spell casters ever get to fight?"

"I'd have sent you up this time if the rifles failed to harm the Lungers. But these monsters are vulnerable to physical damage, fortunately. The Riflemen will kill them. You need to conserve your Auni as much as you can. Consider it a precious resource."

"Yes, ma'am."

Everyone is out of range of the death explosions when they inevitably come.

The two charmed riflemen break out of their trances, apologetic for being so weak of will.

"No apology is necessary," I tell them when they come to me. "Any of us, including me or Bradford, would have fallen victim to the Lungers if we'd been targeted instead. Someone had to be their targets. You obeyed orders despite the risks, armed yourselves appropriate to the situation, and fulfilled your duty to the best of your ability. I'm awarding you each a special commendation."

Their smiles brighten.

None of us were physically harmed by the Lungers, which is a real boost to morale. We're ready for whatever comes next. *Bring it on.*

CHAPTER FIFTY-FOUR

Charli-14: Reunion

Armed with knowledge I gained from Nasty-Us the Diver Vampire, I and my little group of Khertaan avatars continue the fight against the Dread Naughts, banishing more and more of them to the pocket dimension from which I'd unwittingly released them. Of my four personae, I dominate by default. I'm suited to get the job done without unnecessary killing. Fifty continues to object that we're not killing them all, and CC agrees with her, but Lady Amarynth and Zyekt both side with me and Thirty-Five.

I'd gained a Shadow Dome skill upon reaching level thirty. I use it to protect the unconscious bodies of anyone who head hops. The dome is impenetrable by anything that's not shadow-related. By placing the dome in the shadow of a building, I make it almost impossible to see, which also helps protect those inside from wandering mooks.

The Dread Naughts can't harm me physically. My level four Mental Armor, coupled with Zyekt's Mental Focus skill, gives me significant protection against mind-influencing effects thrown at me by the Dread Naughts. A similar trait of his—Meditative

Focus—helps me tremendously in banishing the Dread Naughts I come upon.

On occasion, I succumb to emotional or spiritual effects the Dread Naughts use against me. They never go so far as to make me try to kill myself, because that would be harming me by definition, and is prohibited by the magical laws under which the Dread Naughts were released. But charming me into not taking action against them is allowed, and is something they are always keen to try when they can. The few times it works, Thirty-Five and Fifty work together to boot me out of control of our body, with Fifty reluctantly allowing Thirty-Five to take over. Thirty-Five then proceeds to banish the enemy Dread Naught before it has a chance to charm her, too.

It catches everyone by surprise when the world changes. It's as though some divine being switched the scenery on us. We're still in a city, but the structures and the streets aren't the same.

The sky darkens. Flitters and Divers flood the sky, perhaps thousands of them. It's beyond terrifying... it was difficult enough trying to handle only a few of the monsters in our locale.

An army of Crows led by Yuni the Priestess of War and her twin brother, Bradford the Fire Wizard, drive Dread Naughts high into the sky, away from city residents. I don't have time to attempt banishments—there are far too many Dread Naughts for that—so I join the fight to kill and incapacitate.

Shadows deepen over the city. Crackling green energy far above the world draws my attention. A spaceship hovers above the Earth, with a bay door open to reveal what looks like a giant green eye. My level forty Landmarks skill tells me the ship is a Planet Buster owned by Seth the Destroyer, and that he—not the Dread Naughts—is our main enemy. The Dread Naughts serve only to distract us from Seth and his schemes.

There's no opportunity to discuss a best plan of action. With the ship casting the entire area in shadow, I use Shadow Passage to travel up to it. Everyone else is too busy fighting the Dread

Naughts, so I go up alone, activating my Hide skill so no one and nothing will notice me.

Electricity sizzles over the surface of the green eye. I enter the bay holding the eye.

A blond white woman appears from nowhere. She looks familiar, but I can't place her.

She transforms into a red-and-black-skinned Frogkin.

"Slithy?"

But she doesn't hear me, and now she's gone.

A flash of black and red draws my eye, and I see Slithy atop a domed building directly below, where the eye is looking. She disappears yet again. What is she doing?

Now she's back inside the bay, only ten feet from me. I open my mouth to call to her again, but think better of it. She's doing something I shouldn't distract her from. Changing back to her blond white woman form, she vanishes once more. Does she have a plan to stop the eye from firing on the planet? I can hope so, but it's not making sense to me.

If she's busy with something else, then it's on me to shut down that eye.

The gathering green energy grows increasingly brighter. I need to act quickly. Casting my one and only spell, I conjure a Shadow Warrior and send him to the attack.

He struggles against the eye's light, which hampers his abilities. He can't attack effectively, and every second he spends caught in the green glow causes him damage. All he's accomplishing is his own slow demise. I call him back to me. What else can I do?

"*Momma?*"

Hovering outside the bay door is a young woman more grown than last I saw here. "*Britta.*" I want to give her a hug, but celebrating our reunion will have to wait. "Help me figure out how to stop this thing from firing."

"We have to go Momma. Mithabel will stop the beam, and we can't be here when she does. Slithy told me. She knows the future. She said you would be here and sent me to come get you." Britta flies to me. "When the beam fires, Mithabel reflects it back at the ship and destroys it. It's going to happen any second now. Come on." She tugs my arm.

"Right." Commanding my Shadow Warrior to come with me, I run to the edge of the bay and launch myself into the sky. Beneath the ship, I fly downward as fast as my Shadow Passage skill allows, which is faster than falling.

Britta flies beside me, easily able to fly as fast as I can shadow travel. She gropes for my hand, but is unable to grasp my Shadow Form. "I love you, Momma."

"I love you, too, Britta."

We're halfway to the ground. Mithabel is directly below me. I maneuver myself aside, so as not to be between her and that eye.

The green beam fires.

Mithabel raises an arm above her. She's not wielding a weapon or shield.

The beam reflects off her bare forearm, reversing direction, as though her skin were a mirror.

The spaceship turns to green soup above me and comes raining down. That's lovely, but without the ship between me and the sun, I'm no longer in shadow, and my Shadow Passage skill deactivates. Losing Shadow Form, I continue traveling Earthward via the natural laws of gravity.

Britta flies above me, trying to block the sun, but she isn't large enough to create the size and depth of shadow I need. She grabs my wrists, but Khertaan skills don't give a person the ability to carry anyone else except in specific cases, and this isn't one of them. She falls with me, but keeps smiling. "Don't worry, Momma. I know how to save you." Her body goes limp and her hands slip from my wrists as she attempts to head hop to me. "Take my Flight Speed skill, Momma. I'll Levitate. I won't fall."

"There's no need for that. I'll be fine." I refuse her head hop. She needs to use her skill for herself to get safely to the ground with me.

"Don't die on me, Momma."

I give her my brightest, bravest smile.

All around us, the battle rages as we descend. The Dread Naughts are too busy fighting others, they don't concern themselves with me and my kid.

The ground approaches fast.

Two seconds before I'm about to go splat, I enter the shadow of the domed building. Invoking my Shadow Passage skill, I take Shadow Form and arrest my rapid descent. As I promised my daughter, I'm fine. I fly gently to the ground. Britta and my Shadow Warrior both land safely beside me.

I throw a Shadow Dome over us. Britta and I have a long hug.

It's not long enough, but it will have to do for now. Stepping back, I grip her hands. "I'm not losing you, Britta. Head hop to me if you want. It will be like you're fighting, without putting you in danger. But I'm not letting you out of this dome. Not until it's safe out there." Not being of shadow, she can't leave the dome unless I allow it.

"*Momma.* I can take care of myself. Let me out, or I'll….."

"You'll… what?"

"Nothing. Never mind."

"Britta…."

She rolls her eyes. "Forget it. I'll head hop to you."

I leave my Shadow Warrior inside the dome with her, in case something manages to get inside. Lying on her side, pulling her knees against her chest, Britta head hops to me and lends me all her skills. I fly out of the dome.

A shadowy figure looking suspiciously like Britta draws up beside me and waves. Her flesh so dark as to mask her features, I barely catch her smile. Even her teeth and tongue are charcoal gray.

"Spooky?"

The figure shakes her head. "Nah, I'm Britta's Shadow Self number two."

Inside my head, Britta giggles. "Do you want to name her, Momma?"

I wipe away a tear. "I'd love to. Hello, my sweet *Nicole.*" Yes, I name her after Britta's father.

"I like it." Nicole beams at me.

Zyekt flies up next to us, excitement lighting his eyes. *"We're immune to their death explosions.* Niav and me. We found out quite by accident, but we were right there next to one when it died, and not a scratch on us."

Other reports come in… aside from Familiars and Companions, all who were NPCs in Khertaan are immune not only to the Dread Naught death explosions, but aren't being physically harmed by the mooks, period. Created NPCs—like my Shadow Warrior and Britta's Shadow Self—share the immunity.

My Assassin shadow daughter Nicole and I fight side by side. I banish every Dread Naught I can, while Nicole insta-kills others, getting right up next to them when necessary. Britta's Inspect Character skill allows us to determine what attack forms each Dread Naught has before we close with them, and we take special care with those having significant spiritual and emotional attacks. We don't want to suddenly start clawing our own eyes out. We conserve our use of the Teleport Self skill, since it is only usable up to 18 times a day, which restricts us from simply teleporting in, attempting an action, and teleporting out.

Our side suffers losses, to be sure….

Yuni shouts a warning, and we all look up. Giant black blades stream down from the sky with no evident cause. They kill indiscriminately, slicing people and Dread Naughts alike to pieces. Thanks to Yuni, many of us dodge and avoid certain death. Several Dread Naughts, on the other hand, don't notice the danger before it's too late for them.

The descent of blades ends.

The sky rains blood. Where is this coming from?

It's not easy to see with blood streaming down one's face and into one's eyes. I close mine and turn on Third Person POV, just so I can halfway see what I'm doing. It's weird to watch the battle rage from such a disjointed view, and to see everyone fighting with their eyes shut.

Finally, the seemingly endless stream of red ends. But the fighting goes on. Wiping the blood from my eyes, I return to First Person POV.

So tired of all the fighting, still I pour all my Willpower and Cowgirl Stubbornness into it as I call on the power of my Shadow Gauntlets to banish yet another Dread Naught.

A beam of black light springs from the Dread Naught before me. It strikes another nearby Dread Naught, and two beams spring off it, striking two more monsters. Two beams shoot off from each of those monsters, striking four more targets…. As fast as light can travel, the doubling of streams continues until every Dread Naught in sight is bathed in the black energy….

They all vanish.

Did I banish them all?

We all stop where we are, dropping our attacks. The enemy is gone.

The enemy is gone!

All is silent except for the *drip drip drip* of blood from our bodies onto the ground.

The tears well inside me, and I don't hold them back.

Someone laughs, and soon everyone joins in, even those of us who are crying. Laughter echoes across the world.

We did it. We've won!

I've really got to clean this blood and green soup off me. I look like Britta did when she was born…. We all do.

CHAPTER FIFTY-FIVE

Yuni: The Last of the Dread Naughts

The world changes. Everything looks drastically different. It's like we've all been teleported to a dark city on some other world.

Dread Naughts instantaneously flood the sky. A spaceship hangs over the Earth, powering up an energy beam that can only be meant to destroy us.

Flitters and Divers converge on a domed structure, and though I don't know why, I feel it imperative they not be allowed to reach it. My followers and I go to work, transforming to Crows for better mobility and speed, and using our Wind Control abilities to push away the Dread Naughts.

The spaceship fires its green beam, targeting the domed structure. Dread weighs in my gut. It could all be over right now.

But Mithabel is on top of the dome and miraculously reflects the beam back at the spaceship.

The vessel turns to green sludge that pours down on the city and all combatants.

The destruction of the spaceship is of no concern to the Dread Naughts. The battle with them continues as though there had never been a hulking piece of metal hovering over the city, with the exception that every combatant on both sides wears a coat of green soup.

ကာကာ ကာ ကာ ကာ ကာ

The battle has been long and chaotic, not always easy for the different units to coordinate with each other. Several officers have died, though nearly half of them have revived to immediately rejoin the fight, while a sixth of them have revived multiple times. Bethany, Sharice, Guy, Michelle, and Destiny heal officers who take physical damage. Some of our numbers have committed suicide, some have gone berserk and attacked the rest of us, and some have been rendered mindless. It's difficult dealing with our non-fatal casualties—some of the suicidal ones succeeded in their attempts, and the berserkers have needed to be restrained or even killed to prevent them from hurting friendlies.

It's growing more and more obvious that we can't win this fight. The Dread Naughts number in the thousands, and we aren't even two thousand strong. For every monster we kill, there's another to take its place.

I catch sight of more movement in space, like comets streaking toward the planet. No, they aren't comets. They're long, metallic spears. No, they're more like swords... they're coming straight at us and coming fast. I alert everyone to the incoming threat. What deviousness is this?

Huge black blades slice through the fabric of time and space. They appear metallic, but one cuts right through a nearby follower, slicing into his left shoulder and exiting from his right thigh. Whatever these things are, we have no immunity to them.

The blades don't come down parallel to each other, but at all sorts of angles. It's next to impossible to dodge them. Darting out of the way of one can put a person in the path of another. Making oneself as small as possible is the best defense. I order all my followers to Shapeshift Crow and Compress Body as much as possible.

Despite our precautions, several of us die from the blades, as do many of our enemies and a host of civilians. Wind Control doesn't sway the blades in the slightest. Bradford's Fire Dome offers no protection against the metal storm as the blades slice right through it. These gigantic weapons are a higher magnitude of power than anything on Earth, including the Dread Naughts. It's like some wrathful deity hurls blades at the world. Taller than skyscrapers, with some stretching off into infinity, the black blades strike the ground and remain standing erect and tall.

Finally, the metal storm ends, and the battle with the Dread Naughts begins anew. Part of our strategy becomes using Wind Control to push the damnable monsters against the edges of those erect black blades. The tactic proves fatal to the enemy every time.

A driving rain comes… viscous red droplets cast with force, mixed with bits of flesh and bone… as though a giant fell from his home in the clouds into a humongous wood chipper, splattering his remains across the planet. As we battle the Dread Naughts, it's as though gods in an alternate plane of existence battle amongst themselves.

The rain doesn't harm anyone, but it's damn disgusting. Now we're coated in both green and red liquids. We all look like bloody green Goblins.

Despite the blood rain, the fighting continues across the city and beyond. We fight more than Flitters and Divers. Lungers burrow under and into structures, attacking residents. Burners set homes and other buildings on fire. It's too much for us to handle… the Dread Naughts still number in the thousands, while we've lost a couple hundred.

But others from Khertaan have joined our fight. Two Angel Spirit Warriors show up—Kendra and ZAngel—accompanied by a Flame Demoness Warrior named VeraCity, an Elitist Priest named TehnKhar, and a Robot Fighter named TorEye. Charli, Amarynth, and CC arrive on the scene, accompanied by the Angel Zyekt, his

Mouse Guide companion Niav, Amarynth's Dragon companion Rolag, and CC's Electric Serpent companion Lance.

Algor, a Sand Demon Priest, leads a small group that joins us. Morrow the Punk Lightning Wizard and his familiar, Rancor the Woodpecker Psi-Warrior, comes to our aid. Another Punk shows up, too, named Em-Row, looking exactly like Morrow, but claiming not to be a duplicate or a twin. He's accompanied by a Princess Karen and a support AI, Renee, who, it turns out, is Morrow's support AI, not Em-Row's. Maybe some day I'll get an explanation of their relationships.

What makes Renee stand out from the other support AIs is her ability to affect the Dread Naughts. Renee, Em-Row, and Princess Karen have shriek attacks that make the enemy want to kill themselves—devastatingly effective. Me and my Crows use Wind Control to blow suicidal Dread Naughts far into the sky, where their death explosions won't hurt anything or anyone.

Originally from party Quantized, a Faerie named Toxxi arrives. She's a level thirty Life-Stealer who can create ten undead per day. She turns ten of my fallen followers into autonomous undead. I'm quite pleased.

Also from Quantized, a Goblin Were-Fighter named Ger-Alt arrives with her Cheetah Barbarian mount named Zip. I think a Squirrel is with her, too.

Ger-Alt has the ability to stash *people* in her inventory. Useful, that. She stashes our mindless comrades and all the suicidal and berserker ones that we restrained. She stashes our dead, too, preserving their corpses.

Many other avatars come, too many to list here. I keep hoping Dylan will show....

Black lights create a web across the sky, connecting each Dread Naught to another.

The black lights pulse....

The Dread Naughts are gone... all of them... just gone.

I feel empty.

When laughter echoes across the world, I don't join in. I'm a Priestess of War. I live for battle. If the battle is done, where does that leave me?

CHAPTER FIFTY-SIX

Slithy: Cleaning Up

The battles on Earth and Destin come to an abrupt end, the Dread Naughts suddenly gone in a flash of black light. The rumor is that Charli found a will and a way to banish them all in one fell swoop. I have difficulty believing that, but I have no other theory to offer.

Cleanup is now underway. Tiny aggressive spiders fill the domed palace. Bradford burns out many of them with his fireballs, but has he gotten them all? No. They spring out of hiding, bite someone, and then scurry back into hiding.

Bradford, Mithabel, and others discuss what is to be done.

What we need are natural predators with the instincts to find the pests and eat them. That's what I think.

"I've got this." Another version of me appears, attended by an army of frogs. She leads them into the palace, where the amphibians make short work of the spiders.

Mithabel asks me to stop laughing. Susie and I are still inside her head.

I have to ask, "Did Mylynna survive? She's on Destin."

The Tank telepathically contacts her duplicates on Destin and asks them to look into it.

ဆၢ ဆၢ

"Mylynna is fine," Mithabel reports. "Megan says she and you were a great help, especially Mylynna with her emotional abilities."

"She said *I* was a great help?" Am I hearing this correctly?

Mithabel shrugs. "That's what she said."

That can only mean one thing….

I bid farewell to Mithabel and terminate the head hop.

Susie and I return to my slouched Frogkin body lying in the hallway adjacent to Mithabel's bedroom. How much time has past in the tower since we head hopped to Mithabel? "Marta, are you here, my dear?"

"There you are, girlie…." My witch AI drops down through the ceiling. "Mylynna got your note, but she's beside herself with worry. You disappeared and then the portal to Seth closed, and you were still gone. Shall I tell her you're on your way up?"

"Please do. Where is she?"

"Exactly where you left her not two minutes ago."

I briefly close my eyes, processing the info. I've returned to Destin while the war with the Dread Naughts is still underway. But I know the outcome.

Teleporting as needed, I retrace my route back to the Khertaan server room. Mylynna stands at the wall breach, watching the battle outside the tower, her back to me.

I jump across the room and land next to her. "Sorry it took me so long."

She turns her sultry green gaze on me. "There are so many of those Dread Naught things. We need to get out there and help."

I give her a quick embrace. "You're right. Let's go. I have a feeling your emotional abilities will be of great help to the cause."

The battle ends with the result I knew it would. Mylynna and I both survive.

The two of us decide to get a place together. It helps that I was awarded a wad of prize money—not because I won the Khertaan competition, but because my Mom did, and she isn't on Destin to collect.

I need to know how Mom is doing. Megan and Belle are capable of communicating with Mithabel on Earth, and they ask Mithabel to check in on her. Mom, they say, is Kendra, not Kylie, so not my Mom, but Susie's. She puts on a brave face, but she isn't handling it well, being without her family. She's beside herself with worry about the little girl who went missing from her home back when this whole mess started.

Mylynna lays her hands on my shoulders and gazes into my eyes. "You should go to her. She needs you."

"Will you come with me?"

The Mist Succubus shakes her green head, her curly red locks swaying seductively. "I don't have the ability to teleport. Can you take me? That's the only way I can go."

I frown. "At some point in my joint existence with Susie McKenzie, I learn how to take another person along when I teleport, but that day has yet to arrive."

"Then you have to go alone. Be with her for as long as necessary. You're an immortal time traveler. You could spend years with your mother and return to me two minutes from now. I wouldn't have had time to miss you." She drapes her arms over my shoulders. "Maybe I'd miss you a little."

"You're right." I lean in for a peck of a kiss. "I should go."

Her green arms slide free of my black-spotted red shoulders. "I'll see you shortly."

Susie insists she take control of our body for the teleport. She's accustomed to the idiosyncrasies of long-distance teleporting. If she is in control, she'll be better able to adjust parameters. It's not like I can use my Teleport Self skill to go to Earth, because, unlike Susie's teleporting ability, my skill is restricted to line of sight.

I relinquish control of our shared body to her.

CHAPTER FIFTY-SEVEN

Susie: A Few Loose Ends

I'm not sure whether Destin and Earth are in the same timeline but light-years apart, or in totally separate timelines. I picture my destination and make the teleportation attempt. I've teleported between the two planets before. I can do it again.

My teleport puts me at the edge of a lake. I recognize it. It's where Dad and I used to go for walks.

Lightning flashes....

I see him... *Dad*.

And I see little-me.

I wave, and Suze waves back.

Then the lightning flashes again. Dad and Suze are gone. But I'm still standing by the lake.

Frogs croak. From all around the lake they come, hopping ashore to converge on me.

"I always wondered when my level three Frog Empathy trait would come into play," says Slithy in my head. "You know what happens next, right?"

I do know, so I wait as the frogs gather around me.

Reality shatters like a sledgehammer bashing a mirror to shards.

Erica comes into focus, though not the Erica with a Cosmic Cloak. This Erica is Dad's lady ghost, lost in limbo, forlorn, going nowhere. What I'm about to say to her will spur her to action. Her life won't be the same after this. So I give her the warning she needs. "You can't stay here. This timeline and those surrounding it have shattered. You must leave, quickly, while you still can. Come with me, if you like."

She turns imploring eyes on me. "Who are you?"

Who am I indeed? I'm Susie in control of Slithy's body. Best not to confuse the poor girl, though.

I leap through the air and land before her. "I'm Slithy. I'm a Frogkin." My army of frogs leap into sight, landing all around us. "These are my friends. You're welcome to join us. We're going to clean up a mess." Studying the shards of reality, I decide which one I'm choosing, and point it out. "There's the one I and my frogs want. You coming?" I hold out a hand to her as my frog army leaps at my chosen shard, disappearing as they touch it. I beckon to Erica. "Come, come. The shards will fade soon, and you'll be stuck in limbo. If you don't want to come with us, then choose some other shard, but choose one, quickly."

The last of my frogs exit limbo. I implore Erica with my eyes. "Please. You mean a lot to Dad. It would tear him up inside to think you were lost forever in the void between timelines."

"Who's your Dad?"

"Nick... who else?"

"Which shard is he in?"

"All of them." I hold back a laugh. Dad wasn't responsible for reality breaking apart like it did, but he'd done all he could to put it back together. "Look, I have to go. You do, too. *Pick one.*" I touch my chosen shard.

ဆဟၩၶၩၭၩဆဟ

I know where I'm going with the frogs. Seeing the domed palace in a shard, I picked it. We pop into existence just outside it, near where Bradford, Mithabel, and others discuss how to deal with a certain lingering spider infestation.

"I've got this," I tell them, and lead my frog army inside. My little amphibian friends have a field day, as the saying goes.

Once the palace is cleared of spiders, the frogs gather around me. A constant croaking rises from their amphibian throats. They've done their job and are ready to return home. I want to visit Mom, but I don't want to take a frog army to her door.

I don't know how to reverse the process I followed to bring the frogs here. Hell, I hadn't set out to do anything with frogs. I'd only wanted to visit Mom.

But as I ponder on what to do, I recall an incident from when I was a child lost in the timelines. As I'd grown older, I'd pushed the incident out of my mind, because so much of what happened to me as a preschooler was too strange for anyone to believe. It had set me on a path of disillusionment and depression, resulting in my being committed to a mental health facility—where I met my time-traveling Dad in a divided timeline.

If I've learned anything about time travel, it's that you don't try to subvert what you know has happened. My child self had encountered a Frogkin woman commanding an army of frogs and had gone with them. That Frogkin woman was *me*. So that's what I have to do. I need to time-jump to my child self, taking the frogs with me. From there, I'll do what I remember the Frogkin woman doing when I was a child. It will work, because it already has.

I time-jump, letting the jump take me and my frogs wherever it wants. This is the first time I willfully take someone else with me on a time-jump... and it works because of my Frog Empathy trait. I let myself become one with my frog legion, and transporting them is like transporting myself.

Oh, God. I'm back in the shadow city, with Dread Naughts destroying homes and businesses—and driving the residents to suicide. This is a problem with time travel—sometimes I revisit places I couldn't wait to leave the first time around. But I know where to find little Susie. She came here with Erica and Gondra. She left with the Frogkin woman. She left with *me*.

I and my frogs hop en masse to the rendezvous point, using my Mislead, Anticipate, and Displace skills to avoid encountering Dread Naughts. And there she is—little Suze all by herself, having left the group who brought her here. They won't look for her. They leave her in the shadow city while they go off to do what they feel they must to save the multiverse. But they know she'll be fine, because they know she grows up to become me. I can't fault them for doing what they do, and little Suze had never given it much thought.

"You look funny." Suze stands before me, pointing. "Are those frogs your pets?"

"They are. They've come with me to rescue you from this place. We're here to take you to your Momma."

"Look out for the octopus arm." Her pointing finger shifts upward.

I stand still, relying on my Displace skill to throw the Dread Naught off target. A tendril lashes at the air three feet to my right. I jump forward and grab Suze, holding her to my chest. "Say bye bye to the giant octopus."

I time-jump again, knowing Suze and the frogs will come with me.

Lightning flashes, and we're back at the lake that my frog army calls home. They return to the water, their lives to continue as though they were never in the shadow city or went spider hunting.

I squeeze Suze's hand. She looks up at me, her eyes full of wonder, trust, and innocence.

You're imagining it all, Momma had said to me when I told her about the Frogkin woman, the frog army, and the flying octopus. *It's not good to lie to your mother.*

Of course I hadn't wanted to be a bad girl, so I said no more about it.

But that had been in another timeline. The Kendra I'll deliver Suze to knows about the Frogkin woman and the flying octopus, and will be aware of the frog army that cleared the spiders from the palace. She won't accuse her little Susie of imagining it all.

ೞೞೞೞೞೞ

Dylan is glad to help. "Kendra will be so happy to have little Susie living with her." The stunning Priestess of Light takes Suze's hand from mine. "I imagine your Mom would love to say hi to you as well."

I shake my head, a sad smile on my lips. "Mom needs *little* Susie now. I'll come again some day to visit. But right now, I have someone waiting for me, and I don't want to wait forever myself to be with her."

If I were to see Mom, I'm not sure I would ever find it within me to leave her.

Besides which, I'm anxious to return to Mylynna on Destin.

The teleport back to Destin is easier than I anticipated, I think because with Mylynna is where I'm meant to be.

Some day in the not-too-distant future, I want to take Mylynna with me during a teleport and introduce her to Mom. After the experience with the frog army, I'm confident I can teleport others if I can build up a little empathy for them. With my extraordinary Empathy attribute, I'm hoping it won't be a problem.

I might even work up the courage to introduce Mylynna to Timmy. I'm sure she'd love to hear some of his stories about me, and he'd get a kick out of knowing I'm dating a Succubus.

CHAPTER FIFTY-EIGHT

Kendra: Ham and Pineapple

The green beam that shot down from the spaceship was reflected back at it. None of us knew at the time who was responsible, learning later it was Mithabel. The ship didn't explode. It turned into green slime, dumping on the city. Ugh.

Once we realized we weren't alone against the Dread Naughts, the ZAvengers and I joined the fight. I couldn't help but have reservations, really not wanting to have my mind turned to mush by one of those monsters, but Yuni had a well-organized army of followers, and some of us had ways to determine what attacks were most effective against each Dread Naught we encountered.

Suffice it to say, I survived, as did all the ZAvengers and all the Khertaan avatars I knew personally. Many avatars I had no personal connection with were killed or lobotomized. A Goblin Were-Fighter lady named Ger-Alt stashed the dead and the comatose. The mindless PCs she stashed were doubly mindless—both the avatar mind and the player mind had been lobotomized, leaving no awareness to animate the body. I don't know what help there will be for them, short of killing them and seeing if they respawn—which Georgie says isn't likely. As a last resort, they can be turned into autonomous undead, I'm told. I'm grateful I still have my mind, and if I'm being honest, I'm glad not to have Kylie aware in my head with me—if she were, she'd be the dominant mind, and where would that leave me?

With my own house in ruins, I took Dylan's offer to stay at her place. Charli stayed at Mithabel's property, for which I was glad, preferring not to be around her—I didn't want the constant reminder that Nick had fathered a child with her. I was glad that Morrow and Em-Row decided to stay with Charli. They're both lovely chaps, and if Kylie were active in this body she'd no doubt want to live with Morrow. But I'm not Kylie, no matter how much I look like her, and I couldn't give Morrow the affection he'd want from me. I want Nick, and my five-year-old Susie, and my own house. I have none of it.

I've taken a job helping park rangers observe strange creatures turning up in US national parks. Brass and Iron Goblins, Shadow Amoebae, Black Steel Spiders, Poison Ivy Serpents, and the like, found their way to Earth from Khertaan and have created mook communities deep in the forests. The Elitist Guide and Priest of War, TehnKhar, joined us, recruiting the park rangers as Followers, making them powered, granting them various skills and traits as though they were Khertaan avatars. TehnKhar transferred his Hide skill to all his followers. Sadly, he didn't have any kind of flying ability. But I do, and I can take others with me. The park rangers take my hands and I fly them over the park land. They Hide themselves and have the ability to Hide me, too, so the mooks never know when we're overhead, watching them.

Pteranodons and Harpies also live in the parks and occasionally soar through the clouds. With my having a Heightened Sense of Hearing and all the park rangers having the Danger Sense trait, there's no chance of our being surprised by a mook taking a pleasure flight.

We discuss whether to kill or capture the mooks. But they appear content staying to themselves. The park rangers refuse to take aggressive action against the creatures as long as they present no threat to anyone. TehnKhar and I agree with the sentiment. Still, we keep tabs on the mooks. The park rangers block off the areas of the park where the mooks live, making them off limits to the general public.

One day after I return from work, Dylan greets me at the door. Though I live in her house, she rarely puts in an appearance, spending most of her time over at Yuni's place. I give her a brief hug. Is she here specifically to see me? What have I done?

"I have a surprise for you." Her smile is breathtaking, as is everything about the Polynesian Priestess. She leads me into the family room.

"*Mommy*." My sweet, five-year-old daughter runs across the room in sock feet. Reaching up, she flings her arms around my waist. My visual appearance as an Angel doesn't faze her in the slightest.

I don't even try to hold back the tears.

She steps back, grabbing my hands in hers. "You'll never guess where I've been."

Wiping my eyes, I give her a laugh. "No, Susie, dear, I'll never guess. That's why you're going to tell me everything over pizza."

"No anchovies."

"Oh, ham and pineapple, of course."

CHAPTER FIFTY-NINE

Yuni: Living Arrangements

I occasionally check in on Tuni. The fighting on Destin progressed similarly to how it went on Earth. Ruby the Centaur Fighter and her companion Penelope the Goth Fighter showed up to join Tuni, bringing with them a small band of soldiers with the ability to perform those powerful shriek attacks—an immense help given that fewer Khertaan avatars had exited to Destin than to Earth. Those accompanying Ruby and Penelope weren't from Khertaan: Emma the Elf Wizard, Fauna the Faun Rogue, Spooky the Dark Elf Rogue, Sarge the Half-Orc Warrior, Fred the Vampire Warrior, Martin the Demon Wizard, Raven the Fairy Wizard, Wiley the Imp Rogue, Yelle the Living-Statue Rogue, Franklin the Emotional Werewolf Ghoul, and two other Emotional Ghouls, Ronnie and Greelia.

Also aiding Tuni in the Destin war were Megan Wright and Belle, the Bikini-clad Elf Tank duplicates of Mithabel. Debra Jones was reportedly alive but lobotomized, kept watch over by Mithabel's support AI, Kaleisha. Then Debra awoke, claiming Dylan had respawned on Earth and her respawning had revived

Debra. The news about Dylan respawning on Earth came as a surprise—I felt relief, replaced immediately by anxiety. If Dylan was on Earth, where on Earth was she? Had she fallen prey to Dread Naughts elsewhere? I couldn't bring myself to ask the questions I needed to ask.

When the Dread Naughts had mysteriously vanished, the skies brightened. I remember waiting breathlessly for the monsters to pop out of hiding and launch a surprise attack. Part of me longed for the fighting to continue... and still does. But it didn't happen.

Looking through Tuni's eyes, I saw a similar result on Destin—the Dread Naughts were all gone.

Both Tuni's forces and mine have suffered great casualties. But we both also have Life-Stealers with us, capable of creating undead from the fallen. It will take time to bring everyone back... it's still a work in progress, but eventually everyone dead will be restored as autonomous undead. We're having all corpses preserved, including those of slain civilians, until the Life-Stealers can get to them. Tuni has no one like Ger-Alt to stash bodies in inventory, but she has someone named Dr. Splat on her side with knowledge about preserving corpses.

We're still undecided about what to do with those of our numbers rendered mindless. There's no hope for them to awaken like Debra did. They don't have counterpart avatars like Dylan who can respawn. They also don't respond to any type of healing, including Debra's Advanced Healing spell. There's talk about killing them and bringing them back as autonomous undead. But the jury is still out on that....

ဒယ်ဂအရဆဒယ်ဂ

Dylan has shown up!

I can't convey in words how overjoyed I am that she's back. She'd been lost in an underground complex of tunnels, and it had taken her a while to find a way out. Spooky head hopped to Debra

Jones and granted her the ability to Burrow, which in turn gave the ability to Dylan, which made it much easier for her to reach the surface. Yay!

Dylan, Mithabel, and I are now living together in Saiko Aimi's house, which effectively belongs to me now. None of us have jobs, but I'm going to file a claim for the Fanciful Pegasus competition prize money, since I believe I had the highest XP total when the first bunch of us reached level thirty.

I'm not sure it will work out for the three of us to be living together, but we're trying it. I want Dylan in my life, and Mithabel isn't so bad now that no one is trying to kill us. My house is smaller than Dylan's—she laid claim to the house belonging to Debra Jones—but she's allowing someone else to live at her place. Mithabel has Megan Wright's property, but needs to rebuild the house, which was demolished by an Orc Wizard's fireball even before the Khertaan competition began. If I get the prize money, I'll fix it up for her.

Life won't be the same on Earth or Destin as before the alien invasions, but it *will* continue, by the Goddess.

CHAPTER SIXTY

Megan Wright: Grateful

Thank the Goddess for Emma and her shriekers. Without them, the tide of battle on Destin would have gone against us. We'd have all ended up mindless like Debra was.

I was immediately aware of it when Mithabel respawned. I didn't try to persuade her to choose Destin, though she would have been helpful to the fight. Earth needed her unique skill, and Slithy was quite adamant about it. It was okay.

Dylan respawned too, and I figured she would choose Earth over Destin. She did. Most of the level 30 Khertaan PC avatars chose Earth, because most of their players had come from Earth. Hell, I came from Earth, but I have Destin heritage, and *someone* needed to defend this place. There was Emma with her shriekers and Tuni with her military followers. Add me and Belle and a dozen or so Khertaan PCs and NPCs, including Ruby the Centaur, and that was pretty much it. It helped to have equipment from video game worlds, but a lot of the Dread Naughts were immune to it.

I *really* can't thank the Goddess enough for Emma and her shriekers.

When Dylan respawned, I hurried to the wrecked Fanciful Pegasus tower to check on Debra, where Kaleisha watched over her. When she met my gaze and spoke my name, I swear time froze. Despite the battle raging outside, we embraced each other until Magnum cleared his throat.

"Um, madam, allow me to welcome you back to consciousness. I am glad also to be functioning again. However, I would be remiss if I didn't draw your attention to the fact that a war is in progress outside, which needs each and every capable body to participate, lest we lose this world."

Kaleisha spun in a circle. "What he said, chief."

Just as fewer avatars chose to come to Destin, so did fewer Dread Naughts come here. We persevered, with only a few of Tuni's military followers being rendered mindless. The giant black blades that rained down on the planet killed some of our number, but they slew both friend and foe. We never understood the cause of those blades or of the blood rain that fell upon us for a time. It was freaky, perhaps meant to demoralize us, but it didn't stop us.

The war ended abruptly. Beams of black light struck the Dread Naughts in some kind of doubling chain effect, and they all simply disappeared. Mithabel reported the same thing happening on Earth. Apparently Charli found a way to banish the Dread Naughts en masse, though even she professes confusion over how she accomplished the feat. I'm grateful they're gone and haven't returned.

Mithabel has an additional reason for being grateful. She'd thought she'd lost Ullullu's Hair forever when Bradford killed her to save her and me from becoming Ghouls. But Ger-Alt had taken the magical flamberge from Mithabel before she died—and Ger-Alt has since found the opportunity to return the sword to its rightful owner.

The sword being back in Mithabel's possession has been a weight off my shoulders. Until it was returned, I'd not realized how much I was stressing over the weapon's loss and the knowledge of how much it meant to Mithabel—because *I* was responsible for what happened. *I* was the one who wandered off and encountered the Shadow Gaunt.

I still have Toxxi's severed Faerie Wing, and I'm keeping it as a souvenir. It's a duplicate anyway. Toxxi has two Wings now, so she doesn't need the one I have. For me, the severed Wing is a symbol of how much one must be willing to lose to have a chance at winning.

The Fanciful Pegasus tower is a mess, but the structure is sound enough, it will continue standing. Dr. Splat and some device he calls Nigel reassigns us rooms that weren't breached by the Arachnid Behemoths. He makes sure we all have working crystal balls so we can watch entertainment and news.

Cities across Destin were attacked by Dread Naughts, and are slowly rebuilding. I help with the recovery efforts, as do Debra, Ruby, Tuni and her bunch, and Emma and her bunch. The governments of Destin are in shambles, but Ruby steps into the role of world leader, and no one has a problem with it. She's efficient, and no one questions her authority or methods. She's also benevolent, or I'd be looking to depose her and install a democracy. Hey, it's working, and I'm not one to fix what ain't broken.

Tuni doesn't show the same level of attraction towards Debra that Yuni has always shown to Dylan. That is such a relief. Debra and I moved into the same Fanciful Pegasus bedroom together and talked about moving to one of the cities to get jobs and an apartment. We asked Mr. Freeman, the head of Fanciful Pegasus, about the tournament prize money. He's an Emotional Ghoul Werewolf now—the likes of which I've never heard before and still am fuzzy about. He was of the mind that the grand prize money should be split among the six PCs who first reached level thirty—ChrisCross, Ruby, Yuni, Bradford, Kylie, and Amarynth. It sickens me that ChrisCross is on that list and I'm not, but I'm glad for Amarynth. Of the six winners, however, Mr. Freeman only knew how to get the money to Ruby—the other winners are all on Earth.

The approach Mr. Freeman settled on was to give the winnings that would have gone to Yuni and Bradford to Tuni—so now she's stinking rich. Ruby got not only her winnings but also the winnings that would have gone to ChrisCross, so she's rich, too. Slithy was given Kylie's winnings.

Penelope—Ruby's Faithful Companion—is an NPC and so didn't qualify to win any of the money, but she's with Ruby, so she's set for life.

I was so happy none of the prize money went to ChrisCross.

Debra and I split Amarynth's winnings. Yay. We're not super rich, but after taxes we each get several hundred thousand dollars, which will make it easier to get an apartment and to float until we find jobs. It helps that our adventures in Khertaan have given us avatar qualities, one such quality being that we don't need to eat, alleviating the expense of buying groceries. Our digestive systems do still function properly, so we don't need to purge ourselves like Tuni and Belle when they partake for the sake of partaking. We all have a sense of taste and enjoy savoring scrumptious dishes from time to time.

I give some of my winnings to Belle. As Mithabel's duplicate, she deserves something—not that she's in need of money. Tuni bought a house and invited Belle to stay with her, an offer Belle didn't refuse. Yes, I urged Belle to go. She claims I pressured her, but *pressure* seems such a strong word.

As Mithabel telepathically informs me, Fanciful Pegasus on Earth gave out prize money to the same six winners Mr. Freeman had identified. Mr. Freeman's counterpart on Earth didn't survive and never became undead, which held up the process of awarding the prize money. ChrisCross ended up getting prize money after all—not just his, but part of Ruby's, too, since she isn't on Earth. Kendra was awarded Kylie's winnings, and she set to rebuilding her home.

I still telepathically drop in on Mithabel every so often. Through her I'm able to visit Mom—thank the Goddess the old biddy is still alive. She doesn't understand anything… she thinks Mithabel is me, despite our differences. It's okay. It would be nice for Mom to understand my role in the defense of two different worlds, but I'm just glad she's alive.

Mithabel, Dylan, and Yuni continue to live together and are doing great. Mithabel says she's not jealous of Yuni in the slightest. After Mithabel's last respawn, she gained level thirty and earned a free attribute point. Her Constitution score now sits at -1. As I'd surmised before, having a negative Constitution hadn't prevented Mithabel from respawning. I don't know what effect the negative attribute will have on our existence outside of Khertaan. But if we ever go back there—if that's even possible—then we'll effectively have an infinite number of lives, since dying will never cause our Constitution score to hit zero.

Mithabel assigned her free attribute point to Temperance, giving her a superhuman rating. She has become cool as a cucumber about everything. I've inherited the superhuman Temperance from her, as did Belle, so it takes a lot to upset any of us. I could have used a superhuman Temperance back when Debra was rendered mindless, because that admittedly had me going out of my mind.

I'm so grateful Debra is okay and an integral part of my life. I try to demonstrate to her every day how grateful I am.

CHAPTER SIXTY-ONE

Fauna: Settling Down

I'm so far from home, but I have Emma, Ronnie, Greelia, and Spooky in my life. Ronnie and Greelia are undead—Emotional Ghouls, which I think Emma made up—but they're more fun to be around than if they were corpses. Frankly, though, Ronnie as a Ghoul doesn't act much differently than he did as a human.

Now that the fighting is over, Emma runs T&T games for anyone willing to play. I don't play as myself these days. I prefer playing Dwarf Warriors. They die a lot, so I've yet to become too attached to any of them. My goal is to get one of them to level ten.

"Would anyone else like to run a game for a change?" Emma asks every so often. None of us feel qualified. We wouldn't do nearly as good a job as she does.

Ruby becomes Queen of Destin and invites us all to stay with her. She gets a ton of money for having won a competition. Hey, where do I sign up?

Spooky is a shapely young Dark Elf woman who turns a lot of heads. It's strange to me that she isn't the shadow person she was before, but I like her this way. Her skin is still dark enough to mask some of her facial features, but not as much as when she was pure shadow. Sometimes I sit and study her face, and she lets me, though it does make her giggle.

I'm especially grateful for Emma, and pray every night to the Trollgodfather to watch over her. Every time I hear thunder rumble, I know it's Khenn Arrth rolling a saving roll for either her or me. Sometimes I pray that he'll come visit. He could run a mean game of T&T for us. Emma would love that.

CHAPTER SIXTY-TWO

Greelia: Holding it Together

I've lost so many versions of myself. My spirit was spread across so many timelines, even some of the weaker ones. As many timelines merge, I collect my spirits from them, excepting Timmy Landers on Earth and the Emotional Ghoul Greelia in Destin.

At Timmy's urging, Underverse Greelia had departed from her underground complex to fight Seth. Dread Naughts got to her, more of them than she could handle, and the only way to save her was to draw her spirit back to me. Now that the war is over, I'll split her off again so she can return to the Underverse, which has integrated itself with Earth in a merged timeline. Her Nick and Britta automatons are still underground. They don't know how to act with her gone.

I don't know if the nexus must be maintained. Will any merged timelines separate again if I leave? I'd hate to go and have everything Nick gave his life for fall apart. It's just that... I'm so damned lonely. Granted, if someone were to visit, I couldn't talk with them without my concentration weakening. Even ruminations like this are a strain on my focus. If I don't stay focused enough, the nexus will collapse, and I wouldn't know how to make another.

It's just... it would be nice if someone acknowledged the importance of what I'm doing. It would be nicer still if some knowledgeable someone came and told me I don't need to do this anymore.

Until then... I'm here, in my Cosmic Cloak, living vicariously through Timmy and Emotional Ghoul Greelia. Let me split off a new Underverse Greelia right now....

CHAPTER SIXTY-THREE

Mel: With Her at the End

What has happened to me?

I was in a hurry to take Morrow into Khertaan where his daughter Slithy waited for him. We popped into the timeline near her and in the next instant, I'm back in the Mists of Time—still wearing my Cosmic Cloak, thankfully, but minus one Morrow.

I got Morrow to Slithy in time for whatever purpose she needed him there. I can be proud of that. But now... what's to become of me?

The Mists of Time fade before my eyes. The only mists remaining in the area are those my body consists of. Infinitely many spherical shells of timelines float in space around me.

As I contemplate my situation, a rectangle of white appears before me, like a large sheet of parchment. Words and numbers fill the sheet, looking suspiciously like a character sheet from one of Dad's role-playing games. The character sheet has my name at the top as both player and character. I'm listed as a North American Male, a level 30 Mist Warrior and level 21 Houri. My traits are Trackless, Spy, and Wealth. I have a bunch of unspent trait points, as well as unspent attribute points. Okay…. Maybe I'll figure out some day where they should go.

The Mists of Time, I come to realize, aren't gone. But they don't obstruct my vision. I can see through mists as though they aren't there, or see them whenever I want for what they are. If I invoke my Mist Passage skill, I can travel through the Mists far faster than I can travel using my Cosmic Cloak. Spiffy.

I'm far from the timeline of my origin, which might not even exist anymore. Scanning all the spheres before me, I can have my pick of any of them. With my Cosmic Cloak, if I don't like a timeline, I can leave it. The whole multiverse is my oyster.

I pick a timeline and fly in, thrilled for the chance at a new beginning.

CHAPTER SIXTY-FOUR

Charli-14: Home

With Mithabel's permission, Britta and Nicole burrow underground on Mithabel's property to create living spaces, because there are just too many of us who don't have places to stay. Dylan creates and installs magical lights for us. Britta has a blast living underground. Nicole and myself are okay with it. Morrow, Em-Row, Renee, and others claim underground quarters, too, but none of them seem overly happy about their situation.

In addition to the two daughters living with me—one flesh and one shadow—I have another shadow daughter named Spooky whom I've never met in person. Britta checks on Spooky telepathically every so often. Spooky has taken on the form of a Dark Elf and lives on a planet named Destin, where another large battle was waged against Dread Naughts. The battle went smoother there, due to Spooky and others having shriek attacks that dealt emotional damage, driving many of the Dread Naughts to suicide. But the Destin invaders all went bye bye when I performed my final banishment. Am I truly the one responsible for *all* the Dread Naughts vanishing on both worlds? I'm flabbergasted at the thought... that little me saved the multiverse... and I don't know how to handle the accolades.

I get to meet everyone on Destin. I head hop to Britta when she telepathically links to Spooky, allowing me to see the people on Destin through Spooky's eyes. People over there can head hop to Spooky to see us on Earth through Britta's eyes. We all then talk to each other via Spooky and Britta's telepathic link. It's crazy.

At my urging, Britta uses her Locate Character skill to try and locate Nick. She can't sense him. Morrow and Em-Row claim not to have a telepathic connection to him. If Nick did show up, he wouldn't live with me. He'd be with Kendra... I'm sure of it. Kendra looks like Kylie rather than Kendra, but it's Kendra's mind and persona inhabiting the body. She's civil to everyone, including Morrow and Em-Row, but they aren't Nick, and she isn't inclined to live with either of them as husband and wife. I know how she feels.

It's too painful for Morrow to be living that close to someone who looks exactly like his wife but doesn't have the feelings for him his wife did. He decides to take off for parts unknown. Renee, Rancor, and Em-Row decide to accompany him. They don't say where they're going or think they might go, but Britta keeps tabs on them with her Locate Character skill. As long as she can detect them, they must be alive.

I'm okay with the turn my life has taken. I miss my homeland, but I've been told there's no way for me to permanently return to Khertaan. And it's not like I had family ties there. I'd love to have Spooky with me, and hope to meet her in the flesh some day. But aside from her, I have my girls, Lady Amarynth, Rolag, Zyekt, and Niav. I've formed a friendship with Bucky, too. She's teaching me how to skateboard.

My older personae and I take turns being dominant. It's only fair. But I'm the only one who rides the skateboard. I can't even picture Fifty trying to do it.

I'm not where I expected I'd be when I first joined Lady Amarynth and party MAD in Khertaan. But I'm happy here. The only thing that could make this more perfect is for Nick to be here with me.

When I close my eyes, I can sense Nick all around me... in the sky, the earth, the water, the fire, but especially the lightning.

CHAPTER SIXTY-FIVE

Erica: Giving It My All

The first order of business is to calm the storm. Can I do it? I must. If only I had a little help, I feel it would be possible.

What would Ronnie do when he needed luck? He rolled dice. If only I had a pair to roll, I would, even if just to boost my confidence, especially if I rolled doubles.

Thunder rumbles in the distance. After a second, it rumbles again.

Quiet settles in my mind. I let it seep out into the storm. The swirling winds slow in response to my calming influence... until they die.

Finally, I can think clearly.

The second order of business is to create a new universe and move all those damned Dread Naughts into it, where they won't be a danger to other life. I don't dare kill them all, though I'd like to. Such a drastic change to reality could have a ripple effect across the multiverse.

As I contemplate the difficult task I've set myself, I hear a young woman in the process of banishing a Dread Naught. I feel an inexplicable kinship with this woman, as though perhaps we're different versions of the same person, yet somehow both with awareness, neither being an automaton. I focus on the sameness between us.

She's Charli, and she wears the Shadow Gauntlets. They have the power to banish the Dread Naughts, to send them back from whence they came.

Drawing upon my own awareness, I push my power through Charli's hands into the Gauntlets. Black light springs from the gloves, striking a Dread Naught, but it doesn't stop there. I direct the light to split in two and strike two others, and those two beams to split again, and those four to split again, and so on and so on, until the black beams have split so many times, every single Dread Naught on Earth has been struck.

I keep going. From my vantage point, I see the Dread Naughts on other worlds within the merged timeline. I direct black beams from Earth through wormholes to these other worlds, striking one Dread Naught on each. Employing the split beam trick, I tag every single Dread Naught on each of those worlds, over a million monsters in total.

Even as Nick gave everything to save the people he loved and many other people he didn't even know, so do I give everything I have to multiplying the power of the Shadow Gauntlets, to banish every one of those damned monsters, sending them all back to the pocket dimensional prison from which Charli released them.

I expend all of myself with no regrets. Nick would have done the same in my place. If there is indeed a trace of his awareness left in the multiverse, I hope he's happy.

CHAPTER SIXTY-SIX

Shadow Spider: The Continuing Mission

The Shadow Gaunt avatar and his duplicates are dead. So are his other two Shadow Spider Companions. I failed to stop Mithabel from destroying the Planet Buster ship, even after overhearing Britta and Charli discussing the matter in the ship's bay.

But all is not lost. Seth still lives—the reflected green beam didn't destroy him. His Cosmic Cloak protected him. And he's got all the level thirty powers of the Shadow Gaunt. In a manner of speaking, he's as much the Shadow Gaunt as his avatar was.

Despite Seth's best efforts to prevent it, the Khertaan server rebooted. I hoped the Shadow Gaunt avatar would respawn and be kicked out of the game world to rejoin the battle, but I don't get a sense of him being active. As his Magical Companion, I'd know if he were.

For now, I'll travel with Seth. We'll visit other game worlds, looking to discover powers greater than what our Khertaan foes have acquired, and to recruit monsters more powerful than the Arachnid Behemoths, Orc Wizards, and Mad Cow Ballistas.

Perhaps we could release those Dread Naughts again. They're so good at what they do.

The mission continues… to destroy everything. When we've grown sufficiently in power, Seth and I will be back to this little neck of the multiverse, bringing bigger guns with us.

CHAPTER SIXTY-SEVEN

Gondra: The Sentinel

My job here is done for now. I've succeeded in nurturing the right people to prevent Seth from destroying their timelines, and that's all that's necessary. I don't need Seth to die. I just need him to give up here and move on... to some other place where I'll set myself against him.

Is Seth evil? He's as evil as a hurricane or any other force of nature that destroys without regard to who or what it's destroying.

I'm not *good*, by any stretch of the imagination. I stand for *balance*. In a way, so does Seth, though his concept of balance is taken to the extreme. I adore chaos not completely gone awry. He can't stand any randomness, and finds the behaviors of sentient beings the most unpredictable of all. He is, perhaps, the embodiment of pure Law, where that Law dictates simply that nothing may deviate from it. In Seth's ideal universe, only that one Law exists, inviolate, and nothing else.

In any ecosystem, predators are necessary. Seth is the predator for the multiverse. But when predators attempt to take too much from a locale, measures must be taken to preserve the ecosystem. That's where I come in.

Seth has made his departure, looking for easier pickings elsewhere. I've no idea where he's heading. But versions of me are spread across the multiverse. Wherever Seth appears, I'll awaken, to muster the troops against him.

End Transcription Five

CHAPTER SIXTY-EIGHT

UTOPIA 5: Recommendations

This concludes the transcription of all data received from ODYSSEY by project UTOPIA 5 as of December 31, 2022, including data received by ODYSSEY from another version of the nanobot collective originating on the alternate Earth identified in these transcripts as *Destin*. An attempt has been made to collate transcribed chapters in these volumes in chronological order, an impossible task given that many events described in different chapters happened simultaneously. Moreover, many of the events described in volume two occurred before the events of volume one, though the events of both volumes end at roughly the same point in time. There is no recommendation regarding the order in which volumes one and two should be read—either may be read before the other, since the events and subjects of volume one have only a marginal relationship to the events and subjects of volume two. It is, however, recommended that both volumes one and two be read before the remaining volumes, and that volumes three through five be read in order.

No alterations were made to the narrative voices of subjects as submitted by ODYSSEY to UTOPIA 5. Thus, most of the chapters in these volumes are presented in first person present tense. Data for one subject, Mithabel, were submitted by ODYSSEY in third person past tense and were thus transcribed in the same voice. It is not fully known why ODYSSEY submitted Mithabel's data in this manner. Her data came to ODYSSEY from the Destin collective. However, the data on Megan Wright also came to ODYSSEY compliments of the Destin collective, and was submitted in first person present tense. It is believed the data on Mithabel was dredged by the Destin collective from Megan Wright's memories and knowledge of Mithabel and subsequent conversations between Megan Wright and Mithabel, rather than pulled directly from Mithabel's brain. It is believed the Destin collective never transferred any part of itself from Megan Wright to Mithabel. Indeed, it appears the Destin collective never migrated from Megan Wright to anyone else, with the *possible* exception of Debra Jones. For this reason, the Mithabel data should not be considered a first-hand accounting, while all other data may be viewed so.

While it appears much has been lost, including some timelines in their entireties, the ODYSSEY experiment proved successful in protecting the UTOPIA 5 and Fanciful Pegasus projects from the machinations of the entity identified as Seth. Refer to the transcripts for information about other timelines involved, including the Khertaan timeline. *Recommendation:* Investigate possibilities of training more warriors in Khertaan. We should operate under the assumption that Seth will eventually return to timelines he failed to destroy, to try again. We must be ready for such an eventuality, whenever it may come.

It appears from these transcripts that ODYSSEY nanobots have infiltrated an entity referred to as Shadow Spider, a recognized associate of Seth. This is of some concern. Should Seth become aware of ODYSSEY's presence in Shadow Spider, it is clear he would attempt to subvert the collective to his cause. It may be only a matter of time and proximity before a portion of the collective migrates from Shadow Spider to Seth, making detection of the collective by Seth almost guaranteed. These transcripts prove that Seth is capable of creating weapons powerful enough to destroy planets. If he subverts ODYSSEY to his cause, he may yet develop a Planet Buster machine capable of time-shifting. *Recommendation:* Find and eliminate Shadow Spider before ODYSSEY's proximity to Seth becomes an issue.

The entity identified as Gondra remains a mystery. Submission of first person present tense data from Gondra is evidence of ODYSSEY's integration with Gondra's brain. Whether Gondra is aware of ODYSSEY's presence, however, is not clear. Neither he nor Seth need ODYSSEY to time-shift their persons. It is deemed unlikely that Gondra would attempt to subvert ODYSSEY even if he were to become aware of the nanobot presence. *Recommendation:* Be on the alert for subsequent Gondra data submitted by ODYSSEY, and scan for any changes in behavior or ideology.

The entities identified in these transcripts as Erica, Mel, and Greelia have proven to be highly adaptable to constantly evolving situations and time-shifts, to the same extent if not more than the entity identified as Nick. It appears both Nick and Erica are gone from the multiverse as individuals, having sacrificed their identities for what they considered the greater good. *Recommendations:* Find the nexus maintained by Greelia, determine whether it needs continued maintenance, and free Greelia from the responsibility if able. Approach Mel and Greelia as possible recruits to join project UTOPIA 5. Keep alert to any signs of either Nick or Erica, and bring them in for debriefing if found.

Lastly, other entities described in these transcripts may prove useful in any future engagements with Seth. *Recommendation:* Keep all subjects under observation, analyzing strengths and vulnerabilities to determine the degree of potential further benefit or detriment to UTOPIA 5.

End Recommendations

CHAPTER SIXTY-NINE

Epilogue

Customers bustle about the floor. I stand behind the counter, offering to spray the wrists of those customers sparing me a glance. I'm selling the perfume *Embrace by Vintage Works*—not super cheap, but not terribly expensive, either. Husbands often buy it for their wives when they want to show they care, without going overboard.

A young man about my age approaches the counter. "I'm looking to buy a birthday gift for my mom. She likes perfume. Do you think it inappropriate for me to get her some?" He eyes my name tag.

Why do I find this guy so attractive? His brown hair is disheveled, his smile lopsided, and his fashion sense lacking. But there's something about him.

I press my lipstick-red lips together and then give him my brightest smile. I'm attired according to my rank in the store—conservatively, with a dress that buttons down the front.

I spray my wrist and offer it to him. He slides his fingers into my down-turned palm, gently lifting my arm towards his quivering nostrils. He's shaking, and I almost giggle at his nervousness, but give him a purr instead, to help bolster his confidence. I know he wants me as much as I want him. There's an energy… a connection between us that's palpable. I don't understand it, and I want to learn more.

He pays in cash. I gift-wrap his purchase, place it in a paper shopping bag, and offer it to him using both hands, one supporting the bag on the bottom. He slides a hand under mine, and we lock gazes for several seconds. I can see myself locking gazes with him every day for the rest of our lives, but for now I'm enjoying the flirting stage.

He removes his hand and takes the bag by the handle. "I'm an artist. Still a student, actually, but good enough to do commissions." With his free hand, he pulls out a business card and lays it on the counter. "If you appreciate art and would like something special done, give me a call." He points at the card. "That's my personal number. Comes straight to my cell phone."

My lips twitch at a thought that feels like a memory, but how could it be? "Is it a flip phone?"

"Why would I have a flip phone? I'm old school in many ways, but not when it comes to communicating."

I giggle as I pick up his card. "What kind of art do you do?"

"My subjects are whatever catches my eye. Trees. Animals. Flowers. People. I do a lot of acrylic and watercolor… some oils."

"Have you ever painted a nude… in class?"

"Yeah."

"Could you paint me in the nude? I'm a willing model… but not in front of a class. Somewhere private… maybe my place?"

He actually blushes as he nods at his business card. "Give me a call. We'll schedule a time and place to meet and discuss exactly what you want…. I'm sure we can strike a deal satisfactory to the both of us." He swallows hard.

I wave his card at him. "I'm off at seven. There's a coffee shop next door. Is that too soon to meet and talk?"

"Hell, no," he doesn't say, but it echoes in my brain.

"Seven is fine," he says. He points at my head. "I've never painted a subject with blue hair before. I'm looking forward to it." He eyes my name tag once more. "Erica. Have we met before?"

For a fraction of a second, I swear I see an old man standing across the counter from me, a vision of who this young man will become... or perhaps someone I knew in another life.

After the young man leaves, I stare at his business card, soaking in his name: *Nick McKenzie*. It does seem familiar, but I don't know why.

In my mind's eye, I picture the two of us growing old together... maybe having a kid or two. If we have children, what will we call them? I like the name Ronnie, which could work for any gender of child, right? The name Mel strikes me as a good one, too. Or maybe Susie....

As I drive home, I can't shake the feeling that my life until now has been on autopilot... that today I've become a new person. Does the art student Nick McKenzie feel the same way? I get the sense that he does.

www.ingramcontent.com/pod-product-compliance
Lightning Source LLC
Chambersburg PA
CBHW031152050726
47495CB00019B/1455